GW01375407

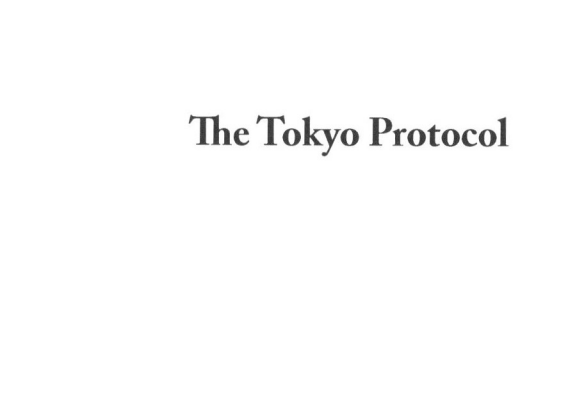

The Tokyo Protocol

The Tokyo Protocol

A *Nippon Noir* novel

Ray Barton

Sarsen Press
WINCHESTER

First published in Great Britain in 2023 by the Sarsen Press,
22 Hyde Street, Winchester, Hampshire SO23 7DR, UK

Copyright © Brian Moeran

The moral right of Brian Moeran to be identified as the author of this work has been asserted in accordance with the Copyright, Designs and Patents Act 1988.

All rights reserved. No part of this book may be reproduced in any form or by electronic or mechanical means, including photocopy, recording, or any information storage and retrieval systems, without permission in writing from both the copyright owner and the publisher, except by a reviewer, who may quote brief passages in a review.

This book is a work of fiction. Names, characters, businesses, organizations, places and events are either the product of the author's imagination or used fictitiously. Any resemblance to actual persons, living or dead, events or locales is entirely coincidental.

ISBN 978-1-916722-06-4 (cased)

For David Pyne

A voracious reader and dear friend

Be extremely subtle, even to the point of formlessness.
Be extremely mysterious, even to the point of soundlessness.
Thereby you can be the director of the opponent's fate.

Sun Tzu

The Chinese and the Japanese are different enough
to make them disagreeable neighbours and similar enough
to intensify their hearty dislike of each other.

Lin Yutang

Prologue

On the night of 8 February 1904, without declaring war, the Japanese fleet under Admiral Heihachirō Tōgō ordered a surprise attack on the Russian squadron in Port Arthur, inflicting serious losses and imposing a blockade on the harbour.

This initial success encouraged the Japanese Army to land at two points on the Korean peninsula and engage with the Russian army. Neither side was able to win a decisive victory, however, until Admiral Tōgō fell upon the Russian Baltic Fleet in the straits of Tsushima between Japan and Korea, and inflicted a dramatic and decisive defeat.

Japan's military success against Russia led to its acquiring at the Treaty of Portsmouth the territories of Korea and Formosa (present-day Taiwan): in short, to its becoming an imperial power in Asia. In Russia, on the other hand, the calamitous course of the Russo-Japanese war led to considerable unrest. The country's humiliating defeat at the hands of an Asian power that until very recently had been preindustrial and isolationist added to people's national anger and disgust, and obliged the Czar, Nicholas II, to end unlimited autocracy in favour of a constitutional monarchy. A dozen years later, after the Czar's further disastrous participation in World War I, Vladimir Lenin was planning the successful October Revolution which led to the establishment of the Union of Soviet Socialist Republics in 1922.

Following Lenin's death in 1924, Ioseb Besarionis dze Jughashvili, better known as Joseph Vissarionovich Stalin, assumed leadership of the Soviet Union. While he was busy consolidating power in Moscow by dealing with those who, like Trotsky, Kamenev and Zinoviev, were competing with him to become Lenin's successor, far away in Siberia Japanese soldiers posed a constant threat along the Amur River border. Recognition of this obliged those in Moscow to seek a mutual non-aggression pact with Japan, but their advances were rebuffed by Tokyo, which claimed that the time wasn't yet ripe for such a treaty. It had its eye on Manchuria and the resources it needed to feed its growing population, and build ships and armaments for its modern military forces.

At the same time, Moscow held out high hopes of the success of the Communist Revolution in China since this would lead to the security of Soviet Far Eastern possessions and the Chinese Eastern Railway – the Trans-Siberian shortcut route running through Harbin in Manchuria to Vladivostok. But that Revolution was faltering under the onslaughts of the Nationalist Generalissimo, Chiang Kai-shek, and wasn't going to come about in the immediate future.

In 1929, two years before the Manchurian Incident enabled the Japanese Kwantung Army to invade and take over the north eastern provinces of China, a respected Chinese journal in the new capital of Nanking, Current Affairs Monthly, published what it referred to as *The Tanaka Memorandum*. This comparatively lengthy document was said to be a summary of the proceedings of a Far Eastern Conference, convened in Mukden the previous summer by the recently appointed Prime Minister of Japan, Baron Gi'ichi Tanaka, and attended by ministers and selected very senior officers of the Imperial Japanese Army and Navy. In its General Considerations, the Memorandum read as follows:

> Japan cannot remove the difficulties in Eastern Asia unless she adopts a policy of 'Blood and Iron.' But in carrying out this policy we have to face the United States which has been turned against us by China's policy of fighting poison with poison. In the future if we want to control China, we must first crush the United States just as in the past we had to fight in the Russo-Japanese War. But in order to conquer China we must first conquer Manchuria and Mongolia. In order to conquer the world, we must first conquer China. If we succeed in conquering China the rest of the Asiatic countries and the South Sea countries will fear us and surrender to us. Then the world will realize that Eastern Asia is ours and will not dare to violate our rights.

The Tanaka Memorandum caused uproar in China. It was also a wake-up call for those Western Powers which, like Great Britain and the United States of America, had until then pursued friendly relations with Japan. It also scared the wits out of Stalin and his Soviet Government in Moscow. While the Japanese decried the document as a fake, the rest of the world took an opposing view and began to prepare accordingly. *The Tanaka Memorandum* had revealed Japan's secret ambition to conquer Asia and, ultimately, the rest of the world. The stage was set for World War II.

Japan's defeat in that war led to the victory of the Red Army under Mao Zedong in China. Communist rule during succeeding decades in both Russia and China, therefore, was underpinned by Japan's, ultimately rejected, flirtation with imperialism in East Asia.

This is the background against which events in *The Tokyo Protocol* take place.

# PART ONE

On the Run

It was a moonless night – the thickening landscape congealed into a married calm with the sky, black as a Zen monk's ink painting. All the better for invisibility. And for stealth.

She moved noiselessly along a network of paths among the rice fields until she came to a track and a bridge across a canal. It was a little late to be early, but that was in the nature of stealth. Her slight figure, clothed from head to toe in black, the garb of the ninja assassin, crossed the bridge and followed the track until she could make out a dim light coming from the house. She skirted a high red-brick wall encircling the front courtyard and followed it round until she came to the rear entrance. Her senses well attuned to the dark-eyed night, she left the house behind her and made her way through an orchard, until she came to a path and a fisherman's lean-to shelter standing on the bank of another stream. This was the way they'd approach.

All she had to do now was wait. In time her prey would come, like insects to the spider's snare. She was the night's black agent, harbinger of ill-timed death, joined now by grave silence – that true friend who never betrays.

Shanghai 1927. The first days of August had brought with them an oppressive heat. The temperatures were punitive – well above 35 degrees during the day. Unforgiving. Now, in the night, grey-black clouds above the flat horizon were punctuated by an occasional flash of pale blue lightning that illuminated the checkerboard of rice fields and waterways stretching across the Yangtze plain. From time to time, an ominous, but still distant, rattling of thunder rent the wide cheeks of the sultry air. Otherwise, it was eerily quiet. Even the frogs, it seemed, had come to an agreement not to engage in their usual cacophony. The silence was one of anticipation – like those last minutes of jittery calm in the trenches before the storm of war.

The only thing that moved in the enveloping night was a small wooden sampan, deftly manoeuvred by its owner standing in the stern with a long sculling oar. In front was his loan passenger, wearing a loose-fitting Chinese tunic that disguised his slightly stocky frame. His sleek round face was hidden, like that of the oarsman, by a broad-rimmed conical bamboo hat.

The sampan moved silently beneath a row of weeping willows along the flooded waterway used to irrigate the rice fields. On either side were dykes obscuring the movement of the flat-bottomed boat, and the occasional straggling lines of farmers' hovels demarcating a settlement here, or whole village there. Somewhere a dog barked as the boat passed, and there was the occasional plop, too, of a fish breaking the water's surface. From time to time, the passenger moved a hand quickly to brush away an annoying mosquito. But the two men themselves were silent.

Little by little, the sampan approached the northern outskirts of the city. The rice fields gave way to a few new houses dotted here and there along tracks just wide enough for a water buffalo and cart. Long-legged white egrets stood motionless in the irrigated rice paddy, waiting patiently to impale a frog or small snake with their long, sharp bills. Nightfall danced to the tune of death's black veil.

The oarsman threaded his craft now this way, now that, as he followed his passenger's raised hand indicating in which direction to steer, before turning sharply into a narrow creek. There he eased his sampan to the water's edge and brought it to a standstill. His passenger stood up, stepped towards the stern to hand over some coins, and, with a muffled word of thanks, alighted onto a grassy bank. With a wave of his hand, he turned and walked away past half a dozen burial jars, a lean-to shelter, and then a fishpond, until he came to a low wall. There he opened a gate and continued along a well-trodden path through an orchard of mulberry trees.

'So, you've come, Shin-gan,' a voice called quietly. 'I wondered if you'd make it.'

'Shao-shan? Is that really you?' Su Bai-li asked, peering uncertainly into the dense darkness.

A sudden flash of lightning revealed a tall, wiry figure with a very black, bushy beard standing under a loquat tree by the path. It was indeed Chou En-lai.

The two old friends embraced, as another roll of thunder rent the silence.

'You came by water, then?'

'It seemed the best way to avoid attention. A bit circuitous, perhaps. But it has been rather a lovely evening for a boat ride. You should try it sometime, Shao-shan,' Bai-li smiled.

'I may have to. Sooner than I thought, too. Not even the French Concession is safe these days.'

'So I've heard. You'll be heading back south, then? To Canton?'

'Where else can I go, Shin-gan. It's our last stronghold. Here we've been decimated.'

Bai-li nodded thoughtfully.

'Remember, new beginnings are often disguised as painful endings.'

He paused, before smiling and reaching out to touch his friend's face. 'But that's quite a beard you've grown, Shao-shan, since you've been in hiding.'

'I use it to camouflage my Little Mountain,' Chou En-lai laughed.

'If you're not careful, it'll transform you into a Da-shan – a Big, not just Little, Mountain,' Bai-li clapped his younger friend on the back, as he sniffed the humid air.

'I'd say it's going to rain. Not yet. Later, though.'

'Let's hope it does. A bit of rain will keep those cockroach spies at home and leave us in peace. There's nothing they dislike more than standing around getting wet.'

'A bit of thunder should help, too. Even grown men are afraid of thunder. Still, one needs to be careful.'

'Always, Shin-gan. But come. Let's go find the others.'

Chou put one arm round his friend's shoulder and together the two men started through a kitchen garden towards the big house, its tiled roof almost imperceptibly etched in the dark. At one point he stopped, bent down and cut a watermelon with a knife that he drew from the pocket of his cotton jacket.

'Surely, Ch'ing-ling already has something for us?' Bai-li said reprovingly.

'Probably. But fresh watermelon is the best way to combat this heat.'

'True. But are you sure it's going to taste good?'

'No, I'm not, Shin-gan. You can never tell what a watermelon is going to taste like until you've cut it open and eaten a slice. It's like a marriage.' Chou laughed loudly and slapped his friend playfully on the back.

'If you say so, Shao-shan. I wouldn't know. How is Ying-ch'ao, by the way?'

'Well, thank you. As beautiful and as committed to the cause as ever.'

'A good wife, then.'

Chou En-lai nodded.

'A good wife.'

'But no children.'

'Now's hardly the time.'

'Indeed,' Bai-li inclined his head.

'You should find a wife for yourself, Shin-gan.'

'I probably should. But, as you say, now's not the time. Too much uncertainty.'

It was Chou's turn to nod, as they passed through some large double wooden doors into a courtyard, round a brick wall that prevented snooping passers-by from peering in, and crossed to a veranda running the length of the southern wall of a substantial house. A dim light came from inside. Chou knocked rapidly twice on the window, and then twice again.

'Madame Sun said we should go in by the side door. Come.'

He led Bai-li along the wide veranda to the end of the house where a door was ajar. Taking off their soft-soled shoes, the two men stepped into a room lined with books. Although it was hard to see in the dark, Chou unerringly made his way through what had been Charlie Soong's study when he was alive. Bai-li made out a handsome Arts and Crafts desk facing the north window, and books in both English and Chinese lining two walls.

They passed through an open door into a dining room, furnished with half a dozen Chinese-style straight-backed chairs set round a rosewood table. Above it hung a handsomely decorated crimson, black and gold Tiffany chandelier. Along the back wall stood two Byrdcliffe cabinets, and a – slightly incongruous – linen press, on which had been placed a tall yellow faience vase. A handsome, inlaid, part-ebonized cherrywood and maple cabinet stood in the corner by the window.

All of this Bai-li noted approvingly as the two men made their way towards the source of the dim light inside the house – a foreign-style parlour with three plush, green-upholstered Egyptian Revival chairs and a sofa set around a large Stickley hexagonal table.

On one side of the room, the fingers of one hand distractedly playing a nursery rhyme on the ivory keys of a Blüthner grand piano, while her other hand rested on its ebony wood lid, sat Soong Ch'ing-ling, the middle 'Red' sister of Charlie Soong's three famous daughters. Petite and square-jawed, she wasn't particularly beautiful by Chinese standards. No melon seed-shaped face, nor almond eyes, nor eyebrows arching like willow shoots across her forehead. But her features were delicate and her skin as smooth as fine porcelain. Her bearing was dignified and graceful, as befitted the young widow of the 'Father of China,' Sun Yat-sen.

Ch'ing-ling was wearing a dark magenta silk dress, with a lace handkerchief tucked into the cuff of one sleeve, matched by two ruby studs in her earlobes. She had pulled her hair back from her face, twisted it, and wrapped its plaits in two circular coils at the back of her head. A picture of contained and modest elegance. The kind of elegance Bai-li loved, and which, he knew, loved him in return.

As he moved towards her, he became aware of the scent of an Oriental perfume. Ginger flower, underpinned by sandalwood. The perfect summer perfume for a stormy night ahead.

Ch'ing-ling stood up from the piano to greet her two visitors.

'You came, Bai-li,' she said simply in English, taking his hand and searching his deep brown eyes. 'Shao-shan was worried you might not make it.' Like her perfume. her voice was soft, alluring, and unexpectedly sweet.

'We came,' Bai-li acknowledged. 'It's good to have you back in Shanghai, Mei-mei. It's been too long.'

Bai-li was the only one – apart from Ei-ling, her older sister – who was intimate enough to call Ch'ing-ling 'Younger Sister.'

Ch'ing-ling squeezed his hand gently – a fraction longer than politeness required – before turning towards her bearded visitor.

'I once knew Chou En-lai by sight,' she gave a gentle laugh as she took his hand in turn. 'But I'm not sure I do now. Is it really you, Shao-shan?'

'It is indeed, Madame Sun,' Chou answered formally.

'Please, Shao-shan. Let's dispense with formalities. There are so few of us left now.'

Ch'ing-ling gestured to the two men to sit down on the Egyptian-style sofa.

'I see you've brought some refreshments, Shao-shan. Let me relieve you of that heavy weight and cut it up for us to eat.'

'I'm afraid I took the liberty of stealing it from your kitchen garden.'

'Did you now?' Once more the gentle laugh. 'You'd better keep that bit of information to yourself. The night is full of listening ears. Imagine how happy the Generalissimo would be to execute you if he found out you've become a thief, as well as dedicated Communist and labour union organizer.'

Chou gave one of his boyish grins. Ch'ing-ling continued,

'Anyway, let me go into the kitchen and prepare this splendid watermelon. I know where everything is, even in the dark. So, just stay where you are and make yourselves at home.'

She left the two men in the dimly lit parlour. Above their heads, a large ceiling fan circled quietly. There was a Western-style fireplace in the middle of the back wall of the room, with a surround of Soochow tiles with yellow dragons on them. Above it was an oil portrait of old Charlie Soong, while on the mantelpiece stood a fine old ormolu and ebony clock. It had stopped, its two mother of pearl hands pointing to five and nine on the clockface.

'The time her father died,' Bai-li intoned as he followed his friend's gaze. 'Twenty-five minutes past nine on the third of May 1918.'

'And only fifty-six years old, wasn't he? Too young.'

'As you say, too young. Sun Yat-sen, too. If only they'd been given more time.'

'Things are what they are, Shin-gan. We have to make do with what Dr Sun bequeathed us.'

Bai-li bowed his head at his friend's gentle rebuke, even though he was about ten years older than 'Little Mountain' Chou. The light revealed him to be slightly short and stocky, with close-cropped hair and round-rimmed tortoiseshell glasses that masked two bushy eyebrows and magnified his deep brown eyes. His mouth was small, but when he smiled, as he often did when with friends, he revealed two rather charming dimples in his cheeks. They were persuasive, too, when the need arose.

The two men had met in Japan where they had audited classes at Kyoto University and met up with all sorts of revolution-minded Chinese students in Japan. Later, firm friends, they had sailed for Europe where Chou had organised a Communist Youth League, before joining the Chinese Communist Party, of which Bai-li was already a founding member.

More recently, Bai-li had saved the other's life when Chiang Kai-shek had made use of his army and Tu Yue-sheng's Green Gang to stage a violent coup – already known as the 'Shanghai Massacre' – earlier that year and Chou was caught hiding in the Commercial Press Building. Assigned to act as second interrogator by General Pai Ch'ung, Bai-li, who the General unquestioningly believed was on his side, arranged for his friend to escape. This was why Chou En-lai called him Shin-gan, or 'Heart and Liver'. Bai-li was like Shao-shan's two most vital organs.

Ch'ing-ling came back into the room, bearing a small bowl of loquats in one hand and, in the other, a large dish of fresh watermelon slices, their black seeds gleaming in the oil lamp's light.

Behind her emerged a second figure who, as he stepped into the light, Bai-li quickly realised wasn't Chinese. Tall and with a leonine head, the newcomer had a slightly sensuous mouth under an extremely bushy moustache. Above it, a shock of neatly coiffed, long and slightly wavy dark brown hair was brushed back from a high, wide forehead, and fell to the nape of its bearer's neck. Even when on the run, Stalin's chief Soviet agent in China, Mikhail Borodin, cut an impressive figure.

'Comrade Chou,' he exclaimed in English, coming forward to shake the hands of his old comrade. 'It's been too long.'

'It has, indeed, Comrade Borodin. And I'm afraid, it's only going to get longer. One wonders when we'll meet again, what with you making your way back to Moscow, and I heading south to Canton.' He smiled sadly.

'Things will get better. This is no time to be despondent, Comrade Chou,' Borodin boomed, before turning quizzically towards Bai-li. 'And you, sir. I don't believe I've had the pleasure –'

His voice tailed off. Ch'ing-ling came to the rescue.

'Mikhail. May I introduce you to Su Bai-li. One of the half-dozen founding members of the Chinese Communist Party.'

'A pioneer, then. It's an honour to meet you, Comrade Su,' Borodin said as he shook Bai-li's hand. Like Ch'ing-ling, he spoke English with a mid-Western American accent. 'But how come I haven't come across you before? Down in Canton, for example. Or at the Whampoa Military Academy. Like my friend Comrade Chou here,' he smiled.

Bai-li pushed his tortoiseshell glasses up more firmly onto the bridge of his nose and glanced uncertainly at the others around him.

'It's all right, Bai-li,' Ch'ing-ling said quickly. 'We're all friends here. Without secrets. Isn't that right, Shao-shan? Mikhail?'

'But of course,' the two men nodded their assent. All turned their attention to Bai-li.

'The fact that you haven't heard of me, Comrade Borodin, I regard as a compliment,' he began.

'You do? How's that?' The Soviet agent's curiosity was piqued.

'As Ch'ing-ling mentioned, when I was in Moscow back in 1921, I was invited to become one of the founding members of the CCP.'

'Along with Mao Tse-tung?'

'Along with Mao. I was then ordered by the Comintern not to reveal that I was a Chinese Communist Party member, but to work undercover. I have, therefore, appeared to throw my lot in with Chiang Kai-shek and the Nationalists in the Kuomintang.'

'The emphasis being on "appeared," I take it?'

Bai-li inclined his head.

Chou En-lai took over.

'This is why, Comrade Borodin, we've invited Bai-li to join us this evening. He's the only one among us who's not on the run. As Director of the Kuomintang's Internal Affairs in Shanghai, he usually knows what Chiang Kai-shek is up to and can, as a result, advise us accordingly. We need his inside knowledge if we're to survive.'

'Gentlemen, I'm forgetting my manners again,' Ch'ing-ling interposed. 'Do please sit down and help yourselves to this appetising watermelon that Little Mountain here stole from my kitchen garden.'

They did as invited, while Ch'ing-ling continued in her gentle voice.

'Mikhail, there's something else I think you should know.'

'There is?' Borodin asked.

'Bai-li is by nature self-effacing and tends not reveal too much about himself. Maybe that's why the Comintern ordered him to go undercover. But he has a special relationship with our mutual enemy, Chiang Kai-shek.'

'He has?' Borodin was caught short with his mouth full of watermelon. A black pip fell conveniently into the palm of his hand.

'Well, I wouldn't say a special relationship as such,' Bai-li demurred. 'It's more – how can I put it? – a point of contact.'

Borodin wiped his moustache with one hand.

'And what is this "point of contact," as you so imprecisely put it?'

Bai-li smiled enough for one of his dimples to make a brief appearance.

'As you know, Comrade Borodin, in China we rely on personal networks – people we know from another place or time in our lives – to get things done. Sometimes we make use of family or lineage connections. Sometimes we rely on colleagues at work, or on members of a common association of some kind,' he paused. 'And then there are the friends we make during the course of our education.'

'And Chiang Kai-shek is such a friend?'

Bai-li inclined his head.

'He was in the year above me at school in Ningpo, so we knew each other quite well. We also ended up attending the military academy in Tokyo at the same time. However, unlike the Generalissimo, I chose not to serve in the Imperial Japanese Army. Instead,' he glanced at Chou En-lai and smiled. 'I met up with this pirate here and went with him to France, before moving on to Moscow.'

'In all fairness to Bai-li,' Chou En-lai addressed Mikhail Borodin, 'I think you should know he hasn't lived his life solely in the lap of Nationalist luxury. Before being appointed to his current elevated position, he helped me organise strikes and worker protests against Japanese textile mill owners in and around Shanghai. At one point, he even became a ricksha puller in order to coordinate a strike involving other ricksha-men in the city. If I have a suggestion, Comrade Borodin, it is, don't be fooled by his soft appearance. If ever you were to engage in an arm-wrestling match with Bai-li, you'd quickly lose.'

After their laughter had died down, Ch'ing-ling added, 'Bai-li also met my husband at our house in Rue Molière just before he died.'

A final seal of approval.

'And borrowed his glasses, too, when he'd forgotten his own.'

Again Bai-li pushed the tortoiseshell glasses up onto his nose. 'They seem to have become a permanent loan.'

'And the lenses fit you?'

Bai-li nodded.

'Better than the frame, perhaps. It's probably a bit presumptuous of me, but I like to think that I share with our much-mourned Doctor the same vision for the Republic of China.'

There was a brief silence before Mikhail Borodin took over.

'So, Comrade Su, I assume you're here to give advice in these difficult times?'

'Only if it should happen to be appropriate.' Bai-li inclined his head modestly once more.

'So, what are your thoughts? The Party's in disarray, its members rounded up, put in gaol and many summarily executed. I myself am on the run, ordered back to Moscow where I must face Stalin's wrath. As for your so-called "pirate," the Generalissimo has put a price of twenty thousand Mexican silver dollars on his head. Only Ch'ing-ling is able to lead a normal life without interference from the Nationalists. It seems that, as Madame Sun, she's untouchable.'

'My thoughts, Comrade Borodin?' Bai-li smiled his disarming dimpled smile. 'I'm not sure I'm in possession of enough information to have arrived at any thoughts as such. At least, not yet. So perhaps you can fill me in on what went on in Hankow last month. There are all kinds of rumours, but I distrust people's prattle. After all, those who speak tend not to know. To act, one needs hard facts.'

Borodin brushed back a stray lock of hair from his forehead.

'I guess we should ask ourselves first, what went wrong,' he began. 'For that I blame Stalin himself. And Manabendra Nath Roy.'

'Still Head of the Far Eastern Section of the Comintern?'

Borodin nodded.

'Stalin sent me a secret message earlier this year, ordering me to conduct a partial confiscation of landlords' holdings in and around Hankow. He also told me to mobilise an army of workers and peasants.'

'That sounds a little impractical, given the circumstances,' Bai-li interjected. He was sitting very still.

'Totally. In my opinion, it was little short of a fairy tale dreamed up by someone overseas with neither knowledge nor understanding of what was happening here on the ground.'

'An opinion, I assume, that you have preferred not to relay back to Stalin in Moscow.'

Borodin grinned behind his moustache.

'Well put, Comrade Su. I had no intention of carrying out those orders. As I saw it, the time wasn't right.'

'Understandable,' Bai-li looked at his two hands lightly clasped in his lap. 'Please continue, Comrade Borodin.'

'Somehow Roy got hold of the message and passed on its contents to Wang Ching-wei.'

'Head of the Wuhan Nationalist government.'

'The same. News then got out. Whether through Roy or Wang, I've no idea. As a result, local landlords protested furiously at the idea of losing their private property. They started beating up tax inspectors and gathered gangs of ruffians to guard their land. Wang became frightened and made a great show of refusing to carry out Stalin's orders. He hinted publicly that I was the culprit.'

'Culprit?' Bai-li removed his glasses. 'Accused of what exactly?'

'Of wanting to start a rebellion against the landlords.'

'But you didn't? Start one, I mean.'

'Nor want one right then, if truth be told.'

'Ah!'

Bai-li had by now extracted a handkerchief from the pocket of his tunic jacket and was carefully polishing the lenses of the round-rimmed spectacles bequeathed him by Dr Sun.

'And then?' He asked mildly.

'Then?' Borodin repeated the word angrily. 'Then, before we knew where we were, Communists and Nationalists were at each other's throats. As you probably heard, on July 15, the Communists were expelled from the left-wing faction of the Kuomintang in Wuhan.'

'Effectively ending the First United Front.'

'Effectively ending the working alliance between the KMT and the CCP, yes.'

'And your own role as a Comintern agent in China, I assume.'

'I was ordered to leave China the following day.'

'But you're still here?'

Borodin chuckled again.

'I refused to leave until Fanya, my wife, was released from prison in Jinan.'

'It was ridiculous,' interposed Ch'ing-ling. Over the years the two women had developed a close friendship, based on the shared experiences of having lived as foreign women in the Mid-West. 'A trumped-up charge.'

'And was she?' Bai-li finished wiping the lenses of his glasses, but left them with his handkerchief, untended in his lap. 'Released, I mean.'

'Eventually. Thanks to a well-placed bribe.'

Bai-li blinked queryingly at the Russian.

'By the Japanese, of all people.'

'The Japanese?' Bai-li raised his bushy eyebrows in a look of feigned surprise. 'Someone, I suppose, must have bribed them in turn to bribe the judge. Any thoughts who that might have been, Comrade Borodin?'

'The KMT, I guess. I wouldn't know.'

'It would make sense, wouldn't it? It's the sort of thing Chiang Kai-shek would do. Play all sides. And of course, not tell anyone.'

Seemingly satisfied with the results of his polishing, Bai-li put his glasses back on his nose and glanced quickly round at the others. 'Let's face it, the Nationalists could hardly be seen to be directly involved in releasing an enemy prisoner, could they?'

Bai-li's handkerchief found its way back effortlessly into the pocket of his dark blue tunic.

'And she is with you now, your wife, Comrade Borodin?'

'Alas, no. We decided to leave separately for Russia. She's taking the direct rail route from Peking through Mukden and Harbin to the Russo-Manchurian border at Manzhouli.'

'And you?'

'Chengchow, Gansu, and on across Mongolia. I leave tomorrow.'

'A long, hard trip. I wish you luck.' Bai-li turned to his old friend. 'And you Shao-shan? When are you off?'

'Tonight, as soon as we're finished here. I'll make my way south somehow. Eventually, I'll find Mao and join his army. After that,' Chou shrugged, 'Who knows?'

Bai-li nodded.

'Take care, my friend,' was all he said.

There was another ominous drum roll of thunder outside. Everyone in the room paused, alert to the possibility of rain. The ceiling fan continued to circle lazily above their heads, stirring the heavy air.

'I blame Chiang Kai-shek for this mess,' Ch'ing-ling spoke up. 'He failed to carry out my late husband's wishes before he died. Instead, he cut off relations with Moscow and the Comintern's Soviet advisers in China, like Mikhail here. He should never have betrayed the Communist cause. We are, after all, all Chinese. We should be united against our real enemy, the Japanese. And to think he's about to become my brother-in-law,' she shuddered.

'It's been decided then?'

'So my older sister Ei-ling tells me. My mother's finally given in. Chiang swore he'd convert to Christianity and become a Methodist and my mother's fallen for it.'

Ch'ing-ling was in defiant mode.

'The Hankow government was the legitimate interpreter of my late husband's thinking. But Chiang paid it no attention. I'm telling you, without the people behind them, the Nationalists will become weak. Their party, the Kuomintang, will no longer be able to aspire to being in any way "revolutionary."'

There was a pause as the three men digested Ch'ing-ling's reasoned outburst. It was Bai-li who spoke first.

'We all accept, I think, that the door to the kind of revolution we envisage has, for the moment, been firmly closed,' he began.

The others listened intently, even though the truth of what Bai-li was saying was uncomfortable.

'But every door has a keyhole, through which one can peer and see what's taking place on the other side,' he continued. 'A seeming impasse, therefore, isn't necessarily impassable.'

He paused, gracing his audience with a dimpled smile.

'Your mention of the Japanese, Comrade Borodin – and you, Mei-mei – reminds us that we're currently facing two enemies: Chiang Kai-shek and the Nationalists, on the one hand, and the Japanese Kwantung Army in Manchuria, on the other. This particular door closing us in, then, would seem to have two keyholes.'

'Meaning, we need two plans? Two keys?' Chou En-lai was quickest on the uptake.

'Precisely.'

'But where do we find them?' Asked Ch'ing-ling in her quiet voice. 'How do we know where to look?'

'You have a plan, don't you, Comrade Su?' Borodin's eyes were sparkling.

'Not a plan as such. That would be an exaggeration. Two half-formed ideas might be a better way of putting it. No more than that, I'm afraid.'

'And they are?'

'First, there is our local enemy, Chiang Kai-shek. Something has occurred to me which may be helpful. As you probably know, when he was still courting the Comintern, the Generalissimo sent his teenage son, Ching-kuo, to Moscow to study.'

'That was a couple of years ago,' Borodin said. 'Surely he's back in China now.'

Another loud peal of thunder rattled the windows of the house. Somewhere in the distance, a dog started barking.

'That's my point,' Bai-li continued impassively. 'Ching-kuo has indeed finished his studies, but now that the Generalissimo has broken with Moscow, Stalin refuses to let the boy return home.'

'You mean, he's holding Ching-kuo hostage?'

'In a manner of speaking, yes, although I doubt Stalin would phrase it like that. A matter of taking out an insurance policy, perhaps.'

'But can't Chiang get him back somehow?'

'The short answer to that question is no. The boy is too valuable a prize for Stalin to release him. He'll want something in return. Something important to the Soviet Union.'

'Like what?'

'Like being given back control of the Chinese Eastern Railway, perhaps? I wouldn't know. Perhaps Comrade Borodin has an idea?'

Borodin stroked his moustache thoughtfully.

'You may be right, Comrade Su. The Soviet Government does want to take back control of its Trans-Siberian rail line. But the Japanese would object, surely?'

'Indeed, they would,' Bai-li examined his carefully trimmed fingernails.

'But what's the plan, Shin-gan?'

'The plan?' Bai-li looked up a little absently. 'Ching-kuo, remember, is Chiang's one and only son. The Generalissimo loves him out of all proportion and would do anything to have him by his side again. As a result, if Ching-kuo continues to remain in Moscow – and I have no reason to believe he won't – then it's reasonable to conclude that Chiang Kai-shek's dealings with the Communists, in particular with the Red Army under Mao Tse-tung, can be influenced by his love for his son. It may alter the whole course of the war between the two sides. To our advantage.'

'How so?' Borodin looked confused.

'If ever he is to get Ching-kuo back, the Generalissimo will know better than to antagonise Stalin by routing what's left of the Red Army. He needs the Soviet Union on his side.'

Outside there was a flash of lightning, another crash of thunder, and the heavens opened with a deafening roar.

'Ah, rain at last!' Ch'ing-ling stood up, crossed the room and opened a window. 'It will be cooler now.'

'And, hopefully, it will help rid us of our confusion,' Chou stood up and stretched, before sitting down again in one of the vacant armchairs.

Ch'ing-ling left the slatted wooden shutter closed to stop the rain splashing onto her grand piano. Then she went and sat down beside her secret lover. Her voice betrayed none of her emotions.

'You were telling us of Chiang Kai-shek's love for his son, Bai-li.'

'Indeed. He writes long letters to him at least once a week.'

'So?'

'So, he never gets a reply. Moscow intercepts all the boy's letters to his father.'

'Always presuming he writes them.'

'He does, I can assure you.'

'Surely, one could be smuggled across the border?' Borodin persisted.

'It's been tried. And failed, which is why I know for a fact that he does write to his father. At this point, though, we have to deal with another problem. This time a personal problem, to do with me, I'm afraid.'

'You, Shin-gan?'

'Yes. It's come to my attention that an ultra-rightist in the ideological wing of the KMT, a Colonel Pan Yu-tang, has suggested to the Generalissimo that I might not be all that I appear to be.'

'You mean, a true Nationalist?'

'In their understanding of the term, of course.'

'Of course,' concurred Borodin. 'But does he have any evidence to support his theory?'

'Not that I know of. But he's looking for it.'

'Will he find anything?'

'It's hard to tell these days, isn't it? I covered my tracks as best I could when I helped Shao-shan out of gaol a couple of months ago. But, as we know, people talk. For money, or under duress, it doesn't matter. Their tongues are loosened. I have to get rid of Colonel Pan, therefore, before he causes trouble.'

'How?'

Borodin was direct and to the point as always.

'Well, it has crossed my mind that I might try to persuade the Generalissimo to entrust him with a letter to his son and have the Colonel travel to Moscow with instructions – as you yourself have already hinted at, Comrade Borodin – to smuggle back a reply from the young man.'

'But how does that help you, Bai-li?'

'It doesn't, of itself. But it does if the Colonel is discovered at the Siberian border to be smuggling a letter to the Generalissimo. A summary trial, I believe is the procedure, with a sentence of ten years at least in a gulag.'

'And the letter?'

'Destroyed. Or, better, retained for Stalin's perusal at his leisure.'

'Like Ching-kuo himself.'

'Precisely. My aim is to make Chiang realise that he cannot – must not – destroy the Red Army, however much he may wish to. And that his true enemy is, in fact, the Japanese.'

'In other words, to get him to look north towards Manchuria, instead of south to Canton?'

'It would help. Otherwise, unless he's persuaded to change course, the Generalissimo might end up where he's heading. And none of us would want that, would we?'

Once more the dimpled smile that charmed them all.

She heard them first. Two reed voices by the water's edge. Then she smelled them. The rank, sour smell of two unwashed bodies. She could scent blood, too, in their murderous sweat.

They were coming along the creek, from the same direction in which Bai-li had come earlier. And the bearded man before him. But they were on foot, not on water.

She sank deeper into the shelter, drawing the black collar of her tunic up over her mouth and the lower half of her face to cover her pale skin and a few stray whisps of auburn red hair. Crouched behind some fishing equipment, her heart beat slightly faster, her pupils dilating. Once she rode the tiger, she could never dismount. She knew from experience there was no turning back. For any of them.

The two men approached, like mosquitoes blown by a gentle breeze towards the black widow's fatal web. The one in front was older, more assured. In his late-forties, probably, with tattoos on his hands and legs. For all that, he recoiled as he passed the burial jars.

'Ugh! Ghosts!' She heard him exclaim. 'I don't like ghosts.'

There was a loud peel of thunder as he spoke.

'And I don't like thunder,' muttered the nervous-looking younger man behind him. 'That makes us quits, *laopan*.'

The older man took a few steps forward until he was level with the shelter where she crouched motionless, her face lowered.

'We'll wait here,' he said quietly. 'It's going to rain, so we'll need shelter of some kind until he leaves the Soong house.'

'Are you sure he'll come this way, Boss?' The younger one asked. He was hardly more than twenty years old, and his voice sounded as edgy as he looked. 'Is that what Big Ears said?'

So, they were members of the Green Gang, Shanghai's feared mobsters, headed by 'Big Ears' Tu Yue-sheng. It always helped to know her enemy.

'What other way is there, *shakua*?' the older man asked. 'We'll wait until he passes us in the dark and then we'll cut his throat.'

'How will we know he's the right guy?' The younger man was wiry, with thick black hair sticking up from his head like an Amur hedgehog. He didn't like being called a 'stupid melon' by his older companion, however affectionate the term might be. It impugned his intelligence.

'By his beard. He's got a big bushy beard. That's what the boss said.'

'Why does he want him killed?'

The older man sighed.

'For a young whipper-snapper, you ask too many questions, *shakua*!'

'Just give me a simple reply, *laopan*. Then I'll shut up, I promise.'

'The monk T'ang-seng said the same when spreading his Buddhist teachings,' his companion snapped sharply. 'And look what happened to him.'

Then he relented. The kid was still young.

'Look, all I know is the order came from the very top.'

'What? Higher than Big Ears?'

The older man shrugged.

'I'm telling you. That's what I heard.'

'But Big Ears doesn't take orders from anyone, *laopan*.'

'Who says he doesn't? Who ordered us to kill all the communists in the spring? Eh? It wasn't Big Ears, that's for sure. He was just carrying out somebody else's orders, because he was being paid to do so.'

Young *shakua's* mouth fell open as the penny dropped.

'Not the Generalissimo?'

There was a silence broken only by another roll of thunder.

'Who else? Look, *shakua*, it's better not to ask questions. Big Ears is paying us well. That's all that matters.'

Suddenly the heavens opened. The rain was torrential, bouncing off the hard earth, quickly forming pools of dirty water. The two men stepped hurriedly in under the shelter and looked out into the night, their backs towards the crouching tigress.

'That's some downpour, *lo*.' The older man said, brushing the rain from the sleeves of his robe.

'Is this guy with a beard another communist, *laopan*?' The younger man continued his train of thought.

'Maybe, but who cares? We do what we're told, *shakua*. Remember, Green Gang members don't climb trees to catch a fish.'

The younger man gave his companion a baffled look. He took out a pack of cigarettes and offered one. A peace offering.

'I got these from a Japanese rōnin,' he continued. 'He said they'd make me happy. Try one, *laopan*.'

'What are they called, then?'

'Bat.'

'Bat? What kind of a name is that?'

'I dunno. A name that appeals to dwarf bandits, I guess.'

'Not sure I'm very fond of bats, to be honest.' The older man gave an exaggerated shiver, then helped himself to a cigarette. As his companion lit it for him, the flare of his match briefly illuminated the shelter. With her head down, she held her breath. But neither of them noticed her.

'Thanks, *shakua*.'

'But if this Big Beard guy's a communist, *laopan*,' the younger man scratched his crotch. 'He must be an important communist.'

'Maybe.'

Give him his due, he stuck to his guns.

'If so, then Big Ears should be paying us more. I mean, there's probably a price on his head.'

'If you value your own life, *shakua*, you need to put ideas like that out of your young head.'

'Yeah! Got it, *laopan*,' the other responded sulkily, staring bleakly out into the night. The rain continued to pour down in front of them both, creating puddles under the eaves of the shelter and rivulets along the path outside.

The older man inhaled deeply and let out an appreciative sigh, along with a lungful of smoke.

'This is good, *lo*,' he said, as if to mollify his companion. 'You were right, *shakua*. One thing you can say about the dwarf bandits, they know a thing or two when it comes to making stuff.'

The other nodded, still silent. Then he struck a second match and, cupping his hands around it, lit his own cigarette.

'Well, this rain isn't going to stop for a while, is it? Why don't you make yourself useful and find us something to sit on?'

'What! Out there in this rain?' The young man said aghast. 'But it's wet, *laopan*.'

'No. Behind us, *shakua*.' Maybe he really was a silly melon.

'There's got to be something in this shelter,' he jerked his left thumb over his shoulder. 'Take a look round. See what you can find.'

Shakua looked back a little nervously.

'It's dark back there.'

'Of course, it is, you thickhead. It's night-time. Get a move on. I don't want to be standing here all night.'

'OK! OK!' The younger man muttered and turned back towards where she was waiting, *finca* combat knife in hand, thumb firm along the back of the blade. Opportunely, a long peal of thunder rent the air around the shelter.

He never saw her. All he felt was death's sharp sting as a knife plunged upwards deep into his side, severing his aorta, while a firm hand snuffed out his cry. He was dead before the sound of rain returned outside. Hidden dragon, crouching tiger.

The older man heard nothing. He took another deep drag on his cigarette, held the smoke in his lungs, and then exhaled with a satisfied sigh. His shoulders seemed visibly to relax as he stood facing out into the night, a flash of lightning illuminating the trail of smoke from his mouth.

'What's up, *shakua*? Have you lost your tongue at last?'

He was half turning when she sliced his neck with her razor-sharp knife. The way she'd been taught in OGPU training back in Moscow. A second body joined the first on the hard earth under the lean-to's rice straw thatch. Quickness was the essence of war.

She listened, her heart pumping with adrenalin. What if? But there was no what if. No wolf coming in through the back door of the tiger's lair. No fox to borrow the tiger's might. She'd been too well prepared for surprises.

She wiped the blade of her knife on the younger man's loose robe, then folded it into its black resin handle and put it back in the pocket of her tunic jacket. Having rinsed the blood off her hands in the raindrops dripping from the eaves of the lean-to roof, she waited and listened. Plip-plip-plop.

Once the rain eased, she heaved the bodies, one by one, onto some rice straw matting she found at the back of the shelter and hauled them along the path to the main canal. There she rolled them down the bank into the water and watched them drift, very slowly, away. Two more corpses that eventually would end up in the Yangtze River, before being washed out to sea where the fishes were waiting expectantly, confidant that this bait, like that on the end of a Buddhist monk's fishing line, had no hook.

As for her, she would remain hidden in the shelter until Bai-li and the bearded man had left. Then she would head back into the city, get changed, and go down to Blood Alley to find herself a man. Any man ready to go to bed with a tiger who harboured a dragon within. It was a rule of hers. After every kill have torrid sex, leading to explosive orgasms that would allow her to free-fall into amnesia. The Art of Fugue.

Chou En-lai stood up again and walked across the room to the open window, enjoying the cool breeze that accompanied the torrential rain beating down on the stone flags in the courtyard between the house and the stream beyond. With his back to the others, he took the conversation forward.

'You said, Shin-gan, that there were two keyholes in the door closed to us. Two keys that we need to look for. What's the second?'

'The second?' Bai-li adjusted his glasses once again. 'Ah, yes. The second.'

There was silence in the room as Chou returned to the armchair Ch'ing-ling had vacated. Outside the frogs had woken up and the night resounded with the resurrection of their hoarse croaking.

'The second is trickier. As I said earlier, it concerns the Japanese, though not entirely. What we do or do not do about the Japanese also concerns Chiang Kai-shek and the Nationalists. And, therefore, ourselves.'

'Go on.'

Borodin was impatient. Bai-li gave him a reproachful look.

'You may have been too caught up in your difficulties in Hankow to notice,' he continued, 'But the Prime Minister of Japan, Gi'ichi Tanaka, recently convened what he referred to as a "Far Eastern Conference" in Tokyo. It was attended, I'm told, by senior members of the Japanese Foreign Ministry, the Army General Staff, the Navy, and Ministry of Finance.'

'I heard something about it,' Borodin said, slightly dismissively. 'So?'

'So, the agenda included discussion of Japan's political and economic interests in China – in particular, in Manchuria and Mongolia, which as you are aware, the Japanese regard as their own.'

'Even though Mongolia is ours,' Borodin clenched his fist.

Bai-li continued unperturbed.

'As I understand it, those present at the conference also made plans for the advancement of Japanese commercial activities in China as a whole.'

'Ah-ha! So, they want more strikes? I can still help them there.'

This time it was Chou who interrupted.

Bai-li refused to be distracted.

'I have it from someone who is normally a reliable source that, in his concluding speech at the end of the twelve-day gathering, Tanaka suggested that it was up to the Chinese people themselves to bring about stability and order to our country. Japan, therefore, wasn't going to side with one faction or another and wouldn't intervene if, or when, strife developed.'

'As now.'

'As you say, Ch'ing-ling, as now. Japan would also respect Dr Sun's "Three Principles of the People."'

'Poof!' There was an exclamation of disgust from Dr Sun's widow. 'What do the Japanese know about my husband's doctrine of nationalism, democracy, and the livelihood of the people?'

'Indeed, Mei-mei!' echoed Bai-li, who proceeded smoothly. 'What I'm saying is that, instead of producing a master plan for world domination, as one or two of us had anticipated, and – if I may say so – feared given Tanaka's "blood and iron" approach, those present at the conference are said to have come to a rough consensus that the Japanese Government should support the KMT against the CCP. At the same time, they agreed that Japan should also devote itself to persuading the warlord of Manchuria, General Chang Tso-lin, to consolidate his base in a virtually autonomous Manchuria.'

'In other words, create a buffer state between China and the Soviet Union?'

'A buffer state that will almost inevitably fall under Japanese domination, yes.'

Bai-li sat back and surveyed the other three in the room. There was a more distant clap of thunder as the storm moved eastwards out to sea. The rain was already easing. But the breeze that came through the one open window still brought cool air with it. There would be a few more hours of respite before the temperature rose again. Enjoy these moments in their entirety, he thought. To a mind that is still the whole universe surrenders.

Mikhail Borodin woke him from his reverie.

'This is all very interesting, Comrade Su. But where are you leading us?'

'Yes, yes. Of course. My apologies.'

Bai-li once again inclined his head compliantly.

'As I'm sure you'll agree, we're too weak right now to fight our enemies. Either the Nationalists, or the Japanese. Militarily, the Generalissimo's troops control the whole of central China and north as far as Peking. The Japanese Kwantung Army in Manchuria, not to mention its naval troops stationed here in Shanghai, are also a constant threat. There's nothing we can do openly against such forces. Yet, as I see it, we need to look to our enemy for a chance to succeed.'

'Which enemy, Comrade Su? The Nationalists? Or the Japanese?'

'Both. I suggest, therefore, that we resort to something underhand. Some kind of disinformation that will distract them.'

Mikhail Borodin leaned forward in his chair.

'Disinformation? Such as?'

'Something credible, but at the same time controversial. A Government document comes to mind, published in the Chinese newspapers.'

'Which government, though? Surely not the one in Nanking?'

'I was thinking of Japan's.'

Sun Yat-sen's glasses were slipping down Bai-li's nose once more. He pushed them back into place with an unconscious movement of one hand.

'More specifically, I was thinking of a memorandum – a protocol, I believe is the correct term. The kind of document that is from time to time presented by the Japanese Government to the Emperor for approval.'

'And what sort of protocol were you envisaging, Comrade Su?'

'A summary of the proceedings of the Far Eastern Conference that Tanaka convened at the beginning of last month.'

'But you said those present had agreed to support the Nationalists against the Communists. What's so special about that conclusion that it needs to be presented formally to the emperor for his approval?'

'Quite.'

'You're being obtuse, Shin-gan.' There was a smile lurking somewhere in Chou En-lai's bushy beard. 'Could you perhaps enlighten us? Be true to your name – Pure Reason.'

'Am I? I'm sorry. I thought I *was* being clear.'

Bai-li gathered his hands in his lap and sat up straighter.

'My informant tells me that no written summary of what was discussed at the conference was ever made.' He raised a hand as Mikhail Borodin made to intervene. 'Don't ask me why.'

'That seems unlikely, don't you think?'

'Oh, I do, Comrade Borodin, I *do*. But such things can happen. And, by all accounts, they did happen in this case.'

'Strange,' Chou mused. 'Are you suggesting that nothing was written down because the conference members' conclusions were too inflammatory? Their real conclusions, that is, rather than the ones you've heard through your informant.'

'My thoughts exactly, Shao-shan,' Bai-li said approvingly. 'Experience tells me that informants are often used to convey false information to the other side.'

'Something you yourself never do, eh, Shin-gan?' Chou laughed. 'So, what's your plan?'

Both Ch'ing-ling and Borodin leaned forward and looked at Bai-li expectantly.

'My suggestion is that we concoct our own version of those conclusions. If, for example, we were to produce a document – let's call it for the sake of convenience "The Tokyo Protocol" – that clearly states Japan's determination to attack Manchuria, China, and the rest of Asia…'

His voice tailed away. Once again, Chou was quick to make the connection.

'We would distract Chiang Kai-shek from pursuing our troops in the south and oblige him to look north towards Manchuria and the Kwantung Army.'

Bai-li gave him a slight nod of approval.

'Different methods,' he said, 'But ideally leading to the same result as my earlier proposal involving Chiang Ching-kuo. We must protect ourselves. And to do that, we must attack the enemy's strategies. Chiang's against the Red Army, Japan's against China.'

The others nodded their agreement but said nothing. Bai-li took this as permission to continue.

'A protocol of this nature would also embarrass the Kwantung Army which, as we know, is itching to take over Manchuria and go to war with China. Even if – perhaps I should say when – the document is declared to be false by the government in Tokyo, the Kwantung Army would attack at its peril.'

'Because it will then be seen to be carrying out the so-called Tokyo Protocol's threat, while the whole world by that time will be watching. You're planning a public relations coup, aren't you, Shin-gan?'

'Certainly, it should deter Western Powers' current fondness for Japan,' Bai-li sidestepped Chou's question. 'But there's another effect of such a document, although you, Comrade Borodin, might disagree with my premise.'

'What's that?' Borodin's eyes were sparkling now with a certain admiration for the seemingly unflappable man in their midst.

'A protocol purporting to give details of Japan's planned aggression in Manchuria would force Stalin to pay attention to his Siberian border.'

'Meaning that it would prompt him to send reinforcements to defend it against possible attack by the Kwantung Army?'

'Precisely. Which in itself will – partly, at least – turn Japan's attention away from China.'

'Smart, Comrade Su,' Borodin stroked his moustache. 'Very smart. I have a feeling we need somebody like you to run our country.'

'I'm sure you have intelligence officers of your own who can do that. Much more efficiently than I ever could.'

'Not now that Iron Felix is dead.'

'Maybe not now, Comrade Borodin, but one day in the future perhaps.'

The four of them sat in silence, mulling over what Bai-li had suggested. Perhaps because he was the oldest at 43 years old, perhaps because he had made his reputation as a brilliant organizer, Mikhail Borodin was the first to speak.

'Assuming we're all agreed that you put your plan into effect, Comrade Su, the question then becomes: who can write this Tokyo Protocol? And in what language?'

'Clearly, as I'm sure we're all agreed, the document will have to be published first in China.'

'First?'

'Yes, first. Because our immediate aim is to attract the attention of Chiang Kai-shek and his generals. At the same time, however, we'll be addressing those elements in Japan who do not favour the Army's current drive towards aggression in Asia.'

'So, it has to be in Japanese as well?'

'Obviously, given that the document purports to be a protocol presented by the Prime Minister of Japan to the Emperor Shōwa. So yes, there must be an original Japanese version. "Original," that is, in terms of its apparent provenance.'

'Hang on, Shin-gan. How on earth are you going to convince the Japanese that there is an original?'

'By letting it be known that it can be found in the archives of one of the Ministries in Tokyo,' Bai-li answered impassively. 'Where, eventually, they'll find it. Or not, as the case may be. Either way, they'll be running around in circles chasing their tails as they try to find a Japanese document that's already been published in Chinese.'

Chou opened his mouth to reply, but no words came out. He was, literally, speechless. Mikhail Borodin asked his question for him.

'Have you also planned how to do this, by any chance?'

'Unfortunately, no, not yet,' Bai-li smiled. 'That demands further thought.'

'It sure does,' Borodin was less impressed.

'The thing is, I've often found that it's better not to cling to any one single idea, but to let things flow around it. Things only fall into place if you keep your mind undivided.'

'That sounds suitably impressive in the mouth of a Chinese philosopher, Comrade Su, but it's hardly what one calls "planning," is it?'

'You're right, Comrade Borodin. But I'm afraid it's the best I can do for now. All I ask is that you trust me and let me get on with what I've outlined to you.'

There was a pause once more. Ch'ing-ling pursed her mouth.

'I don't see what else we can do, do you, Shao-shan? But who are you going to get to write the Protocol, Bai-li? And how on earth are you going to get it placed in a Japanese ministry archive?'

'A most pertinent question, Mei-mei.' Bai-li pushed his tortoiseshell glasses up on his nose and gave yet another of his persuasive dimpled smiles. 'I've got one or two ideas, but I'd prefer not to outline them because, as you'll have gathered, they're still unformulated. All I ask, therefore, is that you give me your approval to go ahead regardless.'

It was Ch'ing-ling who gave her blessing first, albeit obliquely.

'You know, I've always believed in striking the serpent's head with the hand of your enemy.'

'As long as you don't get bitten in the process,' Chou grinned, 'Otherwise, Shin-gan, you'll end up being scared all your life at the mere sight of rope.'

'If you're not hanged by it,' Borodin added, with a twirl of his moustache.

How good, Bai-li reflected contentedly, that laughter could still be uttered from the throat of death.

He left the Soong family house the same way as he'd entered it, by the side door out of Charlie Soong's study.

'I'll see you out, Gē-gē,' said Ch'ing-ling quietly, using her pet name of 'Older Brother' for the man whom, as the young widow of the revered Sun Yat-sen, she dared not love openly. 'The gate to the courtyard needs closing. I don't want anyone snooping around right now.'

'Of course not.'

Putting on his soft-soled shoes, Bai-li walked quietly along the wide veranda with Ch'ing-ling beside him. As he stepped down onto the wet flagstones of the courtyard, he put out his hand.

'Be careful you don't slip, Mei-mei.'

She took his hand gratefully and left it there as they started across the flagstones with their shallow puddles of water shimmering on the uneven surface.

Ch'ing-ling pointed to a building running along the western side of the yard, at right-angles to the main house.

'My father used to house his staff there,' she said in her low, soft voice.

'And now it's a bolt hole for a Soviet agent on the run.'

'How I love this house!' She exclaimed wistfully, half turning back towards the building silhouetted against the flashing night sky. She squeezed his hand affectionately.

'I was brought up here, you know, Gē-gē. Together with my sisters.'

'So you've told me before.'

'Believe it or not, this was the first house in Hongkew. Farmers still planted rice in the paddy fields round about. As you can see, our house was in the half-Chinese, half-foreign style that most Shanghailanders love so much. The local villagers would stop and gawp at it as they passed.'

'A Forbidden City in the Shanghai countryside,' Bai-li murmured.

'And now my mother and my younger sister want to sell it. I'm the only one against it.'

'Mei-mei, your father is long gone. Your mother lives in Shanghai, your older sister in Canton. From what you said earlier, Mei-ling is about to make her home with the Generalissimo in Nanking. Your own home in the French Concession is your former husband's house. But for how long will any of you be able to remain where you are? When the Japanese attack, which they surely will one day, we'll all be forced to move. And not for the first time, either. Be careful you don't turn into a turtle.'

'A turtle?'

'Carrying the heavy shell of your house on your back. Burdened for life.'

'So wise, Gē-gē,' she murmured. Again, she squeezed his hand. They were behind the brick wall now, between the main house and the courtyard gates. It was too dark to be seen. 'I have so much to learn from you.'

'And I from you, Mei-mei.' It was Bai-li's turn to squeeze the delicate hand in his. 'But now I must leave you.'

They stopped at the high wooden doors of the gate to the kitchen garden beyond. He pulled one open, let go of her hand, and stepped over the lintel.

'When will I see you again, Gē-gē?'

'When I have news. But soon, I promise.'

'Be careful, dear friend. It's slippery out there after all the rain.'

'I will take care.'

With that Bai-li turned and disappeared soundlessly into the impenetrable night.

PART TWO

Moscow Run

The night train from Shanghai's North Station pulled into Nanking at seven in the morning. Bai-li stepped down from a Second-Class compartment and started walking along the platform.

'Doctor Su?' A young officer in National Revolutionary Army uniform stepped forward as he passed through the ticket barrier. 'Doctor Su Bai-li?'

'Yes. That's me.'

'My name is Pan. Pan Yu-long. General Chiang Kai-shek ordered me to meet you, Doctor.'

'That was very thoughtful of him. But really, you needn't have bothered.'

'I am to escort you to your hotel, sir, and, once you've rested, to the General's quarters.'

'Thank you, Lieutenant,' Bai-li could tell his rank by his epaulettes. 'You're very kind.'

'My duty and my pleasure, Doctor. I'm honoured to make the acquaintance of someone who is so close to the General.'

Bai-li bowed his head slightly.

'Tell me, Lieutenant Pan. Are you by any chance related to Colonel Pan Yu-tang of the Western Hills Group in Shanghai?'

The young man stood to attention.

'Yes indeed, Doctor Su. The Colonel is my father. Do you happen to know him?'

'Alas, not well,' Bai-li smiled reassuringly. 'I have, though, made his acquaintance during my errands for the General while in Shanghai. Your father has a formidable reputation as a true patriot.'

'Thank you, sir.'

Bai-li failed to enlighten the young man about what he thought of those who wore patriotism on the sleeves of their uniforms.

'Not at all, Lieutenant. Since you and your father presumably share the first character of your personal name, I'm sure you, too, are a great patriot. But perhaps you can show me the way to the General's car. I assume he did send you by car?'

'Yes, Doctor. Of course. And I apologise for keeping you waiting. It is this way,' he pointed, a little unnecessarily, towards the station entrance. 'And please allow me to carry your bag.'

The young officer made a move to take it, but Bai-li restrained him gently.

'Please don't worry, Lieutenant. It contains only what I need for an overnight stay. Far too light a load for a strong young patriot like yourself.'

Together they walked through the vast, domed entrance hall to the street outside where a black Packard 8 was parked with its engine running. A chauffeur in military uniform opened the back door for Bai-li and saluted smartly as he clambered in. How he hated ceremony.

The large American car eased away from the station forecourt, with the young lieutenant in the front seat beside the chauffeur.

'The Generalissimo, Doctor, is embarking on a magnificent project,' he said proudly, turning round in his seat to address Bai-li.

'I've heard he's embarking on many magnificent projects, Lieutenant Pan,' Bai-li smiled. 'Which one in particular do you have in mind?'

'I was referring, Doctor Su, to his planned reconstruction of Nanking and his earnest desire to return the Southern Capital to its former glory.'

'Yes, I heard that the Generalissimo has won his battle with the government in Wuhan. So, finally, he can proceed with his plans?'

'Yes, indeed, sir. The two factions have agreed to establish a new unified Nationalist government here in Nanking,' the young man said proudly. Clearly, when it came to patriotism, he had learned a few lessons from his father.

'Not Peking?'

'No, Doctor. Definitely not Peking.'

'Even though that's where the foreign legations are located?'

'I believe the Generalissimo plans to persuade them to relocate to Nanking.'

'A very sensible idea, although I'm afraid the foreign devils may disagree with his plans.'

'Yes, Doctor Su,' was all Yu-long could say as the Packard swerved violently to one side to avoid a pothole the size of a small bomb crater.

The surface of the road was for the most part little more than a rutted cart track, forcing the powerful car to move at the pace of a water buffalo – very slowly. This gave Bai-li time to gaze out of the back seat window as the chauffeur picked his way slowly towards the city centre. China's new capital was vibrant with noise – angry motorists tooting their car horns, policemen furiously blowing their whistles, ricksha men tinkling their bells, street vendors advertising their wares. People with nothing to do squatted randomly at street corners, in alleyways, and public spaces. Houses were for the most part run down and dilapidated, often little more than shanties.

'Yes, the city could do with a makeover,' Bai-li sighed. 'But where will the Generalissimo begin?'

'Sun Ke, son of the Father of China, has already initiated a series of urban improvement projects,' Yu-long said proudly. 'He's torn down part of the old city wall, built new roads, widened streets, and constructed a sewage system for the city.'

'Such energy!' exclaimed Bai-li. 'I'm envious. But what style of buildings does the Generalissimo intend to have constructed?'

'That I don't know, Doctor, but I think he approves of the half-Western, half-Chinese style. Like that of Ginling Girls' College, designed by the American architect, Henry Murphy. Do you know it, sir?

'I don't believe I do.'

'Unfortunately, we will not be passing it on our way to your quarters, Doctor, but I'm sure a visit could be arranged tomorrow should you so wish.'

'Thank you, Lieutenant. An excellent proposition. I'm afraid, though, that I may not have the time. During this visit, at least. I have to be getting back to Shanghai.'

'The Generalissimo, I'm sure, will be eager to show you Purple Mountain before you leave. It is to be the site of the proposed Sun Yat-sen Mausoleum and, I understand, will make use of a traditional Chinese architectural style. Adapted for modern use, of course.'

The young lieutenant's enthusiasm seemed irrepressible. He should, perhaps, have been employed as a tourist guide, rather than as a very junior officer in the National Revolutionary Army.

'Of course,' Bai-li agreed. 'One should always show respect for traditional order and ritual practices.'

His tone of light irony was, as he'd anticipated, lost on his companion. If only he could deceive Yu-long's father as easily.

Later that afternoon, Bai-li was ushered into a large room of the two-storey residence temporarily serving as Chiang Kai-shek's headquarters. The building was bristling with men in uniform, all moving with a sense of purpose. There was work to be done.

'Yen-ching,' the general exclaimed, rising from his chair behind a large desk. He was tall, lean, trim, almost gangly, in appearance. His high forehead made his head look slightly egg-shaped, but his nose was straight, and lips – surmounted by a small, bristly moustache – full.

He stepped around his desk to meet his visitor.

'You were properly looked after, I hope,' he said, shaking Bai-li's hand.

'Yes, indeed, Chi-ch'ing,' Bai-li replied, using the familiar name Chiang had adopted at school. 'Lieutenant Pan was most accommodating. And an excellent guide.'

'Was he now? He asked to be allowed to meet you, you know.'

Chiang gestured to Bai-li to sit down in a black leather armchair.

'Actually, I didn't.'

'He was most insistent.'

'Was he now? I wonder what could have induced him to ask such a favour of you.'

'I was a little surprised myself, to be honest.' Chiang sat down in a similar chair to Bai-li's, set at right angles to a black leather three-seater sofa by the window overlooking an unkempt park. 'I mean, it's not as if he knew you, or anything like that.'

'No,' Bai-li mused. 'Maybe he'd heard about me from his father?'

He crossed one leg over the other and leaned back in the comfortable chair. He wasn't convinced that leather was the best material to absorb the summer heat.

'Wanted to impress me, more likely,' the Generalissimo said. 'On the principle that anyone who comes to see me must be important. Which you are, of course, Doctor Colonel Su Bai-li,' he added with a touch of irony. 'An ambitious young man.'

'But a patriotic one,' Bai-li said quickly.

'Patriotic? Yes, I suppose he is. I hadn't thought of him that way.'

'He was full of praise for your reconstruction of Nanking, Chi-ch'ing. And the way he described things, I could already see the re-emergence of a brand-new capital city to rival Peking.'

Chiang smiled and pushed an ashtray on the low table between them to one side.

'You flatter me, Yen-ching,' he smiled, using the nickname Bai-li had acquired at school because of his short-sightedness. He was the only boy in his class who wore glasses. Courtesy of the Catholic father who ran his orphanage.

'I've never understood why they insist on putting an ashtray here,' Chiang said, à propos of nothing. 'It's not as if I've ever smoked.'

'For your guests, perhaps?'

The general looked at Bai-li sharply.

'Are you pulling my leg again, Yen-ching? You know I'd never tolerate anybody smoking in my presence.'

It was Bai-li's turn to smile. He knew well how to manipulate his friend. And – something he would be wise never to forget – be manipulated by him.

'So, tell me, Chi-ch'ing. How is life as supreme commander of the Kuomintang, now that the Communists have been so successfully dealt with?'

The general slumped back in his chair and pouted his lips.

'I sometimes wonder whether it was worth all the trouble,' he said. 'There's so much work to be done. So many obstacles to overcome. Unification of the country isn't as easy as we once thought, is it, Yen-ching?'

'No. It definitely isn't,' Bi-li agreed sympathetically. 'I must say, I don't envy you.'

'Nobody in their right mind would envy me this job,' came the sharp reply. 'To be honest, old friend, I'm thinking of quitting entirely.'

Bai-li examined the Generalissimo closely, showing neither surprise nor concern at what he'd been told. He knew, though, not to underestimate Chiang Kai-shek.

'Yes, I suppose you could do that,' he agreed. 'It would show others around you aspiring to wield power just how inadequately suited they are to the task. That's a lesson many need to know.'

'By quitting, therefore, I'd merely strengthen my position, you mean?'

'I assume that's your plan.'

Chiang Kai-shek looked sharply at his old school friend.

'Is it that obvious, Yen-ching?'

'I wouldn't have thought it *that* obvious. To most of those around you, at least. But we need to be cautious. Remember, Chi-ch'ing, *everyone's* up to some scheme or other these days. You included. I have an advantage, though, in having known you ever since we were fifteen years old.'

'When you were the boy from the Catholic orphanage wearing glasses.'

'And you a prosperous salt merchant's son.'

'Remind me, Yen-ching. How *did* we become friends?'

'I seem to remember I taught you how to catch crabs on the beach.'

'You taught me?' Chiang laughed. 'Impossible, old friend. I was always the best at catching crabs.'

'Then you must have taught me,' Bai-li gave up the necessary ground. 'But you also helped me with my arithmetic, as I recall. After all, you were the merchant's son who'd learned how to use an abacus and knew how to add and subtract with ease.'

'And multiply and divide.'

'And multiply and divide,' Bai-li conceded. 'You also explained the Confucian classics – something the Catholic fathers neglected to teach me.'

'True,' the General looked pleased. Both with the recollection and himself.

'But in that case, Chi-ch'ing,' Bai-li continued smoothly, 'What could I have offered you that would enable a friendship to develop between us? There had to be *something*. And, in those days at least,' he added, alluding to Chiang's promise to his future mother-in-law to join the Methodist Church, 'you weren't interested in all the stuff I'd learned about Christianity.'

Chiang looked out of the window thoughtfully. After a while he looked back at Bai-li, who was watching him carefully, and exploded with laughter.

'Of course, you're right. There *had* to be something. It was the crabs, wasn't it, Yen-ching? Just like you said.'

'Possibly.' Bai-li bowed his head in silent acknowledgement.

The two men sat looking out of the window.

'So, Doctor Colonel Su Bai-li, what brings you all the way from Shanghai to Nanking?' The General broke the comradely silence, all business now. 'Has Internal Affairs there uncovered plots afoot?'

'Far from it, my General. The Communists are in total disarray, as you know. Soong Ch'ing-ling is back at her husband's home on the rue Molière. For now, at least. Mikhail Borodin seems to have accompanied her there before moving across country to Mongolia and the Soviet Union. Who knows what fate is in store for him there? Stalin isn't one to tolerate failure gracefully.'

'No, I suppose not. And Chou En-lai?'

Bai-li sighed. Just a little theatrically, for effect.

'I'd thought I would be able to bring you good news on that front, my General. But alas! My best laid plans were upset by my men's fear of thunder and dislike of rain.'

'Fear of thunder? What on earth are you talking about, Yen-ching?'

'As you know, perhaps, Chou escaped Hankow and, slightly surprisingly, made his way up to Shanghai.'

'Rather than south to Canton?'

'Rather than south to Canton,' Bai-li averred. 'I had my informants out on the streets, of course, and struck it lucky when two of them happened to spot Chou way out on Jessfield Road. They followed him to Soochow Creek, where he boarded a sampan and headed west.'

'West?'

'Precisely, my General. That was my thought when one of the men reported back to me. The other having followed Chou, of course, in another sampan.'

Bai-li paused.

'The trouble was he lost Chou somewhere in the waterways through the rice paddy surrounding the north-western outskirts of the city.'

'How?'

'Indeed how? Was the question I asked myself, my General. In all fairness to my man, though, it was extremely dark that night. There was no moon. Just thunder rolling in the distance.'

'Thunder? In which case, there was lightning, too? That should have helped him see in the dark.'

'True, my General. But the lightning was too intermittent to enable constant observation of Chou's boat.'

'So, he escaped.'

'So I thought at first. But then I began to think.'

'And when you think, Yen-ching, problems tend to be solved.'

Bai-li inclined his head.

'Not necessarily. Especially when whatever solution I arrive at involves other people.'

Chiang leaned back in his chair and crossed his legs.

'Go on.'

'It occurred to me that Chou En-lai might just possibly be heading to a meeting with Soong Ch'ing-ling and Mikhail Borodin.'

'In order to commiserate with one another over what had happened in Hankow?'

'That. And, possibly, to make some kind of plan for the future.'

'What future?'

'Indeed, what future?' Bai-li agreed. 'If that were the case, though – I mean, that the three of them had arranged to meet somewhere – then the only conceivable place available to them on the northern outskirts of the city would have been Charlie Soong's old family house.'

'The one on the edge of Hongkew, you mean?'

'The same.'

'So, what did you do?'

'What did I do?' Echoed Bai-li in his matter-of-fact voice. 'Why, I sent three men to watch the house.'

'And?'

'Before they'd even got as far as Hongkew, it started to pour with rain. I mean, serious rain. Accompanied by quite a thunderstorm.'

'So?'

'So it transpired that all the men I'd sent were afraid of thunder. And they didn't want to get wet, either. So they sheltered in a fisherman's hut that they came across nearby. Unfortunately, they either fell asleep or had no clear view of the house, because by the time the rain had stopped, its occupants – if there'd been any there in the first place, of course – were gone. I'm sorry, my General.'

Chiang drummed the armrest on his chair with the fingers of his left hand.

'And now he's escaped?'

'I'm afraid so. At least, that's what I've been told.'

The Generalissimo was silent for a moment, debating something with himself.

'To be honest, Yen-ching, I had the same idea.'

'What idea was that?'

'That Chou might try to meet Ch'ing-ling at her father's old home. So I arranged in advance with Big Ears Tu to send a couple of men along to kill Chou once he left the Soong house.'

'And?'

'And they were never heard of again.'

'It might have helped, my General, if you'd told me this. I could have co-ordinated the assassination attempt.'

Chiang stopped drumming his fingers and relaxed slightly.

'Yes, you could have, I suppose. But look at it this way, Yen-ching. I can still hold onto my 20,000 Mexican silver dollars,' He smiled. 'For the time being, at least.'

'Much to Big Ears' disappointment, no doubt.'

'No doubt.'

'If you were to double your reward, perhaps, one of the southern warlords might be tempted to turn Chou in. I wouldn't bet on it, though. Chou has a lot of friends in the south.'

'Including Mao Tse-tung and the whole Red Army. I'll have to deal with that lot soon.'

'If you want unification of the whole country, yes, of course.'

'But I do, Yen-ching. I do.'

'I know you do, my General,' Bai-li uncrossed his legs and placed both arms on the armrests of his chair. 'Which is why, as Director of Internal Affairs, I've come to offer you some advice.'

The General leaned forward slightly.

'Ah hah! So now finally, we come to the reason for your visit.'

Bai-li smiled his irresistible dimpled smile.

'Yes, my General, we do.'

He paused.

'Well, go on then, you tease. There's a limit to my patience. Even with an old school friend.'

'Of course,' Bai-li said, blinking behind his glasses. 'We're agreed, I think, that for the sake of the unification of China, the Communists have to be – how can I put it? – eradicated. And the sooner the better.'

'Agreed.'

'There is, though, one problem interfering with your desire for peace throughout the country.'

'Which is?'

'Your son,' Bai-li said simply.

'My son? Ching-kuo?'

'Yes, Ching-kuo.'

'That bastard Stalin is keeping him hostage. But you know that, don't you?'

'I do, indeed. And that, Chi-ch'ing, is the point,' Bai-li paused.

'Go on,' Chiang said impatiently.

'As long as Ching-kuo remains a hostage in Moscow, Stalin has a hold over you.'

'Because I'm his father, you mean?'

'Because you want to fight the Communists.'

'What's wrong with –?' Chiang broke off as realisation dawned. 'Ah!'

'Yes, "Ah!" Unfortunately.'

'You mean, if I go about wiping out the Communists, I'll never see my son again?'

Bai-li bowed his head again in acknowledgement.

The General slumped back in his chair. For once he looked defeated.

'I write to him every week, you know, Yen-ching.'

'I know you do,' Bai-li said sympathetically.

'But he never sends a reply.'

'I doubt that's the case, Chi-ch'ing. Indeed, I'm sure he does write back to you. After all, there's no greater love than that between father and son. The trouble is his letters are almost certainly being intercepted by the OGPU. Or the People's Commissariat for Internal Affairs. One of the two. Hence the apparent silence.'

'It's not just silence, Yen-ching. It's torture.'

'I'm sure it is. But remember, old friend, what Lao Tzu wrote. Love is a decision, not an emotion. As long as you fail to accept that, you're bound to feel tortured.'

'How on earth can one *decide* to love one's own son?' the General asked angrily. 'Are you telling me now how I *should* feel, Su Bai-li? And ignoring how I *actually* feel?'

'Not at all, my General. I merely wanted to ease your pain.'

'Then do so another way,' Chiang barked peremptorily.

Bai-li looked out of the window once more. Half a dozen dogs were snarling at one another in the park beyond. Was it going to be that kind of afternoon?

'Let's face it, my General, getting Stalin to release your son isn't going to happen tomorrow. Or by the end of the year even. As I see it, you need to enter into a long-term game of persuasion.'

'Persuasion? What kind of persuasion?'

Bai-li raised both bushy eyebrows, as if surprised Chiang hadn't followed his line of thinking.

'The kind that convinces the Soviet leader that you're still his potential ally when it comes to fighting the Japanese.'

'But I am. I will be, when that happens.'

'In the meantime, though, you're fighting the Red Army under Mao Tse-tung and doing your utmost to get rid of every Communist in the country – something that hardly endears you to Stalin. And certainly won't encourage him to hand over Ching-kuo. Remember, too, that he is still supplying your army with weaponry with which to fight the Communists.'

'True,' the Generalissimo mused. 'What are you suggesting, old friend?'

'That you do not devote all your time and energy to destroying the Communists. Sometimes it's wiser not to press a desperate foe too hard. When you surround the Reds, therefore, leave a passage free for some of them to escape.'

'Are you now a general, Yen-ching?' Chiang laughed.

'No, Chi-ch'ing. You are my General. I'm merely offering my advice. From the perspective of one who's spent several years studying the politics of the Soviet Government.'

'And who now seems to be supporting the continued existence of the Communists in our country.'

'Only for a greater good, my General.'

'The rescue of my son from Stalin's clutches, you mean?'

'As I see it, the greater good, my General, is the unification of the north of the country.'

Bai-li paused.

'Go on,' Chiang ordered.

'By not devoting all your resources to engaging with the Reds in the south, you can use the bulk of your armies to unify the northern provinces. That, surely, is what matters right now. You've rid the central provinces of the Communists. Now turn your attention north, because that's where the real enemy lies.'

'The Japanese, you mean?'

Bai-li once again bowed his head in acknowledgement.

'I should never have let Galen go back to Moscow,' Chiang said ruefully. 'He's an extremely able strategist. He could've helped me out with my plans for unification.'

'Then why not ask the general to come back? I'm sure Stalin would be agreeable. In the meantime, I suggest you devote your energy to persuading that old rogue, Chang Tso-lin, to leave Peking and go back to Manchuria. That shouldn't be too difficult, surely? After all, it's his province. That way, you provide a bulwark against Japan's Kwantung Army and lessen the threat Stalin feels along his Siberian border.'

'But I have to get rid of the Communists. Otherwise they'll be a thorn in my flesh for ever.'

'Yes, indeed. But do it later, once you've persuaded Stalin that the two of you are in fact allies with a common enemy – the Japanese. In the meantime –'

'Yes?'

Bai-li could see that his strategy was taking root in Chiang Kai-shek's mind.

'Why not write another letter to Ching-kuo and have it hand-delivered to Moscow?'

'The point being –?'

'The point being that whoever you choose to deliver it can bring back a reply. You will finally know how he is, what he's doing – who, even, he's fallen in love with.'

Chiang snorted derisively.

'A little too young for that sort of thing, surely?'

'I agree, Chi-ch'ing, but let's forget the detail. What I'm trying to point out is that you'd be relieved of your present uncertainty about Ching-kuo's welfare. A letter, I admit, won't bring your son back. But it would provide you with some consolation for the two of you being apart.'

Chiang scratched the top of his head – a habit he had when thinking something through. Bai-li let him scratch.

The Generalissimo wasn't the only one. Outside one dog was clawing at the eye of another, as they rolled in the dust, fangs bared and snapping. Not unlike the Nationalists and the Communists.

Chiang interrupted Bai-li's musing.

'Do you think it would work, Yen-ching?'

Bai-li blinked once more, his eyes made larger by the thickness of Sun Yat-sen's spectacles.

'It's hard to tell, Chi-ch'ing. But I think it's worth a try. If only to give you slight relief from your fatherly concern. There's a risk, of course, that the letter might be intercepted, but…' His voice tailed away.

'In which case, Stalin might stop treating my son as a favoured guest.'

'He might already have stopped, my General. We just don't know. The important thing is to find out, to know what at present we don't know.'

Chiang stopped scratching his head. He had made up his mind.

'Alright. Let's give it a try,' he smiled. 'Better to have tried and lost than not to have tried at all.'

'True, Chi-ch'ing. I prefer, though, to see it as an opportunity brought about by current chaos.'

The Generalissimo was impatient to move on.

'The next question, then, is who am I going to send to Moscow as my emissary?'

'It must be someone of rank, my General. Someone who can genuinely engage in diplomacy. But someone whose absence for three months you won't regret.'

'A good point.'

'Someone like myself, for example.'

Chiang looked at his friend in surprise.

'What? You, Yen-ching?'

'Why not? Remember, I accompanied Ching-kuo when you sent him to Moscow two years ago. Ching-kuo knows and, I hope, trusts me.'

'Out of the question, Yen-ching. I need you here in Nanking.'

'You do? Why's that?'

'Because you're in charge of Internal Affairs, for one thing. Have you forgotten?' Chiang laughed shortly. 'But also because I'm getting married. Haven't you heard?'

'I had indeed, Chi-ch'ing. I should have congratulated you earlier. Please excuse my rudeness.'

Chiang waved his friend's apology out of the window. The dogs had settled their differences, too, and disappeared.

'As I said, I need you here. In December. As one of the witnesses to my wedding to Soong Mei-ling.'

Bai-li bowed.

'I'm honoured, Chi-ch'ing.'

'And you won't even have to come to Nanking,' Chiang laughed. 'A place I know you're not especially fond of. The ceremony will be held in Shanghai. At the Majestic Hotel.'

'I look forward with great pleasure, then, to your majestic wedding, my General. And to meeting the youngest Soong sister who is to become your wife. Surely, a match made in heaven. But there would still be time for me to make a quick return trip to Moscow, surely?'

Chiang waved Bai-li's suggestion away once more.

'Maybe, but you're not going, Yen-ching. I need you here. We must find someone else. The question is who.'

Bai-li paused, as if in thought. Then,

'How about Hu Han-min?'

'Hu Han-min?' Chiang laughed heartily. 'I wouldn't trust him with my undershirt.'

'No. Perhaps not,' Bai-li couldn't help smiling himself.

'Ever since he took that trip abroad, he's been urging me to model the nationalist revolution here on the kind of reforms Atatürk's been carrying out in Turkey. Honestly! Modernisation and industrialisation, I can accept. But I'm not so sure about Westernisation. After all, we're trying to get rid of all the foreign concessions and their damned Westerners.'

'True, indeed, my General,' Bai-li agreed.

'There's Pan Yu-tang, of course,' he continued slightly dismissively. 'Or, how about Ma Hsin?'

'Hmm.' Chiang clearly wasn't that impressed.

'Or Wang Ching-wei?'

'Ching-wei? You must be joking, Su Bai-li,' The General retorted angrily. 'What on earth's come over you, asking me to put my son's and my own welfare in the hands of a man who's not just a rival, but who's been known to stab me in the back in the past?'

'You're right, of course, my General. I was just thinking what a consummate politician Ching-wei is. You never quite know which side he's on, do you? Sometimes, he seems to be more or less a Communist. At others, a centrist, like yourself. Occasionally even an apparent supporter of the rightists. It had occurred to me that Ching-wei might make an able diplomat under the present circumstances – red enough to put the Soviets at ease; liberal enough to represent your interests.'

'I don't know,' mused Chiang. 'I suppose he might do. As you say, he's senior enough to engage in diplomatic meetings with other senior Soviet officials.'

'Maybe even with Stalin himself,' Bai-li gently pursued a candidate he knew the General would never accept. Victory comes in apparent defeat.

'And to avoid detection of your son's letter on his way back from Moscow,' he continued, 'The Soviets wouldn't dare search him.'

'Maybe not. But still…' Chiang was not convinced. 'Think what I would have to offer him in return, Yen-ching.'

'There's always that to be considered,' Bai-li agreed.

Chiang started scratching his head again. Then,

'To be honest, Yen-ching, I'd be more than a little hesitant about letting Ching-wei negotiate with Stalin over the fate of my son. He's had too many disagreements with me over the years for me to trust him to represent my interests before his own. He's interested only in his own advantage.'

Bai-li pursed his lips thoughtfully.

'A fair assessment, my General. It was thoughtless of me even to consider him.'

Chiang waved away his friend's apology.

'But what about Pan Yu-tang? You mentioned him just now.'

'Did I?' Bai-li looked puzzled. 'Ah yes, so I did. But it wasn't a very serious suggestion, Chi-ch'ing.'

'Why not? The Colonel's part of the Western Hills Group. An ardent Nationalist.'

'Indeed. And a patriot.'

'And a patriot.'

In his enthusiasm Chiang missed Bai-li's irony.

'He's also a senior diplomat. And cunning, too. Remember how he dealt with the Japanese over the Manchurian border problem a couple of years back? Masterful!'

'Yes. I'd forgotten that.'

'He doesn't have the clout of someone like Ching-wei, of course. But that wouldn't stop him from sounding out senior Soviet officials about the prospects of Ching-kuo's return to China. Or of having Galen coming back to help me unify the north.'

'No. No, I suppose it wouldn't. But he is a member of the Western Hills Group. Surely, Moscow would be suspicious of his far-right views?'

'But that's the point, Yen-ching. Didn't you know? Colonel Pan isn't officially a member of the group. He's always been careful not to align himself with any one faction.'

'Very wise, under the circumstances. I hadn't known.'

'And he has this son, Yu-long, whom you met earlier and who's working right here in this building. He's only a couple of years older than Ching-kuo. Maybe he should go as well. The two of them would get on well together, I'm sure.'

'You mean, Yu-long could build trust with Ching-kuo and later act as a regular courier for correspondence between you and your son, my General? What an ingenious idea!'

'That's fixed then,' Chiang clapped his hands excitedly. 'I'll summon Colonel Pan to Nanking and inform him of the plan. Thank you, Yen-ching. You've been most helpful.'

Bai-li bowed yet again.

'It is, of course, my pleasure, Chi-ch'ing. My only concern is that, somehow, we won't succeed in getting a letter from Ching-kuo back to you.'

'Because Colonel Pan and his son are searched at the border, you mean?'

Bai-li nodded.

'I've heard,' he said, 'That in winter Russians like to fold up newspaper and put it in their shoes to keep out the cold.'

'So?'

'So, I don't know about such things, of course, but I was wondering whether this might be a good way for Colonel Pan or his son to smuggle Ching-kuo's letter back across the border.'

Chiang looked doubtful for a moment, then clapped his hands again in delight.

'Yen-ching!' He exclaimed. 'That's a brilliant idea!'

'If it works,' Bai-li replied modestly, before adding hastily: 'But it's only hearsay. I really wouldn't know.'

'It will work, old friend. It will. Come. We should celebrate. There's an excellent dumpling restaurant nearby. And old friends should always share food when united again.'

Bai-li smiled his dimpled smile, as he followed Chiang Kai-shek out of his office. Had he really despatched two birds with a single stone? Who knew? Apart from the east wind, of course.

Three days later, the Generalissimo greeted another visitor.

'Colonel Pan. It's been a long time.'

'Too long, my General. I'm honoured you should remember me.'

'Remember you? How could I forget a senior member of the Western Hills Group in Shanghai? A man who once rode by my side into battle. A man who has over the years fought the same enemies as I have done. Are you mocking me, Pan Yu-tang?' Chiang said playfully, as he put an arm around the Colonel's shoulder.

He liked to use such gestures of intimacy, albeit sparingly. They tended to make his real intent difficult to fathom. A bit of feigned flattery and friendship always helped.

Pan Yu-tang was short and stocky, and had clearly put on weight in recent months. His uniform was too small around the stomach and waist, Chiang noted with distaste. The buttons of the Colonel's jacket seemed ready to burst.

He gestured politely towards the leather armchair, occupied earlier in the week by Su Bai-li.

'Please. Do sit down, Colonel.'

Once again, he took the other chair and gazed intently at the plump round face of his visitor. He wasn't impressed by what he saw. On Pan Yu-tang's head were a few wisps of stray hair, plastered down with some kind of offensive-smelling hair oil. Both his mouth and his nose were small, and he sported a rather ridiculous moustache that made the Generalissimo think of sick rice.

'So, how's life in Shanghai, Pan Yu-tang? Quieter now that the Communists have been rounded up?'

'Very much so, and much the more pleasant a city as a result. Thanks to you, my General.'

Chiang noticed that, although the Colonel's hooded eyes gave him a sleepy look, they were at the same time sly. His flattery had been less than sincere.

'I suppose the British police are maintaining order in the International Settlement?'

'And elsewhere as called for. Big Ears Tu's gangs are always there to help.'

'Indeed,' Chiang nodded, fully aware of the role the Western Hills Group had played in arranging for Tu Yue-sheng to go after the Communists, in exchange for yet another opium monopoly.

'I so rarely get there these days,' he sighed.

'Not even to visit your fiancée, my General?' Pan enquired.

'Alas! From time to time she joins me here in Nanking, instead.'

'A sensible precaution, if I might say so.'

'Precaution?' Chiang looked at the Colonel enquiringly.

'Yes, my General. I've always found, with women, that it's better to lay the ground first. If, as I suspect, you intend to live here with Soong Mei-ling once you're married, it is, I think, better that she gets to know Nanking beforehand. In my experience, women tend not to like surprises.'

'I wouldn't know, Yu-tang. So, thank you. I value your experience. And your advice.'

The colonel's hooded eyes narrowed as he bowed as low as his ill-fitting starched uniform permitted.

'It is indeed a privilege, my General.'

There was a knock on the door and the Colonel's son, Yu-long, entered bearing a tray.

'I'm sure you'd welcome some refreshment, Colonel, after your arduous journey,' Chiang smiled. 'And, perhaps, your son as well.'

Yu-tang said nothing as the young man set the tray with its teapot, cups and saucers on the table. As he straightened up, he glanced at his father before saluting both men and leaving the room.

'Yu-long has become a most capable and reliable assistant,' Chiang said, as he poured out some Pu-erh tea for his guest. 'I shall miss him when he's gone.'

'Gone?' Echoed the Colonel. 'Is he being transferred?'

'In a manner of speaking, Pan Yu-tang,' Chiang reassured his visitor. 'But only temporarily, of course.'

The overweight officer adopted a sleepy look, doing his best to look unconcerned.

'I trust my son hasn't offended you in some way, my General?'

'Offended?' Chiang was enjoying himself. 'Why! Not at all.'

'Then, if you don't mind my asking, why is he being transferred?'

'Because I have need of him elsewhere.'

'Of course, my General,' Pan bowed again.

There was a pause.

'But aren't you curious to know what need I have of Yu-long elsewhere? And where that "elsewhere" might be?' Chiang teased his visitor.

'Why yes, of course, my General.'

Pan waited a little breathlessly while Chiang mulled over his reply.

'Colonel Pan, your son is to be sent on an assignment to Moscow.'

'Moscow?' Echoed Yu-long in consternation.

'Yes, Moscow. He is to accompany a senior, well-respected officer on a diplomatic mission of some delicacy.'

'I see,' nodded Yu-tang, although clearly he didn't.

'Aren't you going to ask what that mission might be, Yu-tang? Really! And there I was, thinking that you members of the Western Hills group were an inquisitive lot,' Chiang grinned again. It wasn't often he had so much fun. 'Clearly, I was wrong.'

'No, no, my General,' interposed the Colonel hurriedly. 'It's just that – just that I felt it not in my remit to enquire about a matter that was so delicate, if you see what I mean.'

'I do, indeed, Colonel. I would have expected nothing less from an officer such as yourself.'

Pan Yu-tang once again inclined his body as far as his uniform permitted, too flustered to note the back-handed compliment.

'The senior and well-respected officer whom your son has been detailed to accompany to Moscow –'

Chiang broke off. Yu-tang leaned forward expectantly.

'Yes, my General?'

'Is none other than yourself, Colonel Pan.'

'Me?' Yu-tang looked suitably surprised.

'You.'

'But to what do I owe this honour?' He asked, his eyes already regaining their slyness. 'And what do you wish me to do in Moscow?'

'So you accept this commission, I take it, Colonel Pan?'

'But of course, my General. Your wish, as they say in English, is my command.'

'As it should be, Colonel Pan. I am, after all, your commanding officer.'

'Yes. I mean, no. I mean, I didn't mean to suggest…' Yu-tang's voice tailed away in confusion.

Chiang sipped his tea, put down his cup and looked the Colonel straight in the eye.

'Enough of this polite shilly-shallying, Colonel Pan. Let's get down to the business at hand. You know, I assume, that I have a son?'

'Of course, my General.'

'And that my son, Ching-kuo, is at present a hostage to Stalin in Moscow?'

Yu-tang looked genuinely surprised.

'No, my General. That I hadn't been aware of.'

'Well, take it from me, he is. I want you to take a letter from me to Ching-kuo and hand it to him when you meet in Moscow. Ask him to write a letter to me, if he hasn't already done so, and bring it back with you to Nanking. Understood, so far?'

'Yes, my General.'

'Good. I am ordering your son, Yu-long, to accompany you on this long trip through Siberia because he is young – more or less the same age as Ching-kuo. I think the two of them will get on well together, so I want Yu-long to get to know Ching-kuo, to help him in any way he can, and so build a bond of trust with him. That way, he'll be able to tell me things that my son would never write down in an ordinary letter. Am I being clear?'

'As always, perfectly clear, my General.'

'Meanwhile, I want you, Colonel, to get in touch with various senior Soviet officials. I will provide you with letters of introduction. Your job is to sound out their views on the Siberian border and how best to deal with the Japanese Kwantung Army in Manchuria. Any information you can glean will be extremely helpful to the cause.'

'The cause, my General?'

'Unification. The whole of China must be united if we are to combat the Japanese.'

'Of course, my General. That goes without saying.'

'Good. I'm glad you see it that way.'

'But, if you will forgive my asking, General, why choose me for such an important task?'

'Because it *is* an important task, Colonel. But also because you have very cleverly kept a low profile over the years with regard to your factional affiliations. You cross the sea, as the saying goes, while hiding under the sky. The Soviets will find themselves having to tread warily in their discussions with you.'

'I see.' Colonel Pan looked flattered.

'There's something else,' Chiang continued smoothly. 'Of a more delicate, personal nature…'

His voice tailed away.

'Yes, my General?'

'Stalin, as I said, is holding my son hostage. I need to know what chance there is of getting him back. That means I need to know how the Soviets regard my – how shall I put it? – my engagement with the Chinese Communist Party. Although you should never put it in these words, Colonel Pan, I want to know how I should treat the Communists here in order to for my son to be released and join me here in Nanking. That is the real purpose of your trip to Moscow.'

Pan Yu-tang nodded his head thoughtfully two or three times.

'I see,' he said. 'And you think I'm the best person for such a delicate mission, my General?'

Chiang's response came without hesitation.

'Why else would I have summoned you here all the way from Shanghai, Colonel Pan? You're well known for your diplomatic skills. For years you've negotiated agreements between different factions of the Kuomintang. You also totally fooled the Japanese over a Manchurian border issue. And you've adopted a tough stance towards the Communists during their ill-fated alliance with the KMT – a stance that turned out to be correct.'

'Thank you, my General.'

'I also haven't forgotten that you speak Russian quite fluently, Colonel. Who else could I possibly send?'

Pan Yu-tang gazed down at the table in thought for a few seconds.

'Well, there's Su Bai-li, of course,' he looked at the Generalissimo with his hooded eyes. They weren't sleepy anymore, but full of craft. 'Didn't he accompany your son to Moscow when you first sent him to study there?'

'You're well informed, Colonel Pan. Yes, he did indeed. But Bai-li's return to Moscow might well raise suspicion among the Soviets. And suspicion is what I wish to avoid. Remember, one important part of your job is to smuggle back a letter to me from my son.'

'It's that part of the assignment that worries me slightly, my General. To be honest, I don't know very much about methods of border smuggling.'

'Nor do I, to be equally frank,' Chiang laughed. 'But I'm sure you have colleagues who can give you advice, Colonel.'

He poured more tea into his visitor's cup.

'Actually, I've heard one way is to cut up a document, wrap it in newspaper, and put it in your shoe.'

'Newspaper in your shoe?' The colonel echoed helplessly.

'Yes. Didn't you know? Surely you noticed when you were there? Russians like to put newspapers in their shoes to help keep their feet warm. An ingenious idea, don't you think?'

Yu-tang looked slightly less worried.

'Most ingenious, my General.'

'Good,' Chiang got up from his chair abruptly and stood towering over his visitor. 'Then I take it you will accept this assignment?'

'But, of course, my General.'

Yu-tang stood to attention.

'Excellent. Might I suggest that we eat dinner together this evening. Along with your son. We can then discuss matters in greater detail.'

'Thank you. We would be honoured, my General.'

All that was needed to grind an iron rod into a needle was hard work and persistence.

'Remember. Someone will always be following you.'

His father's words still echoed in his mind. He'd quickly learned, though, how to lose his tail. Backtracking along pavements, using the reflection in the glass of a shop window to check who was walking at the same speed on the other side of the street, stepping into doorways and waiting. Getting onto a bus and then off again as the doors closed, leaving behind him a frustrated informer. The usual tricks.

He'd also quickly learned to recognise the Chekists by their long flowing leather coats and amber worry beads. OGPU secret police agents had been less obvious and therefore, of course, more dangerous. Experience had taught him, though, to detect the bulge of a badly concealed weapon – an ability that once, he was convinced, saved his life, or a lengthy period of confinement in a gulag. Under the expressionless pale blue eyes of four shaven-headed coffin-bearers, he walked without flinching past Chiang Ching-kuo, who already had his arms out to embrace him Russian style. Without pausing, he continued straight on out through the gates of the Danilovskoye Cemetery. When he turned back, the coffin-bearers and their shoulder holsters were gone. It wasn't going to be his funeral that day.

Winter had come early that year. It was only October, but Moscow was already bitterly cold. But even at minus ten degrees, the temperature didn't deter those ordered to follow the Chinese visitor's every move. Occasional sprinklings of snow made it easy for his babysitters to stay out of sight while following his footsteps in out-of-the-way places. So Pan Yu-long learned to walk in the tracks of others who had walked the same way before him. Once or twice, out in the suburbs, he came across animal tracks and walked along beside them to make it look as if he was some local Russian walking his dog.

The most obvious place to meet and the place that, in spite of its crowded spaces, offered the most privacy was Sun Yat-sen University – or what the Soviet regime liked to call the Sun Yat-sen Communist University of the Toilers of China. Located at Number Sixteen Volkhonka Street in what was an old and rather beautiful part of the city, it was a pleasant half hour walk from the Hotel Metropole where Yu-long was staying.

In the meantime, his father seemed to be spending all of his time, day after day, visiting one Soviet dignitary after another, and only came back to the hotel late in the evening. If at all.

Just who he was having meetings with the Colonel didn't elaborate. Mikhail Borodin was mentioned early on, but when Yu-long asked his father how that encounter had gone, the Colonel had given little more than a grunt by way of reply. Yu-long decided it wiser not to enquire of his father anymore about his activities. In truth, this was just as well. On the morning of only his fifth day in Moscow, the Colonel had bumped into – or, rather, been bumped into – by a buxom blonde whose figure demanded his attention.

'A thousand apologies!' He exclaimed in Russian, bending down as best as his stoutness permitted to help the lady gather up half a dozen potatoes from the pavement and put them back into her net shopping bag. 'Please forgive my clumsiness.'

Surprisingly, perhaps, she did, for she proceeded to accept his invitation to join him for a cup of tea in a nearby establishment. Her name, she said as she left a perfect imprint of her pink lipstick on the tall glass in front of her, was Anastasia. A beautiful name. Yes, thank you, she thought so, too. But then it had been given to the wife of the Czar, Ivan the Terrible – a fact of which she wasn't all that proud since the Revolution. Yu-tang should call her Stasya.

The Colonel presumed Stasya was married. It was kind of him to ask, but no, as a matter of fact she was a widow. Her husband had been killed in the Great War, God rest his soul (this accompanied by a token crossing of her well-endowed bosom with the fingers of one hand). Had he been fighting for the Germans? Yu-tang found it hard to imagine a Russian on the side of the British. Good Lord, no (accompanied by further crossing of that palpitating bosom). She meant the Great Civil War, silly. The one that put paid to the Romanovs. Didn't he know about Russian history?

Anastasia played hard to get, but not that hard. By late afternoon the following day, the Colonel found himself without his clothes on in a rather large bouncy bed, with Anastasia riding astride him. As he settled into a rhythm that his ageing body – and, let's face it, his wife – had long forgotten, Pan Yu-tang was grateful that Mikhail Borodin had suddenly cancelled their appointment that morning. As each would have agreed, though for different reasons, there were better things to do with one's day. And, indeed, the days that were to follow.

In the meantime, at Ching-kuo's suggestion, Pan Yu-long began to audit classes in Marxist and Leninist theory. After all, he had little else to do. His father seemed to be permanently busy, doing one thing or another.

They rarely met, even in the Metropole's splendid breakfast room, with its fountain in the middle and, high up on an internal balcony, a string quartet playing chamber music by Mendelssohn and Rimsky-Korsakov. When asked how his negotiations were going, the Colonel replied brusquely that it was not for his son to enquire about matters of state. Diplomacy should always be conducted in secret.

Auditing classes at the Sun Yat-sen University, then, seemed like a good way to fill in Yu-long's time.

'It'll be good for you, Yu-long,' the Generalissimo's son said encouragingly. 'Those Communist leaders had some interesting things to say, you know.'

'But I'm not a Communist,' Yu-long said rather helplessly.

'Neither am I. But you can learn from them without becoming one.'

And so Yu-long found himself attending lectures by Borodin, Trotsky and, once, even by Stalin himself, although the new leader of the Soviet Union addressed the students in Russian, since he professed not to understand English. Since Yu-long didn't understand Russian, Stalin's lecture went right through, or over, his head. Nevertheless, he basked contentedly in the aura of the great man.

Ching-kuo introduced his new friend to a few other Chinese students at the university – Tso Ch'uän, Teng Hsiao-p'ing, and Wu Hsiu-ch'uän.

'You'll find they're ardent Communists, but they're good men all the same,' Ching-kuo advised Yu-long. 'By associating with them, you'll make the secret police less suspicious of you. If you're clever enough, you'll convince them that you, too, are a good comrade. Then you won't have to worry about taking that letter of mine back to my father,' he grinned.

His father, though, had known his son well when he'd come up with the idea that Yu-long become friends with Ching-kuo. There was only a two-year age gap between them, and the two young men had quickly hit it off. Ching-kuo was more than happy to have Yu-long meet him at university, as well as here and there about the city. They talked as they walked, and Ching-kuo grilled the new arrival about what was going on in China and about his father's plans for the future.

'It can get quite lonely here,' he admitted one afternoon as the two of them sat in the student canteen sipping black tea with lemon. 'It's not that I'm not treated well. So far I have been. I've been given a small apartment and I'm supplied with enough food rations to live off comfortably. Some of my fellow students here are quite envious of me.'

'Will it last, though? I mean, now that your father's broken with the Communists.'

Ching-kuo smiled wryly. Like his father, he was a big man, but big in all directions. He lacked his father's tall, gangly frame. As a result, he came across as less off-putting, more sociable, than Chiang Kai-shek. He was, though, remarkably mature for a young man who wasn't quite eighteen years old.

'That's the big question, isn't it?' He said. 'Frankly, I don't think so. After all, I've completed my studies. Although I've registered for a university degree, I doubt whether Stalin's going to tolerate my leading what I'm sure he'd regard as an idle and luxurious existence. No. I'll be sent off to work somewhere soon.'

'In Moscow?'

'I doubt it. More likely some remote town in the Urals where I'll be made to work in a coal mine or steel factory. Something like that. I've started training, you know – we have facilities here at the university – because I know the work's going to be tougher than anything I've ever known. And I'd prefer not to waste away and die quite yet,' he laughed bitterly.

'Stalin would never let you die, Ching-kuo. You're too – you're too valuable.'

'You're right Yu-long. I've been transformed into a commodity, haven't I, to be randomly exchanged at the whim of whoever owns me. But commodities tend to lose their value over time, don't they? In the end, they become worthless and then they're either given to charity or thrown away. It makes me wonder what's in store for me.'

'Surely, Stalin won't keep you here forever, Ching-kuo. Eventually, he'll hand you back to your father.'

'That's what I long for, of course, Yu-long. But I mustn't show it and I dare not hope. The thought of disappointment's too painful to bear. I think that's the worst part of my life right now. Not knowing. Not knowing whether I'll ever be allowed to leave Moscow and go back to my homeland.'

Teng Hsiao-p'ing suddenly appeared at their side.

'Hey, you two! A couple of us are going for a drink. Want to join us?'

There was a loud rasp of metal on stone as Ching-kuo pushed his chair away from the table they were sitting at.

'Why not?' He exclaimed. 'Come on, Yu-long.'

Teng led them out of the building along Volkhonka Street until they reached ulitsa Lenivka and walked towards the river. After twenty paces or so, Teng turned through the open doors of a stately yellow building into a courtyard. From the far corner came the sound of music – very Russian music played by what sounded like an accordion, balalaika and *domra* lute.

Teng led his two companions up three steps and through an ornate carved door into an open room with half a dozen round tables and chairs. On the back wall stood a masonry stove used both to warm the room's occupants and heat up the food and drink they ordered. Beside it was a three-man band playing with all the energy of young lions chasing an antelope across the savannah. Or, in this case, steppe.

The students crossed the room and sat down at a table by the window where Wu Hsiu-ch'uän was waiting for them. A dour-faced girl came across to take their orders. Unlike the band, she seemed about as energetic as a stalk of whipped asparagus. Maybe she didn't like Chinese students.

'Yes?' She said sourly.

Teng took the lead and ordered.

'Let's start with a jug of *medovukha*, Olga. Nicely warmed up, too, to keep out the cold. Oh, and a plate of blini, too, please.' These days people were polite to one another. After all, everyone was now a comrade.

Olga nodded, but didn't smile as she turned towards the stove. Perhaps she didn't like Chinese students who spoke bad Russian.

'So Pan Yu-long, what brings you to Moscow?' Wu asked, looking the other directly in the eye.

'I'm hoping to get enrolled properly at the university,' Yu-long replied with as deadpan a look as he could muster. On the train to Moscow, he'd spent time getting his story straight for occasions such as this. 'My father's busy arranging it.'

'And who's your father?' This time it was Teng who asked the question. His look was no less direct.

'Colonel Pan Yu-tang. He's been serving under Wang Ching-wei in Wuhan.'

Olga returned with a jug of warm honey-flavoured *medovukha* and placed it with an audible thump on the table. The band started playing *Dark Eyes*.

'And yet here you are, in the company of Chiang Kai-shek's son. How did that come about?'

Yu-long looked at Ching-kuo and smiled.

'A bit of a coincidence, actually,' he replied. 'The Generalissimo somehow got to hear that my father and I were coming to Moscow, and asked us to deliver a letter to his son.'

'Which Yu-long kindly did. And politeness turned into friendship once we got to know each other a bit. A ray of good fortune in the midst of quite a lot of bad luck these days.'

'Good fortune, hopefully, that you'll turn to the Communist cause, Ching-kuo. I assume your father doesn't know of your sympathies?' Wu enquired.

'How can he, Hsiu-ch'uän, when anything I write to him is intercepted by the OGPU? You can rest assured, he knows nothing, although – to be honest – I'd like to engage in a political discussion with him.'

'I doubt he'd listen,' Wu said dismissively.

'Except I'm his son.'

'In that case, let's drink to when that day comes, Ching-kuo. *Bydem zdarovi!*'

'*Kanpei! Za lyubof!*'

'*Za lyubof?*' asked Yu-long as he put his empty glass down on the tabletop. 'What's that mean?'

'What do you expect?' Teng laughed. "To love, of course.'

'Didn't Ching-kuo tell you?' Wu put in mischievously. 'And you thought he was your friend. He's got his eye on dark-eyed Olga there. Tell that to the Generalissimo when you get back home,' he laughed.

'That's enough, Wu Hsiu-ch'uän.' Ching-kuo was clearly not amused. 'I have far better taste. Unlike you, it seems. Olga! Vodka, please,' he called loudly across the room, while the band reminded those present how much in love it was.

'One bottle? Or two?' Olga shouted back.

'Two to start with.'

She crossed the room with two bottles held between the fingers of one hand and four glasses in the other.

'I didn't know you Chinese could drink,' Olga finally smiled. It was a rather pretty, shy smile. Well worth waiting for, Yu-long reflected.

'We're not Chinese,' Teng replied loudly. 'We're Communists. All good Communists know how to drink. So open our bottles, dear Olga, and Ching-kuo here will serenade you all night. Far better than the band there,' he jerked his head across the room, 'Of that I can assure you, comrade.'

Three hours and four bottles of vodka later, the band's members had packed up their instruments and shuffled out into the night. Other customers had followed, one by one, until there was only one old man left, nursing his glass. He had scabs all over his face and his *ushanka* fur hat was motheaten – as was the mongrel lying at his feet with one ear cocked. How a dog could give away the presence of an informer.

Yu-long appreciated the secret policeman's attempt to blend into his surroundings, but was disappointed that he hadn't realised that the pistol in his ankle holster showed whenever he crossed his legs. A careless mistake that he himself wouldn't have made if tasked to report on four Chinese students in a drinking establishment.

Those students, let's face it, were very much the worse for wear. That, after all, was the object of the exercise. But Yu-long had managed to pace himself better than the others. As he'd learned from his father, things – unusual things, important information, normally unspoken thoughts – were often communicated by tongues loosened by alcohol. The Generalissimo was wise to be a teetotaller.

'Hey! Yu-long! Your glash ish em-ty,' Wu raised his head from the table and with shaky hand poured the last of the vodka into his glass. Some of the liquid spilled onto edge of the tabletop and dripped onto the floor. The mongrel across the room licked its lips absently and sniffed around for morsels of food that might have fallen nearby.

'Thanksh, Shiu-ch'uän,' Yu-long did his best to sound as drunk as his companion.

'Shink nussing of it. Hey! Teng! Wake up!' He shouted in his companion's ear. 'Party time!'

Teng raised his head.

'The party's over, Hsiu-ch'uän. The vodka's finished.'

Wu looked at the empty bottle lying on its side.

'The vodka may be finished, Teng Hsiao-p'ing, but the Party isn't over,' he said with a lucidity that made Yu-long wonder just how drunk he was.

'Yes, it is, my friend. We're going home, aren't we, Ching-kuo?'

Ching-kuo nodded and began to stand up.

'Olga!' He called. 'How much do we owe you?'

'I don't mean thish party, you shilly melon!' Wu clearly had something he wanted to communicate.

'What party, then?'

Olga came over with a piece of paper on which she'd tallied the bill. Standing a little unsteadily on his feet, Ching-kuo brought out a handful of coins and paid her.

'The Communisht Party, of course. It may look like it'sh finished,' Wu exclaimed, turning to Ching-kuo. 'Thanksh to your father. But 'tznot.'

The old man in the corner was scratching a scab on his nose, but his ears were alert, and his eyes watched the four young men carefully.

'Communishts forever!' Wu drained his glass and thumped it upside down on the tabletop.

'Come on, Hsiu-ch'uän. It's time to go,' Yu-long put one hand under his companion's armpit and helped pull Wu to his feet. 'I'm sure we're not finished yet.'

Wu looked at him sharply.

'Eh? Wash that a "we" I heard there, Pan Yu-long?'

'Of course it was, Hsiu-ch'uän,' Ching-kuo intervened smoothly. 'Didn't you know? Yu-long may be working for the Nationalists, but he's really a double agent.'

Wu Hsiu-ch'uän smiled his drunken smile and embraced Yu-long.

'You're not a shpy, are you, little white face?'

'Of course, I'm not. Ching-kuo's pulling your leg.'

Wu looked hard at Yu-long.

'Maybe,' he said. 'And maybe not. But I know of one double agent who'sh fooled all the Nationalists. Even Chiang Kai-shek himshelf.'

'Come on, Hsiu-ch'uän!' This time it was Teng bringing his friend to order. 'Enough! Let's get out of here. Good night, Olga.'

Olga gave her departing guests another of her pretty smiles.

'Good night, comrades. Enjoy your hangovers!'

But Wu wasn't to be deterred, even as he staggered towards the door, with one arm over Yu-long's shoulder for support.

'It's Shu Bai-li,' he whispered in the young man's ear. 'He's going to shave the Party. Jusht you wait and shee.'

'I knew it,' Pan Yu-tang exclaimed the next morning, after his son had relayed what he remembered of the night before. Anastasia was visiting a relative near Podolsk and had stayed there overnight.

'Finally, some hard evidence that Su Bai-li's a double agent. We have to tell the Generalissimo.'

'But it's not evidence as such, is it, father?' Yu-long's head was clear, thanks to a brisk walk home through the night, followed by several cups of hot water in his hotel room. 'It's still only hearsay.'

The Colonel's face lost some of its excitement.

'True,' he mused. 'So how can we convince Chiang Kai-shek of what's going on?'

'I can tell him, of course,' Yu-long suggested. 'The General seems to trust me. Maybe he'll listen.'

'Maybe he will,' his father agreed. 'But will he act? Somehow we have to unmask Su Bai-li. I mean, who knows what tales he's telling the Generalissimo in order to advance the Communist cause?'

'Do you think Bai-li suspects us, father?'

'Us? Of what?'

'Of our suspicion that he's some kind of double agent.'

Yu-tang paused to think.

'Possibly,' he conceded, 'In the sense that everything these days seems possible. But I doubt it.'

'So you don't think Bai-li had something to do with the Generalissimo sending us both on this mission together?'

'To Moscow, you mean?' again his father paused, his hooded eyes half-closed in thought. 'Unlikely, I think. The whole thing struck me as being Chiang's own idea. He even suggested how I might smuggle Ching-kuo's letter across the border.'

'Maybe it's a trap,' Yu-long said excitedly. 'To get us out of the way.'

Yu-tang helped himself to a slice of brown bread and sausage.

'Out of the way of what, Yu-long? Why should he want to do that? We're hardly the Generalissimo's enemy, after all. Still,' he added with his mouth full, 'Anything's possible, as I said. We should be prepared, my son.'

'What do you suggest, Father?'

'As I see it, there are two things we need to do before we go back. First, get Ching-kuo to suggest Bai-li's a double agent. Something he's overheard Chinese Communist students talking about. Chiang is far more likely to listen to his son than to us.'

'I'll talk to Ching-kuo, then, and remind him of what Wu Hsiu-ch'uän said as we were leaving the bar. I think he heard. I'll make sure he relates it to his father.'

'Good. Which brings us to the second thing we need to do.'

'What's that?'

'Get hold of a miniature camera and photograph Ching-kuo's letter. So, even if I get caught smuggling the original across the border, you'll have a copy on microfilm. Whatever happens, we'll be able to deliver our evidence to the Generalissimo. I reckon Bai-li's days are numbered.'

'Is it time, then, for us to make the long trip home?'

'It is, Yu-long. Just give me another week. I've a couple of important meetings coming up.'

As usual, he didn't say with whom. He'd miss Anastasia's nocturnal enthusiasms.

The carriage attendant opened the compartment door.

'Next stop Zabaykalsk,' he said. 'All passengers must get off the train with their baggage. For customs inspection,' he added a little unnecessarily, before slamming the compartment door shut again and moving on along the first-class carriage. Chiang Kai-shek had allowed his emissaries to travel in style.

Colonel Pan stood up, reached for his uniform trousers and began to put them on. He liked to travel in comfort in his shirt, long-johns and long woollen socks. Outside silver birch trees huddled endlessly along the edge of the Trans-Siberian Railway, their branches barely covered with snow. The ground was broken occasionally by black tree stumps.

'What's happened to the weather?' He knotted his tie efficiently and put on his uniform jacket. 'Is the snow melting?'

Yu-long looked out of the carriage window.

'It looks like it, doesn't it?'

'Yet soon it'll be up to here,' The Colonel placed the palm of one hand horizontal at shoulder height. He slipped on his shiny, well-polished black shoes.

'I'm glad I packed extra-large sized footwear,' he smiled a little grimly. 'I don't know how I'd have managed to stuff my shoes with newspaper and wear them otherwise.'

'They look alright, I think.'

'I hope they're alright. Remember, Yu-long, if anything goes wrong and they find Ching-kuo's letter, go straight to the Generalissimo in Nanking and tell him everything. You've got the microfilm?'

'Safely hidden away in my –'

'Don't tell me!' Yu-tang ordered. 'It's better I don't know.'

The Colonel looked at his son approvingly. A fine young man.

The carriage jerked suddenly as the train began to slow down. A few minutes later, it drew into Zabaykalsk by the ice-bound Amur river.

'Nearly home,' Yu-long said, reaching up for the suitcases on the baggage rack above their seats.

'Nearly back in Manchuria, at least. Now the fun begins,' muttered his father, suddenly feeling less sure of himself.

Father and son stepped down onto the platform and, together with a couple of dozen other passengers, began hauling their baggage towards the station's single two-storey building set back from the railway line. The sky was overcast, and the temperature hovering around zero degrees, but the weather really was quite mild for the time of year.

'Passports!' A Soviet officer in uniform ordered once they were inside the station building.

As a matter of habit, Yu-tang checked the officer's epaulettes in order to determine his rank. Annoyingly, he had none. He assumed, though, that a customs official at a remote Siberian border post was unlikely to be as senior as himself.

Colonel Pan stood to attention, drew himself to his full height – still a good two inches shorter than that of the Soviet officer – and presented their passports.

The Russian began leafing through them casually.

'And what has been the purpose of your visit to the Union of Soviet Socialist Republics?' he asked in English.

'As a full colonel in the Republican Army of China, to hold diplomatic meetings with senior officials in Moscow,' Yu-tang replied in Russian, eager to impress. 'Very senior officials.'

The officer nodded, but said nothing, as he continued to leaf through the pages of their passports – a bit unnecessarily. Neither Pan Yu-tang nor his son had ever been abroad before. The only stamps in their passports were on the very first page. The rest of the pages were in pristine condition, unmarked by alien entry and exit stamps in smudged ink.

'Place your baggage here, please!' The officer indicated a long low table beside the lectern behind which he was standing. It was a command, rather than a request.

'Are you carrying contraband or smuggling goods contrary to the regulations of the Soviet people?'

'Not that I'm aware, Officer,' Yu-tang stood to full attention.

'You speak Russian.' It was a comment, rather than a question.

'As I said, we are diplomats despatched by General Chiang Kai-shek to conduct diplomacy of a highly sensitive nature.'

The customs official seemed unimpressed.

'Open your suitcases,' he ordered.

He signalled to two soldiers standing nearby to come forward.

'Search the Colonel's belongings,' he ordered once again. 'Thoroughly.'

As the soldiers carried out their commanding officer's instructions, Yu-tang took a cigarette case from his pocket, opened it, and extracted a cigarette. He then proffered it to the officer in front of him.

'Cigarette?'

'If you insist,' the officer accepted Pan's offer. Yu-long stepped forward to light both men's cigarettes.

'Nice case,' the Russian commented approvingly.

'Thank you.'

'Made of silver, too. A gift, perhaps, from one of your diplomatic friends in Moscow?' The officer enquired casually.

'Not at all,' Yu-tang replied stiffly. 'It was a present from my wife in Shanghai. For my fiftieth birthday,' he decided to add age, as well as rank, to his status.

The officer remained unimpressed.

'So you brought this cigarette case – this valuable object – with you when you entered the Union of Soviet Socialist Republics?'

'That is correct, yes.'

The customs official once again leafed through Yu-tang's passport. He held up an empty page at the back enquiringly.

'Where, then, is your entry declaration form?'

'Entry declaration form?'

'All goods of value – as I'm sure a Colonel of your age and diplomatic experience is aware – must be declared upon entry into the Union of Soviet Socialist Republics and entered into the traveller's passport,' the officer stared at Yu-tang dispassionately. 'It is the law. And yet, here,' he tapped with a pen the passport in his hand, 'There's no such record, as I'm sure you can see.'

'Well, yes. I suppose –'

'From which I deduce,' he continued, with barely concealed triumph, 'That you failed to declare this cigarette case upon entry into the Union of Soviet Socialist Republics. Am I not correct?'

'I didn't realise I had to.'

'Obviously not. And yet it is the duty of every visitor to study and adhere to the customs regulations of the Union of Soviet Socialist Republics when entering its sovereign jurisdiction. For whatever purpose. Even diplomacy.'

The officer paused. Yu-tang waited.

'But perhaps you are not telling me the truth, Colonel Pan. Perhaps you were not in possession of this cigarette case when you entered the Union of Soviet Socialist Republics?'

'What do you mean?'

'I mean that maybe this cigarette case – this *silver* cigarette case – is a gift you received here in the Union of Soviet Socialist Republics. From one of your diplomatic friends in Moscow, perhaps?'

'No, Officer. As I said –'

'It is, as I have already intimated, forbidden to carry valuable items of silver across the border. In, or out.' The customs official reached out a hand towards Yu-tang. 'You will, therefore, surrender the item to me for confiscation according to paragraph thirteen, section two, sub-section one, of the Security Protection Regulations of the Commissariat of the Soviet People.'

'But,' Yu-tang was prepared to argue, but thought better of it and handed over his silver cigarette case.

'I would be grateful, Officer, if you could provide me with a receipt so that I may retrieve my property when I next pass through the Soviet Union.'

The customs officer looked at the Chinese colonel. Without saying a word, he slipped Yu-tang's cigarette case into his pocket.

The soldiers had by now taken everything out of the trunk and two suitcases on the table in front of them. One was carefully examining their linings; the other inspecting Yu-long's toilet bag, from which he took out a round wooden box of shaving soap. He opened the lid, prodded and sniffed its contents before returning it to the toilet bag. He then looked across at his commanding officer and shook his head very slightly.

'Perhaps, Colonel Pan, you and your son could take off your shoes?'

'Our shoes?' Yu-tang echoed.

'Your shoes.'

'But why?'

'Colonel Pan, senior customs officials of the Union of Soviet Socialist Republics are not accustomed to being asked questions. Especially those that begin with "why." And especially when they are addressed to Senior Commander of Customs and Excise, Vilen Nikitin. Take off your shoes.'

The two men did as ordered. The wooden floorboards beneath their feet were cold.

The Senior Commander looked down at the shoes worn by the Chinese diplomats.

'Might I ask why, Colonel Pan, you have newspaper in your shoes?'

Yu-tang was tempted to tell the Russian that senior officers in the Republican Army of China were not accustomed to being asked questions that began with "why." Wisely, he thought better of it.

'Because it's cold.'

'Cold?' Commander Nikitin looked puzzled. 'It's not cold, Colonel Pan. Haven't you noticed? The weather is extremely mild for this time of the year. Even the snow outside seems to be melting.'

Yu-tang stood to attention and said nothing.

'But I'm told we're about to get a really cold blast from northern Siberia. Later tonight, I believe,' Nikitin continued conversationally. 'Then you'll certainly need newspaper in your shoes. Perhaps you should have set out on your return trip from Moscow a day later,' he laughed coldly.

'We thought it would be cold here,' Yu-long interceded. 'Cold enough to protect our feet with newspaper.'

'Our feet, Lieutenant?' He turned towards Yu-long. 'And yet you don't have any newspaper in your shoes. Why is that, I wonder? Perhaps because you don't feel the cold as much as the Colonel here?'

'That is true, Senior Commander Nikitin,' Yu-long blurted out, eager to protect his father.

'Or perhaps it was because you noticed that the weather was quite mild and that you didn't need newspaper in your shoes?'

'Yes. You are right, Commander Nikitin.'

'In which case, you must have left the newspaper that was in your shoes in your compartment. Am I right, Lieutenant Pan Yu-long?'

'Yes indeed, Commander Nikitin.'

'And yet,' Nikitin gave the young man the benefit of his most supercilious smile. 'I'm informed that our agents failed to find any newspaper in your compartment. Or in the rubbish receptacles in your carriage.'

'Perhaps –'

'Or anywhere on the train,' continued Nikitin relentlessly. 'Which suggests, doesn't it, Lieutenant Pan, that you had no need of newspaper in your shoes in the first place? For whatever reasons. Whereas your father,' his voice tailed away as he turned his attention to the Colonel. He really did look a little ridiculous in a uniform that was too tight for him. 'Your father clearly did have a reason to put newspaper in his shoes.'

'Because of the cold, I can assure you,' Yu-tang said as persuasively as he was able.

'And yet, by your own admission, it isn't cold, is it, Colonel Pan?' Nikitin continued implacably. 'So why not remove the newspaper from your shoes? I'm sure your feet will feel more comfortable when you put your shoes back on. There should be more wriggle room for your toes,' he smiled.

Yu-tang had no option but to do as he was ordered. He took the folded pieces of newspaper out of his shoes and placed them on the ground beside them.

'Now, Colonel, why don't you throw it!' Nikitin commanded. 'Up in the air, like this.'

He scooped up some of the Colonel's clothes and tossed them high into the air above his head.

Nervously Yu-tang did as he was told. The two wads of newspaper flew up into the air and landed with a dull thud on the floorboards. After them floated down a single thin sheet of paper with writing all over it.

'What's this?' Nikitin asked rhetorically, as he bent down to pick up one page of Ching-kuo's letter. He shook the two wads of newspaper carefully, first one, then the other. Five more sheets of paper with handwriting on them disentangled themselves from the black and white newsprint.

'Ah! Now this is unusual. Your Russian newspaper seems to be carrying an article in the Chinese language – something that clearly constitutes a contravention of the Soviet Newspapers' Regulations for the Dissemination of News and Propaganda. Article 11, I believe. Section 2. Subsection c. All newspapers of the Soviet Union,' he declaimed, as if reading the regulations themselves, 'Must be written in the Russian language. Only those articles of specific interest to the Vepses, Enets, Nenets, blah blah blah, or other indigenous peoples, may be written in a language other than the Russian mother tongue. I don't recall any mention of Chinese in this context, Colonel Pan. Do you? I suppose because you Chinese are too numerous to constitute such an indigenous people. What do you think?'

'Indeed, Commander.'

'I thought so. I must, therefore, immediately alert my superiors in Moscow to this breach of national security, don't you agree?' Nikitin gave Yu-tang a disarming smile, as he took the Colonel's silver cigarette case out of his pocket, opened it and helped himself to a cigarette. He didn't bother to offer one to Pan Yu-tang.

'Of course, one should be careful not to jump to conclusions until one has landed safely,' Nikitin lit his cigarette and inhaled deeply. 'But I think it reasonable to expect that I will receive a commendation from whoever's patriotic duty it is to oversee proper adherence to Soviet newspaper publishing regulations. What do you say to that, Colonel Pan? Perhaps you yourself will be cited in the commendation, although as a Chinese citizen you won't, of course, be entitled to a Soviet medal.'

He exhaled the smoke from his lungs into Yu-tang's face.

'Perhaps even Stalin himself will be persuaded to pin a medal to my chest. What an honour that would be, wouldn't it?'

'Indeed it would, my Commander.'

Nikitin was enjoying himself too much to pay attention to his two victims. Once more he drew on Yu-tang's cigarette.

'And, surely, those concerned will deem it right and proper that I be promoted, don't you think? To Very Senior Commander of the Soviet Department of Customs & Excise perhaps? My life's ambition. It will make my parents so very proud. And I will owe everything to you, Colonel Pan.'

Nikitin put one hand down behind the lectern which he used to examine passports and opened a drawer.

'Come, Colonel! We must drink to my success.'

He brought out a half-opened bottle of vodka and two shot glasses, one of which he handed to Yu-tang and filled to the brim. He did the same with his own glass, raised it and said loudly,

'Za vstrechu! To our meeting!'

He downed the contents of his glass and thumped it down on the top of the lectern beside him. Yu-tang had little alternative but to do the same.

'Of course,' Nikitin continued, licking his lips. 'I may have misread these sheets of paper in my enthusiasm. What do you think, Colonel?'

Yu-tang wasn't sure how best to respond. Nikitin's voice was as cold as the barrel of the pistol in the holster round his waist. It was as if the Siberian winter had magically returned.

'It is, I suppose, possible, Senior Commander Nikitin. But I think you are the best judge of that,' he said stiffly.

'Ah! You really are a diplomat, Colonel Pan. I must say, I'd begun to wonder.'

Nikitin paused, as if struck by a thought.

'What if these sheets of paper in Chinese are not, after all, a newspaper article?' He enquired innocently. 'What if they're some kind of secret message. A code? What do you say to that? Eh, Colonel?'

'I assure you, Commander Nikitin, it's just a letter,' Yu-tang stuttered uncomfortably. Why had Chiang Kai-shek suggested he try to smuggle Ching-kuo's letter in newspaper stuffed into his shoes?

'A letter?' Nikitin looked at the Chinese officer in mild disbelief. 'Written in Chinese? Why didn't I think of that?'

He inhaled again, before stubbing the cigarette out on the iron tabletop where the Pans' baggage lay.

'Or, perhaps, it's not in Chinese at all. I wouldn't know. Perhaps it's written in some sort of code? This so-called letter is made to look as if it's full of Chinese characters when in fact it's nothing of the sort, is it, Colonel Pan? What appears to be Chinese writing is in fact nothing other than a cleverly contrived set of symbols, isn't that right?' Vilen Nikitin was clearly enjoying himself. It wasn't every day he received a bribe to carry out his duty.

'No, Commander Nikitin. I can assure you –'

'A set of symbols which, when decoded, reveals a dastardly Chinese plot to bring about the downfall of the Union of Soviet Socialist Republics? Is that what this so-called "letter" contains, Colonel Pan?'

'No, Senior Commander, you have misunderstood everything.'

'Everything?'

'Yes, Commander. This is a letter from the son of Chiang Kai-shek to his father, Generalissimo of the Nationalist Revolutionary Army in Nanking. A simple letter of affection from a young man for his father whom he hasn't seen for more than two years.'

'A most touching explanation, Colonel Pan. But how do I know you're telling the truth?'

'But I am,' Yu-tang said desperately. 'Surely, you –'

'Ah!' Nikitin had been leafing through the pages of a folder on the lectern in front of him. 'It's as I feared, Colonel Pan. Once again you have contravened the Security Regulations of the Commissariat of the Soviet People.'

'I have?'

'You have. As a detainee of the Soviet Government, Chiang Ching-kuo is not permitted to get in touch by any means with any official of the Nationalist Republican Government of China. It says so right here,' he tapped the pages in front of him.

'But I'm not a government official.'

'Maybe not, strictly speaking. But you've still tried to impress upon me the fact that you're an important diplomat, Colonel Pan. Which suggests that you are, indeed, a member of the Chinese government.'

Nikitin held up his hand to forestall Yu-tang's objection.

'And anyway, this letter, if it is one, is – by your own admission – addressed to Chiang Kai-shek who is, in your own words, the "Generalissimo of the National Revolutionary Army" in Nanking. So, you see –' he raised both hands in a helpless gesture.

Yu-tang stood in silent admission. The game was well and truly up. He did his best, though, to put a brave face on things. His son, after all, was looking on with dismay, seemingly ready to attack Commander Vilen Nikitin with his bare fists – as if that would help.

Yu-tang restrained him with a single severe look.

'What do I see, Commander Nikitin?'

'That you, Colonel Pan, must be placed in detention until a People's Tribunal can be convened to consider your crimes.'

Nikitin jerked his head towards his underlings.

'My crimes?'

Two soldiers came forward and pulled Yu-tang's arms roughly behind his back. They then frog-marched him out of the customs hall.

'Father!' Yu-long called desperately.

Colonel Pan Yu-tang didn't look back as he was led towards his fate.

'As for you, Lieutenant Pan,' Nikitin said smoothly as he handed Yu-long his passport. 'You may proceed across the border. Have a safe journey.'

With that he marched casually through the same door taken by Yu-long's father, as the young man repacked his suitcases and prepared for an uncertain future.

Something wasn't right.

Once again, Bai-li ran through in his mind the report that had reached him through his intelligence agent in Harbin from a certain Vilen Nikitin, Senior Commander of the Soviet Union's Department of Customs & Excise in Zabaykalsk.

Why had Pan Yu-tang placed folded newspaper in his shoes while his son Yu-long had not? It was true. Only the Colonel had been taking Ching-kuo's letter to his father. But he would have insisted, surely, that his son place newspaper in his shoes, too, so as not to attract Nikitin's attention. Like father, like son.

But he hadn't.

Which suggested that Yu-long might have been carrying something else, something perhaps more important, and that Yu-tang's use of newspaper had been designed to deflect the attention of the Soviet customs official.

Unless he was very stupid, of course. But Pan Yu-tang wasn't stupid. On the contrary, he was a rather sly and crafty individual.

So the question was, what else could they have been smuggling through Soviet customs? Another report, this time from Anastasia, insisted that the Colonel had been in her, let's face it charming, company throughout the entirety of his stay in Moscow. So what could the Pans have found out? What did they have in their possession that encouraged them to accept unquestioningly the Colonel's possible arrest?

For arrested he had been, held in a cell in the basement of the customs house at Zabaykalsk, then summarily tried a couple of days later before a tribunal of three judges hastily summoned from Chita, with Commander Nikitin and his two underlings appearing before them as the only witnesses. A Chinese-speaking lawyer had been appointed to act on behalf of the defendant, but to no avail. Not only did Pan Yu-tang, Colonel of the National Revolutionary Army of China, insist on speaking Russian throughout the brief proceedings. He was found guilty of trying to smuggle with intention a silver cigarette case; and, with yet further intention – a term, the lawyer explained, that signified the seriousness of the accusations levelled against the Colonel – a letter from Chiang Ching-kuo, currently detained at the pleasure of the Soviet People in Moscow, to his father, Chiang Kai-shek, de facto head of the Kuomintang Nationalist Party in China.

Each infringement of the Regulations regarding National Security in the Union of the Soviet Socialist Republics was punishable by up to five years of hard labour in one of the newly established Siberian gulag prisons. The judges were lenient. Or so they persuaded themselves during their brief deliberations. Taking into account Colonel Pan's defence regarding his age and diplomatic status, they sentenced him to a total of seven years in one of the 'corrective' labour camps currently being constructed by convicts in the tundra well north of the Lena River. Collectively, they doubted he would survive beyond the following winter.

Meanwhile, Lieutenant Pan Yu-long had proceeded by train to Harbin. There he had alighted and made his way by ricksha to the Hotel Moderne on Kitaiskaia ulitsa in the district of Pristan. Upon arrival, encouraged by the attractive receptionist's demeanour, he had almost at once blurted out the whole story of his father's detention at the border. Moved by his tears, the receptionist – another, far more charming and, let's face it, sexier – Olga decided at once to take the distraught young man under her wing. Perhaps, once he was rested, he would like her to act as his guide and show him the famed Sungari River that flowed nearby?

He would, indeed. As soon as he had unpacked, if that was convenient.

It was, indeed. It so happened that Olga would be off duty at 6pm. They could meet right there in the hotel's vestibule once she had changed her clothes. Unlike the handsome lieutenant's, the hotel's uniform lacked a certain – how might she put it? – lustre, if he knew what she meant.

He did. The hole in his heart was beginning to mend already.

Half an hour later, Olga walked her new-found paramour along the so-called 'Chinese Street' until they reached the embankment of the frozen river. There, in the comfort of the enveloping darkness and out of sight of prying eyes, she slipped her arm through Yu-long's and guided him along the promenade – famous during the summer months when the local inhabitants went boating and swimming in the river, but in early December deserted, apart from two drunken vagrants who watched the couple passing by from the shelter of a straw-thatched fisherman's lean-to.

In the meantime, back in Room 44 on the first floor of the Hotel Moderne, a well-turned out Chinese military intelligence officer was going methodically through Yu-long's suitcases and belongings. At first, as he'd anticipated, he found nothing. This did not worry him. He merely wished to understand what kind of man Lieutenant Pan Yu-long was.

A second search suggested that the young officer was vain when it came to his appearance. His shirts and civilian suits were clearly made to order, and he seemed to enjoy wearing rather dashing underwear, while his toiletries bag was filled with creams, pomades, and various olfactory delights.

A third search – initiated as one of the vagrants made his way quickly towards the hotel to advise the concierge that Lieutenant Pan and the receptionist had begun to retrace their steps – revealed, on the underside of a round cake of shaving soap firmly fixed in its wooden bowl, a strip of miniature film.

This the intelligence officer removed and hurriedly took to the Harbin office of the China-Manchuria Trading Company. There it was examined under a microscope, enlarged, developed on photographic paper, and the prints placed in a sealed envelope. This was then handed to a trusted courier with an order to take it at once by plane to Doctor Colonel Su Bai-li, Director of Internal Affairs in Shanghai.

While the delectable Olga's sympathy for the newly-arrived young guest extended through the night and for the duration of his brief stay,

Bai-li digested the contents of the telephone call he had received from the office of the China-Manchuria Trading Company in Harbin. The next morning, while Yu-long, hungry from his previous night's exertions, breakfasted in the hotel dining room on buckwheat porridge and a plateful of *syrniki* cheese pancakes, washed down by black tea steeped in cinnamon, cloves and lemon juice, in Room 44 upstairs the microfilm was put back into its hiding place. By early afternoon, just as Yu-long was boarding the efficiently-run Japanese Manchurian Railway train to Mukden and from there onwards to Peking, Bai-li held in his hands a copy of the letter from Ching-kuo to Chiang Kai-shek. It made for explosive reading.

After the customary salutations and apologies for failing to find a way to communicate with his father, Ching-kuo began to relate a story told him by Pan Yu-long, concerning someone called Su Bai-li who, Ching-kuo understood, was a close friend and adviser to his father. The evidence presented by Yu-long suggested that Bai-li was very definitely not the Generalissimo's friend, but a double agent working for the Communists – a piece of information he had gleaned during a drinking session with some fellow students at the Sun Yat-sen Communist University of the Toilers of China.

At this point, Bai-li took off his glasses and began to polish them distractedly. He had managed to get rid of one potential rival intent on unmasking him, only to find another taking his place. Pan Yu-long had to be dealt with. But how?

The train from Peking pulled into Nanking Station late at night. Not for the first time in recent months, it had been delayed – this time by a small explosion near the tracks between Tianjin and Jinan. The Japanese, it seemed, wanted to create a false flag incident to lure the Nationalist Revolutionary Army into attacking their positions, but the officer in charge of the Chinese troops nearby wisely paid no attention. The train, though, stayed where it was in the middle of the countryside for a further two hours before finally heading south.

Pan Yu-long alighted from his first-class compartment, called a porter to carry his baggage, and started walking down the platform to the ticket barrier. There he was met by an officer in the full winter uniform of the Chinese Republic's Internal Affairs, complete with *chieh-fang* cap, shoulder loops and red collar tabs.

'Lieutenant Pan?' The officer greeted him politely. 'How nice to see you back in Nanking. The Generalissimo is eager to hear all about your trip.'

Belatedly, Yu-long realised that he was being addressed by none other than Su Bai-li.

'Doctor Colonel Su,' he stuttered. 'I'm sorry. I didn't recognise you. It's been a long trip.'

'So I understand, Lieutenant. You must be very tired.'

'Yes. Your uniform…'

His voice tailed away, emphasising perhaps just how exhausted he was.

'Ah yes, my uniform. I do my best not to wear it,' Bai-li gave one of his disarming dimpled smiles, 'But sometimes duty calls, as I'm sure you can appreciate.'

Yu-long found it difficult to interpret whether Bai-li's remark was part of an innocent conversation, or something slightly more ominous.

'Yes indeed, Colonel.'

'Please allow me to escort you,' Bai-li said graciously. 'The Generalissimo will see you at eight o'clock sharp tomorrow morning, and there are matters we need to discuss beforehand. I have a car at our disposal.'

'Thank you, Colonel Su. You are most kind.'

'It's the least I can do under the circumstances. Your father's arrest at Zabaykalsk must have been quite a shock. And emotionally upsetting, I'm sure.'

Pan Yu-long looked surprised.

'You've heard, then?' He asked.

'Of course, Lieutenant. I am, after all, Director of Internal Affairs in Shanghai, where your father resides. It's my duty to be informed when a senior officer of the National Revolutionary Army – when any Chinese citizen – in my jurisdiction is arrested by officials of a foreign power.'

Bai-li paused, but Yu-long said nothing.

'The information I have, however, is only second – occasionally third – hand, Lieutenant. As you might expect. That's where I hope you'll be able to assist me in my enquiries.'

'Of course, Colonel. Do you know what's happened to my father since his arrest?'

Bai-li looked sympathetic and gestured to Yu-long to get into the waiting car. He joined the young man in the back seat as the chauffeur loaded Yu-long's trunk and suitcases into the cavernous boot of the Packard 8.

'I'm afraid you must brace yourself for bad news, Lieutenant. From what I've heard, your father has been sentenced to seven years hard labour in a Siberian prison camp.'

'What! But that's monstrous.'

'Yes, it does seem excessive. After all, as I understand matters, a false accusation was made regarding a silver cigarette case.'

'It was disgraceful. The customs officer – a Commander Nikitin – claimed my father had received it as a gift from some official in Moscow, when it was a present from my mother for his fiftieth birthday. Nikitin demanded that my father hand it over and he just put it in his pocket. He stole it. He even smoked, uninvited, one of the cigarettes inside the case.'

'Quite unacceptable, I agree, Lieutenant. I've made representations to the Governor of Chita and, in the strongest possible terms, suggested that he remove this Commander Nikitin from his post forthwith.'

'Thank you, Colonel Su,' Yu-long bowed his head as the car lurched over another of Nanking's renowned potholes.

'Under the circumstances, it was the least I could do,' Bai-li patted the other's thigh encouragingly. 'The other accusation, however, is more difficult to deal with. As I understand it, your father was trying to smuggle a letter from Chiang Ching-kuo to the Generalissimo. Is that really true?'

'It was what the Generalissimo asked us to do,' Yu-long wailed. 'Unfortunately, we were caught.'

Bai-li looked at Yu-long sharply.

'We?' he asked. 'But you weren't arrested, Lieutenant.'

The Packard came to a halt outside a large two storey building, its steps flanked by two cast-iron elephants leading up to an ornate double door with brass knockers.

Yu-long looked at Bai-li enquiringly.

'I thought it best to continue our discussion in quiet surroundings where we won't be interrupted. We have a lot to get through before you meet the Generalissimo tomorrow morning.'

The chauffeur opened the door and saluted smartly as his two passengers alighted. Bai-li led the young lieutenant up the steps and through the double doors. Inside was a vast marble atrium, its ceiling as high as the building itself. Followed by Yu-long, Bai-li set off across it towards a door in the far corner beside a sweeping ornate staircase. He pushed the door open and led his visitor down a long corridor stretching to the back of the building. At the very end, he opened another door and Yu-long found himself in an interrogation room. It had no windows – just a metal table with four chairs set around it.

'Do please sit down, Lieutenant,' Bai-li gestured towards one of the chairs and sat down opposite his visitor. He placed his bulging brief case on the tabletop to one side.

'I should start by apologising for the surroundings,' he began, in order to put Yu-long at ease, 'As you may be aware, my office is at present in Shanghai, not Nanking, and I regret that I was unable to persuade any of my colleagues here to offer us, at such short notice, the use of any office in this building. Something to do with security, I was told. This –' he gestured a little helplessly as he looked round the room, 'Was all I could obtain. Please excuse me.'

There was the sound of footsteps outside, followed by a quick knock on the door. A soldier entered with a tray holding a tea pot and two cups, before saluting and leaving the room again. Yu-long realised it was the chauffeur.

'So, let us start, shall we? From the very beginning, please.' Bai-li was suddenly very much the intelligence officer.

Yu-long composed himself.

'It all started when we got to Zabaykalsk,' he began.

'No, Lieutenant Pan, I mean the very beginning,' Bai-li said gently, as he poured some tea from the pot into a cup and pushed it across the table towards Yu-long. 'Right from when you were ordered to travel to Moscow.'

And so, between grateful sips of jasmine tea, Yu-long related everything he knew. There were gaps, of course, because he hadn't been present when the Generalissimo first talked to his father. He also had very little idea about what his father had been up to while he, as instructed, was courting the friendship of Ching-kuo.

'But he must have given you some indication about who he was seeing?' Bai-li asked. 'Who in particular in the hierarchy of Soviet politicians and, perhaps, diplomats he was engaged in discussions with?'

'Actually, he didn't.'

'Really? Why was that, I wonder?' Bai-li started polishing his glasses absent-mindedly.

'One reason, I think, was that we were operating on very different schedules,' Yu-long was getting into his stride, in the way that interrogators wanted of those they questioned.

'What kind of schedules?'

'Well, we'd agreed in advance that I should spend as much time as I could with Ching-kuo, while he pursued his diplomatic contacts.'

'In advance?'

'Yes, on the train to Moscow. We had plenty of time to discuss our assignment during the trip. According to my father, the Generalissimo himself had suggested that I spend time with his son. I thought it a great honour.'

'Honour? In what way, exactly?'

'Because he is the Generalissimo's one and only son. The idea was that Ching-kuo and I should get to know each other so that he could trust me.'

'Trust you? Why *trust*? Surely, all you'd been assigned to do was bring back a letter from Ching-kuo to his father?'

'Yes, but the Generalissimo thought it best that Ching-kuo trust the person who was going to take his letter back to China.'

'But it wasn't you, but your father who undertook that particular task, wasn't it? I mean, he was the one arrested in possession of Ching-kuo's letter.'

'Well, yes, but –'

'So why didn't your *father* spend his time building trust with Ching-kuo?'

'What? And leave me to engage in meetings requiring skilled diplomacy?'

Yu-long's outraged defence of his father was, in a way, touching. 'It's hardly as if I'm qualified for that. I'm just a young, inexperienced lieutenant. And anyway –'

'Anyway?' Bai-li murmured encouragingly.

'Anyway, I don't speak Russian.'

'While your father, of course, does. And rather fluently, too, so I hear. By the time we get him back from Siberia, I'm sure he'll be bilingual.'

'Surely, it won't take that long?' Yu-long asked uncertainly.

'One never knows, Lieutenant, when it comes to diplomacy. Something I'm sure your father will tell you about in due course.'

Bai-li turned his attention once again to polishing his glasses.

'I'm a little unclear about your motivations, if I may use such a word, Lieutenant. I mean, there you are, father and son, alone in Moscow, tasked with carrying out an assignment – one part of which, to smuggle a letter from Ching-kuo to his father here in Nanking, is patently clear. The other part, Lieutenant, is less so. What was a senior officer of the Chinese Nationalist Revolutionary Army and secret member of the Western Hills Group doing negotiating with communist officials in Moscow? I mean, what on earth could they have had in common? Was your father trying to persuade them to bring back the Tzar, or something?'

'No, of course not,' Yu-long spluttered with anger, as he often did when his father's reputation was questioned.

'Then what was he discussing in Moscow, while you were enjoying life auditing classes at the Sun Yat Sen University in the company of young Ching-kuo? And, as I understand it, associating with several other Chinese Communist students there,' Bai-li continued relentlessly. 'And who was he discussing such matters with?'

Yu-long was too exhausted to answer Bai-li's questions clearly.

'I don't know,' he wailed in exasperation. 'My father was carrying out the Generalissimo's orders. He was – he is – an exemplary officer of the Nationalist Revolutionary Army.'

'Yes. Yes, of course,' Bai-li said more to himself than to the young man sitting opposite. 'Exemplary.'

He paused. Somewhere in the distance there was the sound of a door banging, followed by footsteps clacking in the corridor.

'Tell me more about the letter, lieutenant.'

'Ching-kuo's, you mean?'

'Unless there's another that you've failed to mention.'

'No, of course not,' Yu-long muttered.

He really did wish he was lying in bed, catching up on lost sleep. It had been a very long day. Indeed, a very long week. It seemed like an age since his father had been frog-marched out of the customs hall in Zabaykalsk, under the smirking gaze of Commander Nikitin.

'What did Ching-kuo write about in his letter to his father?' Bai-li persisted gently. 'His undying affection for the Generalissimo? His assurance that he was being treated well in Moscow? The sort of things a young lad writes to his father when called upon to do so?'

'I suppose so, yes.' Yu-long still hadn't found his voice.

'The sort of things you yourself will soon be writing to your father, no doubt. Once we've ascertained where he's being held, of course.'

'Will I be allowed to write to him?'

There was a glimmer of hope in the young man's eyes.

'I don't see why not. Although, I suspect, your father's replies to you, if there are any, will be intercepted. Rather like the unfortunate Ching-kuo's. Was there anything else he mentioned in his letter? You haven't really told me very much.'

Yu-long racked his brain, trying to recall things Ching-kuo had told him when they'd been together.

'No. To be honest, I don't really remember. He talked about his studies. And the friends he'd made at university. Oh, and the fact that he thought Stalin would soon force him to work. He'd started doing physical exercises in order to become strong enough for whatever task he was given.'

'Work? What kind of work?'

'He thought he might be sent to a steel works or cement factory.'

'Did he now?'

'In the Urals.'

'The Urals? That's a long way from Moscow.' Bai-li finished polishing his glasses for the umpteenth time and put them back on his nose. His face resumed its slightly owlish look.

'And all this he wrote in his letter to the Generalissimo? It must have made for quite a long letter – a most appropriate way for a son to show his filial duty. And affection for his father, of course. I'd say ten or twelve pages, at a guess. Would that be about right?'

'Six,' Yu-long blurted out. 'He wrote six pages.'

'Six? Only six?' Bai-li nodded. 'He clearly takes after his father. Admirably to the point in all he says and writes. And you read his letter, did you, Lieutenant?'

'He asked me to.'

'Did he now?' Bai-li raised his bushy eyebrows. 'And contents of such a personal nature, too. I'm impressed, Lieutenant. You must have become very close friends.'

Once more, Yu-long was reduced to silence.

'And there was nothing else?' Bai-li continued. 'Nothing about the political situation in Moscow, for example? Or,' he added pointedly, 'Here in Nanking?'

He reached for his briefcase on the tabletop and opened it. Yu-long said nothing.

'Nothing political, then, I take it?'

'Not that I'm aware of, Doctor Colonel Su.'

A give-away that, Yu-long's use of his full title at this stage of the interrogation.

Bai-li looked at his briefcase thoughtfully.

'So that was all, was it? A few personal assurances involving paternal affection, good health, and Ching-kuo's study at university. Nothing seditious at all,' he paused.

'As I said, not –'

'That you're aware of. Yes, I heard you the first time, Lieutenant.'

He poured more tea into his cup and sipped it thoughtfully.

'So what could have induced Commander Nikitin to confiscate that letter at the border?'

'The fact that it was written by Chiang Kai-shek's son,' Yu-long said earnestly, surprised at having to explain this basic fact to the Director of Shanghai's Internal Affairs.

Bai-li nodded.

'And it had nothing to do with the fact that its contents could be construed as politically motivated?'

'What contents?' Yu-long asked, his voice just a little too loud.

Bai-li put one hand into his briefcase and brought out Yu-long's shaving soap.

'The contents recorded on microfilm at the bottom of this wooden bowl. What else?' Bai-li asked rhetorically

He was all business now as he turned the shaving bowl upside down, shook it and let the soap fall on the tabletop, the microfilm clearly visible.

'Let me see if I have understood everything correctly, Lieutenant,' he continued remorselessly. 'Chiang Ching-kuo, currently held hostage by Joseph Stalin in Moscow, sees fit to denounce one Su Bai-li – that is, myself – and to claim that the said Bai-li, who works closely with the Generalissimo, is in fact a double agent working on behalf of the Communists. Have I got that right, Lieutenant?'

Yu-long gulped.

'Now why, do you think, would the Generalissimo's son see fit to denounce one of his father's oldest friends and close adviser who happens to be Director of Internal Affairs for the Kuomintang? What's more, how did he come by such information? After all, he lives in comparative isolation in Moscow and has limited, if any, access to news from China. Other than through his friends at university, of course.'

Bai-li's normally warm dark brown eyes were now like amber glass.

'I need assistance, Lieutenant. Can you perhaps help me answer these two questions?'

Yu-long shook his head. His eyes were riveted on the shaving soap on the tabletop in front of him.

'From your silence, Lieutenant, I'm led to conclude one of two – possibly three – things. The first scenario is that Ching-kuo had his arm twisted by Stalin himself to denounce a loyal patriot of the Chinese Nationalist Party, probably with an offer of freedom should the outcome of his denunciation remove one Su Bai-li from his position. Does that make sense to you, Lieutenant?'

Yu-long nodded a little helplessly.

'It does? I'm not so sure myself. So let me describe a second scenario. Ching-kuo's denunciation had absolutely nothing to do with Stalin who is, after all, too preoccupied with more serious matters of state to worry himself personally over the Generalissimo's son. No, the idea of denouncing Su Bai-li came from Ching-kuo's Chinese Communist classmates at Sun Yat Sen University. Eager to attract attention before they return to their homeland, they concoct a story that they envisage will embarrass the Generalissimo who is, after all, now their bitter foe.'

Bai-li leaned back in his chair and toyed with Yu-long's shaving soap on the tabletop, twirling it round and round as he spoke.

'There is, of course, a third scenario, isn't there, Lieutenant?'

'There is?'

'That, for one reason or another as yet to be ascertained, you yourself, or your father, invited Ching-kuo to write a denunciation of myself. This, I admit, sounds a little implausible. Unless, of course, I do happen to be a double agent for the Communists. But it might have been a ruse devised by your father to deflect my attention away from the fact that, over a period of well over a month, he was engaged in secret communications, in Russian, with high-placed Soviet officials in Moscow. What do you say to that, Lieutenant?'

'No,' exclaimed Yu-long loudly. 'Never!'

'Perhaps you're right, Lieutenant. Perhaps such behaviour is indeed beneath the dignity of such a worthy officer as Colonel Pan,' he paused and gave the shaving soap one last twirl. 'In which case, it must have been those Chinese students who are to blame. Teng Hsiao-p'ing, and Wu Hsiu-ch'üan, you said? I must ensure that they're punished in due course.'

He stretched his arms above his head, then looked at his watch.

'Goodness me, is that the time?' he asked carelessly. 'My apologies, Lieutenant. You must be exhausted.' He put the shaving soap back in its wooden bowl, and handed it to Yu-long. The microfilm he kept for himself.

'You'll be needing this soon,' he said. 'But first, we need to work out what to do with you Lieutenant.'

'Me? But –'

'Your father has been arrested and sentenced to seven years hard labour in a Siberian gulag. It is your filial duty to do everything in your power to get him released.'

'Yes, but how?'

'By serving the Generalissimo and your country to the very best of your ability, Lieutenant. And by thinking of your father in the way that, as you now know, the Generalissimo thinks of his son. All day, every day. This will encourage those in positions of power to act on your behalf in negotiations with the Russians. Do I make myself clear?'

'Yes, Colonel Su,' Yu-long sat up straight in his chair. 'I understand.'

Bai-li wasn't yet prepared to release his stranglehold on the young man in front of him.

'There's something else, Lieutenant.'

'Yes, Colonel?'

'The Nationalist Government is in a precarious situation, as I'm sure you're aware. The country must be united. In other words, contrary to whatever the Generalissimo – or even you yourself – might think or say, the enemy is not the Communists in the south, Lieutenant, but the Japanese in the north.'

Yu-long nodded. All he wanted to do was sleep. Would Bai-li never let him go?

'From now on, therefore, I want you to work for me, Lieutenant Pan Yu-long. Since I cannot be by his side all the time, I want to know who the Generalissimo talks to, what he discusses, and what he intends to do as a result. You will be my eyes and ears in Nanking. Is that clear?'

'Yes, Colonel.'

'Understand one thing, Lieutenant. It is your patriotic duty to ensure that the Generalissimo faces China's real enemy, the Japanese. The Nationalist Revolutionary Army must unite to fight the Japanese. Not the Communists. The Communists are a spent force. That is what Chiang Kai-shek must be made to realise.'

Mention of his patriotic duty seemed to perk up Yu-long.

'Yes, Colonel Su. It will be an honour, sir.'

'Good. Because, remember, it only takes one word from me to the Soviet authorities to bring about adverse effects with regard to your father. And neither of us, I'm sure, would want that, would we?'

Bai-li stood up. The young lieutenant followed suit and stood stiffly to attention.

'No, my Colonel,' he saluted.

'And now, I think, it's time for bed, don't you? The car is waiting for us.'

Bai-li patted Yu-long affectionately on his back as they walked out of the interrogation room. The East wind had cleared away the obstacles Bai-li had feared. Now to move forward to more pressing concerns.

It was bitterly cold again. Minus twenty-six degrees, with a northerly wind that made it feel more like minus forty. The snow didn't help much either as she made her way across the packed ice of the Amur River. Manchuria was behind her, Siberia ahead.

The door to Pan Yu-tang's cell was unlocked and thrown open by a uniformed guard who ordered him out. Slightly reluctantly, he stood up from the iron bedstead with its lumpy mattress. It was good to get away from the bedbugs, maybe, but he was afraid of what was to come. A long, uncomfortable trip north to a gulag, and then who knew what ice-cold horrors awaited him. One thing he did know, though. He'd lose a lot of weight in the months to come.

The guard marched him past a row of empty cells and up a flight of steps to ground level. There two more guards were waiting for him. One of them handed him his overcoat.

'Put this on. It's cold out there.' He plumped an *ushanka* fur hat onto the Colonel's bare head. 'You're going to need this, too.'

The other handed him some folded newspaper.

'And this, too, perhaps?' He smiled. 'For your shoes.'

Both guards laughed, as Yu-tang struggled into his coat. Eager not to annoy them, he put the newspaper into his shoes.

When he was ready, the guards took hold of his arms and marched him through the prison gate towards a truck parked outside with its engine running. They opened the back and pushed him in roughly.

'Where are you taking me?' Yu-tang asked, a little needlessly.

'Home!' barked one of the guards as he slammed the *back door* shut. Then he got into the front cab beside his companion, who put the truck in gear and drove slowly away from the prison where Yu-tang had been held for the past ten days.

He doubted he'd heard the guard correctly. A man sentenced to seven years hard labour wasn't going home in a hurry. He wondered idly what he had said – the name of the gulag, perhaps? – as the truck slithered along the snow-packed road. The guard's accent certainly wasn't one he'd been used to when speaking Russian in Moscow.

Suddenly, he yearned for Stasya's comforting tones as they'd lain in bed after making love. Only a few weeks earlier. The web of his life had truly been of a mingled yarn. The stuff that dreams were made on. Nightmares, too.

He was awoken from his reverie by a sudden jolt as the driver brought the truck to a halt and switched off the engine. Outside was eerily quiet. He heard the guards getting out of the cab. Then the tailgate was flung open, and he looked out onto a vast expanse of ice and snow.

'Come on, Colonel! Out!' One of the guards pulled at his arm as he clambered down from the back of the truck. Then he gestured towards the ice and snow in front of them.

'Home!' he ordered peremptorily.

'Home?' Yu-tang looked confusedly at his minders.

'To Manchuria!'

'I don't understand.'

The guards laughed at his perplexity.

'Walk across the Amur River,' said one, as the other began to light a cigarette, turning his back to the wind. 'When you reach the other side, you'll be in Manchuria.'

'But the ice?'

'The ice is thick enough. Don't worry. Look! Someone's coming this way to meet you. It has to be safe.'

Sure enough, Yu-tang could make out a slight figure making its way across the ice through the snowstorm.

'You're really letting me go back home?' he asked doubtfully.

'Orders,' the guard smoking a cigarette nonchalantly. 'We always obey orders, don't we, Valodya?'

'Always Pyotr Nikolaevich,' Vladimir affirmed, as he borrowed his companion's cigarette to light one of his own. 'Hurry up, Colonel! It's cold out here and we'd like to get back to the warmth of our barracks before we freeze our balls off.'

Hesitantly, Pan Yu-tang turned towards the River Amur and took a few steps down its bank, convinced that he was about to be shot in the back for escaping. But he reached the ice that marked the water's edge without incident. When he turned back, he saw that both guards were facing away from him, totally unconcerned. He waved farewell anyway. Fear wasn't going to strangle his propriety.

'Colonel Pan Yu-tang?' A woman's voice addressed him in English.

He turned hurriedly.

'Yes?' he said. He realised he was being addressed by the figure he'd seen crossing towards him on the ice and snow. She was young and her looks were striking. She was wearing a reindeer coat and trousers tucked into reindeer boots. For better mobility, he assumed. Furs could be so cumbersome. On her head was an *ushanka*, with ear flaps tied around an attractively dimpled chin and covering most, but not quite all, of her flaming red hair.

'I am to accompany you across the Amur River to Harbin,' she said. 'Then you may proceed to Peking and home to Shanghai.'

Yu-tang could hardly believe his ears.

'You mean, I'm free?' he asked incredulously. 'But how? Why? I mean, who's responsible for my release?'

'I'm told it was a certain Doctor Colonel Su Bai-li, Director of Internal Affairs in Shanghai, who effected your release. I understand you know him.' The woman had started walking back across the ice towards the

Manchurian border. He hurried to catch her up.

'Yes, of course,' he said. 'But how did Colonel Su succeed in doing that?'

'I've no idea, Colonel. I'm just a messenger.'

She bent down to tie an errant lace on one of her boots. Yu-tang stopped out of politeness, but she waved him on.

'Don't stop. It's too cold. And we need to get across the river before the Soviets change their minds.'

He walked on across the thick ice, wondering why such a petite and rather beautiful young woman had been assigned to take him to his freedom.

He never found an answer to his half-formed question. Seconds later there was the sound of gunshots and he fell to the ice with two bullets in his back.

Putting her pistol back in the pocket of her reindeer coat, she walked past him without a further glance. If he wasn't already dead, he would be by the time the two guards on the riverbank had finished their cigarettes and come to retrieve the body of a prisoner who'd tried to escape. They'd had no choice but to shoot him in the back. Otherwise he might have reached the other side. The Union of the Soviet Socialist Republics didn't approve of people going over to the other side.

In the meantime, she'd find herself a man when she reached Harbin. A Russian, probably. She needed to be careful, though. The excess of men in the city's population meant that prostitution was rife. And with prostitution came all kinds of venereal and other diseases. Perhaps she should seek out a woman, for a change. There was a receptionist at the Hotel Moderne she'd heard about. Olga something or other.

PART THREE

The Pitch

Joao Serino was foreign correspondent in Shanghai for the left of centre Japanese newspaper, the Asahi Shimbun, having made himself a name by writing about political, economic and social relations between Japan, China, Manchuria and the Soviet Union. In addition to Japanese, he spoke Chinese and English more or less fluently, and could read Russian and German with the aid of a dictionary. He was also fluent in Portuguese. In other words, he wasn't your usual Japanese male.

Something else distinguished him from other Japanese. Joao had two surnames. The other one was Sereño. Born and brought up in Nagasaki, he was the last male member of a Portuguese trading family which had, over a period of two hundred and fifty years, learned to speak, read and write Japanese considerably better than the dockers and hauliers whom it employed. In a vain effort to be accepted as something other than *gaikokujin* 'outlanders', Joao's great grandfather had formally changed the family name to Serino. When written in Chinese characters Serino meant Parsley Field – not your average Satō, Suzuki or Tanaka. Joao and his mother were the only two people in the whole of Japan called Serino.

Having two names was part of Joao's family's schizophrenic existence. At home family members spoke Portuguese, ate Portuguese food (spiced with Chinese cuisine learned from relatives in Macao), slept in beds rather than on futon, and wore Western clothes. They referred to themselves proudly as *Os Sereños*.

Outside the family home's compound gates, however, they spoke Japanese, wore Japanese clothing and footwear, ate Japanese food and, when in the company of their Japanese mistresses, slept on futon laid out on tatami matting in Japanese-style houses. They were the *Serino-ya*.

Joao was, therefore, Japanese, but not Japanese. Thirty-one years old, he was still single, in part because he didn't look entirely Japanese. Although his mother was a native of Nagasaki Prefecture in the southern island of Kyushu, his father was Portuguese. He had inherited from him very dark hair that was slightly wavy, rather than straight and black like a 'true' Japanese. At just over five foot ten inches, he was also much taller than most Japanese men. His nose was straight, with a high bridge that was more European than Japanese. His eyes, although dark brown, had a Douro Valley softness lacking in most Japanese.

He was also still single by temperament. A romantic at heart, he had rejected all attempts by his mother and his editor-in-chief to introduce him to a suitable young woman with a view to arranging their marriage. He wasn't yet ready to settle down. These were uncertain times, he said in his defence. Too many men were ready to cry 'havoc' and let slip the dogs of war.

His posting to Shanghai, therefore, came at an opportune moment. It enabled him to get away both from well-intentioned marriage brokers and from the stifling claustrophobia of Japanese society.

So he started calling himself Sereño when in the company of foreigners in Shanghai. Serino he reserved for interaction with fellow Japanese. There were two reasons for this. First, the Japanese were extremely unpopular among Chinese – a feeling with which Joao greatly sympathised. Japanese textile mill owners in Shanghai treated their Chinese workers with contempt; Japanese navy ratings and soldiers treated all Chinese as if they were dirt. Severe beatings were often the order of the day; bayonet killings of the night.

Second, Joao was very conscious of the fact that he was a Eurasian inhabiting a cosmopolitan city full of Europeans, Asians, and other Eurasians like himself. Unlike in Japan, where he was obliged to be 'Japanese' at all times, in Shanghai Joao could enjoy being his half-Portuguese self.

For the first time in his life, he felt as if he fitted in. He wasn't too tall. His eyes weren't too round, his nose too high, or his hair too light and wavy for a Japanese. He was a well-built Eurasian, handsome, with finely chiselled features, thick black hair parted on the left, and strong dark eyebrows. Unlike in Japan, where his non-Japanese features could attract adverse attention, in Shanghai he felt at home.

And what wasn't there to like about his new home? Streets choc-a-bloc with charabancs and trams, rickshas and sedan chairs, pushcarts and coolies balancing long bamboo poles on their shoulders, at either end a basket filled with squawking ducks or black-glazed wine jars; the cries of street vendors and fortune tellers, of professional story-tellers and itinerant barbers; the wail of a blind musician's two-stringed *erhu* and the clacking of mah-jong tiles.

Alternately known as the Paris of the East or the Whore of the Orient, Shanghai was a city where East met West, but neither prevailed. A city whose inhabitants were of every kind, colour, and ideological persuasion. A city where corpulent, well-oiled bankers with pasty complexions and clammy hands consorted with stunning Eurasian women in their cheongsam, with side-slits up to their come-hither thighs; where down-at-heel gamblers tried their luck with flat-chested and over-rouged sing-song girls, who were too anaemic and weary of life to want their attentions; where vulgar, loud-mouthed colonialists gathered for tiffin in hotel ballrooms to see how vulgarity was dressed; where upstart millionaires ordered servants around like grand marshals, while blowing their noses on linen napkins and sipping egg-drop soup with their knives; and where the hollow cheek of a Chinese coolie was a wealthy taipan's thickset jowl.

Shanghai was a vibrant, elegant, cosmopolitan city reeking of opium, hardship, starvation and greed; a city populated by gangsters and retired brigands, by conmen and cheats; a city where even the beggars were dishonest. And yet it was the safest city in China to live.

Autumn had come and Joao was proceeding at a leisurely pace along the Bund. At the end of the wide thoroughfare, he took a detour through the Public Gardens, before making his way past the bandstand to Garden Bridge. He crossed Soochow Creek and turned into North Soochow Road. It felt good to walk the streets of the city again without breaking into an uncomfortable sweat.

He went past the Shanghai General Hospital and from there over the border of the International Settlement into Chinese Shanghai, with its Japanese-owned silk filatures, notorious for their child labour, abysmal wages, appalling safety measures, and – unsurprisingly – plenty of trade union activity. Communists, he knew, had been heavily involved in three Shanghai uprisings between October 1926 and March 1927. Their leader, Chou En-lai, had also been captured, or so it was rumoured. Yet he had managed to escape. How, nobody knew. Unusually, there hadn't been a hint of gossip in the city's streets and less salubrious alleys.

The Zeitgeist Bookstore was at Number 130, one of a row of small red-brick houses on the corner of North Soochow Road opposite the General Post Office. A couple of men lazed around on the other side of the street, taking note of who went in and out of the store. Peddling information – to the Shanghai Municipal Police, the Gendarmerie, or Tu Yue-sheng – provided gainful employment for those prepared to idle away their days on street corners, and nights with pimps and drunks in the bars along Blood Alley, or with the Natashas on the rue de la Soeur Allegré. The street of the happy sisters.

The Zeitgeist was small – maybe twelve by eighteen feet in size: not much bigger, and poorly lit. But its shelves were well stocked. There were books in Russian, German and English – a lot of the titles written by Russian and other Bolsheviks, but also classical and modern literature, from Dostoyevsky to Ilya Ehrenburg and Olga Forsh.

As he made his way slowly between two bookcases, stopping from time to time to examine a title more closely and even, once, to remove a book and leaf through it, he heard a man's voice behind him.

'Hello. I've seen you here before, haven't I?'

'It's possible,' Joao replied politely. 'This isn't the first time I've come here.'

'Looking for anything in particular?'

His interlocutor was of more or less the same age as Joao, about thirty years old. He had large ears, a prominent nose, thin-lipped smile, and a receding hairline that emphasised his high forehead. To Joao, who had a good ear for languages, his accent placed him as a New Zealander.

'I was hoping to find a copy of Alexandra Kollontai's *A Great Love*. Do you know it?'

'I can't say I do.'

'It depicts Inessa Armand's love affair with "a revolutionary leader," who is none other than Lenin himself.'

'I hadn't realised our Great Leader was subject to such passions of the flesh,' the New Zealander said, slightly disapprovingly.

'Both Kollontai and Armand had interesting ideas about sex, marriage, and women's rights.'

'Really? How interesting, Mr –'

'Sereño. Joao Sereño.'

'Rewi,' the New Zealander extended his hand. 'Rewi Alley. Pleased to meet you.'

Joao took his hand in a firm grasp.

'And I you,' he said with his most charming smile.

'I can't help you with the Kollontai book, I'm afraid. But ask Isa over there. She'll know.'

'Isa?'

'Irene Weidemeyer. She runs the Zeitgeist.'

'Thank you. Then I will.' Joao politely took his leave and, after perusing a few more shelves, headed for the till by the door, where two women – clearly sisters – were talking to each other in low voices.

'Can I help you?' One of them asked.

'Are you Irene Weidemeyer?'

'No, this is Isa,' she smiled, indicating the woman at her side. 'I'm her sister Gerda. How may we be of assistance?'

Gerda was of medium height, her figure slight. She had hazel green eyes, a well-formed straight nose, and full Cupid-bow lips that revealed a perfect line of ivory white teeth when she smiled. The most striking aspect of her appearance, though, was her deep auburn red hair that fell in natural waves to her shoulders. She smelled nice and fresh, too, Joao noticed. Of lily-of-the-valley. Love at first whiff?

'I'm looking for a book by Alexandra Kollontai. *A Great Love*. Do you happen to have it?'

'*A Great Love?*' Irene frowned slightly, as she ran through her store's inventory in her mind. She looked very like her younger sister – a little lither, perhaps, but with the same slight figure, together with the same hazel green eyes, straight nose, and Cupid's bow lips. Her hair was the same auburn red, too, though cut shorter in a bob.

'No, I'm afraid we don't,' she concluded, before turning to her sister and nudging her playfully. 'It sounds like something you should be reading, Gerda.'

Gerda blushed very slightly, the colour infusing her cheeks and enhancing her beauty. The top two buttons of her blouse, Joao noticed, were undone. There was just a hint of cleavage in the opening that revealed her lightly freckled skin.

'Never mind,' he said. When he spoke, his voice was quiet, controlled and sure of itself. 'I'll just take this, then.'

He put a copy of Bukarin's *ABC of Communism* on the tabletop between them.

Gerda looked at the title on the spine and turned to her sister.

'Be careful, Isa dear. There's a communist in your store.'

'Well, I wouldn't say "communist,"' Joao said hurriedly, clearly unaware of the effect his handsome features were having on the two women. 'I mean, not in any active way.'

'But a sympathiser, perhaps?' Irene raised her eyebrows in enquiry.

'A sympathiser?' He pondered her question for a moment. 'Yes, I suppose I am,' he admitted, 'Although I hadn't really thought of it that way.'

'How do you think of it, then?'

'Well, I'm interested in reading writers who have something important to say. What I find important, that is. And that means my reading all sorts of books by all sorts of writers. Including communist ones,' he finished with a shy smile.

'Like Nikolai Bukharin,' Gerda said playfully.

'I thought I'd brush up my Russian.'

'Besides brushing up on your Russian, what else do you do with your life, Mr –?' Irene paused.

'Sereño. Joao Sereño. I'm a journalist,' he said, removing a small leather wallet from his inside jacket pocket, taking out a card and handing it to Irene. 'For the Asahi Newspaper.'

'The Asahi? That's Japanese, isn't it?'

'That's right. You'll see that the name on the other side of my card – Serino – is in fact Japanese.'

Irene looked at Joao more closely. There was a hint of confusion on her face.

'But you said your name was Sereño?'

'That's right.'

'So you're not Japanese,' she paused. 'Or are you?'

'Half of me is, I'm afraid.'

'Why "afraid"?'

Joao pursed his lips a little.

'Because, to be honest, I'm not that keen on the ultra-nationalists currently running the government in Japan.'

'Which half of you is Japanese, then?' asked Gerda, still playful. 'And what's the other half?'

'Portuguese,' Joao said proudly. 'As for which half…' He shrugged his well-built shoulders. 'Maybe I should leave that to your imagination.'

'Be careful, Mr Sereño.' Now it was Irene's turn to be flirtatious. 'My sister's imagination has few limits when it comes to men.'

Joao decided it was time for him to move on.

'How much is the book?' he asked, pointing to the volume that was still lying on the table between the three of them.

'Don't worry about it,' Gerda said, waving his proffered note away. 'Think of it as a present.'

'But –'

'I know. There's always a "but" when it comes to favours received in China, isn't there? It's probably the same in Japan.'

'So, what favour are you going to ask in return?' he asked with a smile.

'Come to one of our meetings.'

'Meetings? What meetings?'

'The ones we hold from time to time to discuss how to make the world a better place.'

'Communist meetings, then?'

'Making the world a better place isn't a prerogative exclusive to communists, you know,' Irene retorted. 'But yes. Those who come to the meetings tend to be communist sympathisers. Of one sort or another.'

'Like you, Mr Sereño,' Gerda smiled in such a manner that he flushed slightly.

'And when is your next meeting?'

'On Friday,' Irene answered, pushing a mimeographed sheet of paper into his hands. 'At 6pm. Viktoria Sotov will be speaking about Communism and the family. Do please join us. It's all very informal.'

'Yes, Mr Sereño, do come. Please.' Was that entreaty in Gerda's voice? 'We need new intellectual input. Otherwise, you get the same old people churning out the same old ideas. I have a feeling you'll inject a fresh viewpoint into the discussion.'

'Well, I'm not sure about that, but –'

Gerda wasn't going to be put off by Joao's modesty.

'And then we'll find out which half of you is, or isn't, Japanese, won't we?'

Her infectious laugh sounded unexpectedly inviting, as he found himself enveloped in the warmth of her hazel green eyes. *A sereña.*

The Friday meeting had started by the time Joao got to the Zeitgeist. He'd been delayed by an urgent request from Mori, his editor in Tokyo, to find out what he could about the Shanghai branch of the Takahashi Bank. It seemed there was a financial crisis looming in Japan – a long-term result of the great Kanto earthquake in 1923 – and Mori wanted to know whether that crisis was simply local to Japan, or extended into its colonies and elsewhere.

About a dozen men and women were sitting on chairs set in more or less a circle around the edge of the central space in the bookstore. They were listening to a woman who was clearly Russian holding forth about the family in Soviet Russia. Viktoria Sotov, he assumed.

Mouthing his apologies to Irene and Gerda, who were sitting one each side of the speaker, and nodding at Rewi Alley, Joao sat himself down in the last remaining chair.

'The family is always in a process of change,' Viktoria Sotov continued from where she'd left off when he'd opened the shop door. 'The customs and moral principles of family life change as the general conditions of life change. And in Soviet Russia there have been radical changes – the liberalisation of divorce and abortion laws, the decriminalization of homosexuality, cohabitation of unmarried couples permitted. These have ushered in a host of reforms that have made women more equal with men.'

'But, as I understand it, Comrade Sotov,' interrupted an energetic young man, hardly out of his twenties, 'They've also led to an epidemic of divorces, as well as to countless children being born out of wedlock.'

The young man's accent betrayed him as, perhaps, Polish, although he'd been pointed out to Joao in the Foreign Correspondents' Club as an Austrian journalist called Hans Shippe. And comrade Sotov, he realised belatedly, was the wife of Vladimir Sotov, Head of the Russian News Agency, TASS, in Shanghai.

'It's more important, I think, to examine the underlying causes of such phenomena,' she continued, side-stepping Shippe's point. Viktoria clearly had the makings of a politician.

'It is the universal spread of female labour that has contributed most to the radical change in family life. The family breaks down as more and more women go out to work. The woman who is wife, mother and worker has to expend every ounce of her energy to fulfil these roles. And yet she has to work the same hours as her husband in some factory, printing-house or commercial establishment. And then on top of that, she has to find the time to attend to her household and look after her children. Woman staggers beneath the weight of this triple load.'

She looked round at her audience which, apart from the Weidemeyer sisters and a diminutive Chinese woman with porcelain skin listening attentively behind them, consisted entirely of men. Viktoria Sotov continued unabashed.

'Life has never been easy for woman, but never has her lot been harder and more desperate than that of the millions of working women under the capitalist yoke in this heyday of factory production. Capitalism has placed a crushing burden on woman's shoulders. It has made her a wage-worker without reducing her cares as housekeeper or mother.'

'I think we can all accept your argument, Viktoria.' This time it was Rewi who spoke, 'But isn't the position of women, and their grievances, related more to class than to gender?'

'That's a very male-oriented way of looking at things, Rewi,' Irene spoke up in support of the evening's speaker on her left.

Another voice spoke up, this time South African.

'But to discuss matters as if they are of primary concern to women surely promotes separatism within both the proletariat and the party. And it's the bond between party and the people that's paramount. I'm sure Madame Sun would agree.'

'I do, Frank,' the diminutive Chinese woman answered in a voice so low Joao had to strain his ears to hear her. 'But "the people," as you refer to them, do not consist wholly, or even predominantly, of men. That's something we should never forget.'

'Although it tends to be, doesn't it, by Bolshevik leaders? I mean, look at the way Lenin himself treated Inessa Armand.'

Everyone turned at the sound of Joao's voice to examine the newcomer.

'I'm sorry,' he said apologetically, 'Have I spoken out of turn? I'm afraid I'm not conversant with your meeting's procedures. My name's Joao Sereño. I, too, am a journalist,' he added with a nod at Hans Shippe.

'Welcome to the club!' Hans said. 'It's always good to get a new perspective.'

'Please don't worry about procedures, Mr Sereño. There aren't any. At least, not to worry about,' Rewi reassured him in a friendly voice.

'I agree with Mr Sereño, though,' Irene said firmly. 'Procedures or no procedures. The Soviet leadership is dominated by men. And that's not right. Look at Viktoria here,' she laid a hand gently on the arm of the woman beside her. 'She's an experienced journalist and editor in her own right, with many years devoted to working for different newspaper organizations in the Soviet Union. And yet it is her husband who's appointed Head of TASS in Shanghai. I hope you don't mind my saying so, Viktoria, but that's not right.'

There was a pause as one or two heads nodded sympathetically.

'I think, too often, women are perceived to be mere appendages of men.'

'What do you mean by that remark, Mr Sereño?' The South African called Frank asked.

'Well, for example, and I hope you will excuse my saying so, it strikes me that in the eyes of many of her admirers the reputation of Madame Sun here stems not from her being a revolutionary in her own right, which she surely is, but as the widow of Dr Sun Yat-sen.'

Joao stopped in confusion, and bowed his head apologetically.

'I'm sorry,' he mumbled and fiddled with the leaflet he was holding in his hand.

'Please don't be sorry, Mr Sereño,' Ch'ing-ling came to his rescue. 'I think my Chinese colleagues here would agree with you. And if they don't,' she added in her gentle voice as she looked at Bai-li, 'They should.'

There was a pause. When Joao dared to look up, he saw Ch'ing-ling and Gerda both smiling at him encouragingly.

'I think there's a danger here, if you don't mind my saying so,' a mild English voice intervened, 'Of our getting side-tracked. Comrade Sotov was discussing changes in the family in Soviet Russia – a topic that I myself find extremely interesting. I wonder if she might be allowed to continue.'

'Thank you, Henry Baring,' Viktoria smiled briefly.

'Women's work,' she continued, as though she had never been interrupted, 'Is becoming less useful to the community as a whole. This is because the machine has superseded the wife. Few working women these days can be bothered to make candles, spin wool, weave cloth, or knit their own stockings when time is money. Why pickle cucumbers or make other preserves when such products can be bought cheaply in stores down the street?' She paused. 'What I'm saying is, the family no longer produces. It only consumes.'

'So what can communism do for contemporary women?' Baring asked politely.

'I think that, instead of the working woman having to struggle with spending the last free hours of her day in the kitchen preparing supper, communist society should organise public restaurants and communal kitchens. Instead of her being obliged to clean her own home, other men and women should be employed to do the job for her every morning while she's out at work.'

Viktoria paused for breath before continuing.

'Not only this, but the workers' state should gradually take upon itself the task of looking after working women's children. In other words, the state should replace the family. And in my opinion, it will,' she finished.

'So, what you're saying is that just as housework will wither away, so will the obligations of parents to their children?'

'Certainly. It will be a gradual transition at first, but finally society will assume full responsibility for obligations that until now have been taken on by the family.'

Comrade Sotov sat back in her chair and looked round the room at her audience. She had said all she wanted to say.

'Well, that was quite fascinating, Viktoria,' Rewi quickly took over. 'Thank you so much for taking the time to come and talk to us this evening. We greatly appreciate your insights.'

Several of those present took this as a hint to clap politely. Some stood up, others remained seated, chatting to one another. Joao wondered whether he should leave.

'You're not going yet, surely?' Gerda's lily-of-the-valley scent reached him before her words.

'Well, I made a bit of a fool of myself. I'm sorry,' he said apologetically. 'I shouldn't have said anything, given that I'd never attended any of your meetings before. I'm afraid I may have offended Soong Ch'ing-ling. And that wasn't my intention.'

'But you didn't, Mr Sereño,' a gentle voice said beside him. It was Madame Sun herself. 'It's rare to hear a man as perceptive as yourself when it comes to women's issues.'

Joao bowed.

'Thank you,' he said.

'Gerda here tells me you're working for a Japanese newspaper – the Asahi, isn't it?'

'That's correct.'

'My husband always spoke very highly of your newspaper, Mr Sereño. Perhaps you would like to visit me at home one day soon? There are many things I'd like to discuss with you that might, I think, interest your readers.'

Joao could hardly believe his luck. When did the widow of Sun Yat-sen ever give an exclusive interview? Mori would fall over backwards with surprise. He'd made a scoop.

'Thank you, Madame Sun. I would be delighted. And honoured.'

'Good,' Ch'ing-ling-gave him one of her delicate smiles. 'But, given your earlier intervention, why don't we dispose of this "Madame Sun" business. Please call me Ch'ing-ling. After all, you're going to interview me.'

'And I'm Joao. Thank you.'

'Why don't you get in touch with Gerda here when you have the time to visit me, Joao? She will arrange everything. Won't you, Gerda?'

'But of course.'

'Good. But now, I'm afraid, I must be going. It was a pleasure meeting you, Joao.'

She held out her hand for Joao to take in his.

'Goodbye, Ch'ing-ling. The pleasure, I assure you, has been entirely mine.'

And with a wave to a Chinese man wearing a loose blue cotton jacket and trousers, with bushy eyebrows and heavy tortoiseshell glasses on his nose, Ch'ing-ling quietly left the gathering.

'I'm sorry, Gerda. I don't know what came over me this evening. Are you sure I didn't offend Chi'ing-ling?'

'Don't be silly, Joao. This isn't one of your International Settlement committees. We don't have a pecking order determining who can say what and when,' she smiled her Cupid's bow smile, revealing two front teeth that he found irresistibly attractive. 'And anyway,' she added, 'I thought your comments were entirely to the point. It's time men stopped imagining they're the centre of the universe.'

'But they are.'

'Unfortunately, yes. You're right about that, Joao.'

They stood facing each other, a lot of words between them unspoken other than in their eyes.

'Well,' Joao said eventually, 'I should go. My editor –'

'Your editor has suddenly ordered you to write an article and submit it before midnight,' Gerda laughed.

'How did you know?'

'I didn't,' she smiled. 'But I guessed. You men aren't *that* difficult to see through, you know.'

'Ah!' He smiled back. 'So, can you tell me what my next question is going to be?'

'Will I join you for dinner one evening soon,' she said, and found herself laughing at the surprise on his face.

'You see? What did I tell you?'

Joao laughed at himself.

'And, by the way,' Gerda continued, 'Before you ask, the answer is yes.'

It wasn't long before most of those gathered for Viktoria Sotov's talk had left the Zeitgeist and made off into the night.

'Well?'

'Well what?'

'What did you think of him?' Bai-li asked.

'I liked him. Rather a lot actually, if you really want to know.'

'I don't,' he answered shortly. 'I asked you, Gerda, what you thought of him. Not whether you liked him. There's a difference, you know.'

The two of them were conversing quietly in a corner of the room, while Isa was stacking chairs and putting them away in a back room.

'I think he's smart and I think he's serious. You could tell that by his interventions and by his reading habits. I also think he's not afraid to speak out when he believes it right and proper to do so. At the same time, though, he's modest – as, I suppose, you'd expect from someone brought up to be Japanese. And he also has a playful streak that – dare I say it? – I liked.'

Bai-li was observing her carefully through his round tortoiseshell glasses.

'And?' he prompted.

'I wasn't so sure about his apparent penchant for flannel suits. Maybe it's just the season. But I suppose the burning question is: is he European? Or is he Japanese? He seems a bit of a chameleon. The kind of man who can be Portuguese in one social setting, like this evening's, and Japanese in another.'

Bai-li nodded.

'Go on.'

'That made him difficult to read. It was hard to work out what was going on behind that handsome appearance of his.'

'Always assuming something was going on, of course.'

'Clearly, it is, Bai-li. You could see that for yourself,' she added playfully.

'Is he the kind of man you could trust, do you think?'

'I've no idea. After all, I've hardly talked to him for more than ten minutes all told. But yes,' she thought back on her conversations, 'I think he probably is. Trustworthy, that is.'

'Thank you, Gerda. You've been most helpful,' Bai-li did his best to charm the petite red-head with his dimpled smile.

'With regard to your liking him,' he continued. 'Might that extend to spending more time with him? I need information, you see.'

'I understand, Bai-li. But you can relax. We've already agreed to meet in a more agreeable atmosphere, where the future of the Soviet family isn't likely to be a topic of our conversation.'

'I'm glad. Thank you, Gerda. I appreciate your help. As always. I realise I ask a lot of you.'

And without further ado, he waved farewell to Isa, slipped his hands into the sleeves of his loose cotton jacket, and went out of the bookstore, leaving behind one cultural zeitgeist for another.

They arranged to meet at the Foreign Correspondents' Club on Broadway, in a building that also housed something to do with the US Army and, way up on the seventeenth floor, a gambling club run by Russian gangsters. Like one of its customers who'd lost his fortune and jumped off the roof in despair the night before, the temperature had plummeted. It was a bitterly cold afternoon in November.

Gerda arrived in a swirl of Siberian sable that hid both her body and her tangled red hair. She took off her coat and *ushanka*, and assigned them to the care of a Chinese cloakroom attendant by the door. As she crossed the lounge to where Joao was already waiting, her look suggested she would tangle his eyes, too, once she got the opportunity.

He had to admit, though, she was the kind of woman who made him feel warm inside. A dangerous sign.

Outside, it began to rain – or was it sleet? Surreal grey-white umbrellas falling from the wintry sky. Having spent an uncomfortable morning interviewing Shanghai's premier gangster, Tu Yue-sheng, Joao was just happy they weren't opium-stained long fingernails.

'I've just been to a wonderful performance at the Lyceum Theatre,' Gerda announced, a little breathlessly, as she sat down in a chair beside him. She was wearing a green Cashmere sweater over a pale pink blouse and wide-leg pants. Her earrings were of amethyst, her smile a ruby red.

'You have?' He enquired politely.

'By a young girl called Peggy Hookham,' she added.

'Really?'

'Yes. She performed the most elegant movements. Her *fouetté* and *grand jeté* were quite magnificent. And only eight years old,' Gerda sighed. 'She has the makings of a star you know.'

He didn't. Ballet wasn't his strong point when it came to polite conversation. But he knew he should say something appropriate. It was, after all, their first date.

'If so,' he suggested, 'She should probably change her name.'

'Why's that?'

'Because neither Peggy nor Hookham sounds to me particularly stellar.'

'Maybe you're right, Joao. Any suggestions?'

'If she's a Peggy, she's probably a Margaret. In which case she should make it sound Russian, perhaps. Like Margarita?'

'Sounds like a drink to me,' Gerda snorted.

'Or French, of course,' Joao continued determinedly. 'How about Marguerite? Or Margot?'

'That sounds a bit better. And Hookham?'

'I've no idea. Something connected with seduction?'

Gerda looked at him quizzically.

'Sorry,' he said. 'That was one of my silly attempts at a joke. How about some tea?'

A waiter appeared as if by magic – unless it was thanks to one of Gerda's own seductive looks – and Joao ordered scones, butter, jam and a pot of Lapsang Souchong tea.

'I wanted to be a ballet dancer, you know. When I was younger.'

'But?'

'But I got injured and had to stop for a few weeks. I never went back to rehearsals. I don't know why. Afraid of what else might happen to my body, perhaps.'

'Your body, if you'll excuse my saying so, looks well attuned to dance. Or one of the martial arts, perhaps. It has the right proportions.'

'So tell me, Mr Sereño – or is it Serino?' She decided quickly to change the subject. 'Which half of you am I talking to this afternoon?'

'Which half would you like?'

'Can we start with the Japanese half? I'm not sure I entirely trust Mr Sereño's motives. Mediterranean men are known for their passions.'

'But Portugal isn't on the Mediterranean, Gerda. It faces the Atlantic.'

'All the same, I suspect passion.'

'If you say so,' Joao shrugged. 'What would you like to know?'

'Everything about you, Joao,' she said, stretching a gloved hand across the table and placing it on his. 'Your parents. Where you were born and brought up. Why you're a journalist. What makes you interested in China. How long ago you came to Shanghai. All that sort of thing.'

'And then it will be your turn?'

'Then it'll be my turn. Promise.'

She took her hand back and placed it in her lap, as she sat back in her chair and made herself more comfortable.

'All right, then,' he began, 'I was born in Nagasaki. Into a long-established Portuguese trading family. My father was Portuguese, but my mother's Japanese. They decided to call me Joao because, in Japanese, the three Chinese characters making up my name mean "Helping Asia Man." That may explain why I became interested in China and came to Shanghai. I wouldn't know.'

'A half Japanese man who helps Asians? I like that.'

'The first few years of my life I felt a bit schizophrenic, though.'

'Schizophrenic?' Gerda echoed. 'How so?'

'We seemed to lead two totally different lives. There was our Portuguese life in the seclusion of our home in the hills above Deshima. That's the name of the port foreigners were confined to back during Japan's feudal period when all socialisation with the Japanese was prohibited. And then there was our Japanese life whenever we ventured out into the streets of the city.'

'And they were different?'

'Very,' Joao said firmly. 'More so than you could ever imagine.'

The waiter arrived bearing a tray with silver teapot, Limoges cobalt and gold gilt cups and saucers, and matching plates with scones and jam. He set everything down on the table and left.

'More than that of Westerners living here in the International Settlement?' Gerda continued where Joao had left off. 'It strikes me as the same kind of difference.'

'You may be right. But my impression is that the Chinese – at least, the Chinese in Shanghai – are far more open to foreigners and their ideas than the Japanese were when I was young.'

'In what way?'

'In what way?' Joao paused. 'The Japanese, I think, are more closed because history has made them so. Two hundred and fifty years of isolation from the outside world made them pretty wary of foreigners. They may have borrowed ideas from France to reform the country's education system, or from Prussia to modernise its army, but fundamentally they're like horses.'

'Horses?' Gerda repeated in surprise.

'They wear blinkers,' Joao grinned.

'Don't we all, Joao?'

'Yes, but not to the same extent. Japanese seem always to see things through the prism of something they call "Japan." I mean, we've laughed about my being half and half, right?'

Gerda nodded as she sipped her tea.

'When I was a boy, like all other children my age, I was sent to the local primary school in Nagasaki. The very first day, the other kids in my class started calling me "gaijin," or "foreigner." Even though I'd been born and brought up in Japan, and spoke Japanese fluently. It didn't matter that my mother was – is – Japanese. My father was a foreigner. Ergo so was I.'

'In other words, when you're in Japan you're not half and half at all?'

'I wasn't then, certainly. Not at school. Things are a bit better now, though.'

'How so?'

'I've learned to adapt, I think. But still, I have to face what the Japanese like to call "*yosomono ishiki*," an acute awareness of someone who isn't one of them. So when in Japan, I suppress my foreign-ness. I do my best to look Japanese, sound Japanese, think like a Japanese. In that way, I become Japanese.'

'And when you're abroad?'

'When I'm in Shanghai, I do my best to look, sound, and think like a Portuguese. Or a European, at least. I have to in my job, given the way the Japanese are thought of here.'

'Especially by the Chinese.'

'And understandably so. There are times when I'm ashamed of that half of me.'

'Don't be, Joao.' Gerda's voice was soft and sympathetic, as if she really cared for the man beside her.

'The thing is, when you're born a "half-caste," as the Brits would probably call me, you're always a "gaijin," always an outsider, wherever you go. For some people, that can be depressing, but not for me. Because I'm an outsider, I can observe everything going on around me. I think that's what makes me a good journalist.'

'Perhaps even a spy,' Gerda laughed, as she finished her tea.

'Perhaps,' Joao joined in her gaiety. 'After all, there's not that much difference between the two.'

'There isn't? Why's that?'

'Both are in the business of obtaining information, right?'

Gerda nodded encouragingly.

'Often, they have to do it without others noticing, don't they? They both have to protect their sources, too, and answer to a higher authority – in my case, an editor back in Tokyo.'

'But a journalist doesn't work for his country, in the way a spy does,' she countered.

'I'm not so sure about that.'

'Why not?'

'Because a newspaper has its readership, and journalists have to satisfy those readers. As a result, they end up writing articles that their audience is interested in reading. In that way, they appeal to a kind of national consciousness.'

'I hadn't thought of it like that,' Gerda nodded her head thoughtfully.

'I know it's a bit different from what a spy does, but it strikes me there's a basic similarity in their overall work and objectives. Both journalists and spies ask questions. They elicit responses. Then they analyse and act.'

'But journalists don't go around killing people, the way spies do.'

'That's true,' Joao admitted, not noticing the slight hint of poignancy in her voice. 'At least, not directly.'

'What do you mean?'

'Well, I sometimes wonder,' he continued, 'What the effect of our articles is on our readers. I mean, we never really know, do we? We write. We publish. The newspaper sells a greater or lesser number of copies every day. Our editor is, or is not, happy. And yet we very rarely hear directly from our readers what they actually think about a particular article. As a result, I sometimes feel as if I'm writing in a vacuum.'

He paused. Gerda watched him carefully.

'I mean, suppose for the sake of argument, I write an exposé giving full details of the love life of a well-known politician or the shady deals of some business magnate. I do so because, as we like to reassure ourselves in the trade, it's in the public interest. But how does what I write affect those people personally? What if the revelation of his love affair breaks up the politician's family, and his wife kills him in revenge? What if publication of the businessman's embezzlement drives him to suicide? Whether spy or journalist, we should never forget that whatever we do, or don't do, has consequences.'

'Even sitting here in the FCC having tea together?'

'Even sitting here in the FCC having tea together,' Joao concurred. 'I mean, by happening to be in this place, on this day, at this time, we might witness that couple in the far corner being shot by one of Tu Yue-sheng's mobsters. Or you might avoid being present when an anti-Communist throws a grenade through the window of the Zeitgeist Bookstore and blows the whole place up.'

'Joao! Stop it!'

'But you see what I mean?'

'You've made your point,' she said testily. Then softened. 'Since you've clearly thought about it so much, does that mean you're a spy yourself, then?'

'Me? A spy?' Joao seemed genuinely amused. 'What on earth makes you think that? I'm just a boring newspaperman.'

'But only half of you is, right?' She was back in playful mode.

'Right. But which half, Gerda? The one you can see? Or the one that's hidden?'

'If you were a spy, it'd have to be the one that's hidden. The one you don't tell me about.'

'Why?' Joao asked rhetorically. He was enjoying this game. 'Surely a spy wouldn't be so obvious? Why not the other way round? Why not create a mysterious character who seems to be deeply involved in espionage of some kind, when it is the everyday person they see and think of as Gerda Weidemeyer who is in fact the spy?'

'Or Joao Sereño.'

'Or even Serino Joao,' he laughed.

'Hiding in plain sight, you mean?'

'Precisely. Isn't that what spies do?'

'And journalists?'

'Maybe journalists, too. Maybe even a woman selling communist literature on North Soochow Road,' Joao smiled. Gerda was a most exquisite woman and, he'd warrant, fun of game.

The following afternoon, Gerda was invited to more tea – this time by Soong Ch'ing-ling – to be taken in Sun Yat-sen's old home, a peaceful haven set back from the rue Molière in the French Concession.

Bai-li had already arrived when Ch'ing-ling received her German guest in the austere living room on the ground floor of the two-storied red-brick house where she spent her days.

'You know each other, I believe,' Ch'ing-ling smiled.

'I'm not sure anyone can ever know Bai-li,' Gerda replied, sitting herself down on one of the hard-backed chairs set round a tea table. 'But yes, we're acquainted with each other.'

Bai-li adjusted the glasses on his nose.

'I'd have hoped by now, Gerda, that we were at least friends.'

'We are,' Gerda laughed. 'But that doesn't mean I know you, Bai-li.'

'She has a point, Gē-ge,' Ch'ing-ling joined in. 'Look how long we've known each other. I still don't know anything about your private life, other than that you went to school with my future brother-in-law, whom you now mysteriously "advise." You're a puzzle, Su Bai-li.'

'Am I really?' Bai-li blinked a little uncomfortably behind his spectacles. He wasn't used to having his leg pulled by two attractive and intelligent women. 'I hadn't thought of it like that.'

'Anyway,' Ch'ing-ling assumed a more serious tone. 'You asked me to invite Gerda to tea for a reason, I assume?'

'I did indeed,' Bai-li took off his glasses and blinked in the dim afternoon sunlight filtered through the blinds. Polishing time. 'I wanted you to hear what Gerda's found out about Joao Sereño, or Serino as he's known in Japan.'

'Me? Why me?'

'Because, Madame Sun, I trust your judgement in these matters.'

He turned towards Gerda.

'Well?' He asked – not for the first time, she noted.

'Well what?' She responded, also not for the first time.

'You spent a long afternoon with Mr Sereño in the Foreign Correspondents' Club, I understand.'

'You're well informed.'

'It's my business to be so, Ms Weidemeyer,' Bai-li was all formality. 'Did you learn anything new?'

'Anything new that could help you, you mean?'

She waited, but he said nothing.

'Of course I did, Su Bai-li. Do you take me for an incompetent?'

Bai-li looked up sharply.

'Have some more tea, Gerda,' Ch'ing-ling came to her old friend's rescue. 'I'm sure Bai-li thought nothing of the sort.'

'I'm sorry,' he said apologetically, 'I suppose I'm a bit on edge these days. There are things happening that are beyond my control.'

'Like a Japanese journalist who may be more Portuguese than you'd imagined?' Gerda's voice indicated that she had indeed forgiven him. If there was anything to forgive in the first place.

'That among other things, yes.'

'Let me put your mind at rest, then, Bai-li,' Gerda sipped her tea before putting her cup back on the table and leaning against the hard wooden back of her ebony chair. She was all business. A professional.

'To all external appearances, Joao Sereño – or should I say Serino? – may seem to be Japanese. Apart from his English flannel clothes, of course, and very slightly wavy, very dark hair that isn't quite an Asian black. But his mannerisms are Japanese. And I've heard him talking to a Japanese colleague. As you'd expect from someone born and brought up in Japan, both his use of language and gestures make him one hundred per cent Japanese.'

'But?' Bai-li always could tell when a contrary element was about to be aired.

'But somehow it strikes me that he isn't.'

'What makes you say that, Gerda dear?' Ch'ing-ling asked gently.

Gerda turned towards her hostess.

'Two things. One of them he told me himself. The other I noticed while he was talking.'

'What was it he told you that makes you think he isn't entirely Japanese?' Bai-li was sitting very still, his glasses left untended on his lap.

'The way he talked about his childhood, for a start,' she said, turning back to Bai-li.

'How *did* he talk about his childhood?'

'As someone who was excluded from being Japanese, however much he wanted to be a part of everything. He called it *yosomono ishiki*. I believe that was the term he used.'

'Meaning?'

'Meaning he felt extremely conscious about being an outsider. He wasn't a "proper" Japanese because his father was Portuguese. I think, deep down, he's resentful of that.'

'What makes you say that?' It was Ch'ing-ling turn to ask.

'Well, I noticed at one stage, early on in our conversation, that he kept on referring to the Japanese as "they," and not "we." It was as if he recognised that he wasn't properly Japanese, even though I'd asked him to talk to me as his Japanese self, and not as a Portuguese.'

There was a silence in the room. Bai-li looked towards Ch'ing-ling who was gazing at Gerda, who was examining the only man in the room.

It was Gerda who broke the silence.

'Bai-li, I'm afraid you're going to have to be honest with me.'

'Yes, of course,' Bai-li began polishing his glasses. 'In so far as I'm able, that is.'

'Please, no games.'

'If you insist,' he said, a little wearily.

'I think she does, Gē-gē,' Ch'ing-ling said warningly. 'What is it, Gerda dear?'

'Am I right in thinking you're trying to recruit Joao Sereño, or Serino, for something?'

'Well –'

'I'm not asking you what you're going to recruit him for, Bai-li. Just if you intend to do so.'

Her question hung suspended in the air above the three of them. Gerda noticed Ch'ing-ling give Bai-li the very slightest of nods.

'That is the intention, Gerda. Yes.'

'Then there's something else that may be of help,' she continued. 'Joao made it very clear he's a loner. And that this he regarded as a strength, not a weakness.'

'And why was that?' Bai-li sat very still, in observational mode.

'Because, by not fitting into Japanese society, he found himself able – like you, Bai-li, right now – to adopt a detached view of everything and everyone around him, and to observe and analyse all that they said and did.'

'Anything else?'

'Only that that was what, in his opinion, made him a good journalist.'

'And informer, of course.'

'Exactly what I told him, Bai-li.'

'Did you now? And how did he react to that?'

'He proceeded to make an interesting comparison between journalists and spies.'

'Did he now?'

'His argument was that they worked in the same way, asking questions, making use of informants, that sort of thing.'

'And?'

'Like any good spy, he was in many ways non-committal,' she smiled.

'Ah!'

'But there was one thing. One more thing, that is.'

'And that thing was?' Bai-li replaced his glasses on his nose.

'Something I think is rather important in a spy. Joao likes to play games.'

'Any particular kind of game?'

'Ones that confuse. He joked about how a spy should, perhaps, allow himself to be taken at face value, rather than don a mask that concealed what he was really up to. He left me wondering whether, perhaps, he isn't himself already a spy, as well as journalist.'

'Working for the Japanese?' Bai-li asked quickly.

'I've no idea. That's your area of expertise. But, as I said, he likes to play games. My impression is he plays them rather well.'

Once more there was silence in the room. A fly buzzed desperately behind a half-closed shutter.

'I think your Mr Sereño sounds rather interesting,' Ch'ing-ling said eventually, as she poured Gerda another cup of tea. 'Do you think you could get in touch with him for me, Gerda?'

'Of course. But why?'

'So that he can interview me. After all, that's what I promised him at the Zeitgeist the other evening.'

'But is that wise, Mei-mei? Journalists always twist informants' words to fit their own version of truth.'

'I know. But how else am I to corroborate what Gerda's been telling us about him? I assume you'd like a second opinion?'

'I would, indeed.'

'Then, Gerda dear, could you bring Mr Sereño here tomorrow afternoon? I think I'm finally ready to talk about the past.'

'What about the future?'

'The future, too. Over yet another cup of tea.'

The following evening, Bai-li slipped into Number 14, rue Molière, through a back gate in the garden wall, where he wouldn't be spotted by informers. Ch'ing-ling was waiting for him. Briefly they embraced. She trembled as his hands clasped her lightly to him.

'So? How did it go, Mei-mei?' He asked, eager to find out what she thought of the Japanese journalist who'd interviewed her for a full three hours that afternoon.

'I haven't talked so much in years,' she gave one of her gentle smiles. 'Not since my husband Te-ming died.'

She was still holding Bai-li's hand as they sat together on a rattan sofa.

'That was probably good for you, wasn't it?'

'Yes,' she leaned close and put her head on Bai-li's shoulder. 'It was time I talked about my childhood and my family.'

'And that was all, Mei-mei?' He asked gently.

'Of course not,' she glanced up at him briefly. 'As you might expect of a journalist, Joao asked me about the love of my life – my other love, that is – and my relationship with Te-ming,' she used the name members of his family used for Sun Yat-sen.

'And? Was Ch'ing-ling toying with him?'

She lifted her head from Bai-li's shoulder and looked him in the eye.

'Upon reflection, I agree with everything Gerda told us yesterday afternoon. He's clearly a very good journalist. His follow-up questions were always to the point. He knew how to pursue a topic that came up while I was talking. Right to the very end.'

'But that's not necessarily what we're looking for, is it? Although it helps, I suppose.'

'True. But Serino-*san* also knew when not to pursue something immediately. Instead, he'd circle round and come back to it later, when he judged I was readier to answer whatever question he'd asked.'

'Interesting,' Bai-li mused.

'What struck me most was his ability to draw me out. To get me talking about things I'd never imagined I'd be willing to talk about. That's a great skill in a journalist.'

'Indeed. Anyone who can get you to break your silence, Ch'ing-ling, must indeed be skilful.'

'And there was something else,' she paused.

'What was that?'

'He knows how to listen, Gē-ge. He didn't spend his time asserting what he thought about my husband, or my sisters, or Chiang Kai-shek, or the communist cause. He kept his questions simple and then, somehow, hid inside them, watching me as I answered them.'

Bai-li's eyes widened slightly.

'An intriguing way of putting it,' he said.

'As a result, I found myself engrossed in a conversation with myself, rather than with him. If you see what I mean,' she finished, slightly helplessly. 'Am I making any sense?'

'You are, indeed.'

'So, if you ask me what I think,' her voice tailed away.

'That's what I did, Mei-Mei,' Bai-li managed a dimpled smile.

'I'd say he's perfect, Gē-gē' she finished. 'And to judge by the way Gerda behaved in his presence, I got the impression she thinks he's perfect, too. A perfect lover.'

It was later that same evening. They had eaten together and talked. Of things they dared not talk about in the company of others. Of Shao Shan's escape to join Mao's army in the south. Of Colonel Pan Yu-tang's trip to Moscow and his arrest at the border. Of his son's attempt to unmask Bai-li.

'Will it be alright, Gē-gē?' Was all Ch'ing-ling could ask.

'There aren't any owls in your garden, Mei-mei, hinting at disaster,' he answered cryptically.

'You should have given the young man an umbrella before he left.'

'To hint that I hoped I'd never see Pan Yu-long again? That's a bit naughty, Mei-mei.'

'I was always the naughty girl when I was young.'

They were back on the rattan sofa and Ch'ing-ling's head was once again resting on Bai-li's shoulder.

'So, how are you going to recruit our Japanese journalist friend?' She broached the subject that each had been avoiding all evening.

Bai-li pursed his lips and blew air out between them in a kind of frustrated sigh.

'The million-dollar question.' He paused uncertainly. 'I'll have to arrange a meeting. And soon.'

'Why don't you ask Gerda to help you? The presence of a woman he likes will soften the stark reality of your proposal.'

'Possibly. But still –'

'But still what?'

'I still have to decide how best to present myself.'

'As a patriot, Gē-gē. Surely, that would be best?'

Bai-li nodded.

'That makes sense. Thank you. And, as you say, Gerda's presence might act as a distraction.'

He paused. It was time for him to polish his glasses. He unfolded his handkerchief, breathed on first one lens, then the other, and quickly started wiping them clean. Round and round. Just like life itself.

'Maybe,' he said at last, 'I can improve on your idea.'

'Of course, you can, Gē-gē. I'm just a woman, remember!' Ch'ing-ling laughed ironically. 'So what's your better idea?'

'You should be there, too, together with Gerda.'

'Me? Are you planning a party, Gē-gē?' This time her laughter was spontaneous.

'In a way, yes,' Bai-li replied. 'So far as we're aware, Joao Sereno doesn't know Gerda's political affiliation. He may suspect, of course. But he doesn't *know*. And if he's intent upon making her his mistress, which I hope he is, he probably doesn't care. Not yet, at least.'

'Which means?' Ch'ing-ling looked. up at Bai-li curiously.

'Which means that, if the widow of Sun Yat-sen shows up in full evening dress for dinner and dance, the last thing Joao will be thinking about is politics. Moreover, because I'll be accompanying you as your dance partner, I'm not going to have to worry about how to present myself.'

'Never hand a sword to a man who can't dance,' Ch'ing-ling murmured.

'We'll just be a group of friends,' Bai-li ignored her allusion. 'Foreign intellectuals and Chinese patriots enjoying a night out together.'

Ch'ing-ling pursed her lips in though. Then,

'I like it, Gē-gē. But what about your plan to turn Chiang Kai-shek against the Japanese? Mr Joao Sereño may not worry too much, but surely Serino Joao-*san* will?'

'Not if he's how you and Gerda have depicted him. I have a feeling we might all be surprised by the outcome. Joao included.'

In the autumn of 1927, nowhere in Shanghai swung quite like the Majestic swung. At least, so Shanghailanders liked to say. While addicts smoked their opium in the Hollywood *hong*, and gamblers sat at their roulette tables in the Burlington Hotel, while drunks frequented all-night bars in Blood Alley, and philanderers sought the favours of their favourite whores in the sing-song houses along Foochow Road, the international set dressed up for the night – men in their starched shirts, bow ties and black evening dress; women in fashionable ballroom gowns ordered from a Parisian couturier on the rue Wagner, or quickly run up by a simply marvellous little Chinese tailorman working out of a hole in the wall somewhere along the Bubbling Well Road. Then they took to the dance floor of the Majestic Hotel's ballroom, renowned for the model train that circled round its four-leaf clover shape. Ah! Those were the days, though of quite what, it was hard to tell. The frenetic energy that tends to grip a populace before it goes to war, was Bai-li's best guess.

Even at two in the morning, the Majestic ballroom pulsated to the beat of Oriental swing, as Whitey Two-Shoes and the Harlem Brothers in their white tuxedos made the chandeliers tinkle to the Turkey Trot and Twelfth Street Rag, and Ebony Jade, when it suited her Whitey's girl, wooed the

Shanghailanders with her honey voice and revealing ways. She knew how to walk the walk and talk the talk. It was rumoured she could take any man's hair between her thighs and spin a yarn. Like flax on a distaff, full of sound and fury, as she crooned *I Got Plenty O' Nuttin'* while going about her business. Those were the days – or rather, nights – when nobody slept. Especially those in the hotel rooms above.

It was nowhere near the witching hour, though, when Joao and Gerda sat down to dinner at a secluded table for two, half hidden from the dance floor by palm trees in bamboo boxes standing incongruously on a thick-piled Peking carpet. It was several days since Bai-li had suggested to Gerda that she persuade Joao to invite her out. This was one of the more agreeable tasks he'd asked her to carry out for him and she was looking forward to getting to know her 'spy' – as she liked to think of him – a little better.

'I think the occasion deserves a bottle of champagne, don't you?' Joao, too, was clearly looking forward to an uninterrupted evening of pleasure in Gerda's company.

Tonight she dazzled in a green silk dress that clung to her lithe body and revealed a cleavage to excite his – indeed, any man's – interest. Her legs were encased in expensive silk stockings, and her forearms in green satin gloves stretching up to her elbows. Her cupid's bow lips were ruby red, her stunning auburn red hair pinned back to reveal two delicate ears, from which a pair of emerald pendants sparkled in the lamp light. Her perfume was no longer lily-of-the-valley, but a heady mix of bergamot, night-blooming jasmine, rose and vanilla.

'Mmm,' Joao breathed in her scent. 'What is it?'

'Shalimar,' she smiled.

'It's like you.'

'How so?'

'It smells as if it's wearing an evening gown with an outrageously plunging neckline.'

A waiter arrived and laid a large leather-bound menu in front of each of the guests. The wine list he placed on Joao's side plate.

Joao didn't bother to open it.

'I think we'll have a bottle of Pommery Millesime. 1921 vintage, please,' he said. 'Well chilled, but not too cold. We don't want the grapes to lose their taste.'

'Very good, sir. And, if I may say so, a superb choice.' The waiter bowed and disappeared behind a screen hiding the door to the kitchen and wine cellar.

'So Joao, how did it go the other day with Ch'ing-ling?' Gerda began. As Joao had intended, she was impressed.

'You were there, Gerda. For most of the time, at least. How do you think it went?'

'Very well. Ch'ing-ling clearly liked you.'

'She did?'

'But, of course. You could tell by the way she relaxed. And by how much she talked.'

'You mean, she doesn't usually.'

'Ch'ing-ling? Talk?' Gerda laughed and put one hand on her companion's arm. 'Joao dear, if only you knew. Ch'ing-ling's one of the most reserved people I know. She keeps things to herself. Which is one reason I like her so much.'

'She struck me as being very sensitive and thoughtful. Committed, too, and strong-minded. I really liked that about her. She knows what she wants and why she wants it. I suppose being sent to school in the United States at such a young age contributed to that.'

'I expect you're right.'

The waiter came back with a bottle that he showed demonstratively to his discerning customer. Joao nodded and the waiter carefully filled the two champagne flutes he had brought with him.

'Are Sir and Madame ready to order? Or would you like a little more time?'

'Can you give us a couple more minutes, please?'

'Certainly, sir.'

'Before you go, though, is there anything you'd recommend?'

'Well, sir,' the waiter opened Gerda's, then Joao's, menu and pointed to the list of appetisers. 'Our customers seem to be very fond of the lobster thermidor as a starter. I would have thought it an excellent complement to the Pommery, sir. If you don't mind my saying so.'

Joao looked at Gerda and raised his eyebrows enquiringly.

'That sounds perfect,' she said.

'Good. That settles it, then. Two lobster thermidors to start with. Followed by…? What would you like, Gerda?'

'I don't know,' she mused as she scanned the Entrées. 'How about Beef Stroganoff? Or Hungarian Goulash? I feel like something a little close to home this evening.'

Joao didn't miss a beat.

'One Beef Stroganoff, it is then. And one Hungarian Goulash. We'll share.'

Gerda began to think she'd met the perfect gentleman.

As the waiter hurried off to the kitchen to place their order, a gentle voice called out behind where Joao was seated.

'Hello Gerda. What are you doing here?' It was Ch'ing-ling, supremely elegant in a high-collared, long blue cheongsam that hugged her slender figure, but allowed her freedom of movement, thanks to two side slits up to her knees.

'And Joao, too,' she continued smoothly. 'Hello, Joao. You didn't tell me you were coming here tonight,' she added, slightly reproachfully.

'You didn't ask, Ch'ing-ling,' Gerda laughed her infectious laugh. 'But who's that with you, hiding behind the palm tree.'

Bai-li stepped forward with a dimpled smile.

'Just me,' he said. 'Although I wasn't hiding behind anything, Gerda. Rather, the palm tree was hiding me. Hello again, Mr Sereño. My name is Su Bai-li.'

Joao was already on his feet.

'Joao. Please.' He said, holding out his hand, but then dropping it. 'I'm sorry. I'm not sure how to greet you properly. I've heard that a lot of Chinese people don't like shaking hands with Westerners.' He bowed slightly, Japanese style.

'That's true,' Bai-li said politely returning his bow. 'But, since you're not properly a "red-haired barbarian," I can hardly object, can I?' He smiled again and shook Joao's hand firmly.

'Well, if we're going to resort to ethnic epithets,' Gerda gave Bai-li a peck on the cheek, 'I should point out that the only red-haired devil present is me.'

'The only devilish thing about you, Gerda, is your bewitching beauty,' Joao said gallantly, before quickly shifting the conversation. 'But are you two dining alone? If so, I'm sure Gerda wouldn't mind if you joined us, would you?' He turned to Gerda as he slipped an arm around her waist.

'Of course not,' she leaned into him slightly, breathing in the scent of his eau de cologne. Penhaligon's, she decided.

'Why, thank you, Joao. That would be a great pleasure, wouldn't it, Gē-gē?'

Bai-li clearly agreed, for he raised one hand and beckoned forward the *maitre d'hotel* who had been showing them to their table, but who was now hovering slightly impatiently to one side, as he waited for the pleasantries between the two couples to come to an end.

'My apologies for troubling you, Monsieur Valentin,' he said politely, 'But do you think you could arrange for our table to be brought over here? Unless you have a better idea, of course.'

Valentin bowed, paused, and then extended a white-gloved hand in the direction of a glass-roofed conservatory at the far end of the dining room.

'If Doctor Su, Madame Sun and their *esteemed* companions would like to follow me, I have an *excellent* table free by the conservatory window, thanks to an *unexpected* cancellation. It has a *delightful* view of the gardens outside, which I'm sure you will appreciate. They're *illuminated*, of course.'

Valentin clearly believed in italicising his words.

'Of *course*,' Joao decided to play the obsequy game. 'How *kind* of you *maitre*!'

'Entirely *my* pleasure, Mr...?'

'Sereño,' Bai-li said at once. 'Joao Sereño is a very good friend of ours, isn't he, Ch'ing-ling?'

'He is, indeed. And an excellent journalist, too. He's writing my biography, you know.'

Valentin didn't.

'But how *wunderbar*!' He exclaimed in a language that he clearly wasn't used to speaking, to judge by Gerda's suppressed giggle in Joao's ear. 'It must be *such* a wonderful opportunity for you, Mr Sereño. Madame Sun has had such an *interesting* life.'

'Our table?' Bai-li reminded the obsequious maître.

'But of *course*, Doctor Su. Do *please* follow me.'

Five minutes later, when Ch'ing-ling and Bai-li had followed their new waiter's advice and ordered lobster thermidor, followed, this time, by a Waldorf Salad for Ch'ing-ling and Dover Sole à la Meunière for Bai-li, they raised their champagne flutes in toast.

'To friendship!' exclaimed Joao, looking into Gerda's mesmerizingly green hazel eyes.

'To friendship!' she said, clinking glasses, and then with Ch'ing-ling and Bai-li in turn.

'And to love!' added Ch'ing-ling softly, with a sidelong glance at Gerda. 'We should never forget love, should we, Gē-gē?'

'If you say so, Mei-mei.'

'I do, Gē-gē. I do.'

Both Joao and Gerda seemed to blush very slightly. At least, Joao's sunburned skin turned a kind of deep mahogany red, while the very light sprinkling of freckles high on Gerda's cheeks became a bit more obvious. That was all.

Joao concentrated on spreading a white linen napkin across his knees. Then,

'Excuse me for asking, Ch'ing-ling, but why do you call Bai-li "Gē-gē"?'

Ch'ing-ling looked at Bai-li, who answered for her.

'It's simple, really, Joao. Doctor Sun asked me to promise to take care of Ch'ing-ling after his death.'

'And you promised.' It was a statement, rather than a question.

'But of course.'

'Ever since then, I've called Bai-li "Gē-gē," or Elder Brother,' Ch'ing-ling put in.

'And I've called Ch'ing-ling "Mei-mei." But tell me, Joao,' Bai-li was all suave affability, 'How did your interview with my Little Sister go the other day?'

'Well, I think. But you should ask Ch'ing-ling. She's the ultimate arbiter of that.'

Ch'ing-ling took the hint.

'I think it went very well,' she said quietly. 'Joao strikes me as being a very good journalist. The kind who can dig deep into someone's soul and draw out secrets that have lain dormant for years. I'm looking forward to reading what you write, Joao.'

'And I to writing up my notes,' he raised his glass to Ch'ing-ling in silent toast. 'I'm about half-way through right now.'

'You are? In which case, you'll need to come and ask me more questions very soon, won't you? And show me what you've written, of course.'

'There's little I would enjoy more.'

At that point, their waiter arrived with a small trolley of plates of lobster thermidor, together with a second ice bucket – this time for a bottle of Lousada that Joao had found buried at the bottom of the wine list and ordered.

Maitre Valentin appeared out of nowhere to open the bottle. Then he moved round to behind where Joao was sitting and began to pour a taster into his glass.

Joao waved the bottle away.

'This isn't red wine, Valentin. Just a simple *vinho verde*. Fill the ladies' glasses, please.'

Valentin performed his duty and, to his chagrin, found himself obliged to leave their table without being given the opportunity to wax eloquent about the full-bodied nature of the wine's heady floral and peach aromas – with their hint of butterscotch. Unless, of course, it was the wool of the sheep that grazed high above the River Douro. What a wasted opportunity!

Joao felt it necessary to explain why he'd foregone the customary ritual.

'I'm sorry, but I really hate the pretension surrounding how wine is served and drunk in restaurants. All this sniffing and tasting, by people who haven't the faintest idea about how grapes are grown and wine is made, or what the wine they've chosen should taste like in the first place – it annoys me. Wine is to be drunk and enjoyed. At least, that's what I think. Not treated like some kind of exotic geisha.'

'Cheers to that, Joao. Here's to our enjoyment.'

Glasses once again were held high and clinked together.

'You make it sound, though, as if you, at least, know what you're talking about,' Ch'ing-ling tested him. 'That's unusual for a Japanese, if you don't mind my saying so.'

'But he's only half Japanese,' Gerda came to the rescue, before Joao explained.

'Actually, the other half of me spent a couple of years in Portugal after I left university.'

'You did?' Bai-li looked surprised. 'Why was that, Joao?'

'I wanted to meet up with my father again,' Joao said, with a slightly sad smile. 'He left my mother when I was six years old, you know, and went back to his family home in Porto.'

'I didn't. And how was your – your reunion? If that's the right word,' Gerda asked in a way that only a lover could.

'Difficult,' Joao replied, with that same slightly sad expression. 'At first, at least. Things got better after time, though. And,' he suddenly brightened up, 'My father owned a few vineyards up the Douro Valley, so I had the opportunity to learn all about how to make wine.'

'So that explains it. I was intrigued, though, by your analogy,' Bai-li said, raising his glass in silent toast. 'Wine as a geisha – beautiful to behold, delicate to taste, and with a luscious afterglow, as I understand it, lasting well into the following day.'

'Bai-li!' Ch'ing-ling exclaimed. 'So that's what you were up to when you lived in Japan?'

'You've lived in Japan?' Joao asked, curious. 'The hidden pasts that emerge over a glass or two of wine.'

'It was some years ago now. I enrolled at the military academy in Tokyo, together with an old school friend, Chiang Kai-shek. Unfortunately, our pocket money didn't extend to paying for geisha to entertain us in Kagurazaka.'

'Karuzagaka?' Gerda asked, mixing up her syllables. The champagne had clearly gone to her head a little.

'Kagurazaka,' Joao corrected her with a gentle smile. 'It's a geisha district in Tokyo. I'm not surprised, though.'

'Not surprised by what?' Ch'ing-ling asked.

'By the fact that Bai-li couldn't afford a visit to a geisha house. It would have been extremely expensive. Far more than what a poor Chinese student could afford, and well over what I myself now earn in a month.'

'In that case, who can afford to go?' It was Gerda's turn to ask.

'Politicians, mainly. Rich businessmen and senior executives of zaibatsu conglomerates. And gangsters, of course.'

'Gangsters?'

Joao nodded.

'Unlike Chinese students, or most of them anyway, gangsters always have a lot of cash to spend.'

'Like Big Ears Tu.'

'Or, in the case of Japan, somebody like Mitsuru Tōyama. Even Chiang Kai-shek paid him a visit when he was in Tokyo.'

'What did you make of that, Joao?'

Joao waited until their empty plates had been cleared. Then,

'What Chiang Kai-shek does in Tokyo is, I suppose, his own business.'

'Except when it impinges on what's going on in China, presumably?'

Joao looked at Bai-li sharply.

'Precisely,' he said.

'And does it? Impinge, I mean.'

'How can it not, Bai-li? You should know better than all of us here. You're one of his advisers, after all.'

Joao was better informed than Bai-li had supposed.

'True. In a manner of speaking, I suppose I am. But –'

'But he doesn't listen to your advice?' Again, Joao was straight to the point.

'There are times, I think, when he prefers his own advice,' Bai-li adjusted his glasses and blinked, slightly owlishly, at his dinner table companions. 'This can make life difficult.'

'For you?'

'For me,' Bai-li conceded, 'But also for China.'

There was a pause in the conversation as the waiter came and cleared away their empty plates.

'Would you care for another bottle of the *vinho verde*, sir?'

He poured the rest of the contents of the bottle in the ice bucket into first Ch'ing-ling's, then Gerda's glass.

Joao looked at Bai-li and raised his eyebrows enquiringly.

'Why not?' Bai-li said to the waiter, before turning to Joao. 'I've never had Portuguese wine before. This is really rather good, Joao.'

'Thank you,' he inclined his head politely. 'But you were talking about the Generalissimo.'

'I was? Ah, yes, of course,' Bai-li gave Joao one of his dimpled smiles. 'I was commenting on how difficult it can be to give advice to someone who doesn't want to listen.'

'Especially when that someone is about to become my brother-in-law,' Ch'ing-ling shuddered involuntarily.

'I mean, what would you do, Joao, to persuade –?' Bai-li stopped suddenly in mid-sentence, looking embarrassed.

'To persuade what?'

'Nothing. I'm sorry. I was getting a bit carried away,' Bai-li tried to wriggle out of what had nearly been a conversational *faux pas*. 'Perhaps we should change the subject.'

'Ah!' Joao smiled in an understanding manner. 'You were about to say something about my countrymen, weren't you, Bai-li? Something negative, perhaps?'

Bai-li couldn't make up his mind about whether his dinner table companion's ability to get straight to the point was a strength or weakness in his character.

'Well, I wouldn't say negative, exactly.'

He took off his glasses and began polishing them carefully with a handkerchief that he took from the breast pocket of his dinner jacket.

'Something about the Kwantung Army in Manchuria, perhaps?'

Bai-li stopped his polishing.

'My goodness, you *are* persistent, aren't you, Joao?' he laughed. 'I can see what makes you a good journalist. But, as I said, I think we should change the subject.'

'By the way, Ch'ing-ling, have you heard about this marvellous young ballet dancer, Margaret Hookham?' Gerda stepped into the rescue – although which of the two men she was rescuing she wasn't quite sure. 'She's hardly more than eight years old, and…'

At which point, the waiter conveniently arrived with his trolley loaded with food. Carefully, he placed a plate of Waldorf Salad in front of Ch'ing-ling, whose knowledge of ballet was perhaps even more limited than Joao's, and the fish dish in front of Bai-li. He then picked up the remaining two plates and held them hesitantly in the air above Gerda's head.

'I believe Madame wishes to share her Hungarian goulash with Sir?'

'Oh, that's right!' Gerda turned in her seat and smiled. 'Just give one of the plates to me, waiter, and the other to Mr Sereño here. We can work things out for ourselves, can't we, Joao?'

'Definitely.' He turned to explain to the others. 'Gerda and I couldn't make up our minds which we preferred, so we decided to share the Hungarian goulash and beef Stroganoff.'

Ch'ing-ling clapped her hands with childlike delight.

'What a wonderful idea, Gerda! Why don't we do the same, Gē-gē? I'll never be able to eat all this salad anyhow.'

'If you insist, Mei-mei.' Bai-li said, not quite sure he approved of the suggestion.

'But I do, Gē-gē. I do.'

'If Madame would allow me,' the waiter said, taking up her plate and placing it once again on the trolley. 'And Sir.'

Bai-li allowed his own plate to be whisked away from under his fish knife and fork.

'You look as if you're about to cut up the tablecloth,' Gerda laughed gaily.

The others joined in as the waiter deftly parted the Dover sole and placed a slice on Ch'ing-ling's plate. Then, with a clean spoon and fork, he lifted some of the Waldorf salad onto Bai-li's plate.

As they started eating their various dishes, Joao resumed their earlier discussion.

'I think, Bai-li, you were embarrassed earlier because you were going to say something impolite – or, at least, impolite to Japanese ears – about the Kwantung Army. Why don't you tell me what it was? Let's face it, I'm not a "proper" Japanese – especially not after spending a couple of years abroad in Portugal. I'm certainly not a supporter of Japanese militarism, either, and there are many in Japan who, like me, are desperate to avoid war.'

Bai-li slowly finished his mouthful of excellently prepared sole à la Meunière.

'Aren't we all?' he began. 'Which was what I was going to say about Chiang Kai-shek.'

'That he's so desperate to avoid confronting Japan that he spends his whole time chasing the communists?' Joao looked at Ch'ing-ling, but failed to catch her eye as she picked delicately at her salad.

'Something like that, yes,' Bai-li admitted.

'If you ask me,' Joao continued, deftly exchanging the plates of goulash and Stroganoff. 'That's not really in China's interest, is it?'

'That's what Bai-li's been trying to tell my future brother-in-law. But he won't listen, will he, Gē-gē?'

'He can be rather obstinate, I must admit,' Bai-li agreed, still concentrating on his food.

'In my experience, there's usually a way round obstinacy,' Joao said. 'At least, there is in Japan. I haven't met him, of course, but I suspect the Generalissimo epitomises that riddle about what happens when the all-conquering spear meets the all-defending shield. You know it, of course, Bai-li? Those two Chinese characters that, when placed together to form a word, signify a "paradox." In your language, as well as in one of mine.'

Joao paused. Bai-li nodded, fork in air, fish firmly impaled.

'Meaning, how can the spear be made to overcome the shield?'

'Precisely.'

'Your fork seems to have no trouble there,' Gerda smiled with a naughty look in her eye. 'Look at that poor bit of fish.'

They all laughed.

'The question is, how did that Dover sole come to be conquered by you, Bai-li?' Joao continued.

Bai-li frowned slightly.

'Because I ordered it.'

'Yes. And how?' Joao persisted, in full interview mode.

'By finding it on the menu, of course. For a Japanese, Joao, if you don't mind my saying so, you ask a lot of questions.'

'I'm a newspaper reporter, remember,' Joao laughed and sipped his wine. 'If you'll allow me to continue?'

'Please do.'

'So what does ordering a fish dish from a menu tell you about how to get the Generalissimo to think of China's interests and pay attention to the Kwantung Army?'

Bai-li had finished his last mouthful of food and put his knife and fork down on his plate, side by side. He sat very still indeed.

'You're suggesting something written? Not a menu, of course, but some kind of written document?'

Gerda and Ch'ing-ling, too, stopped eating. Both recognised that Joao was about to show his true colours.

'Something like that,' Joao said carelessly. 'Why not?'

'But what kind of document, Joao?' Bai-li said a little helplessly, while Ch'ing-ling could only marvel at her lover's skill.

'Ah!' Joao laughed. 'That's something you'd know far better than I, Bai-li. After all, you're the Generalissimo's adviser. Or is it spy? Whichever, if you're asking the Portuguese half of me, I'd suggest something that would somehow embarrass the Japanese. If there's one thing the Japanese half of me hates, it's to be shamed. Especially in public.'

The waiter reappeared to clear away their empty plates.

'But now, ladies,' Joao once more became the Portuguese gallant, 'It's time for dessert, although how such already sweet women have further need of sugared dishes, I've no idea.'

The four of them joined together in laughter, sweeping away the underlying tension of the two men's conversation.

At least, Bai-li reflected, the baited hook had been cast into the water. The fish had nibbled, but had yet properly to bite.

Later in the evening, Joao found himself alone with Bai-li. Ch'ing-ling and Gerda had excused themselves to go and 'powder their noses,' as women liked to phrase it in polite circles. The four of them had been dancing for the best part of an hour – Joao as intimately as he dared with Gerda, from time to time thrilling at the softness of her breasts or the lithe firmness of a thigh, as the two of them whirled with panache on the dance floor. Meanwhile Bai-li and Ch'ing-ling moved in a subdued harmony, whose circumspect restraint was in its own way no less intimate.

It was time, Bai-li decided, to make his move. The atmosphere was relaxed. The presence of the two women had, as he'd planned, made his pitch if not easier, then considerably less fraught with potentially dangerous obstacles.

'I've been mulling over the suggestion you made earlier,' he started, as he refilled Joao's glass with some Châteauneuf-du-Pape.

'Oh yes?' Joao had slipped into non-committal Japanese mode. 'This wine is rather good, don't you think, Bai-li?'

'I do indeed. Although, unlike you, I'm no expert when it comes to wine.'

'They call it a wine for lovers.'

'They do? Why's that?' Bai-li knew when patience was required.

'Back in the old days, wines from the Rhône valley were shipped from a river port called Roquemaure near Avignon. It was known locally as "the capital of lovers.'"

'That sounds most appropriate.'

'I suspect a lot of wishful thinking was involved.'

'Hopefully, that's not the case with you and Gerda,' Bai-li proffered. 'You seem well-matched.'

'Maybe,' Joao looked embarrassed and changed the subject.

'So what were you mulling over, Bai-li?'

Bai-li paused, as if he wasn't sure what Joao was talking about.

'Oh!' he exclaimed eventually, 'That!'

It was Joao's turn to look confused.

'That what?' he asked.

'If I remember aright, I was wondering what sort of document could exist that would embarrass the Kwantung Army and persuade Chiang Kai-shek to deal with the northern warlords and unite China.'

'Ah, yes! A difficult one, that.'

'Indeed.'

Bai-li looked around the crowded ballroom. The two women were on their way back to their table. He needed more time.

Ch'ing-ling caught his look and promptly stopped to greet two Chinese couples seated by the dance floor. They looked delighted to have been addressed by the revered Madame Sun and invited the two women to sit down with them. Now was the time.

'It seems to me, Joao, that any such document would have to be a Japanese one. In Japanese, that is. I mean, your fellow countrymen are unlikely, surely, to believe anything coming out of China.'

Joao nodded thoughtfully, mellowed by the wine and an evening in Gerda's company.

'That makes sense. So it needs to be an army document of some sort, perhaps?'

'I was wondering along those lines. But what?'

'I'm not sure you should be asking me a question like that, Bai-li. Remember, I'm Japanese myself.'

'But only one half of you,' smiled Bai-li. 'You said so yourself.'

'True.' Joao realised that he rather liked Bai-li. The way he thought things through. The understated way he went about analysing things. That was probably why the Generalissimo had made him his adviser.

'What are you trying to tell me, Bai-li? That I should steal some kind of state secret from the Japanese Army's headquarters in Shanghai?' Joao laughed.

'Not steal, no. That would, I think, be rather difficult. And dangerous for whoever tried to do so. No, it has to be something else.'

'Like what?' Joao's interest was piqued.

'What do you know about the Far Eastern Conference?' Bai-li decided to stop circling round his prey.

'What? Gi'ichi Tanaka's gathering of the top brass to discuss Japan's strategy for Asia?'

'In late July this year,' Bai-li confirmed.

'In the end, not much,' Joao said, drawn in. 'I mean, the Tokyo Government made a lot of fuss about it beforehand, but then nothing came out of it.'

'Nothing at all? No newspaper interviews? No minutes? No records of what was said? No –' Bai-li paused in search of the word he wanted. 'No jottings?'

'Now that you come to mention it, Bai-li, no. Nothing that I'm aware of, at least. I don't know why, but Tanaka went totally quiet once the conference was over. Unusual really, given all the media hoo-hah leading up to it.

'As you say, Joao, unusual. Very unusual, wouldn't you say?'

'Well, when you put it like that, yes.'

'Why might that be, do you think?'

Joao paused for thought. It occurred to him that Gerda and Ch'ing-ling were taking their time powdering their noses. But then he spotted Gerda's flaming red hair on the far side of the ballroom. She was sitting at a table with two Chinese couples who seemed to know Ch'ing-ling.

'I suppose for one of two possible reasons,' he concluded.

'Yes?' Bai-li said encouragingly.

'First, nothing of interest was said at the conference.'

'Meaning, that those who attended merely repeated their usual ideological positions?'

'It's usually the case, isn't it, when you gather the same people together to discuss more or less the same thing they've been discussing over the past couple of years?'

'As a result, therefore, no new ideas came up and Tanaka found himself no further forward with his plans for China and East Asia? That makes sense.' Bai-li seemed to be talking to himself in a kind of dream-like state.

He suddenly jerked back to his wide-awake self.

'And the second reason, Joao?'

'Second, a lot of interesting topics were covered fully by the participants, who came to certain conclusions – conclusions which all concerned felt it wiser not to record on paper.'

'Conclusions likely to cause concern, you mean, if they were made public?'

'Precisely.'

'And what sort of conclusions do you think these might be?' Bai-li persisted gently. Joao had to discover things for himself.

'Something to do with war,' he said eventually. 'It couldn't have been anything else, given that the conference was attended by senior members of the Army and Navy.'

'And the Ministry of Finance, I believe.'

'Which, ultimately, decides if Japan can, or cannot, afford to go to war. My God, Bai-li! Is that what happened at Tanaka's conference? They decided that Japan should go to war?'

'I've no idea, Joao. But something important occurred. Why else are there no minutes of who said what at the conference?'

'No minutes? But that's terrible, Bai-li. The ultra-nationalists have to be stopped.'

'They do indeed, Joao. But how?'

Across the ballroom, Gerda and Ch'ing-ling had stood up and were saying farewell to their new-found acquaintances.

'By finding out what was said and agreed,' Joao replied. 'I'll see what –'

Bai-li took the final plunge.

'Or, since nothing was ever written down, by making it up, perhaps?'

Gerda was striding towards him with a wide, inviting smile on her face and Guerlain's heady Shalimar wafting ahead of her. Ch'ing-ling just behind her looked enquiringly at Bai-li.

'Yes, of course.' In his excitement, Joao hadn't noticed the two women returning to their table. 'There has to be a cover up, a fabrication.'

He stopped as he caught sight of Gerda and Ch'ing-ling. Then quietly, so that he wouldn't be overheard.

'That's the kind of document we need, Bai-li.'

'Joao, my dear,' Gerda quickly had her arms around his neck as he stood up to greet her. She gave him a long kiss on the cheek. 'I've missed you.'

'But you've only been away a few minutes,' he countered happily.

'Yes, but still... Come! Let's have one last dance, shall we, before we move on.'

Playing her part perfectly, thought Bai-li, as he sat down and told Ch'ing-ling what had happened during their absence.

When she spoke, it was with relief.

'The things that happen while women are powdering their noses.'

Ground still had to be covered. He may have hooked his fish, but Bai-li still had to reel Joao in. Any fish in such a situation would try to get rid of the hook in its mouth – head in the opposite direction from the shore, leap out of the water, wrap the line around a rock submerged under the surface. He was in unpredictable territory.

Joao might react in any one of several ways – refusing to admit he'd ever had a conversation with Bai-li in the Majestic Ballroom; passing on what was said, or might possibly have been said, to the Japanese consul or, worse, a senior Japanese army officer; or, if he was lucky, fully embracing Bai-li's proposal. If Bai-li had in fact proposed anything. It hadn't been particularly clear. Which was the way he liked to leave things. At the beginning, at least.

Precisely because Joao was in that liminal space between being a Japanese newspaper reporter and an informant for the Chinese government, the timing of Bai-li's next approach was crucial. Too soon, and Joao would be suffering those pangs of remorse often brought on by the consumption of alcohol; too late, and he would have had time to think things through and, in his own mind, 'see sense.'

Bai-li spent the hours he needed by once more reading through Joao's newspaper articles. These reassured him. Joao's sympathies clearly lay with the Chinese when he was writing about the working conditions of Chinese factory workers and dockers. His more general assessments of the geo-political situation in north-east Asia also leaned towards a united China, and against unnecessary Japanese exploitation of Manchuria, even though he paid lip service, at least, to Tokyo's stated need to feed its citizens back home.

What came across very clearly, and it wasn't something that Bai-li had picked up on during an earlier inspection of his quarry's writings, was that, first and foremost, Joao was a humanitarian. He firmly believed that his fellow countrymen should treat the Chinese, as well as other foreigners, with benevolence, and provide them with the assistance they needed to reduce their suffering and improve their everyday living conditions. He expected the same in return. This reassured Bai-li. How could he fail to persuade a humanitarian, if he was offering him an opportunity to help his fellow countrymen?

Bai-li wanted their next meeting to seem accidental. If it were arranged in advance, who knew what might happen? Joao Sereño might turn into Serino Joao and have Bai-li followed. Or, still in his Japanese-half mode, he might get paranoic and imagine that their meeting was being watched by other informants, of one sort or another. Bai-li shuddered at the thought of what might happen to Serino-*san* if he fell into the hands of the Kempeitai Japanese military police. They would arrest Bai-li, too, he realised, regardless of the fact that he lived in the French Concession, if they thought he had anything to do with espionage against the Chrysanthemum Throne.

So Bai-li had Mr Sereño, or *Serino-san*, followed to see if there was a pattern in his everyday behaviour that would permit a planned chance meeting. It seemed there was. Twice a week – on the Wednesdays and Fridays – Joao would drop in at a bookstore in a small alley off North Szechuan Road. It was run by Uchiyama Kanzō, a Japanese intellectual and Christian who published the work of the well-known Shanghainese writer, Lu Shun, whom Bai-li, as himself a published poet, knew rather well. It transpired that the three of them – Uchiyama, Lu and Serino – liked to while away an hour in the late afternoon twice a week, chatting earnestly over cups of *karigane* tea.

On the following Tuesday, after a hurried trip to Nanking to deal with a distraught young Revolutionary Army lieutenant and only a few days before Chiang Kai-shek's marriage to Soong Mei-ling, Bai-li trudged a little wearily up the staircase to the Uchiyama Bookstore, just as Serino-*san* was coming down. He had a dinner engagement with Gerda, and needed to file an article before enjoying the pleasure of her company.

'Su Bai-li,' Joao exclaimed in surprise, 'What on earth are you doing here?'

'Coming to see my friend, Lu Shun,' Bai-li replied, quite truthfully.

'Lu Shun? You know him?'

The two of them stood in the narrow staircase, Joao one step above Bai-li.

'But of course. How can one not know one of our great Chinese writers!'

'He's upstairs with Uchiyama-*san*, in his usual place with his back to the window.'

Joao stepped back against the wall to allow Bai-li to pass.

'Since you're here, Joao, and I'm in no hurry, do you think you could spare me a few minutes. There's something I'd like to sound you out about.'

Joao glanced at his watch.

'Well, if it's quick,' he said. 'I'm sorry, but I have one or two things to do at the office.'

'Oh, it will be, I assure you.' Bai-li turned and started walking back down the stairs. 'There's a coffee shop a few doors down the street. The Gongfei. Do you know it? A gathering place for Chinese and Japanese intellectuals.'

'The Gongfei?' Joao's curiosity was aroused. 'No. I don't believe I do.'

'Then you should definitely pay a brief visit. I think the ambience will appeal to you.'

'And the coffee, too, I hope?'

'Definitely the coffee, I can assure you.'

'Good! We Portuguese are very particular about our coffee, you know.'

Bai-li laughed and led Joao down the stairs and out of the building. Three doors down he turned into another doorway and started to mount another staircase leading to the Gongfei. As Bai-li pushed open the glass-panelled door, they were met by the sound of laughter as a dozen voices discussed the universe over their cups of coffee.

They sat down at an empty table in one corner of the room and ordered.

'I'll have a *pingado*, please,' Joao said to the waitress.

'A *pingado*? What's that?' Bai-li asked.

'A regular expresso with a splash of milk.'

'That sounds excellent. You do take your coffee seriously, Joao,' Bai-li turned to the waitress. 'Make that two *pingados*, please.'

Once she had gone back to the small counter in the corner, Bai-li turned back to Joao.

'The other evening,' he began, 'We had an interesting chat, if you remember.'

'I do, indeed.'

Joao's tone was friendly, so Bai-li homed in on his objective. Now was not the time to beat about the bush.

'Look! China's in a state of chaos, Joao. Nobody in their right mind can disagree with that. But what is Japan's weakness? The other evening, if I understood you correctly, you suggested it might be reputation. Of course, you, Joao, know them much better than I, but it seems to me that the Japanese are acutely conscious of what others think of them on the world stage. They act accordingly.'

Bai-li paused. Joao nodded his agreement.

'In other words, while they may have earned enormous respect from Britain and the United States because of their ability to defeat a Western Power when they overcame Tsarist Russia during the Russo-Japanese War, they know very well that they need to retain that respect. This is why they take great care to conceal what is going on both within Japan and outside the country in Manchuria, Korea and Taiwan. Would that be a fair assessment?'

'It sounds about right to me,' Joao agreed.

The coffees arrived, in tiny cups. The waitress left them to their conversation.

'So, what would happen if something were to undermine that respect?' Bai-li continued. 'Something that embarrassed the Japanese Government and made Britain and the United States reassess their attitude towards Japan?'

'You mean, like the publication of a document of the kind we discussed after dinner at the Majestic?'

Joao took a sip of his coffee and smacked his lips in appreciation. He should visit the Gongfei again. The ambience, as Bai-li had said, was special.

'Something that reveals the Japanese Imperial Army's intent to invade Manchuria and China.'

'But it hasn't. Not yet, at least.'

'Precisely. That's the whole point, Joao. The Kwantung Army hasn't yet invaded anywhere. But it might well do so in the near future. Indeed, it almost certainly will.'

'I agree with you there, and that's what worries me, too, Bai-li. I'd hate to see Japan go to war. It would be a disaster for us all.'

'It would, indeed,' Bai-li said soothingly. 'And, for my part, I'd hate to see China go to war. With a foreign power, that is. We have enough problems as it is trying to unify this vast country of ours.'

It was most likely at this point, Bai-li reflected later, that Joao saw in the slightly podgy, harmless-looking, bespectacled man with bushy eyebrows what he wanted to see – a fellow humanitarian. A Chinese intellectual who was, like him, a pacifist at heart.

'And the way Japanese trading houses treat their Chinese labourers doesn't help, does it?'

'It certainly doesn't,' Bai-li conceded. One last jerk of his rod and the fish would be reeled in.

'Which brings me to my suggestion, Joao – the suggestion you yourself made the other evening, if you recall. Why not strike before any of that happens? Why not come up with a document – like the minutes of Tanaka's Far Eastern Conference – that halts the Kwantung Army in its tracks, a document that makes both Great Britain and the United States sit up and pay attention to what's going on here?'

Rather suddenly, and unexpectedly so far as Bai-li was concerned, at this point Joao slipped into slightly formal Japanese mode. Much to his consternation, his rod went slack and he thought for a moment he'd lost his fish.

It was now Serino-*san* who spoke.

'I may have been slightly overwhelmed by the effects of wine and romance a few nights ago, Su Bai-li, but I think I made it clear then that I agreed with your suggestion. Or, rather, plan – as it now transpires. The idea of writing the fake minutes of a high-level conference convened by a Prime Minister of Japan who is renowned for advocating a "blood and iron" approach to diplomacy –'

Joao paused to sip his coffee, before continuing:

'Such an idea, as I said at the time, appeals to me. If, and only if there's no other way.'

Deep down inside, Bai-li heaved a sigh of relief.

'That's what has been worrying me these past few days,' he admitted. 'Is there some other way?'

'And is there?'

'None that I can think of.'

'So you want to go ahead with our Conference minutes idea?'

Bai-li did his best to conceal his relief at hearing, again, Serino's use of the first-person plural possessive pronoun.

'Which is where we need your input.'

'You do? Why?'

'Because you're Japanese, Joao. At least, half of you is. And we're not. You know what works, and what doesn't work, when it comes to embarrassing the Kwantung Army and the Japanese Government. You know how best to phrase the document.'

'I'm not sure I'm the right person to ask for help, if you wish to write an official Japanese document, Bai-li. Unlike journalists, bureaucrats tend to write in a long-winded style that's extremely opaque. As a result, the contents of what they've written are so tortuous they can be interpreted in any number of ways,' Joao laughed. He had reverted to the Portuguese half of his identity.

'But Tanaka, I understand, is extremely blunt. He doesn't beat about the bush when it comes to expressing his opinion. Isn't that right?'

Joao laughed again. 'It is, indeed. At the newspaper, we always say laughingly that he'll regret it one day.'

'So why not today, then? Why not write something in his straightforward, no-holds-barred, blunt style and cause a furore that he'll regret?' Bai-li asked. 'It could be rather fun.'

Joao suddenly roared with laughter and punched Bai-li playfully on the arm.

'It could be great fun, Bai-li. There's nothing my Portuguese half would like better than to embarrass the Prime Minister of Japan and the Kwantung Army.'

'And your Japanese half?'

'My Japanese half is sad that it should feel obliged to go against authority.'

'But it is prepared to do so?'

'For the sake of millions of innocent Japanese, yes.'

'Are you sure, Joao? After all –'

'Never mind that,' Joao Sereno was all business now. 'When do we start?'

PART FOUR

The Wedding

For some it was the event of the year, for others of the whole decade. In December 1927, after several years of trying to persuade the future bride's mother that, in spite of his not being a Christian – but promising to become one – he would make an acceptable husband, Chiang Kai-shek finally married the youngest of the Soong sisters, Mei-ling. The ceremony was held in front of one thousand three hundred guests crowded into the ballroom of the Majestic Hotel on Bubbling Well Road.

Outside, vagrants, vendors, neighbourhood shopkeepers, casual passers-by and, of course, one or two pickpockets, made up a small throng of curious onlookers who gaped at the high and mighty arriving in their charabancs and private rickshas, dressed in their morning suits and formal party dresses hidden in the luxurious folds of Siberian fur. It was a wonder nobody thought to rob the hotel cloakroom that day. They would have made their fortune offloading sable, squirrel, and corsac fox in the Hongkew Market.

Among those present were the bride's older sisters, Ei-ling, together with her husband, H. H. Kung, Minister of Industry and Commerce, and Ch'ing-ling, widow of Doctor Sun Yat-sen, Forerunner of the Revolution and founder of the Kuomintang Nationalist Party now headed by the bridegroom, and whose oversized and lifelike portrait hanging at one end of the ballroom dominated the proceedings. Other family members included the bride's mother, and older brother, Doctor T. V. Soong, newly-appointed Minister of Finance, who gave away the bride.

Guests who were considered, or thought of themselves as, the high and mighty included the Senior Consul of Shanghai, Edwin S. Cunningham, and various consul-generals from the International Settlement. Also represented were Major-General John Duncan, recently appointed Commander of the North China Command, and Admiral Mark L. Bristol, Commander-in-Chief of the American Pacific Fleet. Americans, for some reason or another, seemed proud of the fact that they had a middle initial in their names and insisted on using it on occasions such as this. The Major-General, on the other hand, kept quiet about his other names. Archibald Basil, if that is what they were, weren't names which – like Lambert – one could be proud of. At least, not in public.

Among the not so high or mighty – that is, the lesser mortals – were a certain Mr Joao Sereño, noted foreign correspondent for the Asahi Newspaper, and his partner, Miss Gerda Weidemeyer. The latter was accompanied by her sister, Miss Irene Weidemeyer, proprietor of the Zeitgeist Bookstore, who had just returned from a business trip to Harbin and who was accompanied by a certain Wu Shao-kuo. Their presence at such august proceedings had been secured for them at short notice by Doctor Colonel Su Bai-li, recently-appointed Director of the Department of Internal Affairs in Shanghai.

Doctor Su himself was one of the officiating witnesses. Once the guests had assembled, he joined a dozen other men in formal Western-style morning dress, complete with long coat tails and starched shirts with wing collars and bow ties. Together, they moved at a sombre pace down the full length of the ballroom, and bowed three times – first to the red, white and blue flag of the Kuomintang on the right of Dr Sun's portrait; then to Doctor Sun's own blue and white flag on the left; and finally to the image of the Father of the Nation himself.

The witnesses then turned to face the gathered guests as the bridegroom came forward to join them. A few minutes later the bride appeared on the arm of her brother, serenaded by a full orchestra of Russian musicians playing Mendelssohn's Wedding March.

Mei-ling wore a gown of silver and white georgette, draped slightly at one side and fastened with a spray of orange blossom. A little wreath of orange buds was draped over her veil of rare lace, made long and flowing to form a second train of white charmeuse, embroidered in silver and falling from her shoulders. She wore silver shoes and stockings, and carried a bouquet of palest pink carnations and fern fronds tied with white and silver ribbons. She was attended by four bridesmaids, each wearing a dress of peach charmeuse.

Once she had joined her husband-to-be on the raised platform below Sun Yat-sen's image, the marriage certificate was read out aloud, before being affixed with an official seal. Bride and bridegroom turned to face each other and bowed once, and thanked those officiating as witnesses by bowing to them en masse. They then turned to their guests assembled on and around the dance floor and bowed to them once. This was the signal for applause from all assembled, a few of whom felt it appropriate to shout 'Bravo!' to show their appreciation.

There followed numerous photographs – of the bride and groom, with and without their family members, and of the assembled witnesses and others who had officiated at the wedding. The bride then retired with her bridesmaids, while hotel staff hurriedly set out tables for the guests to take tea, which in those days in Shanghai, meant many other kinds of less innocuous, but just as soothing, liquid refreshments. The fact that the bride did not reappear, and that neither she nor her newly-acquired husband was seen again, didn't in any way dampen the assembled guests' determination to enjoy themselves. As a result, the Russian musicians found themselves playing well into the early hours of the following morning as what had started out as a formal celebration morphed into a party that, even by Shanghai standards, was considered to be 'wild.'

As the guests waited for arrangements to be made for food and drink to be served, they milled around and greeted one another. Joao and Gerda came across Ch'ing-ling talking politely to a younger man with sleek black hair brushed back from his broad forehead.

'Serino-*san*!' Ch'ing-ling exclaimed, placing a hand on his arm, 'You know Ken Inukai, son of the former cabinet minister, Tsuyoshi Inukai, don't you?'

'By reputation only, I'm afraid.' Joao bowed politely. In Japanese mode now.

'Inukai-*san*,' Ch'ing-ling continued as she smoothly effected the introductions in English, 'I'd like you to meet the noted scholar and foreign correspondent for the Asahi Newspaper, Joao Serino. And his partner, Miss Gerda Weidemeyer.'

The two Japanese bowed to each other, saying their names – the way one always did – before adding the mandatory '*Yoroshiku onegai itashimasu*.' Please treat me favourably, as and when occasion demands. Every meeting had the potential to create a new set of social relationships.

Ken held out his hand to shake Gerda's.

'I'm delighted to make your acquaintance, Miss Weidemeyer,' he said suavely in perfect American English, while Joao watched carefully – watching, but not watching, as was his wont. Surely this wasn't another mixed-up Japanese? His father would never have allowed it. Born to diplomacy, more likely.

Ken turned back to Joao and looked at his new acquaintance carefully. Weighing and measuring – a bit like the preparations leading up to a boxing match. Better to get in the first feint.

'I'm honoured to make your acquaintance, Inukai-*san*.'

'And I yours, Serino-*san*. You've made yourself quite a reputation in certain circles in Tokyo.'

Joao bowed again, sucking air gently through his teeth in modesty and uttering something that sounded like *yéyé*.

Mesmerised, Gerda watched the transformation of her gallant Portuguese into a humble Japanese journalist.

'I hope such a reputation is good, rather than bad,' he said.

'Definitely. Of that you've nothing to fear,' Inukai laughed and, in American fashion, clapped Joao on the back. A sudden jab that momentarily had him reeling with surprise.

'But why don't we dispense with formality? Please call me Ken.'

'Then you must call me Joao.'

'I've always thought your name so intriguing, Joao. I mean, even though it's written in Chinese characters, I assume it's Portuguese, right?'

'Indeed, it is. My mother gave me very special Chinese characters to write it with.'

'What are they, Joao?' Ch'ing-ling asked curiously.

'Well, Jo means help. A, of course, is the character for Asia, and O for Man.'

'Helping Asia Man?' exclaimed Gerda. 'That's rather beautiful. I wish we had names like that in German.'

'But you do in a way,' Joao said quickly. 'Gerda has something to do with protection, doesn't it? Wasn't Gerda the wife of Frey, the Scandinavian god of peace and fertility?'

'And you, too, are a kind of protector, Joao,' Ch'ing-ling chimed in. 'It seems like you're made for each other.'

The laughter was loud, easing the tension, but soon died down.

'To judge from your writings, Joao, you're very definitely a helping Asia kind of man.'

Joao bowed his head modestly. Better not to show his other side yet.

'That's very kind of you to say so.'

'Your analyses of what's going on here in China are being read very carefully by people well-placed in Japanese government, you know. And that interview with Madame Sun that you've just published,' Ken nodded deferentially towards the quiet, diminutive woman beside him, 'Was, if I might say so, a masterpiece. Even my father was taken with its contents.'

'For that you must thank Madame Sun herself,' Joao bowed again.

'Don't be so modest, Joao. I have to tell you, Ken, Joao here is the only reporter I've ever come across who's been able to draw me out in the way he's been doing in our interviews.'

'Is there more to come, then?' Ken looked pleasantly surprised. 'That's definitely something to look forward to.' He stopped, as his eye caught something across the room. 'But I'm sorry. If you'll excuse me, I have to go. I can see my father beckoning to me in the distance. He's a man I've learned to ignore at my peril.' Once again the easy laugh, as he bowed first to Gerda, then Joao, and finally Ch'ing-ling.

'I hope you'll excuse me and that we can meet up again later. It's been a pleasure finally to have met you after all these years, Madame Sun,' he said formally and took his leave.

Ch'ing-ling almost blushed at Joao's enquiring look.

'When my husband was on the run and in exile, he spent several months in Tokyo, as you probably know. Ken's father very kindly put him up in his compound in Mejiro. Ken was just a boy then.'

'I'm sorry to butt in,' a voice said at Joao's side, 'But are you the noted journalist, Joao Serino?'

Joao turned to face the newcomer, as Ch'ing-ling took Gerda by the arm and led her away through the throng of guests. The trouble with gatherings like this. You could never pursue a conversation to its end.

'Yes, that's me,' he affirmed.

'My name is Pan Yu-long. Lieutenant in the National Revolutionary Army and Aide-de-camp to General Chiang Kai-shek.'

Joao bowed formally.

'I'm delighted to make your acquaintance, Lieutenant Pan. How may I be of assistance?'

Yu-long looked about him nervously.

'I was wondering if you might be able to spare me half an hour,' he said in a voice that was so low Joao had difficulty in hearing him. 'I have a story I think might interest you.'

'Well, if it's about the Generalissimo, I'm sure I'll be able to spare the time you ask for. Everyone wants to read about Chiang Kai-shek these days,' Joao laughed.

'No. It isn't about the Generalissimo, but about one of his advisers, Su Bai-li. Do you know him?'

'Su Bai-li?' Alert now. He feigned as if he was searching his memory. 'I know of him. But only very little, I'm afraid. Can you, perhaps, give me some indication of what it is you wish to discuss with me? I'm not really a political journalist– not of that variety, anyway – and I'd hate to be wasting your time, Lieutenant.'

Again, Yu-long glanced around nervously, and then abruptly pulled Joao a little out of the throng of people around them to a nearby palm tree. Then, having ensured he wouldn't be overheard, he summoned up the courage to speak. Very rapidly and in the same low voice.

'I have evidence to prove that Doctor Su is a Communist spy.'

'Goodness me!' Joao played the part. 'But isn't this Su – Bai-li was it? – Director of Internal Affairs here in Shanghai?'

'Yes. And one of the Generalissimo's closest friends and advisers.'

'If that's the case, Lieutenant Pan, I think what you know should be relayed to Chiang Kai-shek himself, rather than to a foreign journalist.'

'Normally, Doctor Serino, I would do precisely as you suggest. But, under the circumstances…' His voice trailed away.

'Under what circumstances?' Joao raised his eyebrows.

'I can't tell you here. It's too crowded and somebody might overhear us. Please can you meet me later? On the hotel terrace facing the gardens. At – say – five o'clock.'

Joao examined Yu-long's pleading, slightly desperate, face.

'I have to accompany the Generalissimo back to Nanking tomorrow morning. Now's the only time. Please,' he repeated.

Joao shrugged.

'If you insist, Lieutenant. But your story had better be good.'

'It is, Doctor Serino. It is.'

And with that the young lieutenant was gone. Was Joao going to surprise his editor with another scoop?

The thing about being a woman, Gerda reflected, was that men didn't take her seriously. As a result, they let slip all kinds of information that should have remained unspoken. In her presence, at least.

Take that tall, broad-chested officer of the German Reichswehr, Major Otto von Holst, for example, with his deep-set blue eyes and square jaw. Proud member of the emergent Nationalsozialistische Deutsche Arbeiterpartei, better known as the Nazi Party, and obviously eager to impress, the major told her quite openly what Chiang Kai-shek and the Government of Germany were doing their utmost to keep secret: modernising the National Revolutionary Army by buying arms with American money to fight the Japanese, and then transporting everything by train through the Soviet Union. Yet Germany and Japan were officially allies, while China, which had demanded back German concessions at Tsingtao and elsewhere in Shantung Province, was not.

It was, she decided, information that Bai-li might find useful.

She eventually found him sitting in the Conservatory with an older grey-haired man, with goatee beard, large ears and crescent-moon eyes.

'Miss Weidemeyer,' Bai-li exclaimed, as he stood up to greet her. Always do what Westerners did. 'May I introduce you to Doctor Tsuyoshi Inukai, former cabinet minister in the Yamamoto administration. And, I'm sure, soon to occupy the highest post in the government of Japan. Inukai sensei, this is Miss Gerda Weidemeyer, a close friend of Soong Ch'ing-ling.'

"I'm delighted to make the acquaintance of such a beautiful woman,' Inukai had also stood up. He took her hand and pressed it lightly to his lips.

'Thank you,' Gerda blushed slightly. Was there really such a thing as a Japanese gallant? 'But there are so many women here who are more beautiful than I.'

'But none with your magnificent head of hair,' Inukai only now let go of Gerda's hand. 'I have to admit, I've always been a fan of red hair. Do you know that Hollywood actress, Myrna Loy?'

'I'm afraid I don't.'

'Never mind,' Inukai continued in almost unstoppable mode. 'She's a redhead. But not like you. You, dear Ms Weidemeyer, are the epitome of what it means to have beautiful red hair.'

He stopped, seemingly surprised at himself.

'I'm sorry,' he said. 'I may be an old man, but I still appreciate beauty when I see it.'

'An admirable trait, if I might say so, sensei. Don't you think so, Gerda?'

'Indeed,' she smiled and made to sit down in the chair Inukai had courteously pulled out from the table for her. 'But tell me, how do you two gentlemen know each other?'

'Oh!' Inukai gave a gruff laugh. 'We go back some years now, don't we, Su-sensei?'

Bai-li inclined his head in acknowledgement.

'Su Bai-li visited the Generalissimo when he was staying with me in Japan,' Inukai explained.

'Really? I didn't know that, Doctor Su.'

'If you don't mind my saying so, Miss Weidemeyer, there are many things you don't know about me.'

'I'm sure there are,' she said, slightly embarrassed and made to stand up again. 'But I interrupted your *tête-à-tête*. I do apologise.'

'No, not at all,' Inukai placed one hand on her arm to detain her. 'Actually, we were discussing how Sino-Japanese relations might be improved. But that's probably a topic that doesn't interest you as a woman.'

'Why not, Inukai sensei?' Gerda tried out her Japanese. The crafty Old Fox looked pleased. 'Everyone's lives here depend on continued good relations between Japan and China. That should be enough to interest even a woman.'

'Yes, of course,' Inukai looked slightly flustered. 'I didn't mean to imply –'

'No, of course, not,' Gerda patted Inukai on the arm. Always soothe a pampered man.

'The trouble is, they're not very good right now. Relations between China and Japan, I mean.'

'True,' agreed Gerda. 'And that's what you were discussing? Did you come to any conclusions?'

There was a pause as Inukai looked at Bai-li and Bai-li at Inukai.

'We agreed, I think, that the Japanese Kwantung Army's threats and posturing have to be stopped. Somehow.'

'Otherwise, there'll never be peace between our two countries.'

'It sounds to me as if you need to threaten the army,' Gerda said brightly. 'Isn't that something your government can do, sensei? Or doesn't it want to?'

Inukai looked at her in surprise. A look that was tinged with respect. Not only was this woman beautiful. She seemed to have a brain in her deep auburn red head.

'You have touched upon the kernel of the problem,' interposed Bai-li.

'Yes, and in far less time than it's taken successive Japanese governments,' Inukai smiled. 'Perhaps, Miss Weidemeyer, we should ask you to be our Prime Minister.'

'Inukai sensei!' Gerda exclaimed mockingly. 'Has my so-called beauty gone completely to your head? When could a woman ever tell a man how to conduct affairs of state?'

'You're right, of course,' Inukai bowed, unable to learn. 'But still…'

'Of course, you – sensei – are a man of great political experience. You know far better than I how best to go about achieving the stated aims of your discussion with Doctor Su here. But…'

A strategic pause.

'But?'

'The best way to tame a tiger, surely, is to frighten it.'

Bai-li nodded. Women made such good agents. More astute than any man.

'The tiger being, in this case, the Kwantung Army?'

'Talking of armies, Doctor Su, I just overheard a young German army officer boasting that the Generalissimo has arranged for Germany to supply him with arms.'

'Really?' Bai-li looked as surprised as she'd intended him to be. Inukai was listening very carefully, as she'd expected him to. Letting a cat out of the proverbial bag had its satisfying moments.

'That's what he said,' she smiled slightly mischievously, then picked her purse up off the table and stood up. 'But I'm afraid I must be going. Mr Serino is waiting for me. It has been a pleasure to make the acquaintance of such a charming gentleman, Inukai sensei. I do hope we'll meet again soon.'

'Indeed,' Inukai had stood up and took her hand, pressing it once more to his lips as he gazed longingly into her eyes. 'I also look forward to that with great anticipation. And pleasure.'

With a swirl of her silk dress, Gerda turned and left. Making her way across the dance floor she was soon lost in the crowd. Except for her hair, of course.

'A remarkable woman,' exclaimed Inukai, sitting down. 'Where on earth did you come across her, Doctor Su?'

'As I said, she's a friend of Ch'ing-ling's. And I, as you know, was asked by Sun Yat-sen himself to look after his widow when he died,' he blinked behind his tortoise-shell glasses. 'Naturally, I get to meet many of her friends.'

'Of course.' Pondering something. As in a game of chess. He had that calculating look that had earned him the nickname of Old Fox.

'In addition to her physical charms, Miss Weidemeyer seems to have a fine mind, don't you think? For a woman, that is.'

Was he drawing out his queen? And so early on in the game. Never underestimate an opponent. Or a friend. Like Gerda, for instance. Why bring up that bit about Germans supplying the Generalissimo with armaments?

'Don't you agree, Doctor Su?'

'What? Oh, yes. Yes, indeed.' He pushed his queen diagonally forward through a gap left by one of his pawns. 'As you say, a very intelligent woman.'

'What she said about taming the tiger was, I thought, most astute.'

'Extremely perspicacious,' Bai-li agreed. How could he not? It was, after all, a Chinese saying. 'But how do you tame the Kwantung Army?'

'You don't.'

Where was Inukai leading him? Maybe this wasn't chess at all, but a game of *wei ch'i* – Inukai would know it as *go* – and he should be looking back over his shoulder, rather than forwards. Was he being encircled by the Japanese politician's black stones without his realising it?

'But you can shame them.'

'Shame them? How?' Playing the ignorant reinforced every Japanese prejudice about who or what the Chinese were.

'By publicising something the Army wants to do, perhaps, but doesn't dare say out loud?'

'Like declare war on China?' Sacrificing a pawn.

'Something along those lines, perhaps. Yes.'

'But who could possibly reveal a thing like that? Nobody would pay any attention if it came from the Chinese side.'

'True,' Inukai stroked his moustache and beard thoughtfully. 'Why don't you leave it with me, Doctor Su? I may be able to help in some way. The last thing we want right now is a war.'

'That's very kind of you, sensei,' Bai-li took a handkerchief from his trouser pocket and started polishing his glasses. Now for the *quid pro quo*, no doubt.

'I have a favour to ask, old friend.'

'A favour?' Bai-li's look was slightly unfocused.

'I'm an old man. But I'm still young here,' he paused and patted the crotch of his trousers under the table. 'Do you think…?' His voice trailed away.

He was being asked to sacrifice his queen? Let him sweat.

'Do I think what, Inukai sensei?'

'Do you think Miss Weidemeyer might be persuaded…?'

'Persuaded to do what?' A pause. 'To keep you company?'

'Something like that, yes.' Inukai was positively squirming with embarrassment.

'I don't know, sensei. Surely that's something you should ask her yourself?'

'Indeed, it is. But I don't want to make a fool of myself, you understand.'

'No, of course not,' Bai-li paused, put his glasses back on.

'It would just be for a very short while,' Inukai continued nervously. 'During my late afternoon nap.'

'Your afternoon nap?'

'Yes, I take one every day. For no more than half an hour, you understand. At my age, one tends to tire a little.'

'That I can well understand, sensei. I'm sure the time will come when I feel the same way,' Bai-li said soothingly, although it was hardly the way he was feeling. His queen would never allow herself to be sacrificed in this way.

He realised, though, that Inukai had indeed encircled him. Just like that. He should have seen it coming. Bai-li's only consolation was that in *wei ch'i* territory was never necessarily dead forever. He'd have to find a way to retake what he'd lost.

'If you'll excuse me, sensei, I'll see if I can find Miss Weidemeyer somewhere in this throng of guests and bring her to you.'

Inukai leaned back, beaming with satisfaction.

'Thank you, old friend. I'm indebted to you.'

Like a lot of his fellow countrymen when it came to dealing with the Chinese, he had perhaps underestimated Bai-li. After all, where was the danger?

'You want me to do what?' There was fire in Gerda's eyes. It went rather well with her hair. Not the kind of thought he should be thinking right now.

'I know. It's not something I should be asking of you again.'

'It certainly isn't.'

Bai-li pushed his glasses more firmly onto his nose. 'Still, things seem to be working out rather well between you and Serino-*san*.'

'Don't call him that!' Gerda snapped. 'The only reason I agreed to act as bait was because Joao isn't Japanese. Not properly, at least. You knew that. But now you ask me this.'

'It'll only be for a few minutes,' he tried to soothe his agent. 'He's an old man. He'll fall asleep immediately after you've done it.'

'Done what?'

'Done whatever's necessary to help us complete the task we all agreed to,' he gently reminded her.

'What task?' Playing hard to get.

Bai-li looked around to make sure there was nobody within earshot.

'The protocol,' he answered simply.

'Oh, that!' Disdainfully, as only a beautiful redhead knew how.

'Please,' he pleaded. 'Just this once. For the cause.'

'Which cause? Communism? Or Nationalism? I'm not Chinese, you know.'

'Of course not.' He kept his voice low, afraid that they were being overheard. But he had to admire the way she was able to deflect an argument. A sharp turn, just when you think you're going straight.

Gerda looked at Bai-li coldly. Did she have a choice?

'What did you say to him?'

'When he asked?'

'When he asked.' She now the tiger, ready to pounce.

'That he ask you himself,' Bai-li said truthfully.

'And?'

'He said he was afraid of being rejected.'

'So you agreed to face the fusillade instead.'

'Something like that.' He was, he agreed with her unspoken accusation, pathetic. 'You can just say no.'

'But you don't want me to. You want me to go along with his shabby ambition to make love to a white European whose eyes and hair are a different colour from his own.'

What could he say? She was right. Inukai clearly had a typical Japanese man's fascination with Caucasian women. Were their breasts really as large and soft as they seemed in Hollywood films? Were their vaginas in the same place? Did they make love in the same way? Did any woman make love in the same way? Or man, for that matter?

He was saved from finding a suitable reply, because the next moment she surprised him. Yet again.

'Where do I find this Inukai sensei?' Managing just the hint of a smile. 'Maybe I can give him a heart attack. That'd make one less Japanese to fight.'

There was always a choice.

The tables had been put in place and the guests invited to partake of 'tea.' Tea, though, it clearly wasn't – at least, not in the sense that the various English people present normally envisaged their 'tiffin.'

Along the whole of one wall of the ballroom, and another of the conservatory, white linen-covered tables had been arranged in a row and a seemingly infinite number of silver chafing dishes and platters of Western and Chinese food. Guests flocked forwards eagerly to help themselves to the buffet refreshments. Joao, however, had an appointment.

As did Gerda. As she crossed the hotel lobby towards the concertina-doored lift, keeping a discrete distance behind the man she had been charged with making love to, a Floor Manager came forward from his station behind the reception desk.

'Doctor Inukai?' He enquired politely.

Inukai looked at the smooth hotelier in surprise.

'Yes?'

'Doctor Inukai, I'm terribly sorry to bother you, but there has been a – an untoward occurrence with regard to your room.'

Inukai raised his eyebrows.

'An untoward occurrence? What on earth do you mean, young man?'

'I'm very sorry, sir, but there has been a plumbing malfunction in the room originally assigned to you. As a result, we have been obliged to move your belongings to a new room.'

Gerda discretely sat herself down in one of the lobby's plush armchairs.

Better not to arouse attention. Especially if he were to die of the heart attack she fully intended to give him.

'I can assure you, Doctor Inukai, that your new room is exactly the same as the one you were first assigned,' the Floor Manager continued smoothly. 'In fact, it is directly below it – on the first floor, instead of the second. The only difference is that it has a balcony which – if I might presume to say so – offers a rather better panorama of the gardens to the rear of the hotel.'

Inukai didn't bother to object. He had other pressing matters to attend to – or have attended to.

'Right. Thank you,' he said gruffly. 'And the keys to my new room?'

'Right here, sir,' the manager held out a set of keys. 'Your belongings have all been moved and rearranged exactly as we found them, Doctor. Your room is on the first floor, along the corridor to the right once you get out of the lift. Number 155.'

'One five five. Thank you,' Inukai bowed politely and, without bothering to check if Gerda was behind him, moved towards the lift.

The cabin attendant asked him which floor he wished to go to.

'First,' he replied, as Gerda came rushing forward from the lobby.

'Wait, please!'

'Which floor, Madame?'

'First, please.'

Inukai said nothing, but when the lift reached the first floor, he bowed and indicated that his fellow passenger should alight first.

Nothing was said as the two of them walked, one behind the other, to Room 155. Making sure nobody else was in the corridor, Gerda paused while Inukai fumbled with the keys to his new room and opened the door. Again, with an unmistakable excitement in his crescent-moon eyes, he motioned to her to go in first.

The room was in fact two rooms, as befitted an important politician who was likely to become Prime Minister of Japan within a year or two. In the outer 'drawing room,' Inukai's suitcases had been placed in one corner by the window. In the other room, his yukata sleeping robe was laid tidily on a double bed, and, Gerda noticed through an open door, his washing things were properly arranged by the bathroom basin.

Suddenly, Inukai had his skinny arms around her and he was kissing her hair and neck feverishly.

Laughingly, she pushed him away.

'Come now, sensei! Aren't you going to get properly dressed for the occasion?'

'Undressed, you mean,' he grinned boyishly and began to take off his formal dinner suit. She helped him gently.

When he was in his underwear, she said.

'I'm going into the bathroom to prepare myself. Make sure you've taken everything off, sensei, by the time I return.'

She closed the bathroom door and carefully removed her dress, so that she was wearing only a deep red brassiere and underpants, together with matching garter belt and black silk stockings. These, she reflected ruefully, she had put on earlier that day in the expectation that it would be Joao who would enjoy the pleasure they afforded a man.

Inukai was sitting on the edge of the bed wearing a somewhat garish black and gold striped cotton yukata when she re-entered the room. She allowed him to savour the sight of her intoxicating body as she pulled back the fold of his sleeping robe and sat astride his knees.

Again he buried his head in her hair, as she gently took hold of his penis and started rubbing it up and down. She was impressed that a man of his age could get an erection so quickly, and hoped he wasn't like one of those rounded Japanese *daruma* dolls, falling over seven times, but getting up eight. She could do without that kind of persistence.

Slipping down onto her knees on the carpeted floor, she began to caress his penis with her tongue and mouth. The Old Fox gasped, then quickly groaned with pleasure. Before Gerda had time to take away her mouth, he had exploded inside it. She held the semen on her tongue while Inukai quivered and uttered tiny grunts. When she took her mouth away and stood up, he was smiling like a small child at Christmas.

'That was *wunderbar*, Miss Weidemeyer.' A bearded *maître d'*, perhaps, but no Valentino.

Unable to speak because of what was in her mouth, she half smiled, turned away, and headed for the bathroom again. There she spat out the semen, rinsed her mouth thoroughly and washed her face, before applying fresh lipstick to her mouth, powder to her cheeks, and mascara to her eyes. The smell of him still haunted her nostrils, however. She blew her nose loudly on a hand towel.

By the time she'd returned to the bedroom, Inukai was fast asleep, smiling like a contented tiger in his black and gold striped yukata. Somebody else would have to give him his heart attack.

Above his head, a camera had recorded everything that had taken place a few minutes earlier. Feeling suddenly hungry for real food, Gerda quietly let herself out of Inukai's suite and went downstairs to the hotel ballroom in search of her preferred lover.

It was five o'clock. Joao had failed to find Gerda anywhere in the crowded ballroom, and now he had an appointment with Pan Yu-long.

The young lieutenant was already waiting when Joao found his way out onto the terrace. It was cold and he wished he'd brought a coat. Yu-long, also without a coat, was pacing nervously back and forth across the large slabs of stone laid between the Majestic's rear wall and an ornate balustrade separating the terrace from a well-tended flower bed and the gardens beyond.

'Serino-*san*,' he exclaimed with obvious relief. 'I was afraid you wouldn't come.'

'One thing you should learn about newspaper journalists, Lieutenant Pan, is that when they make a promise, they keep it,' Joao admonished him. 'Now, what's this story you were on about earlier?'

'It's about Su Bai-li,' Yu-long began.

Joao sat down on a convenient bench and indicated to the lieutenant that he should join him there.

'So you said earlier. What about him?'

'I have reason to believe he's a communist agent.'

'Believe?' Joao looked at him sharply. 'And on what do you base your belief?'

Yu-long embarked on a long, disjointed story about being sent to Moscow with his father, Colonel Pan Yu-tang, in order to meet Ching-kuo, the son of Chiang Kai-shek. They had been ordered by the Generalissimo to bring back a letter from Ching-kuo to his father.

'So? What's the problem?' Joao was genuinely confused. A nice story – suitable for a gossip column, perhaps – but nothing that implicated Su Bai-li in any way.

But then Yu-long related how he and his father had been stopped at the border and searched by a customs official. Ching-kuo's letter had been found – secreted, of all places, in some newspaper placed in his shoes – and Yu-long's father arrested and, he later understood, sentenced to seven years of hard labour in a Soviet gulag.

Maybe not something for a gossip column, after all. Or any column in the Asahi. There was nothing to interest a Japanese reader.

'This is clearly a tragic story for you personally, Lieutenant Pan,' Joao said sympathetically, 'But I fail to see what it has to do with Su Bai-li.'

'But don't you understand?' Yu-long said, exasperation in his voice. 'It was Doctor Su who sent my father and me to Moscow.'

'But you said it was Chiang Kai-shek himself who called your father in.'

'Yes, but it was Su Bai-li's idea.'

'It was? How do you know?'

Yu-long sat silent.

'Where's your evidence, Lieutenant Pan? I can't just publish suspicion and gossip, you know. I don't work for that kind of newspaper.'

'No, of course not,' Yu-long bowed his apology. 'It was after my father was arrested that Su revealed himself.'

'In what way "revealed," Lieutenant?'

At which point, Yu-long embarked on a second long story that ended up with his lengthy interrogation by Su Bai-li upon his return to Nanking.

'Interrogation?' Joao's ears pricked. 'Were you subjected to any kind of violence? Torture, even?'

Yu-long shuddered.

'No. Nothing like that. Doctor Su just asked me an endless series of questions.'

'As in an interview, then?'

'Well yes, but…'

'How long did these questions go on for, Lieutenant?'

'I don't know. An hour, maybe.'

'An hour?' Joao wasn't impressed. 'That doesn't sound like an interrogation to me. Interrogations go on for several hours – days, even – not a single hour. Wasn't Su Bai-li merely trying to elicit as much information from you as he could, so that he could establish what had happened and take the necessary steps to try and rescue your father from a Soviet gulag? Doesn't that seem like a more plausible explanation, Lieutenant Pan?'

Yu-long nodded.

'Except that he threatened me at the end.'

'Threatened you? How?'

'He said that I had to keep my mouth shut about what had happened. Or else he wouldn't be able to help my father.'

'He said that? In so many words?'

'Not exactly. But he did say that it would only take one word from him to the Soviet customs official in Zabaykalsk to ensure that my father remained in prison,' Yu-long's eyes began to water with tears. A truly filial son. If only Joao felt the same way about his father in Portugal.

'He also said that the real enemy wasn't the communists, but the Japanese, and that I was to spy on the Generalissimo. I was to be Doctor Su's eyes and ears, as he put it,'

'Spy on Chiang Kai-shek? But why?'

'To ensure that Doctor Su knew exactly what the Generalissimo's plans were.'

'With regard to the communists?'

'Yes. And the Japanese, as well.'

'But, surely, that's fair enough? Su Bai-li, as you said, is Director of Internal Affairs. He needs to know such things in order to be able to carry out his duties.'

'Yes, but…'

Another unfinished sentence. So much left unsaid. Joao sat back and mulled over all the young lieutenant had told him. There was a story there alright, but all of Yu-long's suspicions were unfounded. It would be one man's word against another's.

'Look!' he said eventually. 'I'm going to have to do a bit of background work on what you've told me if I'm to write it up as something my newspaper can publish, although I'm not convinced my Japanese readers would be interested. Are there people you can recommend I talk to? Friends of your father's, perhaps?'

'There's the Western Hills group here in Shanghai. My father was a member of the group. I'm sure his colleagues can tell you something.'

'Good. Write down some names for me in this notebook.'

After Yu-long had done so, Joao stood up. 'That's a start, at least. But now, I really have to be getting back to the festivities. My partner must be wondering where I am.'

'Thank you. Thank you so much, Serino-*san*. I knew I could rely on you for help.'

'I haven't helped yet, Lieutenant Pan. But I'll see what I can do. I can get in touch with you in Nanking, I presume?'

'Yes, sir. At the Generalissimo's headquarters. This is the telephone number.'

He handed Joao a printed card which Joao slipped into the pocket of his dinner jacket.

'Thank you. I'll be in touch. Give me a week,' he said and went back inside the hotel building.

Inside, the Russian orchestra had struck up and the ballroom dance floor was filled with couples doing their utmost to avoid bumping into one another as they performed a sprightly fox trot.

'There you are,' Gerda greeted him as he entered the ballroom, 'I was wondering where you'd got to.'

'Well, here I am.' Joao kissed her on the cheek. 'I was looking for you earlier. Have you eaten yet?'

'Not really.'

'Then why don't we get something from the buffet over there and find somewhere to sit down?'

She took his arm as they made their way round the edge of the dance floor. Joao noticed that she'd refreshed her makeup in his absence. Also that she looked a little pale. Not surprising, given the throng of guests. It had been a long afternoon.

'Are you feeling alright?' he asked solicitously, squeezing her hand.

'Me? Yes, of course,' Gerda looked surprised. 'Why do you ask?'

'I don't know. You just look a little – off-peak somehow.'

'Off-peak? That's an interesting phrase, Joao. Have you been climbing mountains in your absence?' She shrugged off his enquiry with a slightly discordant laugh.

A few minutes later, each with a plate of food, they came upon Bai-li sitting alone at a small table behind a clump of bamboo in one corner of the conservatory.

'Bai-li,' Joao exclaimed, 'Do you mind if we join you?'

'No, not at all,' the other replied, rising to his feet in greeting. He quickly pulled out a chair for Gerda.

'Please,' he said.

She thanked him and sat down, but not before giving him a quick nod to indicate that the deed he'd asked of her had been duly performed.

Just as she was taking her first mouthful of shrimp dumpling, she felt a hand on each shoulder and heard her sister's voice.

'So where have you two been hiding?'

'Isa! I could ask the same of you.'

'We've been dancing,' Isa laughed gaily. 'Or at least, in Shao-kuo's case, trying to dance.'

'Not my forte, I'm afraid,' Shao-kuo smiled modestly. 'I clearly need more practice.'

'Don't we all!' Bai-li remarked. 'Ch'ing-ling asked me to dance the other evening. I did my best, but, like you Shao-kuo, I find it hard to tell the difference between a foxtrot and a quickstep.'

'You did alright, though,' Ch'ing-ling laughed as she arrived at his side, Ken Inukai behind her.

'But tell me, Gē-gē – you who are a master of all mystery – how on earth are we going to fit seven people round a table made for two – at most, three?'

'I'm sure our friend Valentin will be able to help us. Valentin!' Bai-li beckoned to the *maitre d'* who happened to be passing.

'Doctor Su!' he exclaimed unctuously. 'What a pleasure to have you as our guest again, sir. And you, too, Madame Sun. Oh, and Doctor Sereño and your quite *charming* fiancée. If I may be allowed to say so, what a *splendid* gathering!'

'I feel certain, Valentin, that you are the best judge of splendour on occasions such as this,' Joao took over. 'I think, Valentin, that this particular gathering is in desperate need of a table and some chairs, if it is to remain gathered. I realise you're incredibly busy, but do you think you could possibly arrange for my friends here to be seated? Although I wouldn't know from experience, I understand that high heels are not the most comfortable form of footwear to stand in.'

'But of *course*, Doctor Sereño. Everything will be arranged at once, if not *sooner*.'

Valentin flicked his fingers in commanding fashion and, miraculously, given the hubbub of guests around them, not one but two waiters appeared.

After they had hurried off to fulfil the *maitre d's* command, Ken spoke up.

'Monsieur Valentin, would you be kind enough to bring us some champagne?'

'But of *course*, sir. Is there any *particular* vintage you would like me to bring?'

'How about the Pommery 1921? Do you happen to have it?'

'But of *course*, sir. Your wish, as they say, is my *command*.'

And with that, he sped away in a flurry of coat tails and powerful cologne.

Two waiters reappeared carrying a table, which they set down and covered with a cloth. Two more arrived carrying four chairs, and everyone sat down.

Gerda opened the conversation with a slight toss of her hair

'Ch'ing-ling, tell me. How do you happen to know Inukai-*san* – sorry, Ken?'

'That's the second time I've been asked that question this afternoon,' she smiled demurely, looking at Joao. 'It's simple, really. Ken's father once sheltered my husband in his home in Tokyo when the Doctor had to flee China. We weren't married then, so I only knew of Ken from Doctor Sun – until this afternoon, that is.'

'Yes, I was still in my second year at high school then.'

'What? In 1913?' Joao asked. 'Me, too.'

'You mean, you're the same age as I am, Joao?' Ken asked excitedly. 'Then we're classmates.'

'Really?' Talk about luck. It wasn't every day he made a connection like this with such a well-placed politician's son.

'This calls for celebration.' Ken turned to address the waiter who was doing his best to make a single bottle of champagne adequately fill seven flutes. 'How about another bottle of Pommery? Room 2 – no, 155.'

'Very good, sir,' the waiter bowed and departed.

Irene was looking confused.

'Excuse my asking,' she said, looking first at Ken and then at Joao. 'But why is being of the same age so important to you both?'

'Because it means we went through the same educational curriculum together,' Ken explained.

'From start to finish,' added Joao, with a friendly glance at his new 'classmate.'

'But you didn't go to the same school, did you?'

'No,' Ken smiled. 'But that doesn't matter. Being *dōkyūsei*, same grade students, is what counts.'

'It's often the same here in China, Isa,' Bai-li put in.

'I believe it's connected to age associations formed by young people in traditional times.'

'That's right,' Ken affirmed eagerly. 'Those initiated in the same year shared everything and felt great attachment and mutual responsibility towards one another.'

'So you'd better watch out, Ken. No misbehaving while I'm around!'

Once their laughter had subsided, Ken continued.

'Seriously, though. I already feel as if Joao and I share a lot in common.'

'How's that?' Asked Shao-kuo politely.

'Well, I've already read a lot Joao's written for the Asahi over the past few years. So I know his interests and how he thinks and analyses what he wants to report. I like what he writes and I find myself sharing his outlook. It makes me feel as if I already know him quite well.'

'Even though you don't?' It was Irene's turn to intercede.

'True. But still, I'd be surprised if he turned out to be all that different in real life.'

'And, for my part, I'd be surprised if I didn't like Ken,' Joao put in. 'True, I don't know him at all, apart from what I've read in the papers about his political activities. Other than that, I don't know his likes and dislikes. I've never read anything he's written – if he has written anything, that is –' a playful smile, 'but I'm ready to bet that, once we do get to know each other, we will, as Ken says, find that we share a lot in common. After all, we're both born in the Year of the Monkey.'

'Which means we're both curious and smart.'

'Which is why we tend not to stick to anything for any length of time. We get bored, don't we, Ken?'

'We certainly do,' Ken laughed. 'We're always playing by our own rules, too. And yet I like to think we have a humanitarian view of life. Nowadays, that means a determination to get Japan back on track. Away from all this pseudo-patriotic ultranationalism.'

'Cheers to that!' Joao raised his glass. 'To peace!'

'Peace!' Went up a chorus of voices, as everyone downed the rest of the champagne in their glasses. The waiter refilled them from the new bottle he had just opened.

'And to friendship between China and Japan!' Ken added. 'It's people like Joao who'll make that possible.'

'I'm not sure about that.'

'I am. You're a journalist, Joao. What you write influences hundreds of thousands – millions – of people in Japan.'

'Maybe, but there are many more millions who read right-wing newspapers and think – no, believe – Japan should take over Manchuria.'

Ken looked at Joao sharply.

'So there's a difference?' he asked quietly.

'Between thought and belief? Of course there is,' Joao retorted. 'People are always saying they "think" this, or "think" that, but what they "think" isn't thought at all. At least, not in the sense of rational analysis. It's belief.

And we know what happens when belief rules rationality's roost.'

'War?'

'War, uprisings, protests, populism, revolution – they're all based on opposing sets of beliefs, surely. All you have to do is look at what's been happening here in China. Landlords versus peasants. Capitalists versus workers. Communists versus Nationalists. Even the Nationalists are divided by different ideologies. And all arguing with one another according to whatever belief they've decided to adopt.'

'And all convinced that they're right and the others are wrong.'

'But surely,' Ch'ing-ling interceded, 'Not everything is based on belief? Marx and Lenin articulated an extremely rational argument in favour of something they called communism.'

'They did indeed,' Joao agreed. 'But, with respect, Ch'ing-ling, their followers make use of the arguments that suit them at the time, when putting forward their ideas. They'll claim that "Marx said this" or "Lenin that," to justify their position in an argument, but they ignore everything else these men wrote that doesn't fit in with that position. In this respect, thought, when it occurs, is at best partial.'

'And therefore biased.'

'And therefore biased, yes.' He paused for a moment. 'But that's enough. We're supposed to be celebrating a marriage, not engaging in serious discussion.'

Joao turned to Gerda, as the orchestra embarked upon *Yes Sir, That's My Baby*. 'May I have the pleasure of this dance, Miss Weidemeyer?' He asked formally.

Gerda laughed and took his proffered hand as she stood up from the table.

'Ladies, Gentlemen, if you'll excuse us for a few minutes,' Joao bowed and led Gerda to the ballroom floor. The Charleston was a recent craze that had Shanghailanders in a flap. As a result, the floor was almost too full for Gerda and Joao to be able to dance in peace.

Tea for Two allowed them more space as, worn out by their exertions in the previous dance, a lot of couples left the floor in flurries of loud laughter.

'I had an interesting conversation earlier,' Joao said, as he turned his partner in a neat pirouette.

'You did? With whom? Anyone I know?'

'I don't think so. A young lieutenant who's the Generalissimo's *aide de camp*.'

'Really? And what did he want with a Japanese newspaper journalist?'

'A good question, really,' Joao manoeuvred Gerda expertly between two couples on a collision course on the dance floor. 'He had a tale to tell about his father and Bai-li.'

'Really? And?'

Joao gave her a truncated version of Pan Yu-long's story. As the orchestra finished playing and those on the dance floor clapped their appreciation, Gerda asked.

'So what do you intend to do, Joao?'

'Frankly, I haven't had time to think about it. It was all a bit cloak and dagger stuff. Not really my kind of newspaper reporting.'

'No, probably not,' Gerda mused and took his arm as they left the dance floor. 'Are you going to tell Bai-li?'

'I don't know. Maybe I should. What do you think?'

'What do I think? Well, you're the newspaper journalist. You're going to have to ask him his side of the story at some point, aren't you? If you're going to follow it up, that is.'

'True.'

They were interrupted by Valentin, the *maître d'*, who came up to them with his customary flurry of coat tails.

'Miss *Weidemeyer*,' he said. There was urgency in his voice, but he still had time to stress his words. 'I've been asked to tell you that there is a *fire* on North Soochow Road, somewhere close to the *Zeitgeist* bookstore. I have been told to *advise* you, therefore, to proceed with all due haste to the scene of the *adversity*.'

'A fire? Oh, my God!' Gerda looked suitably horrified. 'I must find Isa.'

'Your sister has already been advised of the *circumstances*,' Valentin put in, 'And left the hotel ballroom a few minutes ago. She *desired* that you meet her on your premises as soon as *conveniently* possible.'

'Of course. Thank you, Valentin.'

'My *pleasure*, Miss Weidemeyer,' he said, perhaps a little inappropriately, before retreating in haste towards the doors to the kitchen.

'This is terrible. I'll come with you,' Joao said.

'No, Joao. I'm sure Isa will have contacted Rewi and the others for help.' Gerda seemed quite unperturbed. 'You stay here and talk to Bai-li. And, if you have the time,' she leaned close to whisper in his ear, 'You might want to take a room upstairs. I've a feeling we might need it before the night is out.'

And with that she was gone. As he made his way back to the table where he'd been sitting with Bai-li and the others, he felt a tap on his shoulder.

'Hey, Sereño!' It was Hans Shippe. 'Heard the news?'

'About the fire on North Soochow Road? Yes I have, thank you, Hans. Gerda's just left to make sure everything's OK at the Zeitgeist.'

'Oh, *that!*' exclaimed Hans dismissively. 'That's nothing, I can assure you. Some Chinese granny upset her cooking stove. That's all. And it was nowhere near the Zeitgeist. The fire's already been put out.'

Joao heaved a sigh of relief.

'No,' Hans continued, 'What I meant was, the news about a Japanese bank manager committing suicide. Not the sort of thing my paper's interested in, but yours might be.'

'Suicide?'

'Yeah! The real McCoy. According to the grapevine, at least. Harakiri ritual disembowelment.'

'Good God! Any idea which bank? Not the Takahashi, by any chance?'

'That's the one. A guy called Sakamoto. He was the branch manager there, apparently. Although why he should have wanted to kill himself is anyone's guess.'

Joao reckoned that his editor, Mori, would probably be able to make an informed guess once he heard the news.

'Thanks, Hans. I owe you one.'

'My pleasure. Great party, eh! I should have come here earlier.'

And with that he was off, bottle of beer in hand, in search of who knew what alcoholic inducements and feminine delights.

In the meantime, Joao knew he'd better go and check a gory corpse. Not the kind of business that was his pleasure. Hopefully, that would come later with Gerda.

'What is it, Mei-mei?'

Ch'ing-ling had told him in a low voice that she wanted to talk to him in private. The only quiet place he could think of was the hotel's back terrace. When he arrived, she was already there, wearing her Siberian sable, seemingly ready to go home.

'Had enough?' he asked earnestly.

She looked at him carefully in the light that came through the glass doors leading onto the terrace. As if she wanted to memorise his face, his bushy eyebrows arching over her late husband's glasses, his cherubic look and dimpled smile.

'Yes, quite enough, Gē-gē,' she said in her small quiet voice. Even out in the comparative silence of the terrace with the hotel gardens beyond, he had to lean forward to make sure he could hear her. 'I find an event like this quite tiring, to be frank. Too many people. Too many inane conversations.'

Bai-li glanced around him before putting an arm around her shoulder and drawing her to him.

'You're getting old, Mei-mei,' he chuckled, thinking more about himself.

'It happens when you're a widow.' She leaned into him. Warm. Comforting. The only one she could really trust. Except for Ei-ling. And, perhaps, Mei-ling. But they were family. 'There's something I need to tell you.'

Not more secrets. Please. He'd had enough surprises for one day. Joao had just told him about Pan Yu-long – a problem he'd had to deal with at once.

'I'm going to Moscow.'

'Moscow?' The word escaped his lips involuntarily. Of course she was going to Moscow. She had no choice right now.

But what a time to go. Trotsky, Zinoviev and Kamenev has just been ousted from the party at the Communist Party Congress. Stalin was in total control.

'When?' He asked.

'The day after tomorrow.'

'So soon?'

'And yet not soon enough.' She savoured the very slight smell of his body through his shirt. He hadn't put on an overcoat to come outside, so she wrapped her coat around him as best she could.

'I'm so tired, Gē-gē. Tired of being watched. Tired of this so-called wedding reception, where nobody cares a damn about my sister and her new husband.'

'Tired of being watched, Mei-mei? But everyone's watching everyone else here. That's what parties like this are for.'

'No. I meant at home.'

'Rue Molière?'

'They're always outside. Two men at a time. Watching my every move. Chiang may be my brother-in-law now, but he's also my jailer. He's just looking for an excuse to get rid of me.'

'As he is of every other communist sympathiser in the country. It's not just you, Mei-mei.'

'Maybe not, but I might as well help him out by leaving the country. After all, he's family now.'

Bai-li had known it was coming, this decision of Ch'ing-ling's to go into voluntary exile. But so soon? There again, maybe it was a smart move. By waiting until after her younger sister had got married, Ch'ing-ling was showing the Generalissimo that she was a responsible member of his newly-acquired family. She wouldn't embarrass him publicly, but allow him to get on with the most important task ahead: the unification of China.

'Why so soon?'

'Why not?' Detached. Objective. But clever. People would understand very quickly why she hadn't left earlier, after the chaos of July. She had had to wait until this family matter was dealt with before she slipped away. People would realise this and they would approve. Madame Sun would rise even higher in their estimation.

'How long will you stay?'

'In Moscow?' A shrug, as if it were of no importance. 'A month or two, perhaps. Until Uncle Joe throws me out,' she managed a smile.

'He'd never do that.'

'He'll do anything to get Chiang on his side.'

'And then?'

'And then? Berlin, I think. Gerda's arranging for friends to find me a place to stay there.'

'Gerda?' Again the involuntary repetition of a word. 'Yes, of course. Gerda. What are your plans?'

'My plans? How can anyone in my position have plans, Gē-gē? Oh!' Suddenly a little frightened at the unknown. 'I wish you could come with me.'

He held her tightly under the warmth of her fur coat.

'Me, too. But not yet, Mei-mei. Soon, though. I promise.'

'Yes. It's always "soon," isn't it?' Not reproachful. Just a statement of fact. 'It's the times we live in.'

A pause for shared reflection. Like the two plane trees on the surface of the pond with its quietly splashing fountain.

'I'm going to miss you, Gē-gē.' Soft now. Her voice bewitching.

'And I you,' was all he could think of saying. Truth tended to be banal.

'Will you come to me tonight? When this –' she waved one hand in the direction of the hotel wall looming up in the dark beside them, 'When all this is over and done with?'

'Of course, I will,' he kissed the top of her head affectionately. 'Is there anything you'd like me to bring for your journey?'

'Just yourself, Gē-gē. Just yourself. I want to lock you in my memory.'

And you yourself, he thought, shall keep the key of it.

An hour or so later, Lieutenant Pan Yu-long was making his way erratically back to his hotel on the corner of Ningpo and Szechuen Roads, just south of the Soochow Creek. He was more than a little drunk. It had been a stressful afternoon and evening, but at least he'd got his story off his chest and told everything to that Japanese journalist. Now all he could do was wait and hope that Serino-*san* would follow up on the facts he'd told him and unmask Su Bai-li.

'What's a handsome gentleman like yourself doing all alone, sir, at this time of night?'

What indeed? Yu-long raised his eyes from the ground and saw standing before him the slight figure of a young woman, austerely dressed from head to toe in black under a hooded coat made from what looked like reindeer skin. Her lips formed a Cupid's bow and her eyes seemed green. A small amount of hair peeking out from under her hat and hood looked red, but that was probably an effect of a distant streetlamp.

Unless.

He veered to one side of the cobble stones to avoid her, but she was quicker. Taking his arm, she turned him smartly left towards the Soochow Creek and nuzzled her head into his neck.

'Why don't you accompany me to my room?' she coaxed soothingly. 'It's warm and comfortable inside. And I know how to make young lieutenants like yourself warm and comfortable,' she continued, before adding for effect, 'Inside me.'

Yu-long could scarcely believe what he'd heard. In his befuddled mind he realised, of course, that this beautiful woman just had to be a prostitute. But he'd never in his life come across one so beautiful, even though he had a feeling he'd seen her somewhere before. She was Pai Mu-tan personified. A temptress of the night.

As he allowed her to lean against him, with one arm thrown around his shoulders, he felt a sudden prick of pain in his neck. His head almost immediately grew dizzy and he lost his balance, as the woman, who wasn't very tall, showed surprising strength in keeping him upright for a few moments, until the poison worked its deadly miracle.

'Just a quick one, sir,' she said soothingly, as he began to lose consciousness. 'You probably won't remember a thing.'

As Yu-long slumped to the ground, he remembered where he'd seen her before. In the arms of Joao Serino on the dance floor of the Majestic Hotel's ballroom.

'Miss Weide –' He exclaimed before losing consciousness.

Meanwhile, two pairs of hands took over and went through the pockets of his uniform, removing his wallet and other forms of identification. Then they took off the uniform itself and handed it to the woman in black, who turned and walked away into the night. There was a man she would beguile.

Her two accomplices lifted Yu-long's dead body and carried it as far as the creek. There they stepped across one sampan after another until they came to a patch of clear water, infested by water rats and flowing with thousands of gallons of 'night soil' from the city's less than salubrious open latrines. Into this they heaved Yu-long's body with an unceremonious splash. The fatal screech-owl's cry.

It had been, as the now lifeless lieutenant had reflected several hours earlier, a truly shitty day.

In a room on the second floor of the Majestic Hotel, above those occupied by Inukai father and son, Gerda allowed the man who was with her to take off her clothes. Not for the first time that evening, she stood in her deep red lingerie while her companion surveyed her firm, petite and curvaceous body in all its ravishing beauty.

'Gerda!' Standing by the bed, Joao leaned back to admire her, still with his arms around her waist.

'Joao!' She smiled her most seductive smile, and the passion in her eyes matched the angry fire she'd felt earlier. The dragon inside her spread its cupid's wings.

Before they knew quite where they were, the two of them were entwined in each other, exploring secret places as they fell together as one onto the large double bed. They did what was expected of lovers, as they sought out private parts with hands and mouths, arched their bodies, groaned and gasped with the ecstasy of physical pleasure. Gerda, in particular, was almost savage in her inflamed desire and Joao could only delight in her wild abandon.

Afterwards, they lay exhausted in each other's arms, murmuring the kind of words only those who are newly acquainted as lovers know how to murmur. Then, soothed by the sweet nothings of intimacy, they fell asleep – only to wake up a few hours later and rouse their bodies once more to passion. Orgasms achieved, they slept again until first light, when the song of birds in the gardens outside their window roused them to passion once again.

Gerda was in the bathroom. Joao had just got dressed, feeling a little silly to be wearing his morning suit from the day before. But at least, it was now morning. As he stood by a three-mirrored dressing table putting his jade cufflinks into the sleeves of his starched white shirt, he noticed out of the corner of his left eye a brown envelope under the door.

Casually, he crossed the bedroom, bent down and picked it up. It wasn't addressed to anyone; simply to 'Room 255.'

Joao turned the envelope over twice, as Gerda emerged from the bathroom looking radiant in a simple black tunic, set off by amethyst earrings and, of course, her glorious head of auburn hair.

'What's that?' she asked, as she moved her reindeer-skin overcoat from the dressing table chair, sat down and began combing her hair.

'An envelope. I found it under the door.'

'Who's it for?'

'I don't know. It doesn't say. It just has the room number on it.'

'Are you sure it's our room number?'

'Room 255,' he opened the door and looked at the polished brass numbers on its other side. 'Yes, 255.'

'Then why not open the envelope?'

Joao found a letter opener in the drawer of the bureau, thoughtfully provided by the Majestic Hotel's management, and slit open the envelope in his hand.

Inside was a single black and white photograph of an elderly Japanese man wearing a yukata and lying on his back, his bearded mouth slack and open in ecstasy as a woman performed fellatio on him.

It was only when he'd recovered from his surprise at the contents of the photograph that, with a stab of despair's keen dagger in his heart, Joao realised who the woman was.

Joao was angry. He was hurt. He felt ashamed. A green and yellow melancholy brooded on his soul.

He went straight home from the hotel and changed into everyday wear – white shirt, dark blue tie, an English flannel suit and black worsted wool overcoat with black leather gloves. They suited his funereal mood.

Then he made his way to the Asahi Newspaper office in the Foreign Correspondents Club building and wrote up a report for his editor-in-chief about the Takahashi Bank branch manager's suicide. There wasn't much to tell Mori other than that Sakamoto had cut open his stomach with a *wakizashi* short sword in the best samurai tradition and made quite a mess of one room in his house on Elgin Road, out near the northern boundary of the international settlement. It must have been an agonizing death. He'd had no second, no *kaishakunin* assistant, to cut off his head once he'd made the initial cut in his belly.

The Kempeitai, Japan's military police, had already put a lid on everything by the time he'd got there the night before. An unfortunate suicide, an officious officer told Joao. The result of an illicit love affair, perhaps. You'd have to ask his wife about that, though now, of course, was not the time. No, it had nothing to do with his work. Why should it have done? Sakamoto was a successful businessman, the branch manager of an illustrious Japanese bank. It was most unfortunate, but these things could happen. Especially in this day and age. But thank you for your concern. Case closed.

Of course, the case wasn't closed. The fact that it was the Kempeitai, and not Shanghai's municipal police force, that was in charge of whatever investigations might, or might not, be taking place made that clear, and piqued Joao's curiosity. Mori would advise him how best to proceed.

Once he'd wired his report to Tokyo, he walked to the Chocolate Shop on Bubbling Well Road, a Jewish café popular with American and European businesspeople because of its sandwiches and pastries. It was lunch time and the place was almost full. Joao ordered a cup of coffee and a chicken salad sandwich, and sat on a high stool by the counter.

He'd been played – played by Gerda, played by Bai-li, and, in a way, played by Tsuyoshi Inukai himself. After all, the Old Fox knew the two of them were – in a manner of speaking – together, and yet he'd persuaded Bai-li to ask Gerda to make love to him. Just to satisfy his craving for a white woman before he died. Or could no longer get an erection.

She'd told Joao everything, of course. In floods of what seemed like genuinely remorseful tears, she'd related in detail how Bai-li had asked her to get close to him. Not sleep with him. That she had done of her own accord because she'd grown to like Joao. A lot. But she was to get close to him, so that Bai-li would know if he was the right person to approach for the task he'd envisaged: to stop the Japanese from invading China.

As Joao distractedly ate his sandwich, he remembered that it was this that had persuaded him in the first place to fall in with Bai-li's plan to write up a fake protocol based on Gi'ichi Tanaka's Far Eastern Conference proceedings. Japanese with power – military power, economic power, soldiers, capitalists – had to be brought to account. He still believed this, whatever had happened to him personally.

A man's voice interrupted his reverie. A familiar voice that he wasn't sure he wanted to have to listen to right now.

He rose politely to greet the newcomer. 'I have a feeling this isn't a coincidence, Bai-li.'

'I think you can safely say that, Joao. There are a couple of things we need to iron out.'

'There are? Tell me about them,' he exclaimed huffily.

Bai-li ignored Joao's sarcasm.

'First, there's what you told me about Pan Yu-long implicating me as some kind of communist spy yesterday evening.'

Joao stared at Bai-li impassively. He didn't bother to reply.

'As a newspaper journalist, you will, in due course no doubt, be eager to hear my side of the story.'

'It might help.'

'Yes. It might. I'm not sure exactly what the young lieutenant relayed to you, Joao, but I can tell you what I know as Director of Internal Affairs here. In this respect, you might wish to know that I've just received word from one of my agents in Harbin that his father has been killed.'

'Not sent to a gulag, then?'

'It seems not.' Bai-li removed his glasses and searched in his pockets for a handkerchief with which to clean them. 'Somehow, he managed to escape from the cell where he was being held at the border.'

'Escape?' Joao looked incredulous. 'How on earth can a man escape from a Soviet prison?'

'I don't know, Joao. I really don't know.'

There was a sudden crash and clattering of breaking china, as a waitress dropped her tray. This was followed by a brief but total silence in the café, before the conversations around them began to pick up from where they'd left off. Red-faced with embarrassment, the waitress bent down to pick up the broken pieces of cups and saucers from the floor.

'You were saying?' Joao prompted.

'Yes, I was, wasn't I? About Pan Yu-tang. He seems to have made his way down to the Amur river and started to walk across the ice towards Manchuria. Two border guards who caught sight of him shouted to the colonel to stop. When he paid no attention, they had no choice but to shoot him. In the back.' Bai-li paused. 'At least, that's what I've been told.'

'A plausible story.'

'Plausible, yes.'

'Conveniently made up by a soviet spy?'

'That is a possibility. You'll have to make that judgement for yourself, however.'

'And for my newspaper.'

'Indeed. Also for your newspaper,' Bai-li had finally located his handkerchief – it clearly wasn't in its usual place – and was polishing one lens of his glasses.

'And then,' he said finally, 'There's that other matter I mentioned. I came here to find you as soon as I heard what occurred this morning.'

'From Gerda, presumably?' Joao was polite, distant, but still seething inside. 'I hope you enjoyed your little game.'

'It certainly wasn't a game. Of any kind. I can assure you of that. At least, not one involving you.' Bai-li sat down uninvited, and pointing to the remains of Joao's sandwich and coffee, indicated to the woman behind the counter that he'd like the same.

'It was, in fact, a clerical error. With the worst possible consequences,' he continued.

'Meaning?'

'Meaning that the envelope and its contents were intended for the Old Fox himself, not you. Or for that matter, Gerda.'

Joao raised his eyebrows enquiringly.

'You see, Tsuyoshi Inukai had a sudden room change, and had to be moved from the second floor down to the first. His old room was the one that you happened to end up occupying with Gerda last night. Unfortunately, the night-duty concierge wasn't informed of Inukai's room change, however, and ordered one of his underlings to deliver the envelope to Room 255, instead of 155. As we say in Chinese, humans can make mistakes, horses can stumble. I believe in Japanese, you like to talk about how even monkeys can fall out of trees. I rather like that metaphor.'

'It's not a metaphor. It's an idiom.' Joao wasn't going to accept Bai-li attempt to lighten the tone of their conversation.

'Ah yes, of course.' More polishing. 'An idiom.'

Curiosity got the better of Joao. He was, after all, a newspaper reporter.

'So, the envelope was intended for Inukai?' Joao pursed his lips. 'You mean, you're blackmailing him?'

'I prefer to think of it as a form of persuasion,' Bai-li said seriously. 'We need him on our side.'

'We? Isn't that being a bit presumptuous, Su Bai-li?' Joao was still angry when he thought of the previous night's lovemaking with Gerda. She had been played, too, by the man sitting beside him.

'Of course,' Bai-li responded soothingly, 'I quite understand if you prefer not to be involved in the proposal we worked on together the other day. I can see I've destroyed your trust.'

'Trust?' Joao almost exploded with fury. 'Aren't you being overly presumptuous, Bai-li? Who ever said I trusted you in the first place?'

'Ah!' was all he said.

What interested him, though, was what it was that made Joao so angry. Was it because he had been played? Or was it because his girlfriend had agreed to have perfunctory oral sex with an elderly Japanese politician? Either way, shame was a motivating factor. It was Joao's Japanese, not Portuguese, half that was reacting so vehemently.

'Joao, I'll be frank with you. I was astonished – no, shocked – when Inukai-so-called-sensei,' he chose to give the honorific appellation a sarcastic emphasis, 'Asked me if I might somehow be able to persuade Miss Weidemeyer to accompany him to his room for a short while during his late afternoon rest. He seemed to have some kind of fixation on making love to a woman who wasn't – isn't – Japanese.'

'You mean, he had some misplaced idea that the neighbour's lawn is green, while his wasn't.'

'Is that how you'd put it?' Bai-li finally put away his handkerchief and put his glasses back on his nose. Lunch hour was clearly over, for the café had suddenly emptied. 'We like to say that the other mountain looks higher. Or, as Koreans put it, other people's rice cakes look bigger.'

For the first time that morning Joao smiled.

'I like the one about the rice cakes. I hadn't heard it before.'

Bai-li adjusted his glasses with one hand, while holding his chicken salad sandwich with the other. He took a large bite and chewed.

'Inukai may be a respected politician,' Joao was in meditative mode now, 'But in the end he's like all of us. Just another predatory man when it comes to women.'

He stopped.

'No. Not man. Animal! A typical Japanese animal.'

Bai-li swallowed his mouthful and put his sandwich back on its plate.

'Why don't we have a second cup of coffee, Joao, and sit over at that empty table in the corner? We can talk more freely there.'

Joao acquiesced. A first step towards settling their quarrel.

Bai-li ordered two espressos and they sat themselves down in the corner of the café, well away from prying ears.

'Before we go any further, Joao, I want to reassure you of one thing.'

'What's that?'

'That Gerda's affection for you is not something I've somehow managed to arrange. I can accomplish many things, thanks to my position, but one thing I can never determine or influence is an agent's emotions. Indeed, anyone's emotions. As I understand it, Gerda is truly fond of you, so I hope you will forgive her.'

Joao looked down at the tabletop and said nothing.

'Also, in my position I'm not used to acting as a go-between, either. But on Gerda's behalf, I'd like to extend an invitation to you for dinner this evening. A reservation for two has been made at what I understand is an excellent Russian restaurant on Avenue Lafayette, the Baikal. Do you know it? Number 1240. Gerda has already agreed to be there. I hope you can bring yourself to join her. At 8pm.'

Bai-li stopped and watched Joao carefully. Had he chosen the right man to become his agent? Emotions tended to overcome rational thought. But would Joao accept that love was a decision, not an emotion?

There was a long pause, almost half a minute in length. Then,

'I think I'd like that,' Joao said.

Bravo Lao-Tzu. More power to the sage's elbow. And to Joao's.

'It will probably be a little difficult for you both at first,' Bai-li said reassuringly. 'But I'm sure you'll find a way to resume where you left off before the unfortunate arrival of that brown envelope.'

'Which you now have in your possession? What do you intend to do with it?'

'Make sure it's properly addressed and delivered to Tsuyoshi Inukai before his departure for Tokyo.'

'What do you think he'll do once he sees the photograph? Burn it?'

'Maybe,' Bai-li blinked from behind the glasses now firmly back on his nose. 'But that's not the point, is it? Inukai-sensei now knows we have something on him that could prove embarrassing if revealed to a Japanese audience. At the same time, the fact that I have in my possession the negative of that and other similar photographs should encourage the Old Fox to assist as necessary in our – or should I now say "my"? – plan to create the Tokyo Protocol and then secrete it in a ministry archive. He knows all the right people for such deception.'

He paused. Joao was listening intently. Another good sign.

'My concern –' he paused again.

'Yes?'

'My concern is you, Joao.'

'In what way?'

'Suppose – let us for the moment suppose – you agree to go along with the plan we discussed the other day. Suppose you then go to Tokyo. Suppose you're able to strengthen your burgeoning friendship with Ken Inukai and persuade him to take part in our endeavour.'

'That's a lot of suppositions, Bai-li.' He wasn't going to allow himself to be a pushover. Not again.

'True, but if they *were* to come to fruition, it would mean that you would almost certainly end up in the company of Ken Inukai's father as you pursue our goal. How would you feel about that, Joao?'

'Talking to the Old Fox, you mean?'

'Yes.' Expectant. Concerned.

Joao let Bai-li wait before answering. Eventually,

'I don't envisage a problem,' he said coolly.

'Might I ask why not?'

'Inukai sensei strikes me in some ways as being just another arrogant Japanese – the kind I've had to deal with all my life as an "impure" racial bastard, so to speak. I know how to manipulate him to do what I want, if I have to.'

Bai-li leaned back in his chair, sipped the last of his expresso and positively beamed his most charming of dimpled smiles.

'That's what I was hoping to hear,' he said, and Joao sensed the relief in his voice.

After that, however, Bai-li was all business.

'I want you to work for me, Joao.'

'What kind of work?'

The way he asked, Bai-li knew that his prey had now seriously made up his mind to do whatever he was asked. Provided they were in line with his humanitarian sentiments.

'Oh, this and that,' he said casually. 'Whatever you learn that upsets your sense of what is right and proper. It might be gossip you happen to overhear while nursing a beer in the Japanese Club in Hongkew. Or something you see while going about your daily tasks as a newspaper reporter.'

'Journalist, please.'

'My apologies. As a journalist. I'd be very grateful. Come to think of it, and with no disrespect whatsoever to your relationship with Gerda, it's a pity you're not married.'

'Married?' Joao laughed bitterly. 'You really are in the business of relationships, aren't you!'

'It's just that, in my experience, wives often provide such useful information. The way they're always chattering among themselves. Especially at the hairdresser's. And in the public bath, of course. There's nothing like a good hot soak to loosen tongues, is there?'

'I suppose not,' Joao admitted. 'Although I'd never thought of it like that.'

'No. Well, there was no need to, was there?' Then,

'Tell me, is there an *o-sento* public bath in Japan Town in Hongkew?'

'Alas, no. Not that I know of, at least.'

'I thought not. A pity. I remember well from the time I lived in Japan. It was only a brief stay, mind you. Not like your own immersion in Chinese society here in Shanghai,' he paused. A bit of flattery rarely went amiss.

'What were you doing in Tokyo, Bai-li? You never told me.'

'What was I doing? Filling in time, really, after university. I wanted to experience the Japanese first hand. After all, they were already in many ways our enemy. And what is it Sun Tzu says? To know your enemy, you must become your enemy. Something like that.'

'He also wrote, didn't he, that the opportunity of defeating the enemy is provided by the enemy himself?' Joao replied quickly.

'Yes, indeed. That had slipped my mind.'

Bai-li reflected briefly on how fortunate he was to have found this man. And it would never have been possible to recruit him without Gerda's help. Her beauty made it easy to overlook her intelligence and skill as an agent. The Old Fox had somehow grasped that. With him, even lust was the servant of the brain.

'Would you like some more coffee? Or have you had enough?'

Joao had had enough. The taste in his mouth was bitter, but now from the coffee, rather than from what had happened earlier that day.

'By the way,' Bai-li said, à propos of nothing, 'I talked to the Generalissimo about my plan. I needed to run it by him to make sure he was, so to speak, on board.'

'And?'

'He was rather keen on the protocol idea. Like us, he thinks it'll help overcome the rift between Nationalists and Communists as all Chinese unite behind him.'

'And, of course, he wants to be seen as China's undisputed leader.'

'Of course,' Bai-li nodded. 'But he also reckoned, like us, that publication of the protocol would embarrass the Kwantung Army, while – and this, he particularly liked – also alienating Japan's Western allies, in particular Britain and the USA, once they realise what Japan was up to.'

It was Joao's turn to nod.

'So where do we go from here?'

The fish was well and truly landed after all. Bai-li heaved a silent sigh of relief. It had been a difficult morning.

'First, I think you should make use of all your expertise, Joao, and write a draft of the protocol. You're extremely familiar with the political situation in East Asia. As a scholar, you can present details in an objective manner. Unlike the potential bias a Nationalist like me would display if I were to write it.'

'But I've no idea what a protocol presented to the Emperor of Japan normally looks like. Or how it should be written.'

'Maybe not, but that's where Inukai father and son should be able to help. You like Ken, right?'

'Yes. As a matter of fact I do,' Joao smiled. 'We had quite a long chat at one point yesterday evening and we seemed to be on the same wavelength when it came to Sino-Japanese relations. Ken's as worried as I am about what the Kwantung Army might get up to.'

'Then, Joao, I suggest you get closer to Ken. Persuade him to cooperate in producing a document detailing the discussions that took place, or might have taken place, at Tanaka's Far Eastern Conference during the summer. That shouldn't be too hard, should it?'

'I don't know,' Joao looked concerned. 'Remember, he's a pure-blooded Japanese man. Unlike me. He may regard it as a betrayal of his country.'

'Which, at first glance, it may seem to be.'

'Which, in the eyes of militarists, it certainly is.'

'But Ken isn't a militarist.'

'No. Obviously not. But he strikes me as a patriot.'

'Like yourself.'

'Like myself,' Joao acknowledged.

'Then, you must make him realise, Joao, that it's not a matter of betrayal. On the contrary, it's only people like you and him, not the ultranationalists, who can save Japan. That's your opening,' Bai-li said encouragingly. 'Go for it! After all, one can't catch a tiger's cub without entering the tiger's cave.'

'*Koketsu ni irazumba*… We've got that proverb in Japanese, too, Bai-li.'

'Well, there you are, then. Just make sure you manage to persuade the Old Fox to join your venture.'

'You mean, once I've entered the cave, make sure the tiger's on my side? I'm not sure tigers are that cooperative,'

'No, maybe not. But if your mind remains calm, you can think in the face of a tiger. And if you can think in the face of a tiger, you'll surely succeed.'

'I'll keep that in mind. But I'm not sure tigers like being presented with their own image in a photograph.'

'You'd be surprised, Joao. Even tigers are vain.'

'It must have something to do with their stripes.'

'Hopefully not the ones on his yukata.'

Both men laughed. The rift between them sealed in black and gold.

PART FIVE

Tokyo Run

It was a new year. All over the country people had given their homes a thorough spring clean. They'd soaked themselves in steaming hot baths to cleanse themselves of last year's dirt; drunk bottles of warm sake to purify themselves inside; listened to the boom of temple bells at midnight; and visited Shinto shrines, where they'd clapped their hands – not to frighten away the spirits, but to attract the attention of the deities floating invisibly in the world around them. Humanity had need of all the help it could get.

Ken was already sitting in one of the Imperial Hotel's famed peacock chairs. The table he had selected was on one of the indoor balconies above the hotel's main entrance and lobby, and overlooked the wooded landscape of Hibiya Park across the road. The last of the evening's light filtered through long vertical windows onto exposed grey and green volcanic stone, carved in traditional Mayan decorative patterns. An architectural masterpiece. According to the experts, at least.

'Quite a building, isn't it?' Joao said, coming up quietly behind him.

'Hello, Joao,' Ken rose and bowed slightly, before shaking hands with his guest. Still the cosmopolitan. A good sign. 'One of Frank Lloyd Wright's best, I believe.'

'It has to be, to have survived the Great Kanto Earthquake.'

Joao pulled out a second peacock chair and sat down, as Ken called over a waitress and ordered coffee.

'And on the day of its intended opening, too.'

'Was nothing destroyed?'

'There was some damage, but apparently nothing major structurally. A few bits of stonework fell to the ground, as did some of the ceiling fans on this balcony here. You weren't around then?'

'No. I was in Portugal at the time.'

'Portugal? Lucky you. Doing what?'

'Discovering my roots. Or my father, at least.'

'Ah, yes. Of course. You missed all the fun, then.'

'It seems so.' 'Fun' didn't seem like quite the best word to describe the death and destruction the earthquake had caused.

'What saved the hotel from damage? Was it Lloyd Wright's idea that the hotel should float on alluvial mud like – what was his expression? – a tray on a waiter's fingertips?'

'More like a battleship floating on water,' Ken laughed, as the waitress arrived with two cups of coffee, which she carefully placed before the two men. She bowed silently and took her leave.

'But what about your own home?' Joao asked.

'Miraculously, it survived. We live in an old Japanese-style wooden house in Mejiro. The earthquake did far less damage up on the hill where we were than down in Ikebukuro, Shinjuku and the rest of the flatlands.' The last word in English. 'Of course, several tiles came off the roof, and part of the wall round our compound buckled, but generally speaking we were lucky.'

'That's good to hear. The same could hardly be said of Japan as a whole, though.'

First move. *Fuseki*. The four-four star point on the grid. This time, Joao wasn't going to be played. He was the black-clothed *kuroko* – the master puppeteer hiding in plain sight on the *bunraku* stage.

'You can say that again. One hundred and thirty thousand killed. Over half a million buildings destroyed. A financial crisis that we haven't yet left behind. Everything's playing into the Army's hand.'

Black stone in the same position on the opposite corner of the board.

'Manchuria, you mean?'

Bottom corner of the board, underneath Ken's black. Learning which way the wind blew.

'Of course. Manchuria may not have rice, but it supplies us with all the soya beans we need. And, of course, all that iron and coal that can be used to supply the factories that make the armaments the Army needs.'

Filling in. *Joseki* standard sequence.

Ken stubbed his cigarette forcefully into the onyx ashtray beside him. It was only then that he thought to look around him to make sure they weren't being overheard. But it was still late afternoon. Most people were only just finishing work. In half an hour's time, perhaps, they'd need to be more careful. Tokkō police informers were everywhere – even in a swank hotel like the Imperial. Especially, perhaps, in the Imperial. Foreigners were always under observation.

Joao placed a white connecting stone two squares above Ken's.

'So everything's up to the cabinet.'

'Meaning?' Ken was alert. A black stone right next to his first.

'Meaning control has to be exerted by elected politicians in government, or the Army will seize power.'

Threatening a chain designed to surround.

'That's what Tanaka seems determined to do.'

Defensive wall.

'True. But isn't he a bit too close to the Army?'

'Too ready to agree to the Army's demands, you mean?'

'When it comes to Manchuria and the rest of China, yes.'

Joao had made his intention quite clear. Ken sipped the last of his coffee as he contemplated his own next move.

'True,' he nodded. 'We could do with a change of leadership. But, tell me Joao, what brings you to Tokyo?'

Sudden move to an empty corner of the board. *Tenuki*. Was the other position he was entering too dangerous?

'The bank crisis here back in April. It's had a knock-on effect in Shanghai, of course. The branch manager of the Takahashi Bank committed suicide.'

'What? Because of the Finance Minister's gaffe?'

'Seems unlikely. But there are a couple of leads I need to follow up. Shady politicians' deals. Or so rumour has it.'

'I hope my father's not involved.'

'Not so far as I know,' It was Joao's turn to laugh. 'Don't worry. I'll let you know if I find out anything interesting.'

Stones in place. An eye for an eye. Each of them safe for now.

'I have to say I admire you, though.'

'Why's that?'

'Living with your father, I mean. If my brief acquaintance with my own father is anything to go by, I'd guess it can't be easy.'

Ken laughed easily.

'It isn't. But luckily he's hardly home. What he refers to as his "official residence" is down in Toranomon near the Diet.'

'Conveniently close to the high-class bars and clubs in Akasaka?'

'Precisely.' Again the easy laugh. 'My two brothers have moved out, so it's just my mother and I most of the time. Doesn't worry me. I have my own space in an annexe and I don't have to cook.'

'Lucky you.'

'You're not married, either, are you Joao?'

'No. Not yet at least.'

'What about that rather attractive German girl you were with? Gerda, wasn't it?'

Joao gave a wry smile. Did Ken know about what his father had been up to the afternoon of the Generalissimo's wedding party?

'You know how it is in Japan, Ken. Nobody would accept her as my wife.'

'Not with that red hair, no,' Ken laughed. 'But, if you want to be together, why not stay right out of it? Live quietly in Shanghai and enjoy the cosmopolitanism. I know I would.'

'Would you?' An opening. 'But stop to think, Ken. We've already agreed Manchuria isn't safe from the Kwangtung Army. If that's the case, then China isn't safe either. And that means Shanghai would eventually be taken over by the Japanese. Probably sooner rather than later.'

'Why not Germany then.'

'Ken,' Joao wagged a finger reprovingly. 'Have you no idea what's going on there?'

'Hitler, you mean?'

'Yes, Hitler. A nasty piece of work. Power-crazed and, much more dangerous. A demagogue who seemingly can rouse people to do anything he wants. Unquestioningly. I don't think Gerda wants to be a part of that. I certainly don't.'

'That I can see. So where, then?'

'Where could we live together in peace? Assuming we actually want to be together. You tell me, Ken.'

'Hong Kong? Singapore?'

Falling into the trap.

'And who says the Navy hasn't got its eyes on those jewels of south east Asia?'

'The Philippines, then?' Ken now less sure of himself.

'The United States itself might be a safer bet. But Gerda's German and I'm half-Japanese. Neither of us is likely to be perceived as particularly "friendly" immigrants. Especially,' he added as a careful afterthought, 'when you hear the kind of rumours I've heard as a newspaperman.'

'Rumours? What rumours, Joao?'

A quick look round. There were people around them now, well-heeled Tokyo-ites taking cocktails at the Imperial before moving on, as only they knew how and where to move on. Nobody paying the two young men any attention, but better to lower one's voice.

'There are some young Army staff officers – not the senior ones, but mid-ranking – who are convinced that Japan can attack and defeat the United States.'

'What?' Ken genuinely shocked. 'I don't believe it.'

'Then get yourself out and about, Ken. Listen to drunken conversations among officers in the bars of Akasaka. Sooner or later you'll hear it. The same way I did in Harbin and Mukden. And in Japan Town in Hongkew. And that wasn't even Army types talking. To be honest, Ken, it frightens me, this – this arrogance. This certainty that Japan is somehow better than any other nation in the world.'

'Superior, you mean?' Ken was sitting very still.

Weighing up the stones on the board.

'Yes, superior. It's this feeling of superiority that frightens me when I'm in China. I don't know what it's like here. I've been away too long. But I hope there's some sense of measured balance among people who matter here.'

Time to see how things stood. *Yosu o mite*. A probe.

'Like you and your father, for instance.'

'Of course,' was all Ken said, as he signalled to the waitress to bring their bill. When she came with it, he merely signed his name. She bowed deferentially as the two guests stood up to leave.

'Just like Shanghai,' Joao laughed. 'Nobody carries any cash there.'

'Depends on who you are, doesn't it? Come on, Joao. I don't know about you, but I definitely need a drink.'

Bingo.

The latest fad in Shanghai. And all the rage.

Ken took him in a chauffeur-driven black Packard to the Press Club near Shinbashi Station. What traffic there was parted in front of them, and officious policemen whistled them through intersections on the short journey from the Imperial Hotel. Joao said nothing, merely enjoying the smooth ride, but he suspected they were being driven in Ken's father's official limousine. Friends in high places made a world of difference in downtown Tokyo.

The Press Club was located down a side street from the main road running through the lower part of the Ginza. A solid two-storey brick building occupying a whole block, it had been rebuilt following the earthquake. People were still working in the numerous well-lit offices downstairs, finishing reports and articles to be dispatched over the teleprinter for publication in the following day's newspapers around the world. Upstairs there was a library, an archive, and convivial bar, where both foreigners and Japanese who had done their day's work gathered to exchange gossip and pick up bits of information that a bottle or two of beer loosened from the tongues of those standing along the length of a well-polished oak counter top. A pleasant dining room was attached. There conversations could be conducted more privately.

Ken led the way towards the dining room, stopping to greet two or three red-faced men at the bar, exchange a few words, allow a back or two to be slapped, as Joao stood silently by.

'Sorry, Joao. I should've introduced you to some of those guys,' Ken apologised as they sat down at a window table overlooking the *izakaya* bars running back from the station underneath the railway tracks that lay overhead. 'But I was afraid we'd get hijacked into joining their booze-ups and I wanted you all to myself. You know how newspapermen are.'

He did. Most foreign newsmen he knew drank far too much. But you could hardly ignore the camaraderie, if you wanted to get things done. So Joao drank in moderation, careful to smile and laugh as required, playing the game. But always alert, ears and eyes wide open. Never drunk in charge of a glass.

The two of them had a quiet dinner together, undisturbed by the rowdy rabble in the bar, except when the door to the dining room was opened briefly as a waiter came in or went out with an order. Only two other of the dozen or so available tables were occupied, so there was little chance of their being overheard.

And, even if they had been, there was nothing much to overhear.

'I want to know all about you, Joao,' Ken said right at the start, with a frankness that he must have picked up during his year at Harvard. It was refreshing in a Japanese, usually so careful in keeping whatever they knew close to their chests.

Joao realised, of course, that Ken might be playing a sly game, feigning behaviour that was un-Japanese in order to test his loyalties, but he didn't think so. He had to make a snap decision, whether to answer Ken's straightforward questions like for like, or to remain guarded until he knew which way the wind was blowing. His training as a gaijin in Japan suggested the latter course of behaviour. That, surely, was what Bai-li would have expected of his newly-acquired agent. It was what any Japanese would have done. But instinct prevailed. Ken was an ally. And a friend. Not now, maybe, but it wouldn't take long. That was what Ken was looking for, too. Friendship. Hence the straightforward approach as he asked Joao all about his childhood, what it was like growing up in Japan as someone who wasn't entirely Japanese – Ken liked to call him a 'half-ski,' a strange English-Russian neologism that he came up with during the course of a second bottle of beer and which Joao rather liked. Yes, he was definitely a half-ski, although which half was Japanese and which Portuguese he had no clear idea.

By the time they'd finished their meal with a cup of coffee, Joao knew that he'd been right to trust his instinct. Ken was going to be a friend for life, whatever differences of opinion they might have. Not that there seemed to be any. They had similar tastes in reading — Dostoyevsky, Tanizaki, Balzac, and (although better to whisper it than shout aloud) Dickens; and in music, too, although here Ken was convinced that Bach was superior to Joao's favourite, Mozart.

'Mozart is too, I don't know, too light,' he exclaimed.

'The *Missa Solemnis* is hardly light, Ken-*chan*.'

'Too inebriated, then. A victim of his own intoxicating genius. While Bach – Bach's the sober mathematician. At least, that's how I see him, Joao. He works out in advance every juxtaposition of notes possible and then puts them together in combinations no ordinary mortal can imagine. Like in *The Art of the Fugue*.'

By this stage of the evening, they had already started using the diminutive form *chan* when addressing each other, rather than the more formal *san*. Like two kids in the same class at school.

They discovered, to their mutual delight – and ensuing conviction that such commonalities could only be found among *dōkyūsei* classmates – that they went to the same tailor hidden away in a side street behind Mitsukoshi Department Store near Nihonbashi. They even liked smoking the same brand of English cigarettes. How could they not be friends forever?

They'd shared a lot of common experiences at the Imperial University, too – Ken in Tokyo, Joao in Kyoto. Ken revealed that he used to go to meetings of the Shirakaba literary group, something which led to a conversation that Joao wished he had more often, given that it was a central part of his profession – writing. And yet, for some reason never explained, it was something his fellow journalists, both in Tokyo and Shanghai, always seemed keen to avoid. So, over two bowls of *purin* cream caramel ordered for desert (a nod towards Joao's Portuguese heritage), they discussed style – the kinds of words and expressions that should be used in different contexts, even what happened during the course of writing itself. The creative process, if you will.

'The thing is, Ken, you think you're in control of what you're going to write, but you're not. A word or phrase can suddenly push you, like the wind in a sail at sea, in a totally new direction. And, in so doing, it can conjure up new ideas that you hadn't initially thought of. Take you where you'd never thought of going. Wouldn't you agree?'

'I don't know, Joao. I'm not a journalist, like you.'

'That's not the point, Ken. You're still writing. It doesn't matter what you write. It's the writing itself that matters. In your case, policy documents for government and bureaucrats.'

'Yes, and for that very reason I can't let my imagination take over.'

'I'm not suggesting that. I'm just trying to point out how the very act of writing creates new ways of perceiving a problem. And, therefore, of analysing it. That's why I'm not totally convinced by your suggestion that Johann Sebastian planned out everything in advance. He had to leave room for chance. That's what makes him – and Mozart – so great.'

Ken tossed his napkin onto the table, pushed back his chair and stood up.

'I give up, Joao. You win. Now we need a real drink.'

Both chauffeur and black Packard were waiting for them in front of the Press Club outside.

'Brrr. It's cold outside.'

'Yes, sir,' the chauffeur said as he opened the rear door of the car for his passengers. 'They say it's going to snow soon.'

Joao didn't hear what Ken said to the driver as he got into the car after him, but soon they were being whisked back along the same streets towards the Imperial Hotel, with the same or different policemen waving them through with shrill blasts on their whistles. How men loved the accoutrements of power. Uniforms, leather boots, batons, pistols, whistles. How insignificant to be a mere journalist.

Instead of turning left at Uchisaiwaichō, the chauffeur steered the car to the right along the road that followed the contours of the moat around the Imperial Palace. Joao didn't notice anything more about where they were heading, because picking up on his new friend's use of the idea of chance in literary and musical composition, Ken was talking about *go-en* – a favourite concept with any Japanese who was at a loss for a rational explanation as to why something had happened. Not some kind of objectively administered 'fate' so much as a subjective connection between people or things that couldn't be explained immediately in rational terms.

'Ask yourself this, Joao,' Ken was saying, the alcohol going a bit, perhaps, to his head. 'How did you and I happen to meet? I mean, I wasn't supposed to go to Chiang Kai-shek's wedding. I'd been invited to attend a workshop on Sino-Japanese relations here in Tokyo. But then, for no particular rhyme or reason, I changed my mind and agreed to accompany my father. He doesn't like to travel alone, you know.'

'There's your reason, then. Nothing at all to do with *go-en*.'

'Yeah, perhaps. But why did I use that as an excuse to go to Shanghai? Why not something else?'

'You mean, you could have asked your mother to go with him?'

'My mother?' Ken burst out laughing. 'It's hard enough to get her onto a tram to go shopping in Ikebukuro. I can't imagine what she'd do if asked to board a ship and travel abroad. No,' he continued more seriously, 'It had to be me.'

'And look what happened.'

'That's just what I've been saying, Joao. Our meeting was *go-en*. If Sun Yat-sen hadn't stayed with my father when he was in exile in Japan; if I hadn't recognised Soong Ch'ing-ling in the midst of that vast throng of guests in the ballroom of the Majestic Hotel, we'd never have met.'

'You're forgetting something, Ken?'

'I am? What's that?'

'Why did Doctor Sun choose to go into exile in Japan? What if he hadn't been thrown out of his position in the new republic? Once you start explaining things by resorting to *go-en*, you find yourself tracing more and more ramifications, involving more and more people, each with its own set of *go-en* connections. As a result, you go so far back in time you end up rewriting history.'

'You've got me there,' Ken laughed as the chauffeur brought the car to a smooth halt outside a wooden gated building facing onto a narrow alley. There was a clump of bamboo to one side with a single dim light with the word Sakura written in tasteful calligraphy on its glass shade. On the other, a large rock set in small white stones and, leaning over it like an umbrella, a plum tree in blossom.

'Where are we now?' Joao hadn't been paying much attention to the road during their conversation.

'Kagurazaka. The Sakura tea house. My father's favourite geisha hang-out,' Ken smiled. 'Don't worry. He's not going to ask you to foot the bill.'

'Just as well because I don't think I could. Not even with my Shanghai allowance. But does he know we're coming?'

'Of course he does, Joao. He ordered me to bring you here after dinner. Thank you, *Kobayashi*,' he said to the chauffeur who bowed low and got back into the Packard.

Ken pushed open the wooden gate and stepped inside.

There were half a dozen stone slabs laid haphazardly on the ground. On one side was a *kara sansui* miniature Zen garden, consisting of three asymmetrically placed rocks in a raked sea of small white stones; on the other, a large clump of bamboo and maple tree that concealed the entrance to the tea house. The path was bordered by a carpet of thick moss. There was the sound of trickling water somewhere close by and the sudden echo of a *shishi-odoshi* bamboo clapper. Echoes of old Japan.

Ken pushed open the sliding wooden door to the tea house and entered.

'*Gomen kudasai*,' he called in a voice just loud enough to be heard.

There was a quick shuffle of tabi stockinged feet on the wooden floor of the house and a middle-aged woman in kimono appeared.

'*Okoshiyasu*,' she greeted her guests. Then, surprised at seeing who it was, '*Ara, Inukai-sensei. O-hisashiburi de gozaimasu ne.*'

'Yes. It's been a long time,' Ken agreed, taking off his shoes and stepping up into the house. 'Is my father here?'

'Yes, indeed. And has been for some time now. I think Kohana has a certain effect on him,' she laughed coquettishly before glancing at Joao enquiringly.

Ken smoothly took the hint, as Joao took off his shoes and followed him up onto the wooden floor.

'*Okāsan*, might I introduce you to a close friend of mine – a very close friend of mine – Joao Serino.'

'*Hajimemashite*,' the woman bowed low. '*Yoroshū otanomōshimasu*. Inukai-sensei has told me about you. A distinguished scholar and journalist, living in Shanghai, I understand?'

'I'm not sure about "distinguished,"' Joao said, returning her bow. 'But yes, at present I live and work in Shanghai.'

'Not for long, though,' Ken intervened, putting one arm round Joao's shoulder. 'We need him back here in Japan.'

'So that we can enjoy his company more often,' the Okāsan laughed dutifully. She then bowed again and turned away along the ill-lit passageway leading to the back of the tea house.

'Your father is in his usual room, overlooking the back garden. If you'd like to follow me. You'll find that the plum trees are in full flower.'

The Okāsan led the way, the split-toed tabi socks on her feet rustling on the well-worn floorboards as she moved.

After turning right, left, right and left again, she paused, knelt down on the wooden floor and with a discrete cough, followed by a *'Gomen kudasai,'* slid open a *fusuma* screen door.

'Ah! There you are!' Ken's father said happily.

He had reason to be. A simpering young woman in full geisha outfit – traditional *shimada*-style wig, long-sleeved kimono and *oshiroi* white makeup with bright red lips – was leaning gently against him as she poured sake rice wine into his cup.

'*Okāsan*, I think Kohana here needs a little assistance this evening,' Tsuyoshi downed the rice wine in his cup. 'Could you possibly arrange something for these two youngsters?'

'Of course, sensei.' The older woman got up from her kneeling position, stepped outside the room into the corridor, knelt down again, bowed from the hip, and smoothly closed the screen door.

'Well, Serino-*san*, welcome back to Tokyo. I hope my son's been treating you well.'

'He has indeed, sir. Much more than I deserve.'

'Good. Kohana,' he raised his eyebrows in the direction of a bottle of sake on the low table at which they were now all sitting, and jerked his head towards his guests, 'I think these two need all your support until your companions arrive. I'm clearly well ahead of them.'

'Of course, sensei.' Effortlessly she stood up from her formal kneeling position on the tatami matting and came round with a bottle of sake to kneel down between Ken and Joao.

'Kohana,' she said, bowing as she introduced herself. '*Yoroshū otanomōshimasu.*' Then, with the bottle in pouring position, '*Dōzo. Otsukareyasu.*'

The two newcomers dutifully picked up their sake cups. Kohana filled them to the brim.

'*Kanpai*,' Ken toasted Joao, his father and, lastly, the simpering Kohana. '*Yoroshiku onegai itashimasu.*'

Putting his cup down on the table, Joao took a fresh one and offered it to Kohana.

'*Ōkini,*' she said, using the Kyoto dialect affected by geisha all over the country.

She downed the sake, then deftly wiped the edge of her cup with the sleeve of her kimono before offering it to Joao. He accepted it and she filled his cup. He bowed his thanks and quickly downed his second cup. This was a sure-fire recipe for disaster if he carried on drinking so fast.

As Kohana retired to one corner of the *zashiki* room to heat up two more bottles of sake, Tsuyoshi took over.

'Well, you two, what have you been up to this evening?'

'Not much,' Ken replied with a glance at Joao. 'Coffee at the Imperial, followed by dinner at the Press Club.'

'Hrrmph!' The old man clearly didn't approve of the Press Club, although whether it was because of the clientele or the food, Joao wasn't sure.

'We wanted somewhere quiet, Father, where we wouldn't be disturbed.'

'And were you?'

'No. In fact, we had rather a nice chat.'

'Politics.'

'Actually, no.'

'What? No politics?'

'No politics, Father. Just personal stuff. You know how it is with friends.'

'So you're friends now?' Inukai nodded as he stroked his beard with one hand. 'That's good. I'm glad to hear it.' He looked directly at Joao. 'Friends are important, don't you think, Serino-*san*?'

'I most certainly do, sir. Especially when they're hard to come by. I feel incredibly lucky to have met Ken here.'

'Good. Good,' he mused and downed another cup of sake. 'Oy! Kohana!' He called to the woman just behind him. 'We need more sake here.'

At that point, there was the sound of several feet on the other side of the screen door, followed by a low voice calling for permission to enter. Kohana shuffled quickly across the tatami, knelt down and opened the *fusuma* to reveal two more geisha kneeling in the corridor.

'*Ara!*' Ken's father exclaimed in mock surprise. 'Who are these two beauties? Come in. Come in. I have a feeling these two young men are in need of your attention.'

'Father! Really!' Ken exclaimed with a hint of embarrassment.

But it was too late. The newcomers were already in the room and, taking up position beside Ken and Joao, introduced themselves as Asakichi and Chiyotsuru.

Suddenly the *zashiki* was filled with frivolity and laughter as the three geisha, who clearly knew one another well, began to entertain the two young men. Not used to this kind of revelry, Joao looked at Ken a little helplessly, as the two of them were called on to take part in a couple of innocent party games that were clearly designed to help guests relax and forget the exigencies of the outside world. He soon found himself mesmerised by Chiyotsuru, who was paying him particular attention to make him feel at ease. That, he had to remind himself, was her job.

At one point, Asakichi took up a samisen lute-like instrument and began strumming it as she sang a song that probably appealed more to the neighbourhood cats than to two young men who weren't well versed in geisha arts. Nevertheless, they applauded loudly as she brought her song about the twelfth century wars between the Minamoto and Taira clans to an end, and asked her to sing another. When Ken's father chimed in with his praise and insisted that she perform again, Asakichi cast aside her modesty and did as asked. The cats on the back wall of the garden purred with delight.

Next it was Chiyotsuru's turn to show off her skills – this time in dance, as Kohana took over on the samisen and Asakichi turned to sake cup-refilling duty. Chiyotsuru certainly had a way with her fan, which she used with immense skill to narrate a dance that revealed a supple body under her kimono. Even someone as uninitiated in the geisha world as Joao could more or less work out the tale of love told by Chiyotsuru's sinuous moves. He longed suddenly for Gerda and wished he'd been able to bring her to Tokyo. If only this geisha were as approachable.

The party went on, filled with inane conversation, led primarily by Tsuyoshi – he was, after all, the oldest man present and deference need be paid him, especially since he was also a senior politician and former government minister. Flattery prevailed. And yet, somehow, Kohana and her friends managed to make everything they said seem natural, not false. Even in his cups, Joao marvelled at their skills honed by years and years of training. He also recognised that such an ability to dissimulate would make great spies of the three young women. Perhaps one of them already was. After all, what other profession had access to such an exclusive clientele? Politicians, managerial executives in Japan's largest and most important companies, senior bureaucrats. Plus, of course, the occasional underworld figure. A yakuza here; an ultranationalist conspirator there. He should advise Bai-li, if he wasn't already aware of the potential.

All this Joao vaguely put together in an intoxicated haze – some of it, admittedly, feigned. As luck would have it, the tea house provided rather large, deep ashtrays for the men to use when smoking. On the pretext of extinguishing one of his cigarettes or putting out some smouldering ash, Joao was able surreptitiously to pour the rice wine in his cup straight into the ashtray nestling on the tatami matting between his crossed legs. In this way, he managed to consume about half as much alcohol as his two companions, although Chiyotsuru beside him quickly noticed what was going on.

'*Ara*, Serino sensei!' She exclaimed discretely with a tinkling laugh, 'Don't you like your sake? I'll have to drink it for you.'

Which, with an affectionate pat on his knee, she kindly did. And duly suffered, no doubt, the following morning.

Joao had no idea what the time was. He'd rather foolishly left his watch in his hotel room. But he reckoned the party had been in full swing for a good couple of hours when Tsuyoshi suddenly clapped his hands loudly. Voices that had risen to full pitch in their owners' inebriation were suddenly quiet. Asakichi and Chiyotsuru, who had been dancing a kind of waltz with Ken and Joao, let go of their partners and took up a formal kneeling position as each adjusted the collar of her kimono and ensured that everything was in place where it should be. Joao reflected that he might have been able to gird Gerda's loins, but had little hope of charming the wig off a geisha.

'We have greatly appreciated your company, my beauties,' Tsuyoshi spoke to Chiyotsuru and Asakichi, his voice only slightly slurred. 'But now, I'm afraid, it's time for you to leave. Good night and thank you. Kohana, you stay here.'

The two women dutifully bowed and politely expressed their concern that none of the three men present had been unduly tired by their attention. Then they left the room. Kohana positioned herself just behind Ken's father, ready to attend to whatever wish he expressed. Now that they were alone, Joao instinctively straightened his back as he moved quickly and deftly from a cross-legged to a kneeling position.

'Serino-*san*,' Tsuyoshi looked at him sharply, but smiled through his beard. 'Are you still in full possession of your wits?'

'I'm not sure, sensei, that anyone can be in full possession of anything after the pleasure of the last couple of hours.'

'Hmm. I hope I haven't calculated you wrongly.'

'Calculated?'

'We have plans for you, don't we, Ken?' Father looked at son.

Ken nodded.

'We do indeed.'

Was he being played again?

'Am I permitted to ask what those plans might be?' Joao could see the resemblance between the two men. Not physical so much as their ability to give away nothing until it was in their interest to do so.

Tsuyoshi, skilled politician that he was, answered Joao's question with one of his own.

'Tell me, Serino-*san*, what brings you back to Tokyo so suddenly? You didn't mention it when we spoke in Shanghai.'

'True. Simply because I had no idea I'd find myself called back.'

'Called back?'

'By my editor. He wants me to follow up a lead on the Takahashi Bank collapse.'

'The collapse that wasn't, so to speak?'

'Exactly. The collapse instigated by the Finance Minister's apparent slip of the tongue when addressing the Diet.'

'Apparent slip of the tongue?' Any sign that Tsuyoshi had been drinking heavily that evening now gone. He was alert and attentive when faced with political rumour. Always the query. How can this be used to my advantage? Joao's query was the same, however. Journalists and politicians were always ready to trade information. It was an essential part of their jobs. Information, the right information, was power.

'I'm not sure whether you heard, sensei,' Joao began. 'But Hiroshi Sakamoto, branch manager of the Takahashi Bank in Shanghai, committed suicide on the evening of the Generalissimo's wedding.'

'Really? How?'

'The traditional way. Harakiri.'

'The messy way, then,' Ken put in.

'Very. Or so I'm told. The question is, why?'

'And?'

'There's the difficulty,' Joao was still kneeling formally on the tatami matting. Kohana, he noted, was listening carefully, even while tidying the table and placing used sake cups and bottles, dishes and pairs of chopsticks on a lacquer tray behind Tsuyoshi. Visible, but invisible. There, but not there.

'Sakamoto's wife, it transpires, is the younger sister of the Finance Minister's wife. The suggestion is that something – something important, connected with the Takahashi Bank's affairs – was passed from husband to wife in Shanghai, and then from one sister to the other, and onwards to the Minister in Tokyo.'

'You mean –?'

'I mean that what the Foreign Minister chose to say to his colleagues in the Diet may not have been a slip of the tongue, or error of judgement at all. It may have been the unvarnished truth. But we don't know. That's what I'm here to find out. I need to talk to people here in Tokyo as well as back in Shanghai.'

Tsuyoshi mulled over Joao's words silently, as he took another sip of sake poured by the ever-attentive Kohana.

'Or it may have nothing at all to do with the sisters…'

'But it's being made to look that way? As I said, sensei, I'm here to see what, if anything, I can find out.'

Joao paused, before adding as a seemingly unpremeditated afterthought.

'Of course, if there were something that you, sensei, might be able to help me with, I would be extremely grateful. My Akasaka government contacts aren't as good as they once were, now that I'm living abroad.' He bowed low.

Once again, Tsuyoshi avoided the immediate. Instead, he answered Joao's earlier question.

'As I said, Serino-*kun*, we have plans for you. Or, to be more specific, Ken has had an idea that we want to sound you out about.'

'Joao, Prince Saionji, as you probably know, is extremely worried about the rise of militarism in Japan. He's also determined to keep the Emperor out of politics – something that neither the Army nor the Navy wants.'

'In other words, he has a fight on his hands.'

'He does, indeed,' Ken acknowledged, 'and that's where you come in. As the last remaining genro or elder statesman, Prince Saionji has decided to set up an advisory group to the Prime Minister and his cabinet.'

'Will the Prime Minister listen? Tanaka's hardly the kind of man to take advice.'

'True. But remember, Serino-*kun*. It's Saionji who's recommended every Prime Minister's appointment to the Emperor over the past ten years and more. Tanaka will have to listen to what he says.'

'Part of the group's remit,' Ken took over, 'Is to offer advice on Manchuria, China and the Asian continent. Measured advice. Apolitical advice. The Prince would like you to join his group.'

'Me? But I'm just an ordinary journalist.'

'No ordinary journalist, Serino-*kun*. Let me assure you. The Prince has been much taken with your analyses of the situation on the Asian continent, and has specifically requested that you become a member of the Breakfast Club.'

'Breakfast –'

Ken explained.

'Because we are to meet over breakfast from time to time for a round-table discussion. A particular topic is to be selected, a discussion paper circulated in advance, and ideas freely exchanged regardless of the political or ideological persuasions of the group's participants.'

'Like military intervention in Manchuria?'

'Or like Chiang Kai-shek's war against the Communists. Will you join us?'

'But Ken, I'm living and working in Shanghai. I can hardly come to Tokyo for breakfast every now and then.'

'Of course, you can't. And nobody's asking you to,' Tsuyoshi took over. 'But, let's face it, Serino-*kun*, sooner or later your newspaper's going to transfer you back here from Shanghai. That's when the Breakfast Club will be able to take full advantage of your expertise.'

'In the meantime, all we ask is that you write an occasional policy document, based on what you observe and learn in Shanghai and elsewhere in China. For our part, we'll keep you up to date on the content of our discussions in Tokyo and ask for your input as and when appropriate. What do you think?'

It was, of course, an honour Joao could hardly refuse. Still, he shouldn't appear too eager to accept, so he asked various questions about the size and membership of the group, as well as about why some people had been selected and not others. The answers Inukai father and son gave him were reassuring. It was a club of which he could be proud to be a member, a club to whose discussions he felt he'd be able to make a useful contribution. For the sake of Japan.

Seemingly grudgingly, he finally gave his consent.

'Good. That's settled then,' Tsuyoshi turned to Kohana, waiting patiently behind him, listening to everything they'd said. 'We need a toast. One last *tokkuri* bottle, please, Kohana.'

'*Kashikomariyasu*,' she murmured, getting up from her position and moving to the back wall to prepare the sake.

'Ah! How beautiful the plum blossoms are tonight!' Tsuyoshi sighed wistfully. 'Fragrant in the full moonlight.'

'In the spring haze, their scent filling the air – plum blossoms and the moon,' Ken intoned, quoting a seventeen-syllable haiku by the poet Basho.

'Early spring, the first thing they sell is sake and plum blossom. What fragrance!' Tsuyoshi made a prompt allusion to another poem, as in the distance a temple bell rent the stillness of the night.

'A cloud of flowers,' it was Joao's turn, 'Is that the temple bell at Ueno? Or Asakusa?'

Inukai father and son both burst out laughing.

'I know,' Joao said quickly. 'Basho was referring to the cherry blossoms, but it somehow seemed appropriate.'

'It was, indeed,' Kohana came to his support, 'What a perceptive and sensitive young companion you've found. Don't you think so, sensei?'

'Hrrmph!' Exclaimed Tsuyoshi, but there was an unmistakeable twinkle in his eye.

The banging on the door of his hotel room was loud and insistent. Joao did his best to ignore it by burying his head under a pillow, but it was no good. An imperious voice, clearly used to giving commands, called his name out loudly. The banging continued as he sat up and felt for the light switch. Five o'clock in the morning. Not the best time to be woken with a hangover.

'Joao Serino?' Two uniformed men stood in the half light of the corridor outside his room. 'You are to come with us.'

An order, not a request.

'Go with you where? Do you know what time it is?'

'Eastern District Kempei Headquarters.'

That woke him up. Kempeitai? He looked at the two men more closely. Each was wearing a standard khaki army field uniform with high black leather boots, and sported a white armband on which the characters for *ken* and *hei*, military police, were printed in red. Bad news.

'Do you mind if I get dressed first? Or would you like me to accompany you in my night clothes?' A half joke to allay the fear.

'Get dressed! Major Doihara is not in the habit of interviewing suspects in their yukata,' one of the soldiers replied curtly.

Suspect? Definitely not a good sign. A manner of speaking, perhaps? He could only hope so.

Joao made to close the door of his room, but the soldier put his booted foot in to stop him. Then he watched casually as Joao found some fresh underwear in a chest of drawers by the window, struggled into it under his yukata robe, which he then discarded and put on a clean shirt hanging in the wardrobe. He knotted a silk tie Gerda had given him a few weeks previously and put on the same suit he'd worn the previous day. As he prepared to leave, he took his hat and overcoat off the pegs on the back of the hotel room door, and followed his visitors down the corridor.

At the top of the stairs, one of the military policemen bowed and signalled to him to go first. There was no way Joao was going to escape, even if the thought had crossed his mind. Which it hadn't. Not at that hour of the morning.

Downstairs the lobby was empty. Unsurprising, given the hour. A sleepy bellhop watched the three men exit the hotel from the comparative safety of the concierge desk. Then he reached for the telephone on the desk in front of him.

Joao was bundled into an army car and driven at speed through the city's empty streets, across town in the direction of the Imperial Palace, but before getting that far the car swerved right down an alleyway and came to a screeching halt outside the back door of an imposing building. The man beside him in the back seat got out and pulled Joao after him. No niceties now that they were no longer in the public eye.

He went up a short flight of steps, half stumbling as one of the military policemen shoved him from behind. He was led into a vast hallway with corridors leading off left and right to offices of some kind. The military policemen stopped at a large desk set up at the foot of an ornate staircase.

'Name?' An official seated at the desk asked in a bored voice.

'Serino,' one of the MPs answered for him.

The official checked a list of names in front of him, running his finger down the page until he came to the one he wanted.

'First name, Joao?'

'That's correct.'

'Room 7.' The official picked up a *hankō* signature seal and pressed it onto the paper beside his name. Katō, he read, in red ink. What a common name! He was proud to be a Serino. One of two in a country of more than seventy million people.

The military policemen, each firmly holding one of Joao's arms, led him away from the desk across the hall and down a corridor. Joao noticed the sequence of numbers — odd on the left, even on the right. One of the MPs opened the fourth door on the left and the other pushed Joao unceremoniously into the room. They closed the door firmly behind him.

Joao took in his surroundings. Bare bulb on the ceiling. A steel desk. One chair only. No windows. No nothing. An interrogation room.

He thought he might as well sit while he could. Who knew what lay ahead?

It was more than three hours before he found out. The door was suddenly thrown open and an officer came into the room. In his mid-forties, he was short and slightly stout, with a minuscule black moustache that highlighted a small, merciless mouth slanting downwards, like his eyebrows. His eyes were hooded, calculating and observant. The sort of eyes that missed nothing.

'Good morning, Serino-*san*,' he said politely, as Joao stood up. 'Do please remain seated. My apologies for the early call, but I have a busy day ahead of me, so I thought it opportune to have a chat before the inconvenience of my other –' a slight pause, 'guests.'

'Is that what I am, too? A guest?'

'Guest?' The officer looked at him amiably. 'Goodness me, no, Serino-*san*. You're a suspect.'

'Suspect? Suspected of what, might I ask?'

'You might indeed. A fair question, if I might say so. The trouble is, I don't yet know. But we're getting ahead of ourselves. Oy!' He suddenly shouted loudly. 'A chair.'

There was a muffled 'Hah!' from one of the military policemen outside the interrogation room, followed by a hurried scamper of boots along the corridor.

'First, let me introduce myself. My name is Doihara. Major Kenji Doihara of the First Field Division of the Kempeitai. My job, and that of those under my command, is to preserve the peace. A worthy ambition, as I'm sure you'll agree.'

'Of course, Major.' Always use rank to flatter. 'But do you have any reason to believe that I'm preventing you from carrying out your duties? So far as I'm aware, I haven't disturbed the peace you mention in any way.'

'Haven't you? Well, that's one relief, at least.' Doihara took a packet of cigarettes from his pocket and offered one to Joao.

At that moment, there was a knock on the door and one of the military policemen came into the room with a chair.

'Ah!' was all Doihara said as he turned its back to face Joao and sat astride it. He then flicked on his lighter as the soldier withdrew with a low bow.

Joao accepted the cigarette and Doihara's offer of a light. He wondered how long the major would be able to keep his pose. His legs were too short to hold a position like that comfortably for more than a few minutes.

'Have you come across these cigarettes in Shanghai by any chance, Serino-*san*?'

'Bat?' Joao read the brand name on the packet Doihara was holding in his hand. 'Not British American Tobacco, I presume?' Then, seeing the look on Doihara's face, 'No, I can't say I have. Why do you ask?'

'Oh, just curiosity, I suppose. They're made in Japan, but for some obscure reason connected with the government's cigarette monopoly, they're not sold here. A pity, don't you think? I've always regarded them as rather good.'

Joao inhaled the tobacco. Doihara was right. Good flavour. And smooth, too. A taste he thought he recognised, but couldn't put his finger on where or when. Or who he was with at the time. Still the taste was recognisable. A tip of the tongue phenomenon.

'Anyway,' Doihara interrupted his thoughts, 'We were discussing the reason I've had you brought in here for questioning.'

'Yes, indeed. And you said I was suspected of something.'

Doihara exhaled the smoke in his lungs into the air above Joao's head.

'Not exactly.' His thin lips cracked into what might have passed for a smile in anyone else. But a Kempeitai officer wasn't just anyone else. 'I said you were a suspect. I didn't say you were suspected of anything in particular.'

'True. But you presumably have some idea of what makes you suspicious of me? Otherwise you wouldn't have had me woken up so early this morning and brought in here for interrogation.'

'Questioning, please, Serino-*san*,' Doihara corrected him again. 'Interrogations aren't as pleasant as this, I can assure you.'

'No, they probably aren't,' Joao gave an involuntary shudder. 'But still, the question remains. You have suspicions about me, Major. But suspicions of what?'

Doihara leaned forward, resting his arms on the back of his chair.

'How about destabilisation of the State?' he said smoothly. 'How's that for a start?'

'Not bad,' admitted Joao with a bit more bravado than he felt inside, 'I mean, you're halfway down the race track and I haven't even left my starting blocks.'

Doihara looked pleased. 'A nice analogy, Serino-*san*. I must remember that when talking to my other guests.'

'So, if I might ask, how have I destabilised the State? We're talking about Japan, I presume, and not China.'

'Maybe both. That has yet to be determined.'

'Let's start with Japan, then.'

'My information is that you have been making enquiries about the failure – or the perceived failure – of the Takahashi Bank. Is that correct?'

'Yes. But only indirectly. My initial concern was the suicide of the bank's Shanghai branch manager. A certain Mr Sakamoto.'

'Initial?' Doihara had not smoked his cigarette after the first puff and tapped a long strip of burnt ash onto the floor. Joao followed suit, realising he was a feeling a little dreamy rather suddenly. He'd never enjoyed smoking on an empty stomach. 'So where did your initial enquiries take you?'

'I don't know yet.'

'But you came to Tokyo to follow something up.'

'Yes, Major. A family connection.'

'You're referring to the fact that the wives of the dead branch manager in Shanghai and of the Finance Minister here in Tokyo are sisters?'

'That's correct.'

'And?'

'And nothing, Major. I've only been here two nights and a day. I haven't had time to do anything other than meet with my editor at the Asahi Newspaper.'

'I hope you're not forgetting your politician friends, Inukai father and son?'

Kempeitai officers, he knew, were always well informed.

'Them, too.'

'Did they enlighten you further with regard to the Takahashi Bank? A little inside information, perhaps?'

'No, Major.'

'But you were at a geisha tea house in Kagurazaka.'

Too well informed. Joao knew inside information when he came across it.

'Yes. So what?'

'So you drank sake, I presume. A lot of it. And when a man drinks sake his tongue is loosened. He says things he normally keeps to himself.'

Joao didn't bother to answer. His interest was in how Doihara knew about the geisha party the previous evening. He suspected Kohana.

'So what did Inukai Tsuyoshi have to say about the Takahashi Bank affair?'

'Inukai-sensei? Nothing, Major. They don't call him the Old Fox for nothing.'

'No. Probably not,' Doihara looked at his watch and stood up suddenly. 'My goodness! Is that the time? I'm afraid I have to be going. As I said, I've a busy day ahead.'

Joao also stood up, glad to stretch his legs.

'So, am I free to go, Major?'

'Go?' Doihara turned as he was opening the door and gave another of those humourless smiles that slit the lower half of his face in two. 'No, I don't think so, Serino-*san*. Not yet. I need to talk to you again.'

He left the interrogation room and the two MPs came in and took Joao firmly by the arms.

'Come with us,' they said unnecessarily as they pushed him into the corridor. There were some stairs leading down to the basement diagonally across from where he stood, and the MPs manhandled him down into what turned out to be a row of cells, each with a heavy iron door. Behind him, Joao could hear the grunting sounds of someone being badly beaten, followed by a loud inhuman scream.

Psychology, he told himself as he was literally thrown into an empty cell. It was all psychological. He had to ignore everything going on – or everything he thought was going on – even as the MPs ordered him to take off his jacket, tie and trouser belt, and to loosen and remove the laces in his shoes. With the Kempeitai there were no strings attached when it came to soliciting information. They took his socks for good measure.

The two military policemen slammed the cell door, leaving him standing on cold stone slabs in a state of what in polite society would have been termed 'undress.' But at least he wasn't completely naked. That would come later, no doubt.

He crouched down on his haunches, that classic posture adopted by Asian people while waiting for something to happen. The cell was completely empty, apart from a bucket for slops in one corner. Above it a barred window. There were the remains of what looked like blood on one wall. It was then that, looking up, Joao noticed two chains with handcuffs hanging from the ceiling. In his dreamlike state, he accepted without any hint of shock that he was in a torture chamber.

Was there anything he could do? No. Was there any point in preparing answers to questions that he could only imagine? Not really. Better to take them as they came, tell the truth, and hope Doihara would realise he'd made a mistake. The trouble was the Kempeitai never admitted it made mistakes.

Did he have any hope of prompt release from his situation? Probably not. Was there anything his editor at the Asahi could, or would, do for him? Always presuming, of course, that he found out Joao had been called in for questioning. Unlikely. Newspapers didn't have that much power. What about Ken or his father? Surely, they'd do something once they learned of his whereabouts? But would they find out? And, if so, when?

So many unanswerable questions. Joao realised it would be better to think of something else. Like the Takahashi Bank affair. Why should a major in the Kempeitai be interested in a suicide that Joao was investigating? Obviously, it wasn't just a suicide. Doihara had inadvertently confirmed something he'd been wondering about – that there was more to the Takahashi Bank's insolvency than met the eye. The Kempeitai must somehow be involved. That would explain why they'd been so quick onto the scene when Sakamoto had committed suicide.

And then there was Doihara. By racking his memory – luckily it had always been an outstandingly good memory – Joao recalled a rumour about Doihara. It had never been confirmed and, even if it had been, no newspaper reporter would have dared publish it. It would have been too sensational even for the tabloids. Anything painting the Imperial family in bad light was off-limits.

The rumour was that Doihara had taken photographs of his fifteen-year-old younger sister in the nude and handed them to one of the Imperial princes who immediately took her as his concubine. In exchange, it was said, Doihara had been promoted to the rank of major and offered an appointment in the Kempeitai. He was, apparently, angling for a transfer to China – possibly Manchuria since he spoke Russian fluently and was competent in Mandarin.

It was early afternoon – that much a brilliant winter's sun told him through the barred window of his cell – when they came for him. Different guards this time, but just as rough as they manhandled him out of his cell and along the corridor to where he'd heard grunts and screams earlier. Another bare cell, this time with a table and chair. Joao was made to stand in a pool of blood on the floor, as his guards stripped off his shirt and underwear before forcing his arms upwards and cuffing his hands to chains attached to the ceiling. Once secured, one of the guards hauled the other end of the chains and Joao found himself being stretched upwards, until only his toes were in touch with the bloody stone slabs of the cell floor. Only just in touch.

Here we go, he thought, as Doihara entered the cell. The major sat down wordlessly on the chair and nodded at one of the guards, who immediately punched Joao hard – excruciatingly hard – in the kidneys. His torso jerked forward and he dry retched. There was a sharp pain in both of his shoulders as his feet lost all contact with the ground.

It was the first blow that was always the worst. Other blows might be harder, but you knew they were coming. The first took you by surprise. It disoriented the prisoner, just as intended.

'So Serino-*san*,' Doihara said calmly through a cloud of cigarette smoke. 'Here we are again. You have something to tell me, perhaps?'

The cigarette was different, Joao realised. Not as smooth as the one before.

'I'm not sure what you'd like me to tell you, Major,' he said.

'Why did the Takahashi Bank fail?'

'Because the Finance Minister made a mistake in the Diet and said it had failed when it hadn't. That's what I heard in Shanghai, at least.'

'Wrong answer!'

It was the other guard's turn to hit Joao. No less painfully. In the kidneys again. Again his feet flailed helplessly in the air. The pain in his shoulders was excruciating. As he hung there, his toes desperately searching to relieve the pressure in his arms and neck, he suddenly remembered what it was. That tip of the tongue phenomenon. The cigarette Doihara had offered him earlier – the Bat brand – was spiced with opium. No wonder it couldn't be sold in Japan.

Doihara was speaking. Icily.

'Why did your friend Inukai alert the Finance Minister?'

'Alert? Alert him to what?'

Another punch in his gut. This time he did retch and some of his vomit soaked the uniform sleeve of the guard who'd punched him. A little must have splashed onto Doihara, too, because suddenly he stood up, wiping the front of his uniform with a handkerchief, and stepped over to where Joao was hanging.

'You don't ask questions, Serino. You answer them.'

And, swinging his arm to one side, he slapped Joao hard on the cheek. Once. Twice. The third time, his lip split and he could feel blood in his mouth. His nose was bleeding, too.

'What were you doing at the Zeitgeist Bookstore in Shanghai on October 21 last year?'

'What?' Joao exclaimed involuntarily and received another slap on the mouth for his pains. He saw that Doihara had a deep scar across the back of his hand and wrist. The strange things one noticed in the midst of agonising pain. He realised, too, that he needed to engage in a conversation of sorts. As a prisoner he mustn't lose his dignity.

'Buying a book, of course. What do you expect? That I went there to get noodles?'

Doihara actually laughed.

'You foreigners and your misplaced sense of humour,' he said, punching one of Joao's shoulders in a manner intended to be friendly, perhaps, but which merely caused him more pain.

'I would remind you that I am indeed a Portuguese citizen, Major Doihara. You have no right to hold me here.'

'Oh?' Another icy chuckle. Joao could smell his breath and it wasn't exactly Guerlain's Shalimar. 'Not even if you were a spy?'

'I'm not a spy,' Joao managed, spitting out enough blood for Doihara to take a precautionary step backwards.

'So what were you doing in the Zeitgeist Bookstore?'

'Buying a copy of Dostoyevsky's *Crime and Punishment*, if I remember aright.'

'An appropriate title, don't you think? Under the circumstances.'

'At least Raskolnikov knew what his crime was and what punishment to expect.'

Doihara ignored Joao's latest attempt at humour.

'A seditious novel, in many ways. Which you read – or tried to read – in Russian.'

'That is correct. I have been learning the language. Given relations between the Soviet Union, Japan and China, it's become an integral part of my job description.'

'Do you really think you can deceive me, Serino? You're a communist, aren't you?'

Joao noticed that Doihara had dispensed with polite forms of language when addressing him. The first step in a dehumanisation process, no doubt.

'No, I'm certainly not a communist, Major.'

'But you purchased a Russian book in a bookstore that is known to be financed by the Communist Party of Russia.'

'Forgive me, Major. My sources in Shanghai tell me that the Zeitgeist isn't financed by the Communist Party of the Soviet Union as such, but by its international branch, the so-called Comintern. Money comes, I believe, from its representative in Berlin.'

Doihara waved his correction away with another lit cigarette.

'The same thing in the end. A communist organisation.'

'You may well be right, Major.'

'And you consort with communists.'

'I do?' Joao managed to look incredulous.

'A German woman. Gerda Weidemeyer.'

Joao laughed, in spite of the pain in his shoulders.

'I hardly think Miss Weidemeyer's a communist, Major Doihara. More like a good German Nazi, if you ask me.'

That remark earned him both a slap on the face and a hard punch in his stomach, followed by two more – one for each shoulder.

He cried out in pain.

'And then there's your Chinese communist friend, Soong Ch'ing-ling.'

'Whom I interviewed for my newspaper,' Joao gasped through his pain. 'Maybe you haven't read it?'

Doihara ignored that.

'And you speak Russian. It's clear where your sympathies lie.'

'Is it?' Joao was annoyed by the stupidity of Doihara's line of questioning. Against his better judgement he decided to go on the attack. He wasn't going to allow himself to be beaten up by a Kempeitai bully. 'Then how about you, Major? Where do your sympathies lie?'

'What?' He was annoyed, realising his mistake. No longer in complete control.

'You speak Russian, too, Major. By all accounts fluently. Certainly far more fluently than I do. By your own logic that makes you an ardent commu – Aagh!'

That was as far as he was permitted to go, as Doihara stubbed his cigarette out on Joao's cheek. Now he had a burn to go with the rest of the pain in his stomach and shoulders.

At just that moment, the door to the cell was thrown open.

'Doihara! You will release this prisoner,' ordered a commanding voice. Joao couldn't see who it belonged to, but was grateful for the timely intervention.

'But, Colonel,' Doihara was standing rigidly to attention, as were the two guards.

'Now!' barked the Colonel.

'Yes, sir!' Doihara barked back, before jerking his head at the two guards, then in Joao's direction.

'You will arrange for Serino sensei to be given back his clothes and provided with washing facilities. You will then escort him to the front door of the building, where a member of the Imperial Palace is waiting for him.'

'Imperial Palace?' Doihara mumbled uncertainly.

'The Imperial Palace, Doihara. You're not the only one with friends in high places. Now move! And report to my office when you've carried out my orders.'

'Sir!' Doihara almost shouted, his accompanying salute only slightly tarnished by the specks of vomit on the chest of his uniform jacket.

Outside Kempeitai Headquarters a familiar black Packard was waiting. Kobayashi the chauffeur smiled when he saw Joao and gave him a white-gloved salute of his own.

'Welcome home, sensei,' he said, as he helped Joao get painfully into the back seat before closing the rear door of the car.

As the Packard moved out into the late afternoon traffic in the direction of Takebashi, Joao asked his first question.

'How did you know where I was?'

'Me, sir? I didn't know. But Prince Saionji instructed me to meet you in front of that rather infamous building we've just left behind us. He was, if I may say so, very angry.'

'Prince Saionji? But I don't even know him.'

'No, sensei. Maybe not. But the Prince clearly knows you,' the chauffeur smiled. Then added, 'But are you alright, sensei? You look as if they had a right go at you.'

'They certainly did,' Joao rubbed each of his shoulders where they'd been more or less wrenched their sockets. 'But I'll probably survive. You came in the nick of time, Kobayashi-*san*. A few more minutes and Buddha alone knows what might have happened to me. Thank you.'

'Not at all, sensei. But I'm not the one who deserves your thanks.'

'Maybe not, but still. Anyone who arrives like a knight in armour and drives me away from Kempeitai Headquarters deserves my thanks.'

Kobayashi smiled at him in his back mirror.

'But, surely, this is Inukai sensei's car, isn't it?'

'That is correct, Serino sensei. He's instructed me to take you to Kagurazaka.'

'Oh no!' Joao exclaimed involuntarily. 'Not another evening at the Sakura tea house.'

The chauffeur laughed.

'No, sir. Not this evening. I'm to drive you to a private bathhouse nearby.'

'A bathhouse?'

'Yes, sensei. Prince Saionji and Inukai sensei agreed that a long hot soak might be the best remedy for a body that had probably been quite badly beaten. After that, I am to take you to the Imperial Hotel where a room has been reserved for you.'

'The Imperial? But I'm staying at the Dai'ichi.'

'Don't you worry about that, sensei. Your belongings have already been packed and taken to your new accommodation.'

The Packard had already entered the maze of narrow streets around Kagurazaka. After a couple of minutes, Kobayashi brought the vehicle to a smooth stop beside a high wattle fence. In front of it a young woman was standing in a simple informal kimono. She bowed low as she opened the rear door for Joao to alight.

'Good evening, sensei. Welcome,' she said in a voice that struck Joao as vaguely familiar.

He grunted with pain, as he stood up straight and put his hand to his back. Clearly that part of his body had suffered, too, from all that hanging in the air.

The young woman moved towards him quickly and put one arm round his waist to help him.

'It's OK,' he said, trying to wave her away.

'No, it's not alright, sensei,' she said firmly. 'Do as I tell you.'

Then to the chauffeur, 'Kobayashi-*san*, I'll bring his clothes the moment he's in the bath.'

Kobayashi bowed, went round the front of the Packard and got back into the driving seat.

The young woman slid open a wooden door and called out softly.

'*Gomen kudasai.*'

'*Hai!*' Another woman's voice, followed by the sound of bare feet on the floorboards.

'*Irasshaimase,*' she knelt down in the raised part of the *genkan* hallway and bowed deeply. Then she stood and motioned to her guests to follow her along a dimly lit corridor. '*Dōzo kochira e,*' she intoned, sliding open a screen door to reveal a four and a half-mat tatami room. Beyond it was a second sliding wooden door, this time with glass panels frosted with steam from a bath beyond.

'*Dōzo go-yukkuri o-yasumi ni natte kudasai,*' the older woman intoned as she slid the screen door closed behind them .

Joao felt suddenly exhausted and, closing his eyes, allowed himself to fall full length onto the tatami.

'Sensei!' The girl cried in concern, gently holding his head and placing a pillow under it. 'Are you alright?'

He opened his eyes.

'Where am I?' he asked, now confused. 'And who are you?'

'Me?' She laughed coquettishly, putting one hand in front of her mouth in a manner that he recognised.

'You… Are you really?' he asked, looking at her perfectly oval face carefully. 'Chiyotsuru?'

'You *do* recognise me, sensei. For a moment, I thought you'd forgotten all about me.'

'I'm sorry,' Joao tried to sit up, but she held him down with one hand firmly on his chest. 'I hadn't expected to see you again. At least, not so soon.'

'And not dressed like this either, I'm sure,' Chiyotsuru gave one of her tinkling laughs.

'But why?'

She put one hand gently to his split lip.

'Sssh. Inukai sensei asked my Okāsan to let me look after you this evening. Not as a geisha, but as an ordinary young Japanese woman. And that's who I am this evening.'

'Not Chiyotsuru, then?'

'Definitely not Chiyotsuru.'

'Then who?'

'Yukiko.'

'Yukiko? You mean, you're a snow child? That's a lovely name.'

'Better than Chiyotsuru?'

'Definitely better than Chiyotsuru. Although Crane of a Thousand Years isn't bad,' he added quickly.

'Sensei!' She reprimanded him laughingly. 'So you're still the flatterer, in spite of whatever those nasty Kempeitai soldiers did to you today.' She put one hand under the back of Joao's neck and another behind one shoulder. 'But now it's time to find out just what they did do and make you better. Come on! One. Two. Up you come!'

Joao winced, but managed not to cry out as Yukiko helped him sit up. Then, very gently, she undid the buttons of his shirt and slipped it off. Next his undershirt. He was too exhausted to feel any sense of embarrassment at being half naked in front of her. Then she pulled off his socks. After that it was time to take off his trousers. She did it so quickly and expertly he hardly had time to notice he was now almost completely naked.

Yukiko led him towards the bathroom door, which she slid open, then allowed him to step down onto wooden boards under a thatched roof. There was a large wooden bathtub under it, completely open to the gathering darkness and giving off a deliciously refreshing smell of cedar. Steam rose in gentle spirals from the water's surface. Beyond was a Japanese garden with, again, plum flowers blossoming in profusion in one corner, and raked gravel and rocks in another.

Joao sighed with a mixture of pleasure and relief. Already the terrors of the day seemed but a distant memory.

'Sensei,' Yukiko smiled, but with a hint of embarrassment, as she spoke to him over her shoulder. 'I need your underpants.'

'You do?'

She nodded. 'To be washed,' she explained, before turning her back to him. 'Kobayashi-*san*, the chauffeur, is waiting.'

'Ah!' he said. 'Right.'

He took off his underpants and handed them to Yukiko who, without looking round, took them and left the bathroom.

'I'll be back in a few moments, sensei. In the meantime, get in the water and soak yourself.'

And with that she was gone. Joao dipped a wooden ladle into the water and rinsed himself before stepping over the edge of the bath and easing himself very slowly and carefully into the steaming hot water. It wasn't quite boiling, but it seemed like it to a body that was battered and bruised and that hadn't experienced the pleasure of a Japanese bath for a couple of years.

He sat on a bench-like ledge running along the bottom of the wooden tub and sank down until the water came up to his neck. He wrung out a *tenugui* hand towel, folded it carefully and placed it on his head. The muscles in his shoulders were incredibly sore — torn probably – but the hot water helped him relax. He closed his eyes and allowed himself to drift into a dream-like state half way between being awake and being asleep, lulled by the sound of the *shishi odoshi* in the garden outside.

It could have been three or thirty minutes later when he was aroused by the gentle sound of the door behind him being slid open. He was too tired to turn round although he realised it must be Yukiko.

'*Ojama itashimasu*,' she said from just behind him as he saw first one foot, then a second, step into the water beside him. He looked up. Yukiko had pinned her shoulder-length hair up at the back and was completely naked – her breasts small with prominent thick nipples, and a tuft of black hair sticking out from just above her vagina.

She smiled as she, too, eased herself into the hot water. There was no sexiness in her behaviour. It was as if being naked in a bath with a naked man was the most natural thing in the world.

'How are you feeling, sensei?' She asked, as she wiped her upper arms with her own *tenugui*.

'Tired,' Joao said truthfully. 'Very tired. And very sore.'

'It's been a long day, hasn't it, sensei? When you're ready, I'll wash you.

Gently, I promise.' She smiled again, and he realised what a beautiful full-lipped smile she had when her mouth wasn't bedecked with vermilion lip paste and her face plastered with *oshiroi* white make-up. Her skin wasn't quite ivory white, but it had a translucent sheen that gave off an aura of purity coupled with youthful energy.

Yukiko sensed what he was thinking.

'I know. I'm not white enough, am I? My Okāsan is always telling me so. I'll never get to the top of my profession. Not like Kohana or some of the other girls.'

'Not white enough? I think you look just right,' Joao said honestly. 'Like a real woman.'

'Sensei! Are you flattering me again?' Yukiko laughed coquettishly.

'No. Just being honest.'

'Honest? That's not something I'm very used to in my world. Thank you, sensei,' she said and, kneeling in the water in front of him, gently wiped his face and shoulders with her towel.

'Tell me, Yukiko-*san*, where are you from originally? Somewhere near Nagasaki?'

'*Ara*, sensei! How did you know? Is it my accent?'

Joao grinned.

'Yes, there was a moment back there when you slipped into the Nagasaki dialect. Most people wouldn't have noticed, but…'

'You did?'

'Because I'm from Nagasaki myself.'

'Really?' Yukiko clapped her hands in childlike delight. 'Which part?'

'Deshima in the city. And you?'

'A farming village way out in the sticks. You wouldn't have heard of it.'

'No? Try me.'

She looked at him, frowning very slightly.

'Tajiri.'

'Tajiri?'

'See? I told you you would never have heard of it.'

'You're right. I haven't. What's your surname, Yukiko?'

'Me? Ōhara.'

'There. You see!' Joao exclaimed happily.

'See what, sensei?'

'Ōhara was my mother's maiden name, too. Before she became Serino.'

'Perhaps we're related, then,' Yukiko laughed.

'Perhaps. But somehow I doubt it. There are too many people called Ōhara in Nagasaki.'

Yukiko nodded and was silent for a moment.

'Serino? That's an unusual name, sensei. Is it a Nagasaki name? I've never heard it before.'

'It's made up,' Joao was beginning to feel relaxed with her. 'My father's family is Portuguese. Their name is Sereño, but they changed it to Serino about a hundred years ago. In order to fit in.'

'*Yoso mono ishiki?* Outsider awareness? We had that sort of thing in Tajiri, too. Amongst Japanese families. Our neighbour came from across the prefectural boundary in Kumamoto – just a few miles away. Even though he'd been living next to us for a couple of generations, the other Japanese in the village still called him "that outsider who recently arrived here,"' she laughed. 'But that's Japan for you, isn't it. Always making others into outsiders.'

Joao was surprised.

'You're very enlightened, Yuki-*chan*,' he said, using the diminutive form of address usually reserved for children and lovers.

'I like to read during the day, when I've nothing else to do. After all, I have to hold my own with clients. So I read all about art and literature. History, too. Even a bit of philosophy, although I find that pretty difficult.' She laughed modestly. 'But enough of this, sensei,' she stood up suddenly, her black tuft of pubic hair right in front of his face. 'Come on. It's time I washed you.'

'In that case, you should stop calling me sensei,' he said. 'My name's Joao.'

'OK, Joao-*san*. Up you get!'

And with that she put two surprisingly strong arms under Joao's armpits and helped lift him up. Then she got a small wooden bath stool from nearby and set it by the bath overlooking the garden.

'You sit down here,' she commanded, seemingly not to notice his or her own nudity. 'And enjoy the view.'

She dipped a small basin into the bath tub and filled it with water. Then she rubbed a lot of soap into her *tenugui* towel before very carefully starting to wash Joao's back. She was especially careful as she soaped his shoulders.

'Is this alright, Joao-*san*? Not too painful? Look!' She suddenly exclaimed, pointing one soapy hand in the direction of the garden. 'It's snowing.'

Joao looked out into the night.

'My Snow Child,' he smiled.

'And my Parsley Field,' she replied with a giggle as she began to soap his chest and stomach. 'With a daikon radish growing in the middle of it.'

Joao's mouth opened, too astonished by her allusion to his penis to say anything.

She grinned.

'Don't look so surprised, Joao. Remember, I come from a farming family.'

Later, they were back in the bathtub together, gazing contentedly at the thick flakes drifting down on the garden beyond. The stone lantern already had a covering of snow, as did one corner of the pond where ice had formed. Yukiko had gently massaged Joao's body and he now felt completely relaxed, the pain in his shoulders and bruises on his stomach, not to mention his split lip and the burn on his cheek, all receding under his companion's careful ministrations. Yukiko was sitting close beside him, with her head on his shoulder. The ache was bearable.

'Tell me, Yukiko, do you have a patron?'

'Why do you ask?' He could feel her breath in the crook of his neck. Steady, soothing.

'I don't know, really. I mean, I don't know anything about how your world works. I assume your parents got paid when you were taken away and that you have to work off that debt somehow.'

'Yes. It's hard,' was all she said.

'I'm sorry I'm not in a position to help,' he said, the romantic. 'I'm not rich or important like Inukai sensei.'

'You don't have to be, Joao-*san*. There are other things that matter to a woman.'

'Yes, of course.' He let his head rest on hers. 'Still, it must be difficult.'

'How so?' She looked at him enquiringly.

'Well, look at Kohana. I don't know how old she is – more or less your age, I guess – but she's being courted by Inukai sensei. It can't be much fun making love – or being made love to – by a seventy year old bearded politician. And yet, she probably feels she has to, in order to work off her debt.'

'Kohana has other ways.'

'What do you mean?' He looked at her sharply. Was Bai-li right? Was a bath house a good place to come across secrets? Naked truths.

'Kohana has a patron.'

'A patron? But I thought Inukai –'

'Inukai sensei provides Kohana with plenty of gifts. But there's another man, she once let slip, who's paid off her debt.'

'Really? Lucky woman. Any idea who?'

'He's in the Army, I think. Or the police. She didn't really say.'

'An Army officer? He'd have to be really senior to be able to afford a geisha.'

'That's what one would have thought. But apparently he isn't.'

'And yet he's purchased her freedom?'

'It seems so. My feeling is there's a bit of give-and-take involved.'

'How so?'

Yukiko hesitated.

'I don't really want to tell tales. Kohana's my elder sister, after all. In the geisha world.'

'Fair enough.' Better not to press too hard. A journalist's instinct.

Together they sat in silence admiring the snow.

'I don't know his name,' she said after a while. 'As I said, I think he's in the Army or with the police. Kohana says he's got a scar across the back of one hand. She finds it rather sexy, even though the man himself isn't.'

'A scar?' Putting everything together now. The hot bath was beginning to clear his head as well as mend his battered body. 'If he's with the police or the Army, I bet he wants information. That's the *quid pro quo*, I expect.'

She didn't say anything, but Joao knew by the way she leaned into him that he was right. Women knew the power of words when they were necessary. And of silence when they weren't.

Even later, the two of them were alone together in his new and opulent room in the Imperial Hotel. After drying him and applying various salves to help heal his tortured body, Yukiko had led him back to the four and a half mat room where she'd left two *furoshiki* bags. One contained a fresh set of clothes which, reluctantly, he put on – reluctantly because that meant that Yukiko, too, got dressed and deprived him of the simple beauty of her nudity. The other she then untied to reveal a large lacquer box filled with *nori-make* and *inari-zushi* rice balls. These he wolfed down hungrily, one after the other, while Yukiko watched him with an almost motherly smile.

'Are you a little hungry, Joao-*san*?' She laughed.

He was. After all, he hadn't eaten all day.

'Be careful, though,' Yukiko reminded him. 'Your stomach took quite a beating earlier. Treat it gently and eat slowly.'

He did his best. So did Kobayashi-*san* waiting patiently outside in the Packard and then driving them slowly down the snow-covered alleyways of Kagurazaka, trying not to skid on the slippery slope. He left them at the hotel, with a promise that he'd be back at five o'clock the following afternoon to take Joao to meet Inukai sensei and his son at their home in Mejiro.

Joao checked in. The receptionist seemed already apprised of the fact that he'd be accompanied by Miss Yukiko Ōhara. At least, he didn't bat an eyelid when the young woman followed the hotel's very important guest to his room on the second floor.

And there they were alone again. There was a hesitancy between them, though, as if putting on their clothes had somehow covered the spontaneity of their earlier conversation in the bathhouse. There was an expectation, too, of something that was to come, but which neither of them was sure of. A sudden shyness that overcame the ease they'd experienced in the bath.

It was Yukiko who made the first move. And she made it in such a way that he couldn't possibly have resisted, even if he'd wanted to.

'Joao-*san*, let me look at your wounds before we go to bed. They may need more of my salve.'

It was the 'we' that broke the incipient awkwardness between them. A simple word buried in the depth of a sub-clause that allowed him to do whatever she suggested. So he let her unbutton his shirt and take off his vest.

'Sit on the bed,' she said, and herself got up onto it, kneeling behind him. She opened her bottle of eucalyptus salve and began rubbing his back and shoulders gently.

'How are your shoulders now?'

'Much better, thank you. You have healing hands.'

She seemed pleased, as she got off the mattress and looked at his face.

'That's a nasty burn on your cheek. Let me put more ointment on it.' She unscrewed a small jar and dipped a forefinger into it. 'Lavender's the best cure for burns, you know.'

'Lavender? Where do you find lavender in Japan?'

'Way up north in Hokkaido. The parents of one of the girls in my house sends this to us from time to time.' Gently, she smeared some of the ointment on Joao's cheek. Then she knelt down in front of him, carefully examining the bruises on his stomach.

'Lie back.'

He did so and again she applied some salve. The room was filled not just with the fragrance of lavender, but of eucalyptus mixed with the cedar wood of the furnishings and screens.

'What a lovely smell!' He exclaimed. 'It reminds me of my house in Nagasaki when I was a boy.'

'Lucky you!' She exclaimed. 'All we had was manure and night soil slops!'

Joao winced.

'That wasn't very romantic,' he laughed.

'Wasn't it? How about this then?'

Before he knew where he was, she had undone his trousers and pulled them off, so that all he was wearing was his underpants.

'Your turn,' he said, half rising from where he was lying on the bed. But she stayed him with one hand, stood up and stepped behind a gold-painted screen at the far end of the bedroom. There, the top of her head just visible, she took off her kimono and folded it carefully before laying it on the top of the screen. Next came the pair of tabi socks she'd been wearing. No bra. No underwear.

She stepped out from behind the screen. Joao saw that she was naked from the waste up and once again enjoyed the unadorned natural beauty of her body. She was wearing a *fundoshi* long strip of white cotton wound around her waist and between her legs. She let her arms hang down by her side so that he could appreciate her body as she glided nonchalantly over the floor towards him. When she reached the bed, she picked up a hotel yukata robe placed in readiness and slipped it on, before sitting on the bed beside him.

'You're wondering if I'm going to make love to you, aren't you?' She said in her matter of fact manner.

He gulped with embarrassment.

'Well -'

'Joao, there are two things you should know. First, I'm not going to give away my virginity that easily. I'm keeping that for a man I know I can love for ever. And who will love me in return. Although I may like you very much, I'm far from convinced you're that man.'

Joao nodded.

'Second, even if I had already decided that you were the man for me, I'm not sure you're in any fit state to make love to a woman tonight. At least, not to a woman like me. I'd be far too demanding.'

He had to laugh at Yukiko's direct manner. So different from her geisha persona.

'*Kawaii*. Sweet,' was all he could say.

'Sweet?' She repeated contemptuously. 'Joao-*san*, you may think me sweet on the surface, but I'm tough underneath. I have to be. It's my job.' She pushed him gently down onto the bed, as she slipped under the futon to lie beside him. 'But I promise you one thing.'

'What's that?'

'If I want to make love to a half-Japanese man who speaks the same dialect as I do, then I will. But not tonight, Joao. Tonight you need to rest.'

'If you say so.'

He closed his eyes and began to drift off to sleep, lulled by the warmth of her body curled up against his — her knees behind his, her waist against his backside, her breasts nestling against his shoulder blades.

'Do you think we will make love one day?' He heard himself asking, his voice slurred in his drowsiness.

He was asleep before he heard her reply.

The next thing he knew it was light. Yukiko was kneeling beside him on the bed. She had untied his yukata and was applying her eucalyptus salve to his shoulders, stomach and kidneys, before very gently massaging the lavender ointment on the burn on his cheek. He closed his eyes contentedly and almost immediately went back to sleep.

When he next awoke, it was late morning. It had stopped snowing and Yukiko, the Snow Child, was gone. She'd left him a brief message, thanking him for allowing her to look after him. She would look in on him that night and apply more of her ointments as necessary. He shouldn't wait up for her, though, because she'd probably come very late, after work. As was to be expected of a geisha, her handwriting was exquisite. There was a hint of lavender, too, on the envelope in which she'd placed her note. He folded the thick *washi* paper carefully, put it back in the envelope, and tucked it into the breast pocket of his jacket. Then he added a folded handkerchief to make sure it didn't fall out.

Although still suffering from soreness, he was surprised how well his body had recovered from the day before. A combination of the steaming hot bath and Yukiko's ministrations had seen to that. So after a late Japanese-style breakfast of raw egg, dried seaweed, pickled daikon radish and rice, he took a taxi to the Asahi Newspaper's head office.

'Serino!' Mori, his editor, called him into his office the moment he saw him. 'What the hell happened? We heard you'd been arrested.'

'Detained, I think, would be a more appropriate way to describe it.' Joao sat down gingerly opposite his boss. 'Detention plus a beating for good measure.'

'So I see.' Mori was concerned as he examined his star journalist's face. 'We got word quite quickly.'

'You did? How?'

'A bellhop at your hotel. We pay him to keep an eye out on what goes on there with the guests. Luckily, he was on duty when the Kempeitai came to arrest – sorry, detain – you. I got no joy out of them when I went to enquire at their headquarters, so I took the liberty of going to see the Old Fox.'

'Inukai Tsuyoshi?'

'Well, you'd told me you'd met him and his son at Chiang Kai-shek's wedding back in December. I thought he might be able to pull a few strings.'

'Which he seems to have done.'

'To judge by the way you're sitting here in front of me, yes,' Mori laughed. 'Inukai was pretty shocked when I told him what had happened. His son, Ken, was seriously angry and promised he'd deal with it. Said something about Prince Saionji. Is there some connection you've made that you're not telling me about, Serino?'

'It only happened the night before.'

'What did?'

Joao explained how he'd been invited to join the Breakfast Club.

'Sounds like a story.'

'No. Please excuse my saying so, but definitely not. We need to keep this under wraps for now. It's going to provide us with all sorts of political feedback and the occasional scoop, once the club starts meeting regularly.'

'Does this mean I have to bring you back to Tokyo?'

'Not yet. I think it'd be better if I stay in Shanghai for a while longer. Another six months, at least. The paper still needs my input on what's going on in China.'

Mori looked at him thoughtfully through his glasses, nodding his bald head up and down as he weighed up what Joao had told him.

'Fair enough. But what about that Takahashi Bank manager's suicide? Any leads?'

'Rumours. But nothing tangible. At least, not enough for a story.'

This time Mori scratched one of his rather prominent ears. Then he scribbled something on a notepad on his desk.

'Try this guy,' he said, tearing off the sheet of paper and handing it to Joao. 'Goes by the name of Sano. Works for Mikawa Trading Company and is involved in what they're up to in Manchuria. Procurements, I mean. I know he's not happy with a lot of what's going on over there, although I'm not sure why. He was into his cups at the time and not entirely coherent. But, by all accounts, he's reliable. If you can get him to talk, what he tells you will be the truth.'

An hour later Joao was sitting opposite a middle-aged salaried employee in a rundown *shokudō* eatery near Kyobashi. Like Mori, he didn't have much hair on the top of his head. Like Mori, too, he wore glasses, and his suit, with badly knotted tie, suggested that he and Mori went to the same tailor and would probably have got on rather well at a casual meeting in a cheap Shinbashi bar. Whether it was the fact that he'd been offered a free *katsudon* lunch, or Joao's rather ruffian-like look, or just because he felt like it, Sano was clearly ready to open up and talk. And without the encouraging effects of alcohol either.

'Look, Serino-*san*,' he said, looking round to make sure he wasn't being overheard. 'I shouldn't be saying this, OK? So it's all off the record.'

Joao nodded his agreement.

'As I'm sure you're aware, Mikawa Trading Company does a lot of business in Manchuria. Mantetsu – the Manchuria Railway Company that the Japanese Government set up some years back – distributes everything for us. In fact, a lot of our orders come straight from Mantetsu, so we get a pretty good discount when it comes to freight rates. We ship all the Manchurian soya bean crop, all its coal and iron back to Japan and sell it here'.

Joao wasn't quite sure where Sano was going.

'So you make a good profit?'

'Certainly.'

'And the money's paid into your bank here in Tokyo?'

'A lot of it. But not all, by any means.'

Seeing the confused look on Joao's face, Sano began to explain in the kind of voice a parent uses to a child who has failed to understand something simple. Joao was surprised how often this kind of approach worked.

'Look! We make a lot of money out of selling soya beans and minerals here in Japan, right? But we have to buy all that stuff in the first place. Which means we have to pay for everything in Manchuria before we make our profit here. And that means we need money in Manchuria, don't we? A lot of it we get from the finished goods we're sending from Japan and selling in Manchuria. But sometimes there's a shortfall. Clear so far?'

'Yes. Thank you, Sano-*san*. In other words, Mikawa has to borrow money from somewhere?'

'That's right.' The lad was beginning to see the light.

'In Mukden? Or Harbin, perhaps?'

'Neither, Serino-*san*. Shanghai.'

'Shanghai?'

'Yes, that's where the real money is, after all.'

'So the Mikawa Bank in Shanghai helps finance your company's trading in Manchuria.'

'Not the Mikawa. The Takahashi Bank. Very few people know it, but the Takahashi's an offshoot of the Mikawa financial group.'

Joao stopped taking notes. Ostentatiously, he put his notebook back in his jacket pocket. He knew from experience to do this whenever his informants began revealing information they should be keeping quiet about. It put them at ease. The fact that they weren't being recorded made it seem somehow as if whatever they said evaporated in mid-air and disappeared for good. The trouble was they forgot the part played by memory. And Joao had trained his memory well over the years.

'So where does the Takahashi Bank get its money from? I mean, enough to finance Mikawa Trading Company's business in Manchuria. Real estate?'

'Drugs,' Sano said simply.

'Drugs? You mean, opium?'

'Yes, of course.'

'Through the gangster, Tu Yue-sheng?'

'Who else?' By the tone of his voice, Sano wasn't entirely happy. 'Tu keeps a lot of his money in the Takahashi Bank branch in Hongkew. Some of it the bank uses to buy opium from Tu, before selling it at a profit to Mikawa Trading Company, which ships it here to Japan.'

'And then what?'

'It sells the opium, again at a profit, to Teikoku Tobacco.'

'Teikoku Tobacco?' Suddenly Joao realised where this conversation was going. 'To put in their Bat cigarettes.'

Sano paused, coffee cup poised in mid-air.

'You know about Bat?'

'Only that I was offered one by a Kempeitai officer yesterday morning. It made me a bit – I don't know – a bit dreamy.'

'Well it would, wouldn't it? That's the whole point.'

'Point?' Play the idiot just to make sure.

'Yes. Look! By spiking each cigarette with a tiny amount of opium, Teikoku Tobacco can turn the whole of the population of China into drug addicts. Then the Army can conquer the country without firing a single shot. At least, that's the plan. I heard it was the brainchild of some mid-ranking Kempeitai officer. He's really raking the money in. Gets his cut and spends most of it on geisha girls in Kagurazaka. Or so I've heard.'

'What do you mean?'

'Look, Serino-*san*!' Again the didactic parent. Was this guy really so thick? Journalists were supposed to be smart. 'We sell the opium to Teikoku Tobacco, right?'

'Right.'

'Teitoku Tobacco makes a special brand of cigarettes that it's not allowed to sell in Japan. So it has to export it, right? The obvious place is Manchuria. Who better to ask to do this than Mikawa Trading Company, which supplies it with the opium in the first place. So Mikawa exports millions of cartons of Bat cigarettes to Manchuria where it then distributes and sells them throughout China to an unsuspecting populace.'

'Making a profit.'

'Of course, making a profit.'

'Don't tell me, Sano-*san*. A profit which it deposits in the Takahashi Bank in Shanghai.'

Sano looked pleased with his pupil. Finally, the penny had dropped.

'I believe it's what Karl Marx referred to as the circulation of commodities,' he said wryly.

'Going round and round. And the Kempeitai takes a cut somewhere along the line. Mukden? Harbin?'

'No. Shanghai.'

Bingo again. Definitely all the rage. Joao told himself he ought to try it sometime.

'Where it deposits its money in the Takahashi Bank?'

'Well done, Serino-*san*. And now, I'm afraid, I have to be going. My lunch hour's over. Remember, though. You never heard any of this from me. In fact, we never met.'

And with that he was gone. Outside it was snowing again.

Next stop Shinjuku. He boarded the Yamanote loop line at Tokyo Station, the long way round. He could have taken the more direct Chuo Line route, but he needed to write down all the mental notes he'd made during his interview with Sano. Occasionally, just occasionally, he reflected as he wrote, a journalist struck it lucky.

Half an hour later, he got off at Shinjuku Station, and took the East Exit. As he walked slowly downhill towards Kabukichō, Joao passed an arcade where some young lads were playing on a pachinko machine – the very latest craze, or so he'd heard, and the only place in the country you could find one. There were a few seedy bars, a couple of cinemas and several cabaret clubs – all of them still closed. Kabukichō only woke up in the early evening.

He stopped at the entrance to a rickety building and climbed the stairs. At the top were a couple of rooms, filled with people playing mah-jong. Apart from the occasion cry of '*chi*' and '*ron*', the only sound in the smoke-haze came from the slap and rattle of ivory tiles. And the occasional curse, or cry of despair.

'Well, if it isn't Seri-*chan*!' One of the players stood up from a game he'd just finished. 'Long time, no see. What brings you to this neck of the woods?'

'Kuro-*chan*, how's tricks? Still ahead of your game?'

'Could be worse,' Kurogi pursed his lips. 'Thanks.'

'I need information.'

'You always need information, Serino. That's the only reason you come and see me.'

'Not entirely,' Joao said. 'I like to see a friendly face from time to time. Tokyo's such an anonymous city.'

'Yeah? Depends on where you live, I guess.' Kurogi led the way into a back office of some sort and pointed to one of two chairs that had seen better days. He lit himself a cigarette as he sat down.

'Well, what can I do for you, old friend?'

And they were old friends. Since primary school in Deshima, twenty years ago. Kurogi, 'Blackie,' had been the tough one, ready to beat the shit out of the foreign boy as and when the mood took him. But one day Seri-*chan*, 'Parsley,' had stood up to him and kneed him hard in the goolies, putting an end to that particular fight. And to any others that might have taken place thereafter. Kurogi had been impressed and often came to his rescue when one of the other bullies tried to take it out on the 'softy' in their class.

And now he was a yakuza – well, to be more truthful, more like a *chimpira* – a second-grade tough, whose job was to go round all the gambling dens and brothels and 'collect.' And woe betide anyone who didn't or couldn't for some reason pay up. They'd be seriously beaten up. Carved up with a knife – Kurogi's special skill – if they were serial offenders.

'Anyway, where've you been, Seri-*chan*? Haven't see you around now for a year or more. Found yourself a woman at last, have you?'

'No. As a matter of fact, I've been in Shanghai.'

'Shanghai? Now there's a place I wouldn't mind going to. Masses of business opportunities. My kind of business opportunities. Or so I hear.' He grinned.

'You heard right, Kuro-*chan*. Drugs, prostitution, gambling, rackets of all kinds. A good place to get rich,' Joao lit a cigarette of his own. 'And get yourself killed in the process. Too many people in your line of business end up in the river, and float off downstream to be eaten by the fish.'

Kurogi tapped the ash from his cigarette onto the floor.

'You're right, Serino. I'm probably better off here. Anyway,' he stared at his face. 'What happened to you? You look like you've been in the wars yourself.'

'I had a chat with someone in the Kempeitai.'

'Kempeitai? That's bad news. Anyone I know?'

'I doubt it. A stout gentleman with a stupid little moustache going by the name of Doihara. Claimed to be a major.'

'Kenji Doihara?' Kurogi looked at him sharply. 'Now that happens to be a name I *do* know. Cocky little bastard.'

'You can say that again. He beat the shit out of me yesterday. Without rhyme or reason. Wanted to know what I knew about the Takahashi Bank.'

'What do you know about the Takahashi Bank?' Kurogi was looking at him curiously.

'I don't. Other than what's been in the news. Why? Is there something I should know?'

'Don't ask me, Seri-chan. I just collect money and give it to my boss. I don't move it around the way he does. Or, for that matter, Doihara does.'

'You mean, Doihara has money?'

'Masses of it. Spends most of his time partying in Akasaka and Roppongi, although he's been known to slum it here in Kabukichō. The word is he's even got infatuated with a Kagurazaka geisha and bought her out.'

'Serious money, then?'

'Serious.'

'Drugs?'

Kurogi laughed.

'You were always the cunning one, Seri-*chan*. While the rest of us spent our time honing our fists, you used your brain. How did you know?'

'Actually, he gave the game away himself.'

'The arrogant prick. How?'

'By offering me a Bat cigarette spiked with opium.'

'He didn't?'

'He did. It helped when it came to being beaten up, though. I wasn't quite sure if I was there or where, if you see what I mean.'

'I do, indeed. I tried one myself once, just to see what they were like. Always need to test the product, you know,' he laughed his gruff, guttural laugh.

'So you know all about Bat fags?'

'Of course I do, Seri-*chan*. I oversee the opium being off-loaded from every ship that docks in Yokohama. Part of our business, you know, dockers. Then I have to get it loaded onto a freight train up to Utsunomiya where the Teikoku Tobacco factory is. Takes forever. A real pain of a job.'

'But you get a cut?'

'Of course, we do. We're not a charity, you know.' Again the guttural laugh.

'So you sell it on the streets here in Kabukichō?'

'Most of it. But you know how it is. There's always someone else higher up the food chain, who wants their share of whatever's going on.' He shrugged. 'That's how it works.'

'So who gets that share from your yakuza gang?'

'The Kempeitai. Bastards!' He spat on the floor.

'Bastards? How many of them?'

'Just the one, Seri-*chan*. Just the one,' he sat back in his rickety chair and puffed at his cigarette. Then he exhaled the smoke into Joao's face. Still the bully.

'Who's that, then?'

'Your new friend, Doihara.'

Kobayashi was waiting for him with the Packard in the forecourt of the Imperial Hotel at five o'clock as promised. Joao was a minute late. The receptionist had handed him a note as he left his key at the desk.

'From your wife, Serino sensei.'

It was from Yukiko. She promised to join him in his room later that evening. She didn't know what time exactly, but she would come when her work was finished. She hoped he wouldn't mind and wait up for her. She needed to make sure his body was alright.

Whether she had meant the *double entendre* or not, he wasn't sure, but it brought a smile to Joao's still far from mended face. He liked Yukiko. There was something enigmatic about her. On the one hand, she was well versed in the arts and immensely skilled in allusion. On the other, she could be extraordinarily direct. And then she had an understated, but slightly mischievous, sense of humour that he really appreciated.

'Oh! Kobayashi-*san*. There you are. Punctual as ever.'

'Thank you, sensei.'

The chauffeur held the black door of the automobile open for him once more before getting into the driving seat. The engine was already running. As he eased the car into gear and accelerated slowly out of the forecourt towards the main road, Kobayashi looked at Joao in his back mirror.

'The younger Mr Inukai will be waiting for you at his home, sensei. His father, I regret to inform you, has been delayed and will not return home until later.'

'Ah! OK. Thank you.'

The chauffeur eased the car out into Hibiya-dori and along towards the Imperial Palace.

'Tell me, Kobayashi-*san*, are you from Tokyo?'

'Yes, indeed, sensei. Born and bred in Asakusa. Like my father and grandfather before me.'

'A real *Edokko*, then.'

Kobayashi laughed.

'That's right, sensei. Tokyo actually was called Edo in my grandfather's time. There aren't that many of us left these days, of course. We tend to live in low-lying places like Asakusa, and the Kanto Earthquake killed a lot of us three-generation Tokyo-ites.'

'Ah, yes. Of course.' Joao sat silently for a while. Then,

'Excuse my asking, Kobayashi-*san*, but how long have you been Inukai sensei's driver?'

'Me, sir? Ooh, longer than I can remember, really.'

Seeing his passenger's frown, he continued. 'Actually, I started out as my boss' gardener.'

'Gardener?'

'Yes, sensei. As you'll see when we get there, the Inukai family has a very pleasant old *yashiki* residence, with a large garden. There's always plenty of work to do there.'

'But you became a chauffeur. How come?'

'Inukai sensei had become an important politician and needed somebody to drive him around. So he asked me to do it.'

'And what about the garden? Did anyone tend it in your place?'

'Yes, my son, sir. He'd just left school and needed a job. I taught him a few things while I was learning how to drive.'

'That must have been difficult.'

'What? Learning how to drive? It's a piece of cake, sensei. Any old fool can do it. All you need to do is turn the steering wheel left or right from time to time, and make sure your feet don't get mixed up on the pedals. Of course, there are more vehicles on the road now, compared with when I started a few years back, but I've had all the experience I need, so hopefully we're not going to have a crash.'

Joao laughed.

'Even if we do, Kobayashi-*san*, I'm sure it won't be as bad as my clash with the Kempeitai yesterday.'

'Yes, sir. I'm very sorry about that, sensei.'

'Thank you, but there's nothing to be sorry about. It wasn't your fault.'

'No, sensei. Maybe not. But I don't like to witness injustice. Maybe it's my *Edokko* temperament, but it's not right – especially when the perpetrators get away with it. It makes you wonder what's happening to Japan these days, doesn't it? Military policemen doing whatever they please here in Tokyo – and probably in the rest of the country, too, for all I know. And then there's the Army in Manchuria ready to run riot, regardless of whatever cabinet ministers like Inukai sensei tell them. All this talk about democracy and the new Japan – sometimes I think it's all a bit of a sham designed to make us shut up and accept what's going on without complaining.'

Kobayashi kept his eyes on the road, with only an occasional glance at Joao in his back mirror. They were driving along past Takebashi now, heading for Iidabashi. It was a busy time of the evening and there were plenty of other bicycles, carts, the occasional tram, and motor vehicles and pedestrians all negotiating their way along the same route.

'Do you have any other children, Kobayashi-*san*?'

'Me, sensei? No. Just the one, alas! My brother, though, has three daughters more or less the same age as my son, so we're pretty close as a family. It wouldn't surprise me if my son ended up marrying the oldest girl in a couple of years' time. They're a good match.'

'Cousin marriage, eh?'

'That's right, sir. Cousin marriage is often the best, they say.'

'Maybe you're right.' When arranged marriages were the norm, it was usually safer to choose a bride from a family you knew.

'What does your brother do, then, if you don't mind my asking?'

'My brother, sensei? Oh, he's the smart one, he is, in our family. Always reading books as a child. Not manga comics, mind you. Real books. He ended up working as an archivist.'

'An archivist? Now that is unusual. You're quite a family, aren't you. A gardener who learns to drive. A younger brother who becomes an archivist. Not many *Edokko* families can say that about themselves. Where does your brother work?'

'Well, I'm a bit ashamed to say so, sensei, but he's employed by the Army Ministry.'

'The Army?'

'Yes, sensei, a bit ironical, really, seeing as my brother's a pacifist. Well, to be honest, we all are really. But there you go. Life's a funny old thing, isn't it.'

'You can say that again.'

'Anyway, now you can understand why, personally, I got pretty pissed off when I learned you were being interrogated by the Kempeitai. Anyone who suffers at their hands is my friend. I mean it, sensei. If there's anything I can do to help, don't hold back. Just ask.'

'Thank you, Kobayashi-*san*. That's very kind of you. I appreciate it. But maybe you should be careful when making an offer like that. I may well take you up on it.'

Kobayashi fixed his eyes firmly on Joao.

'Good, sensei. I look forward to that. Remember, I'm an *Edokko*. We have our pride. If we say we'll do something, we do it.'

By now they were climbing slowly up the long hill to Mejiro. The temperature had risen slightly and there'd been a bit of a thaw from mid-afternoon, so the Packard was able to negotiate the slush with ease. At the top of the hill, Takahashi turned right along a narrow street and a couple of blocks in, right again into a dead-end alley. He brought the car to a halt outside an imposing wooden *mon* gate.

'Here we are, sensei. The Inukai residence.' Kobayashi gave a gentle toot on the car horn, as he switched off the engine and got out to open the door for Joao.

'Thank you, Kobayashi-*san*. I greatly appreciated our chat.'

'Don't mention it, sensei. It was a pleasure. And don't forget what I told you, sir.'

'I won't. You can be sure of that.'

Each of them bowed to the other. It was incredible how things that he had fretted over because they seemed so difficult, suddenly became easy.

A small door built into the closed wooden gates behind him opened and Ken came out into the street.

'Joao,' he exclaimed, as he bowed in greeting. Then he came forward quickly and put his arm around Joao's shoulders. 'How are you? Is everything alright?'

Joao tried not to wince at the pain.

'Fine, thanks to you and your father. I'm very grateful to you both, Ken-*chan*.'

'Don't thank me,' he said quickly, taking him by the arm and leading him through the small side door. 'Thank Prince Saionji. He was the one who pulled all the strings to get you out. It must have been a terrible experience. And frightening, too.'

'Frightening, indeed. And painful.'

Ken led his friend along a path away from the main house. The snow had been swept from the flag stones, but the trees and bushes in the garden were still laden with snow. Clearly, the thaw hadn't managed to make its way up to the top of Mejiro hill.

'Mind your step,' Ken said, as if he was reading his friend's train of thought. 'It's quite slippery here and there.'

They walked parallel to the main house to a smaller dwelling half hidden behind three carefully trimmed pine trees, their trunks protected by plaited straw. As they came abreast of the trees, Joao found himself looking out over the city, with the lights of Ikebukuro on the left and, way over to the right, those of Shinjuku, where he'd been talking to Kurogi earlier that afternoon.

'Wow!' was all he could say. 'You live here, Ken?'

'Not quite a four and a half mat tea house, but simple all the same. It suits my needs.'

He led his visitor into a pebbled entrance where they slipped off their shoes, before stepping up into the house.

'Just the two rooms,' Ken said. 'One for entertainment; the other for study – and sleeping the occasional guest. There's a small kitchen where the maid from the main house prepares my food when I need it, and an open-air bath the far side there,' he pointed in the direction of the Shinjuku lights. 'Maybe that's where we should start the evening. We both need to clean up after a day in the city.'

So, once again, Joao found himself naked in a bath tub with another person – this time a man. The bath itself was quite small and intimate, big enough really for just two people, but it had a spectacular view, unimpeded by the usual compound wall.

'There's quite a drop in front beyond the garden,' Again Ken seemed to be reading his thoughts. 'So my father reckoned he didn't want to spoil the view from the *engawa* veranda of our two houses. He just bought up the plot of land below and put a wall round that to stop potential burglars.'

'It's beautiful,' Joao intoned. 'Certainly better than anything I've come across in Shanghai. It reminds me of Nagasaki. Our house in Deshima has this kind of view. It makes me wonder why I ever left.'

'You'll go back, Joao. One always goes back to one's family home. It's where your soul resides, even when you're far away somewhere – like in Tokyo or Shanghai. We always return to where our soul is.'

They sat silently together in the bath, occasionally sinking up to their necks when their shoulders felt cold.

'So, what did they do to you, those bastards at the Kempeitai? I noticed a few bruises here and there as you undressed. And whatever happened to your face?'

'They slapped it around – hence the split lip and the cut above my eye. And then my newly acquired friend, a Major Doihara, decided to stub his cigarette out on my cheek.'

'The bastard!'

'That's what I thought. Luckily, it was at that moment a colonel walked in and ordered him to release me. Prince Saionji saved me in the nick of time. I have a lot to thank him for.'

'Including the ministrations of a rather beautiful young geisha called Chiyotsuru, I gather. Makes me sort of want to be interrogated by the Kempeitai myself.' Ken laughed.

'Was Prince Saionji responsible for her, too?' Joao had thought it must have been Ken's father who'd arranged for Yukiko's company. 'In which case I owe him even more. We kind of hit it off, Yukiko and I.'

'Yukiko? So that's her real name, is it? A perfect fit for the weather. Don't tell me you've fallen in love, sensei!' He said ironically. 'Remember, that's what she's been trained to do. Steal a man's heart. Her future depends on it.'

'True. But I had the feeling she felt genuinely sorry for me.'

'Compassion isn't the same as love, though, is it, Joao? But you don't need me to tell you that. Come on! Let's get dressed. There's some sushi and sashimi waiting for us inside.'

A few minutes later, the two of them were sitting on the edge of the open veranda with two large plates – one filled with tuna, mackerel, yellowtail and octopus sashimi; the other with *nigiri* sushi – tuna, shrimp, and omelette. Joao realised he hadn't had anything proper to eat since breakfast and began wolfing down his food.

'Steady on, Joao. This isn't an Olympics race, you know. We've got all the time in the world.'

'Sorry,' Joao bowed his head in apology. 'It's been a long day, and I didn't have time to eat properly.'

'What kind of a long day?'

'Are you ready for a long story?'

'It's still only just evening. We've got plenty of time. Fire ahead.'

So Joao told Ken first about Doihara's rather unexpected interest in the Takahashi Bank, followed by everything he'd learned that day in a couple of interviews. As his story unfolded, Ken stopped eating and gazed at his friend with a look that was a mixture of wonder and surprise – wonder at Joao's ability as a newspaper journalist to dig under the surface of appearances and get hold of the truth; surprise at the sheer audacity and mendacity of Doihara and the Kempeitai.

'This has to be stopped,' he exclaimed angrily once Joao had finished. 'The Kempeitai's job is to police the Army, not make a small fortune selling spiked cigarettes to unsuspecting Chinese peasants. You've got to publish this, Joao. People have to know what's going on.'

'True,' Joao agreed, taking just one more shrimp *nigiri* rice ball, dipping it into wasabi and soy sauce, and then plopping it into his mouth. 'But I'm going to have to write it in such a way that I protect my sources. So I'll wait until I get back to Shanghai. Then I'll make it seem as if it's something I've found out in China, not Japan. That way, nobody will be able to trace things back to the people I talked to today. Doihara won't be able to get his revenge.'

'On them, at least. But what about you?'

'Me? We'll face that problem if or when it happens. It's one of the hazards of being a journalist in times like this, Ken. If the truth comes out, it can be dangerous. But that shouldn't stop me from pursuing it.'

'At any cost?'

'At all costs.'

Now was the time, he realised, for the *nerai* threat. The *go* game had gone on for too long. The board was filling with black and white stones, and it was hard to tell who fully occupied what. Ken would have no choice but to answer his *sente* attack.

'So, how does one take the Army down?'

'What? Oh, I see what you mean. To be frank, I've no idea.'

'Would you support military intervention in China, if it were absolutely necessary?'

'I suppose if it were absolutely necessary. But how do you define absolutely?'

'Or necessary.'

Play elsewhere for the moment. *Tenuki*.

'Or necessary,' Ken conceded. 'I just don't know. I mean, it'd be better, wouldn't it, if Chiang Kai-shek were able to unify the country and make peace with Japan. That'd be the best solution, surely?'

'I agree.' Tighten the play. 'But what if hot-headed officers in the Kwangtung Army were to disregard government orders and take matters into their own hands? It's not beyond the realm of possibility, is it?'

'True.' Ken helped himself to one of the two remaining rice balls before pushing the plate gently towards Joao. 'It is really difficult to control the Kwangtung Army when it's so far away in Manchuria. That's where newspapers can be so useful, Joao. You can put out warning signals.'

'Would they be enough, though? My impression is mid-ranking officers like Doihara in the Kempeitai are a law to themselves. They're not going to listen to anyone unless they happen to agree with them.'

'I suppose not.'

'There's something else, too.'

A forcing move. *Kikashi*.

'What?'

'Every newspaper has two sources of income. One from its subscribers. The other – a much larger source – comes from advertising. If an advertiser doesn't like what a newspaper publishes, it withdraws its custom. In the end, therefore, a newspaper lives or dies according to the health of its advertising. That means journalists like me can't just write anything we want to write. It's my editor's job to make sure I don't overstep the line drawn between the newspaper and its advertisers.'

'So every newspaper has two masters, you mean?'

'Right. In other words, there's no such thing as a "free" press, Ken, whatever journalists like to pretend.'

'But what other options are available to us?'

'Us?'

Atari.

'I mean, to whoever's sufficiently concerned to want to do something. To act on behalf of the country. I mean, we don't want war, do we?'

'Absolutely not.' Careful. 'At least, not yet.'

'Probably never. It would destroy us.'

'Something that would hardly please our new Emperor.'

Suggest proper affiliations. Give wriggle room. Now, though, for the final attacking play. *Yose*.

'Tell me, Ken, do you think it's possible to take a leaf out of the militarists' playbook and forestall them?'

'Forestall them? How?'

'By creating and publishing a document that purports to outline the Kwantung Army's future plans in Manchuria, China and the rest of Asia.'

'What plans?'

On his guard now. But not too much. Closer to curious. Perfect *gote* defensive.

'Well, what we've been assuming. That the Army will take over Manchuria as a prelude to invading China. With or without the Government's blessing. With Tanaka in charge, anything the Army does will probably be tolerated, even if he himself doesn't approve. He is, after all, a soldier through and through.'

'Fair enough, but –'

'But what if those "plans" purported to be something that Tanaka himself approves of? A document of some kind that embarrasses the Army.'

Keep Ken on the defensive. *Kiai*.

'What have you got in mind?'

'What if it were made known that the Prime Minister of Japan, without consulting his own cabinet – of which your father is an esteemed member – was advocating military intervention in Manchuria? Surely that would create a rift in government – a rift from which your father might benefit? If properly forewarned, of course.'

At that moment, there was the sound of the *genkan* door opening at the back of the house, followed by Tsuyoshi sensei's gruff voice.

'Oy! Anyone at home?'

'Father? *Irasshai*!'

Both men got up to their feet as the old man came into the room.

'Brrr! A bit cold in here. Aren't you two freezing, sitting out there on the veranda?'

Ken took the hint and slid the shōji paper screens closed.

'Let's get into the *kotatsu* then. That way we can keep our legs warm.'

The three of them sat down under a low table, with their feet extending below the floor into a shallow pit filled with warm charcoal.

'That's better,' Tsuyoshi grunted contentedly. 'So what've you two been up to?'

'Joao's been telling me all about his experiences at Kempeitai HQ. As well as what he's learned about the Takahashi Bank.'

'The Takahashi? I'm all ears,' the old man said. 'They're talking about nothing else in Cabinet. Day in, day out. Repeating the same old stuff. And doing absolutely nothing. What have you heard, Serino-*kun*?'

For the second time that evening, Joao related everything that had happened over the past two days.

'Well, that's something I hadn't heard before. Not even a whisper of it,' Tsuyoshi said admiringly. 'You really are a good journalist, aren't you.'

'There's more, Father.'

'There is? What?'

This time it was Ken who told him about the discussion they'd been having when Tsuyoshi arrived. The old man listened, stroking his beard as he did so. His eyes were watchful and his mind alert.

'So what in particular were you thinking of in relation to this document you were talking about?'

Sente.

'Something suggesting that the Kwantung Army is ready to attack China. Perhaps the rest of Asia, too.'

'But what's this proposed document's provenance?' Tsuyoshi asked sharply. 'How does it come into being in the first place?'

Joao explained what he'd learned about the Far Eastern Conference: that nothing had been published regarding its conclusions. Apparently, not even minutes had been taken.

Tsuyoshi didn't interrupt him at all. A good sign? Or a bad one? Once Joao had finished speaking, there was a long silence. The old man took a *kiseru* bamboo-stemmed pipe from the sleeve of his kimono, found his tobacco pouch in the other sleeve, and filled the tiny bowl of his pipe.

'I'm really impressed by your grasp of the situation in East Asia,' he said finally, as he puffed contentedly. 'And of Tanaka's "Blood and Iron" approach, although I don't necessarily agree with it.'

Joao waited expectantly. Neither of these topics had been the subject of their discussion, but he reckoned Tsuyoshi needed time to work out how he could make use of everything he'd told him to his own political advantage. Minimize and maximise. Eventually,

'Yes. Such a document could work,' he agreed.

Much to Joao's relief, it was Ken who spoke.

'Why don't we write one, then?'

'We?'

'Why not? You, Father, know the Japanese side of things really well. And Joao here knows the Chinese side. Between you, you could write a protocol of the kind Joao's suggesting.'

Another long pause as Tsuyoshi worked out the long game. Reading ahead.

'We need sake,' he said. 'O-Kyō!' he shouted. 'Are you there?'

'Haiii!' Came a distant voice, followed by the sound of wooden clogs tripping along the flagstones in the garden. The *genkan* door was opened again and a flushed maid put her head through the door to the room where they were sitting.

'Sensei?'

'Sake! There are three cold and thirsty men in here who need warming up. Ooh!' he turned towards Ken, 'maybe I should get hold of Kohana? She'd soon get rid of the cold in our blood.'

'No, Father!' Ken said firmly. 'No more Kohana. Your fascination with young women has got us into enough trouble, as it is.'

Tsuyoshi looked a bit shifty, but covered it well.

'Trouble? What do you mean, trouble?'

Ken explained. As he went through one detail after another, Tsuyoshi's face fell. He began to look like a small boy scolded in class for not remembering his multiplication tables.

'I'm sorry, Serino-*kun*. It won't happen again. I'll tell the Okāsan at the Sakura tea house. I doubt whether Kohana will ever work again. Not there, at least.'

'Anyway, Father, you don't want to share a woman with an arrogant major in the Kempeitai, do you?'

'Captain in the Kempeitai.'

'Captain? What do you mean captain?'

'Demoted this morning. And to be transferred to China.'

'Serves him right.'

'Yes, but he can do as much damage over there as here. Somebody needs to put a bullet in his head.'

'Be careful what you say, Father. Even the pine trees have ears these days.'

'Harrumph!'

O-Kyō slid open the shoji screen door separating the main rooms from the kitchen and, with a bow and a muttered 'Excuse me,' brought in two bottles of sake together with three small cups. Joao used the diversion to get up from the *kotatsu* and walk across the tatami to where he'd left a slim briefcase. He opened it and took out a few sheets of paper.

'I know it was a bit presumptuous of me,' he said, returning to the warmth of the *kotatsu*, 'But I wrote a few notes beforehand outlining what a summary of the Far Eastern Conference might look like. Actually, I made two versions, just for fun – one advocating peace, the other war. My editor's thinking about publishing them together as an editorial to make our readers aware of the limitations of each approach.'

'The military option's the one we want,' Tsuyoshi said gruffly. 'If we're intent on embarrassing the Kwantung Army.'

Joao handed a few sheets to Ken who quickly scanned the first page, before passing it on to his father as he moved to the second.

'"In order to take over the world, we need to take over Asia,"' Tsuyoshi read out loud. 'That's quite a bombshell for an opening line summarising participants' conclusions, Serino-*kun*. You newspaper journalists certainly know how to attract attention.'

'That's one reason Prince Saionji wants Joao on our team,' Ken laughed. 'He knows how to write. Unlike us politicians.'

'Harrumph!' Tsuyoshi exclaimed again, as he continued reading, placing each page face down on the *kotatsu* table top. When he was finished, he sat silently refilling the bowl of his *kiseru* pipe. Analyse, extrapolate and read ahead. The best responses to each play. And the best responses to those responses. And so on. Maximize. Minimize.

'I think it'll work,' he said finally. 'But, to be honest, I'm not entirely happy. Too many imponderables.'

'But can I take it that you agree in principle, sensei?'

'In principle, yes.' He nodded and puffed on his pipe. 'But you'll need to get Saionji's approval before you go ahead. Without his support, this'll go nowhere.'

'Of course,' Joao bowed his head reluctantly. What Tsuyoshi had said was perfectly reasonable, but he didn't fancy trying to persuade the *genro* elder statesman to condone an act that could be interpreted as treason.

'Can I mention your name, though, when I talk to him? Or would you prefer to be kept right out of this?'

'Yes, of course you can. In fact, I'll set up a meeting for you and forewarn him. If Saionji says OK, then I'm with you all the way.'

'You don't usually commit yourself so openly, Dad. What's wrong with you?' Ken laughed.

'I'm looking ahead, Ken-*chan*.'

'Plotting again?'

'You might call it that.'

'You're going to bring down Tanaka, aren't you? I know you, Father. Not in the immediate future, maybe. But sometime fairly soon.'

'Maybe,' Tsuyoshi smiled enigmatically and poured more sake into his companions' cups.

'In which case, don't get mixed up with any more women. Kohana, Gerda – they just cause you problems. I mean, look at –' He stopped in mid-sentence in embarrassment. 'I'm sorry, Joao, I didn't mean –'

'Don't worry. I know all about what happened that evening at the Majestic. Not my most glorious moment, sensei,' he turned to Tsuyoshi. 'But Gerda and I've worked things out between us. Anyway, it's not as if she and I are ever going to get married, or anything like that. She isn't Japanese.' Better to affirm his identity.

'But Yukiko is!' Ken teased, hiding his embarrassment at his father's infidelities.

'Who's this Yukiko? Anyone I know?'

'Yes. And there again, no. You know her as Chiyotsuru. Joao seems to have discovered she's also called Yukiko.'

'Harrumph,' Tsuyoshi exclaimed in the manner he usually adopted when he disapproved of something or saw its amusing side. 'Ken-*chan*! There's work to be done. Get out brush and ink and write these notes up in your best handwriting. Cut out the bit about Sino-Japanese relations where Serino gets a bit too scholarly. But keep the rest. OK? I'll go and give Saionji a call.'

Prince Saionji received him in the Tsukimidō, Moon Viewing Pavilion, in the Kitanomaru Garden of the Imperial Palace. It was eleven o'clock the following morning. True to her word, Yukiko had joined him in his hotel room the night before, a little after midnight, and once more tended to his injuries, before again joining him in bed under the futon. Again she allowed her body to follow the contours of his own back and legs, although this time she placed one arm over his waist as they slept. Like brother and sister, he thought happily.

A member of the Imperial Household was waiting to usher Joao along various deserted corridors to an eight mat reception room. There was a simple flower arrangement reaching out from the mouth of an equally simple Korean moon jar in the *tokonoma* raised dais along one earth and wattle wall, and in the centre of the room an *irori* fireplace on which an iron kettle was gently steaming.

Joao felt relaxed and at peace with himself, but he was glad he'd put on his most formal clothes. When the elder statesman came into the room, he was wearing a black suit with a sober dark grey tie knotted round a starched wing collar. It kept the wrinkles under his chin at bay.

'Serino-*san*, delighted to make your acquaintance,' the prince said, as he, too, knelt down on the other side of the *irori*. 'I hope you don't mind the open *shoji*. The view of the garden is so beautiful, don't you think, with the snow?'

'Indeed, Your Highness. I cannot imagine how it must look in the moonlight.'

'Magical, I can assure you. Too much for even Tessai to capture. And certainly beyond the literary powers of Abe no Nakamaro,' he laughed shortly, testing his guest's knowledge of *bujinga* painting.

'Too much can be made of nostalgia, I tend to think. Especially in poetry,' Joao said, sucking the cold air sharply through his half open mouth, but playing the game. Tessai had painted a picture of the poet contemplating the moon in China. 'But maybe Your Highness disagrees?'

Saionji ignored the question. The young man in front of him was at least erudite. Always a positive.

'First of all, Inukai tells me you have accepted my proposal that you become a member of the Breakfast Club. I would like to thank you.'

'The honour is entirely mine, Your Highness.'

Saionji waved away his thanks.

'I also understand that you have come across a rather unusual form of trade that involves a certain Captain Doihara and, perhaps, other members of the Kempeitai.'

Joao bowed his head in acknowledgement.

'I'm sure you editor wants you to write all about it. And that is right and proper, Serino-*san*. But there are going to be things that your newspaper can't, for one reason or another, publish. I would like you, therefore, to write a full report about what you've learned –' and I mean everything, including the minutest detail that attracts your attention, for circulation to members of the Breakfast Club. We need to formulate a longer term strategy.'

'Of course, Your Highness.'

Saionji scooped a wooden spoonful of tea from a caddy into a small side-handled *kyuusu* tea pot, and poured hot water from the kettle sizzling gently on the *irori* beside him.

'Inukai tells me you have a proposition,' he continued. 'An unusual proposition, I understand.'

'I'm not sure whether it should be termed unusual, Your Highness, or simply insane.'

'Let me be the judge of that. Why don't you tell me about it? But please, be concise, Serino-*san*. I don't have either the time or the patience for long-winded explanations.'

'Of course, Your Highness.'

Joao had expected something like this – Ken had warned him the evening before that the Prince could be impatient with those who strayed from simplicity – and he had spent the morning preparing what he was going to say. He wasn't going to fudge. If he was going to fail, he might as well do so quickly. He could always revert to plan B.

Not that he had a plan B. Yet. Other than to approach Kobayashi's brother.

But first things first.

So he outlined his perception of Sino-Japanese relations and the Kwantung Army's potential belligerence, the need for something that would expose their plans and so alert the Japanese public to the dangers of military intervention. He knew he was still on safe ground at this point. It was the next step – his suggested cure – that was going to give Prince Saionji cause for reflection.

'A protocol?' As he poured out tea into two porcelain cups, the old man's rigidly straight back betrayed his attention. 'An Imperial Protocol. Audacious, to say the least. I'm beginning to see what you meant by its insanity, Serino-*kun*.'

A change in the way he was being addressed by the old man. Did the slight informality of *kun* indicate that his idea wasn't being rejected outright?'

'As you say, Your Highness, audacious. But in my view necessary. Essential even.'

'Please,' Saionji offered the open palm of one hand towards his guest. 'Have some tea.'

'Thank you, Your Highness.'

Both men lifted the handle-less porcelain cups from their lacquer saucers and sipped the green tea thoughtfully.

'Is it to your taste, Serino-*kun*?' The elder statesman asked politely.

'Very much so, Your Highness. Yame *sencha*, if I'm not mistaken?'

Saionji looked at the young journalist approvingly. He'd passed the second test. One more and he'd make a decision.

'Supposing I were to approve of your plan, how would you go about realising it?'

'I wouldn't be able to, Your Highness, without your assistance.'

'How so?'

'You are the only person I've met who knows what an Imperial Protocol looks like. How it should be worded in its address to the Emperor. What kind of calligraphy should be used on what kind of paper. And what seals should be attached. Without your advice on these matters, I'm helpless.'

'Do you have a sample of what you intend to put in your so-called protocol?'

'Yes, Your Highness,' Joao slipped an envelope across the tatami between them. Saionji opened it and took out the sheet of paper Ken had written the evening before. Unhurriedly he read its contents, before laying the sheet of paper down on the tatami beside his porcelain tea cup and saucer.

'Do you recognise the provenance of your teacup?' Saionji asked, *à propos* of nothing.

'Yes, I think so, Your Highness. Nabeshima ware from the Imaizumi kiln.'

'Yes, but which Imaizumi?' Saionji probed.

Joao bowed his head.

'That's a difficult question to answer, Your Highness. The wares are so standardised. It's hard to tell between one generation and the next.'

'But?'

'But, if I were forced to make a guess – which Your Highness is clearly obliging me to do – I'd say tenth or eleventh generation.'

Saionji scratched the top of his bald head as he regarded his visitor. Not just extremely well versed in the arts, but bold. And direct. Seemingly unconcerned by the possibility of failure. A man who had stood up to interrogation by the Kempeitai and who was prepared to take an incredible risk on behalf of his country. And his father was said to be Portuguese. If only more Japanese were like him.

'I assume you've spent quite a lot of time wandering round bookshops in Kanda?'

'Yes, indeed, Your Highness.'

'Of course,' he smiled, 'You're a journalist, aren't you. And one who clearly reads books. Unlike too many of your colleagues.'

Joao said nothing, waiting.

'Presumably, in your wandering, you've come across Iwanami Shoten.'

Joao bowed to signal that indeed he had.

'Round the back of the building, on Kanda Suzuran Street, is a place that sells calligraphy brushes, ink stones, *washi* paper, that sort of thing. The man who runs it is called Suzuki.'

'Hah!' Joao signalled that he had taken all this in.

'Go there and speak to Suzuki. Not the young one, but his father. He spends most of his time upstairs. Explain exactly what you need and give him this,' he slid Joao's envelope back across the tatami. 'He'll know what's required.'

Saionji took a small embossed card from one pocket of his jacket. From the other, he brought out a small vermilion seal and pressed it firmly to the card. 'And this will tell him that the request comes from me.'

Once again the Prince put his hand into a jacket pocket – this time his inside one – and drew out a carefully wrapped packet on which were written in brushstrokes the words *o-iwai*. The Prince once again slid the envelope full of money towards his visitor.

'Your Highness, I cannot possibly accept this,' Joao pushed the envelope back across the tatami. 'As I understand it, you've arranged for my release from Kempeitai Headquarters, as well as for the ministrations of a young geisha, Chiyotsuru, to tend to my wounds. I am too indebted to you already, Your Highness, to be able to take advantage of your money.'

Saionji smiled. When he did so, his nose seemed to grow a little longer than it already was.

'What do you mean "my" money?' he smiled, with a nod towards the envelope in front of Joao. 'I don't recall having given you any money, Serino-*kun*. So far as I'm aware, the contents of that packet have always been yours.'

It wouldn't be polite to refuse, so Joao bowed deeply, uttering his sincerest thanks. The tatami when it touched his forehead was cool. If only he felt the same.

'Well, we are going up in the world, aren't we, sensei?' Kobayashi grinned as he eased the Packard out through the Kikyomon gate and across the palace moat into the traffic running along Hibiyadōri. 'I've never had the pleasure of seeing the inside of the Imperial Palace grounds. Imagine! A simple *Edokko* like me being so close to the Emperor. Thank you, sensei. I'm most grateful.'

'Not at all, Kobayashi-*san*. As I warned you, payback time's coming soon,' Joao laughed. 'Anyway, I've never been inside the palace grounds before either, so that makes two of us. And I'm not even an *Edokko*.'

'Anyway sensei, where to now?' Kobayashi asked.

'Kanda Jimbochō. Iwanami Shoten. After that, I'll look after myself, thank you.'

'Are you sure you're going to be alright, sensei? I noticed a couple of rough-looking guys outside the palace watching you very carefully.'

'What?' Joao looked out of the back window of the car in surprise.

'Sorry, sensei. That was one of my crude attempts at a joke. Everything's fine. Nobody's after you.'

'Not yet.'

'As you say, not yet. But I've got a feeling nobody's going to bother you much here anymore. Word will be out on the street and in police stations and *kōban* boxes around town. I reckon you're untouchable.'

'Even if I ask you to tell your brother to do something for me? Something he definitely shouldn't do in his job?'

'Well, sensei, of course it depends on what you ask. But knowing you, there'll be a reason for whatever it is. And a good one, too.'

Joao paused to give him a chance to change his mind. He liked Kobayashi too much to want to put him or his family in danger.

'OK, then. Would you and your brother mind meeting me tomorrow evening? Will you be free then?'

Kobayashi sucked air through his teeth. Then,

'I don't know about myself, but my brother should be free. He finishes work at six.'

'Then why doesn't he come to the Imperial Hotel and meet me there? I'll wait for him in the lobby at – say – six thirty.'

'Six thirty in the Imperial Hotel. Very good, sensei. You can expect me, too, if I'm free. I've never been inside that building either, although I've hung around outside it often enough. Goodness me! What's becoming of my life. The Imperial Palace one day, and the Imperial Hotel the next. My mates will never believe me.'

Kobayashi dropped him outside the Iwanami publishing house offices and drove off, as smoothly as always. Joao marvelled at his skill. You never quite knew if you were moving or stationary in the Packard. Maybe it was the car, but he doubted it.

Following Prince Saionji's instructions, Joao walked along Kanda Suzuran street until he came to Suzuki's stationery store.

'*Irasshaimase!*' An elderly woman shuffled forwards in her wooden clogs to greet the new customer.

'I'm looking for Mister Suzuki,' Joao said politely.

'Which one?'

'Your husband.'

'He's upstairs,' she motioned with her head towards an open door leading to a set of open. stairs. *'Anata!'* she called loudly. '*Okyakusan desu.* You have a visitor.'

There was a muffled grunt from upstairs.

'He's like that,' the woman said in mild exasperation. Husbands!

Joao negotiated the staircase. Its treads were steep and narrow. At the top was a large work table with two overhead lights. An elderly man in his sixties was hunched over a large piece of Japanese paper, held down at each corner by iron paper weights, each embossed with a thirteen petalled chrysanthemum flower. The Imperial seal.

'How can I help?' He stood up straight, stretching his back. Suzuki was wearing a heavy cotton kimono, with its sleeves tucked into the armholes of a *chanchanko* padded jacket that kept his back warm as he worked.

'Good afternoon, Suzuki-*san*. My name is Serino. Prince Saionji recommended that I come to you.'

'Prince Saionji?' Suzuki looked at him a little doubtfully.

'Yes. He asked me to give you this.' Joao gave him the Prince's embossed card.

Suzuki pushed his glasses up onto his forehead and peered down to read it.

'Well, Mister Serino, what can I do for you? ' He asked, pushing his glasses back down onto his nose.

Joao explained, while Suzuki listened carefully.

'An Imperial Protocol, then. From the Prime Minister, you say? Then we'll need two seals. That's easy enough. I use them all the time. The paper's a bit special, though. Kyōchiyogami. It comes from Kyoto, of course.'

'Of course.' That was where the Imperial Household had been located for hundreds of years, until the Emperor Meiji moved to Tokyo in the mid to late 1800s.

Joao gave Suzuki the note Saionji had scribbled for him. 'The Prince asked me to give you this, too.'

Suzuki took the note, pushed his glasses up on his forehead again, and squinted at what Saionji had written.

'You have to hand it to them, don't you?' Was all he said as he looked up.

'Hand what to whom?'

'Our imperial family, of course,' he said a little disapprovingly, as if to a child who should know better. 'They really know how to write. I mean, look at this calligraphy,' he showed Saionji's note to Joao. 'It's perfect. Quite beautiful. Even a hurried scribble like this is a work of art.'

'Yes, you're right,' Joao sucked some air through his teeth. 'When can I pick up the document, Suzuki-*san*?'

'Eh? Oh, right! The protocol. How about this time tomorrow? I'll have it done by then.'

Joao took the folded envelope of money that Saionji had given him and placed it on the work table where Suzuki was standing.

'The Prince asked me to give you this for your services.'

Suzuki hurried picked it up and slipped it into the waist pocket of his padded jacket.

'He shouldn't have,' he muttered. As if his artistic skill was somehow contaminated by the base reward of money.

Once he had left Suzuki, Joao walked to the Asahi Newspaper office in Kyōbashi. There he filled Mori in on everything he'd learned and thanked his editor for the lead. It was time for Joao to head back to Shanghai. He could check out a few missing details, hopefully get some more information, and write up his article. Mori said he'd make it a two-page spread in the Sunday edition. Maximum effect. People had time to read long articles as they lay sprawled on their tatami floors or sat at the *kotatsu* smoking.

Joao asked for a few days off work. He wanted to see his mother in Nagasaki. He could take a ship to Shanghai from Moji. When Mori checked, there was one leaving in a week's time, the Hakata-maru. He promised to reserve a cabin for him and deliver his ticket to the Imperial Hotel the next day.

'The Imperial! Honestly, Serino. You have all the luck.'

'Maybe. But haven't you forgotten something?'

'Yeah? What's that?'

'My brush with the Kempeitai.'

'Ah!' Was all he said to that. A little embarrassed, though.

Back in his room, Joao made use of the hotel's public bath for guests; then changed into less formal clothes. It was already seven in the evening. As he was deliberating whether or not to put on a tie, there was a knock on the door.

'*Hai!*' He called and went across the room to open it. He found himself face to face with Yukiko.

'Yuki-*chan*. What a pleasant surprise!' He said. 'Do please come in.'

'I'm sorry. Am I disturbing you, sensei? I should perhaps have advised you that I was coming here so early.'

'No, not at all. It's a pleasure to see you again.' He opened the door wide to let her come in, his heart beating with pleasure. She glanced nervously left and right along the corridor to ensure she wasn't being observed and stepped into the room quickly.

'Please. Make yourself comfortable,' Joao pointed to a chair by the window. 'I'm glad you've come. I was just wondering what to do with myself this evening. I'm leaving Tokyo the day after tomorrow, you know.'

'I'm sorry to hear that,' she replied, not meeting his gaze. 'I'd hoped you might be able to stay longer.'

'I'd really like to, but I've finished the research for my story here and need to get back to Shanghai and write it up.'

'Of course,' she said, still not looking him in the eye.

'But, tell me. What are you doing here at this time in the late afternoon? Shouldn't you be getting ready for your clients' calls?'

'Yes, normally that would be the case, but…' Her voice trailed away.

'But you just couldn't wait to see me again. Is that it?' He said jocularly.

'Yes, as a matter of fact it is,' she replied, still gazing at her hands crossed demurely on her lap.

Joao looked at her carefully. She was wearing a dark blue kimono with a mauve pink plum blossom motif, held in place by a matching obi belt. On her feet were white split-toed *tabi* socks and *zōri* sandals with mauve pink *hanao* straps. Understated. Beautiful.

'Is something wrong?' He asked gently. 'Something you want to tell me about?'

She suddenly slipped from where she was sitting on the chair onto her knees and bowed deeply, her forehead touching the wooden floorboards.

'*Hontō ni arigatō gozaimashita,*' she said formally.

'What are you thanking me for?' Joao's expression was one of confusion.

He bent down and put his hands under her shoulders to raise her from the floor.

'Come, Yukiko. Tell me what's going on.'

She allowed him to lift her up until she was standing straight. Then, suddenly, and in a very unjapanese-like manner, she threw her arms around his neck, sobbing convulsively.

'What is it? Please tell me.' He held her gently, not sure what to do about the beautiful body clinging to him in a way he'd hardly dared imagine.

'Surely you know?' Her voice was muffled as she continued to bury her head in his shoulder.

'Know? Know what?'

She broke away and looked up at him. Instead of answering, she put her finger gently to his cheek.

'You're using the lavender ointment, then?' She smiled through her tears. 'Your burn is much better.'

'Yes. Thanks to you. But what is it I'm supposed to know?'

'And what about the rest of your body?' She asked, refusing to be drawn. 'Is that, too, mending well?'

'Yes, thank you. As well as can be expected.'

He paused. All in due course, no doubt.

'I had a visitor this afternoon,' she began, sitting herself down on the chair again and folding her hands demurely on her lap.

'Yes?'

'Prince Saionji,' she glanced up at him. 'Someone you know, it seems.'

'Saionji? I met him earlier today, but I could hardly say I know him.'

'Well, he seemed to know all about you.' The hint of a smile. 'Anyway, he asked for me this afternoon at the Sakura *chaya*. After toasting my beauty with a single cup of sake, he asked me to perform a dance.'

'And?'

'And, of course, I did as he asked. He was the client, after all.' She checked the collar of her kimono with one delicate hand. 'Then he wanted to know my feelings for you.'

'Me?'

'Yes, you. Is Serino-*kun* the kind of man, he asked, whom I might be prepared to marry?'

'Marry?' Joao gulped. 'And what was your answer?'

'Of course, I told him, we hardly knew each other. But I felt that there was a bond between us that could perhaps be tied into the knot of marriage. Even though you'd said nothing,' she smiled sadly.

Joao said nothing.

'I must say, I rather liked the old man. He was courteous. Concerned about you. And generous.'

'Generous?'

'Yes. Having heard what I had to say, he called in my Okāsan and there and then handed her several thousand yen.' She paused, and suddenly tears were welling up in her eyes. 'Don't you understand, Joao? The Prince has paid off all my debts. I'm a free woman.'

'You mean, you're no longer a geisha?' Joao could hardly believe what Yukiko was telling him.

'That all depends, doesn't it?'

'Depends? Depends on what?'

'Depends on who.'

'Who, then?' Confusedly aware of the answer.

'You, silly!'

Once more the full-lipped smile and tinkling laugh.

They spent a long evening together.

Joao took Yukiko to a cheap yakitori restaurant located underneath the Tokyo-Shinbashi railway line. They both felt as if they were walking on air, talking and laughing happily as they made their way through the streets and alleyways towards the station. But, once they'd sat down and ordered half a dozen skewers of mixed meats, they became more serious. and told each other about their childhoods, the things they did with friends – spinning wooden tops on the floorboards of the local shrine; catching *kabutomushi* rhinoceros beetles in summer and pitting them against one another in battle; chasing fireflies in the early autumn; scooping up, or trying to scoop up, with their hands newts and small fish in a nearby stream; playing *oni-gokko* hide-and-seek among the straw stacks in the rice fields after harvest; tobogganing down snow-covered slopes in winter on used fertiliser bags; pounding rice cakes at New Year and failing to get a hand out of the way when the wooden mallet wielded by an adult came crashing down. Ouch! All the games children in the country used to play. Some of them were alien to Joao, the city boy; others not.

Yukiko had lost her mother at the same age he'd lost his father. That gave them a common bond. They talked about the same feeling of loss, of emptiness in the house, and the sadness of the parent left behind. But then, just as she was finishing primary school after her twelfth birthday, Yukiko's father had died of tuberculosis. She and her older brother had been split up. He had been adopted by an uncle and aunt who set him to work in their tiny leather factory. She herself had been taken in by Catholic missionaries in Hirado. The headmaster at her local school was a Christian and had recommended her to their care. The fact that her school grades were excellent persuaded them that Yukiko would, with a bit more education, become an excellent nun. They were right about her excellence, but not about her spirituality.

'I don't know. It all seemed so unreal. A woman giving birth to a child without, apparently, making love to a man. I mean, even at that age, I knew it was nonsense. I'd watched dogs do it. And frogs. I'd even seen poisonous snakes wrapped round each other in ecstasy. The sisters denied all that. But they did teach me to be open and direct. "Always say what you mean," Sister Ximena insisted. "And mean what you say."'

'Sounds like good advice to me.'

'It was. But it also became clear to the sisters that I'd never make a good nun, and I became too old to stay in the orphanage. One day a middle-aged woman in a beautiful kimono came to the convent. She asked me some questions, before examining me carefully and making me take off my clothes. I was so embarrassed, even though I was used to having the sisters see me naked in the bath. Then she nodded and left the room. Half an hour later, she came back with Sister Ximena who had all my belongings wrapped up in a single large *furoshiki*. "Yukiko," the strange woman said, "How would you like to become a geisha? You're going to come with me to Tokyo."'

'Just like that?'

'Just like that. I didn't really have a choice. The woman had already made a generous contribution to the orphanage. Anyway, the thought of going to

Tokyo was very exciting to a sixteen year old girl! So here I am.'

Joao didn't have such an exciting tale to tell. There was the sadness of his parents' separation, followed by his great-uncle's decision to sell up the family business and emigrate to Brazil. But there was no happy ending. So he told her about his fights at school, about how he'd been jeered at and bullied for being a 'foreigner,' about the scrapes he'd got into and the scratches and bruises his mother had had to tend to.

'Things haven't changed much, then,' Yukiko laughed and, reaching out across the table where they were sitting, lightly stroked his cheek.

'In a way, things never do change, do they? They just go round and round, and every time they come round again, we feel as if they're new somehow. Probably because we forget so much of the past.'

'And yet, here we are telling each other about our pasts,' she reminded him gently.

They moved on. To their more recent education – university for Joao, her training as a geisha for Yukiko. She marvelled at his intellect; he at her intelligence. And at a seemingly uncontrollable sense of humour. The tiny restaurant – more like a dive – tinkled with her laughter. Even the owner was impressed.

'It's good to hear so much laughter,' he said, putting down yet another plateful of skewered meat on the table where they were sitting. 'There's not enough of it these days. Please come here again. And soon,' he smiled and made his way back to behind the counter where he prepared all the food.

Within half a minute he was back, with a large bottle of Yebisu lager.

'Here, this is on the house,' he said, plonking it down. 'Look! You've brought in two more customers,' he jerked his head towards the doorway, where the *noren* was being pushed aside by another young couple. 'Thanks again. *Hai! Irasshaimase!*'

Yukiko was a good storyteller, too. Joao was almost envious. After all, it was his job to tell stories, but he always found it difficult to set the right mood when writing an article, even though everyone praised him for what he wrote. It was sheer hard work. For Yukiko, though, every story seemed to come naturally and the two of them would crack up with laughter as she related one mad drunken story after another.

'There was this couple who fell in love,' she began.

'Sounds familiar.'

'Sssh! Anyway, their parents didn't approve, so they decided to commit suicide together. There was a hill nearby with a sheer drop on one side, and they agreed to throw themselves off the top. And they did. The trouble was, there was a farmhouse right below them that they hadn't seen. And they fell right onto its thatched roof, which saved them because of its thick covering of rice straw. They walked away unscathed.'

'What's funny about that?'

'Nothing really,' Yukiko put on her deadpan look. 'The trouble was, the old lady who lived in the farmhouse was out in the vegetable patch nearby. When she looked up and saw the boy and girl falling down from the top of the precipice, she had a heart attack and died.'

That was worth repeating for the benefit of others in the *yakitoriya*. And earned them another bottle of beer – this time from one of the customers.

Eventually, it was time to leave. Joao paid the bill and promised to come back with Yukiko as soon as they could.

Outside it was cold. She slipped her arm through his as they walked. Daring and very modern. After the warmth and frivolity of the *izakaya*, they slipped into silence. It was snowing again. Lightly. Soft flakes seesawing down through the night, lit by the occasional street lamp or bar doorway. Yukiko nestled her head against Joao's shoulder, but said nothing. He could feel her thick black hair tickling his neck. Like her, he was deep in thought, mulling over everything he'd said and heard during the past three hours.

By the time they reached the lobby of the Imperial Hotel, and were laughingly brushing the snow from their heads and shoulders, they had both made up their minds.

Joao asked for the key to his room and together they walked silently up the stairs to the first floor, then along the edge of an inner balcony where he had first met Ken, before climbing another flight of stairs to his room. He inserted the key and turned the lock. Opening the door, he smiled and indicated that she should go in first.

'Ladies first, as they like to say in English.'

She bowed almost imperceptibly as she passed him into the room. As light as a feather. Or a snowflake in the night sky.

He closed the door and, without thinking, locked it. When he turned, she was standing by the window, looking out across the forecourt to the park.

'Joao-*chan*,' she said, with her back still to him. 'Do you remember what I said about holding on to my virginity?'

'Of course I remember, Yuki-*chan*. I remember, too, being disappointed, even though I was in no fit state to make love at the time.'

She turned away from the window and looked at him deep in the eyes. When she spoke, her voice was trembling with suppressed emotion. And desire.

'I'm ready to let go of it now.'

The nearest she could get to saying that she'd fallen in love with him.

After that things moved swiftly. Energised, perhaps, by Yukiko's expertise in making love – she may have been a virgin, but she had been well prepared for their night together by her training – the next morning after breakfast,

Joao sat down at the desk in his room and composed a message to Prince Saionji, thanking him for everything he'd done both for Chiyotsuru and, therefore, for him. The sunlight poured in through the window. Across the road in Hibiya Park, a homeless man was trudging slowly through the sparkling snowscape.

On a separate sheet of paper, Joao scribbled a haiku poem. He showed it to Yukiko, who was reading quietly beside him.

'You're the expert,' he said. 'Tell me what you think.'

She read the three lines, first silently mouthing their seventeen syllables, then speaking them out aloud.

'Hanging out his clothes / On a dazzling sunlit day / Beggar in the snow.'

'You could reverse the first two lines,' she said thoughtfully. 'A dazzling morning / Hanging out his clothes to dry / Beggar in the snow.'

He mulled over her suggestion.

'You're right. I don't need both "dazzling" and "sunlit," do I? Thank you.' He held her hand as she handed him back the sheet of paper. 'I can see already that it's going to be difficult to live without you.'

'Charmer!' She laughed and kissed his forehead affectionately.

'One thing, though, Joao. I don't know what's going to happen between us, but if we do end up becoming man and wife, please treat me like you do now.'

'Like I do now? How do I treat you now?'

'Like a friend. I always want to be your friend before I'm your wife. Do you think you can agree to that?'

'Is there a difference?'

'Of course there is, silly. Friends, unlike husband and wife, always treat each other as equals. If I am to be married to you, that's the kind of relationship I'd like. Sharing everything and never holding back our ideas, our problems, what we want from our lives – even our physical relationship. We mustn't be afraid of what the other may think or do. We have to trust each other. Totally.' She paused. In a most un-Japanese manner, she was sitting astride his lap, looking deeply into his eyes and stroking the hair at the back of his head as she spoke. 'Does that make sense?'

'Perfect sense. I promise to do my very best to be your friend, Yuki-*chan*, before everything else.'

'And I yours,' she said. And this time she kissed him with a passion that he couldn't resist. It was a full half hour before he could return to the writing desk and, in his best calligraphy, write out his haiku for Prince Saionji. The old man was far too erudite not to understand the poem's allusion to the new life that he'd made possible.

Once he was finished, they walked over to the Ginza. As they headed slowly up the busy shopping street towards Mitsukoshi Department Store, he wrestled with the first challenge of his new relationship. The Tokyo Protocol.

It was as they were eating *yakisoba* fried noodles in the tea room attached to the upmarket Meidi-ya grocery store that he finally made up his mind.

'There's something I have to tell you.'

'Yes?' She looked up from her food. The first test? Quicker than she'd expected, but it had to come at some time or another. Better to get it over with and move on.

'As you already know,' he began, looking quickly round to make sure none of the middle-aged women at surrounding tables was paying the young couple any attention. 'I'm not at all happy about the political situation here in Japan.'

'The role of the Army, you mean?' Her look was natural, but she kept her voice low. An ordinary lovers' conversation.

Joao nodded. 'When I was in Shanghai, I was asked by some Chinese acquaintances – in important positions – what might be the best way to stop the Kwangtung Army from invading Manchuria and China.'

She stopped him, with chopsticks raised in mid-air.

'Because they knew of your expertise in Sino-Japanese relations?'

'Yes.'

'Go on.'

'Well, to make a long story short, we agreed to compose a document that we hoped would embarrass the Kwantung Army.'

'"We" being your Chinese friends in Shanghai?'

'Yes, but also my two new friends here in Tokyo. Inukai father and son. They agreed to help me place the document in an Army archive.'

'Isn't this all rather a dangerous undertaking?'

'And frightening. Especially when the Kempeitai starts interrogating me.'

'But that was about something different, wasn't it?'

'Yes. But still…'

'Hmm. Go on.'

'Somebody else also decided to get involved. Albeit indirectly.'

'And who was that?'

'Prince Saionji.'

'Saionji? You mean –' she stopped, as she quickly realised the connection between her lover, the elder statesman, and her release from being a geisha. 'Ah, I see,' she said quietly. 'Well, that begins to explain things, doesn't it.'

'I'm sorry,' Joao began to apologise.

'Why, Joao? Didn't you want any of this to happen?'

'Of course, I did. And still do. It's just that it's all been so unexpected. I never imagined that Saionji would do what he's done for me – for us. I mean, I'd never laid eyes on the man until yesterday morning.'

'You should meet him more often, then. Maybe he'll make you Prime Minister,' she laughed gaily.

A middle-aged woman in elegant sober kimono at the next table looked across at them slightly disapprovingly. Young people these days. They had no idea how to control their voices in public.

'Ssh!' Joao put a finger to his lips with a smile. 'Anyway, I've got to pick the document up from a man in Jimbochō this afternoon. And then hand it over to Kobayashi-*san*.'

'Kobayashi?'

'Yes, Inukai's chauffeur.'

'And what does he have to do with everything?'

Joao explained. When he'd finished, she wiped her mouth with a table napkin thoughtfully provided by the tea house waitress. Then,

'It strikes me, Joao, that you've been incredibly lucky these past few days. First Inukai sensei's geisha party that first brought us together. Then your meeting with Prince Saionji, who arranges everything you need to complete your document. And now a chauffeur's brother who just happens to work in the archive where you want the document placed.'

'Not to mention the story I got out of two informants about the Kempeitai and spiked cigarettes. It's been quite a week.'

'Aren't you forgetting something, though?'

'I am? What?'

She kicked him discretely under the table.

'Me, silly!'

Suzuki was waiting for him upstairs in his stationary store.

'Serino sensei. Good afternoon. Thank you for coming. Everything's ready, as you requested.'

He handed Joao a cardboard cylinder – the kind used to house scrolls. Joao opened it and pulled out a carefully rolled up sheet of washi paper. The Tokyo Protocol now actually existed.

'Thank you, Suzuki-*san*. I'm very grateful to you.'

'Not at all. I'm honoured to do business with anyone recommended by Prince Saionji. Oh, by the way,' he searched around among the numerous bits and pieces scattered over his work table, 'His Highness asked me to give you this.'

He handed Joao the same envelope he had received from him the day before.

'There was far too much money in it. I took what I felt was a reasonable amount for the task entrusted to me. The rest is for you.'

'No, Suzuki-*san*. I couldn't possibly,' Joao tried pushing the envelope back on the table top, but the old man would have none of it.

'You keep it, sensei. You're going to need it now that you're to be married.'

'*What?*'

'Ah! So it *is* true. His Highness was wondering.' Suzuki laughed. 'I'll let him know.'

'Well, I wouldn't say we've come that far,' Joao began.

'Yet.'

'Yet. You're right. But who knows how things will turn out between us.' Joao shrugged, a little helplessly.

'Who indeed, sensei,' Suzuki smiled knowingly. 'But that's the nature of relations between men and women.' He jerked his head in the direction of the stairs down to the shop. 'Just ask the wife. She'll tell you, all right,' he chuckled as he rolled up the scroll, slipped it back into the cylindrical container, and handed it to his visitor.

'Well, I'd better be on my way. Thank you again, Suzuki-*san*. I'm very grateful.'

'Not at all, sensei,' he said, before adding. 'And congratulations.'

Joao mumbled a thank you and almost stumbled as he went down the narrow stairs. Did everyone know everything in Tokyo?

He stopped half way down and turned back. Suzuki was looking down at him from the top of the stairs.

'Forgotten something, sensei?'

'You don't happen to know where I can buy a camera, do you, Suzuki-san?'

'A camera? What kind of camera?' Toying with him.

'I don't know. One that takes clear pictures of documents, I suppose.'

Suzuki gestured to Joao to come back up. Once he was in the workshop again, the old man went over to a cabinet by the window and brought back a small box.

'Is this the sort of thing you're looking for, sensei?' he asked, a little too innocently. 'In my line of business, people sometimes find it helpful to make copies of the work I do for them,' he smiled, as he opened the box to reveal a miniature camera inside. 'I take the precaution, therefore, of stocking something that might be of assistance to them. What do you reckon?'

Joao nodded.

'Yes, perfect, Suzuki-*san*.'

'I thought it might be, sensei,' Suzuki continued smoothly, 'His Highness was wondering if you might want to make a copy, so I took the liberty of taking a couple of photos of the document in your hand soon after I finished it. He thought it would probably be useful insurance should anything happen to the original.'

Joao wasn't sure what Suzuki meant by 'anything,' but was grateful all the same.

'Because the negatives are very small, sensei, I felt it wise to place them in a safe place. You do smoke, don't you, sensei?' He asked a little anxiously.

'Yes, indeed.'

'I thought so. I don't myself. I'm very forgetful, you know. I'd be ruined if my workshop caught fire because I forgot to extinguish a cigarette.'

'Yes, I suppose you would. Very sensible, Suzuki-*san*.'

'Thank you, sensei. You can always tell a smoker, can't you, by his clothes. At least, that's what I've found. There's always a certain smell, isn't there?'

Discretely, Joao sniffed the sleeve of his jacket. Suzuki was right.

'Of course, a lot of smokers are impervious to the smell of their tobacco. They're so used to it, they don't notice it.'

'No. I suppose they don't.'

'But I'm forgetting my manners, sensei. Wittering on about the smell of tobacco. What I wanted to say was I took the liberty of secreting the two negatives in a cigarette.' He picked up an inlaid enamel cigarette case and opened it.

'It's the one on your far right, sensei. The one that's separated a bit from the rest. That's the one you really shouldn't smoke.' He grinned his gap-toothed smile.

Suzuki closed the lid and showed it to Joao.

'As you can see, sensei, it has someone's name on it. Your fiancée's, I believe.'

Joao looked at Yukiko's name in beautiful calligraphy.

'But –'

'Prince Saionji was kind enough to arrange for the inscription. His handwriting is, as I said before, quite exquisite, isn't it?'

'Indeed, it is,' Joao agreed, gazing at the first character making up Yukiko's name. 'A work of art.'

'You're too kind, sensei.'

'Given all you've done for me, I have a feeling I don't really need that camera after all.'

'No. Probably not.' Suzuki inclined his head and closed the lid of the box the camera was in.

Joao turned to leave again.

'Don't forget your cigarette case,' Suzuki reminded him.

'Oh yes. Of course. Thank you. I don't know what's come over me.'

'That's what falling in love does to you, sensei,' the old man grinned again. 'Keep your wits about you. I've a feeling you're going to need them.'

His meeting with Kobayashi and his younger brother, Jiro, was brief but relatively smooth. Jiro listened to what Joao wanted of him, then pursed his lips as he mulled over the task.

'Well, it's pretty easy, what you're asking, sensei. Just a matter of taking this cylinder here into the Ministry and depositing the scroll inside it somewhere in the archive. Do you have anywhere particular in mind? The Chinese Section? The Manchurian?'

'How about the Kempeitai?'

'The Kempeitai? That's a pretty big section. Covers several aisles. Have you got anything particular in mind?'

'Anyone, yes. There are records of individual officers, right?'

'That's right, sensei. Any officer of the rank of major or above.'

'Can you find the file on someone called Kenji Doihara and slip this protocol into it, do you think?'

'Doihara?' He paused briefly. 'Isn't that the guy who interrogated you downtown the other day?'

'That's right. How did you know?'

'*Aniki* here's been telling me one or two things about you,' he jerked his head in the direction of his older brother. 'Getting your own back, then?'

'Something like that.'

'Good for you, sensei. I'm all for a bit of payback. When it's deserved, of course. Consider it done.'

Like his brother, Ichiro, Jiro clearly believed in getting straight down to business.

Joao brought the envelope he'd received from Suzuki earlier out of his pocket and handed it to Jiro.

'This is for your trouble.'

'No, no, sensei. I don't need any of your money. This is a favour.'

'But I can't pay you back in any way.'

'You already have, sensei. By inviting us for a beer at the Imperial Hotel. What more could we ask for? Eh, *aniki*?'

Real *Edokko*.

'I'll let you know once I've placed this in Doihara's file,' he waved the cylinder in the air.

'You won't be checked at all?'

'It sometimes happens, sensei. But I'll put a few other scrolls in with your document and just show one of them to whoever asks. I've found that two or three *shunga* erotic woodblock prints always distract a young soldier's attention. Especially that one with the octopus. Do you know it, sensei?'

'Refresh my memory.'

'The one where an octopus is eating out a naked woman's hairy pussy and wrapping the tip of one tentacle round her nipple.'

'Ah! That print? Indeed, I do know it. One of Hokusai's masterpieces.'

'There you go,' Kobayashi the chauffeur interposed. 'I told you, didn't I, Jiro-*chan*? Serino sensei's a learned man.'

'You did, indeed, *aniki*.'

Eighteen hours later, Joao met Jiro in a ramen shop near the ministry.

'Well?' he asked, a little nervously. 'How did it go, Jiro-*san*?'

'Easy-peasy Japanesey,' Jiro said between loud slurps of his *tonkotsu* noodles.

'Nobody checked you?'

'Only on my way out, sensei. But that's normal, isn't it? They're suspicious of stuff being stolen as you come out of the archive. But they don't expect anyone to take anything in. Still, I had to loan the guard on the door one of my *shunga* prints.'

'Not the Hokusai octopus, I hope.'

'Goodness me, no, sensei. I'd never let that one out of my possession. Not willingly, at least. No. I let him have one by Utamaro. The one with the inscription about a snipe being unable to fly away because its beak has been caught firmly in a clamshell. Do you know it, sensei?'

'I can't say that I do,' Joao admitted.

'No. Well, it's not one of his more lascivious prints. Not like the woman being fucked while riding a horse.'

'If you say so, Jiro-*san*. I wouldn't know.'

'No, probably not, sensei. Ask that young woman of yours. I'm sure she'll be able to fill you in.'

As I fill her, he thought, but said nothing. The things *shunga* do to a man.

Back at the hotel, Yukiko was waiting for him.

'We're going out tonight.'

'We are?'

'We are.'

'Anywhere in particular?'

'Yes.' Yukiko didn't say much when she didn't want to.

She took him to a classy sushi bar off the Ginza. One of those places that had no prices attached to the beautifully written menu placard on one wall and you dared not ask how much each dish cost. Joao was immediately nervous. He didn't have much money in his pocket.

'Don't worry,' she said in a low voice, patting his hand reassuringly under the counter. 'It's all taken care of.'

'Taken care of? Not by Prince Saionji again?'

She laughed her infectious laugh.

'No. Not Prince Saionji.'

'One of the Inukais, then?'

'Not them, either.'

Just then the wooden door slid open and a geisha in full dress, makeup and wig came in, followed by an older woman in formal kimono.

Yukiko stood up quickly and bowed deeply.

'*Okāsan*. Asakichi-*san*. Thank you so much for coming.'

'Chiyotsuru!' They both smiled happily. Then, as if feigning surprise when they saw him, '*Ara*, Serino sensei! What are you doing here?'

'I'm not sure, really. Yukiko brought me here.'

'Yukiko?' They laughed in unison. 'And who is this "Yukiko," sensei? A girlfriend of yours? He'll make Chiyotsuru jealous, won't he, *Okāsan*?'

Chiyotsuru joined in the fun.

'Jealous? Of a man like Serino? You must be joking.'

Which they were, of course.

Everything had been pre-arranged – a surprise party for Joao, maybe, but a farewell dinner for Yukiko's sister geisha, Asakichi, and their Okāsan. And, it eventually turned out, a birthday party for Yukiko herself.

'You can't leave us, Chiyotsuru,' the Okāsan insisted on using her geisha name. 'I'm keeping your room for you, so that you can come to work whenever you want to. That's my present to you.'

Yukiko bowed in embarrassment.

'*Okāsan*, you shouldn't.'

'Maybe not, but I am anyway. Now that the donation I gave Sister Ximena has been covered, you can pick and choose among clients' calls. But please, Chiyotsuru, don't run off with this man forever. Surely, he can't be that special.'

'Yes, *onēsan*. Please come back from time to time,' Asakichi added. 'I'm going to miss your sisterly help and advice.'

'Let me think about it,' Yukiko said, bowing to them both. 'But thank you very much, *Okāsan*, for your kind offer.'

The older woman smiled and turned towards the restaurant owner standing behind the counter in his white cotton jacket and apron tied in front over *jinbei* trousers, with a *hachimaki* headband knotted across his forehead.

'*Taishō*, show this young man here how to make a headless prawn walk across the counter towards him. After that we leave everything up to you. *Omakase*.'

'Righty-ho, *Okāsan*. One headless prawn coming up for each of you for starters.'

'And make it a race, *Taishō*. The winner gets to marry this handsome young man here.'

And, of course, much to everyone's delight, Yukiko's prawn won.

Much, much later, they were in bed together. It was their last night at the Imperial Hotel. Yukiko had just shown Joao how she could make him ejaculate simply by tightening and loosening her vaginal muscles, as she sat motionless astride him. He had come with a force that he wouldn't have believed possible.

She lifted herself off his prostrate body and carefully wiped his penis. Then she washed herself behind the screen and came back to join him in bed.

'Did you like my birthday present?' she asked, knowing perfectly well what his answer would be.

'Except it should have been your birthday present. You never told me.'

'I didn't want to make a fuss about it. Not this year. Anyway, the way your sperm exploded inside me was the perfect gift. It was lovely knowing that my years of training in sex techniques actually have the effect I was told they would. That they can give the man I love such pleasure.'

He said nothing, but held her close to him. As he often did immediately after having sex, he felt sleepy.

'Joao-*chan*.'

'Mmm.'

'Don't go to sleep!' She shook him gently. 'Not yet. I've got something to say to you.'

'What?'

'You remember the other day, how I asked that we be friends?'

'Yes, of course.'

'And that we tell each other everything?'

'Yes. And I did, didn't I, when I told you about the Tokyo Protocol?'

'It can't have been easy, I know. And I greatly appreciated your telling me.'

'Thanks. To be honest, though, I had no idea how you'd react. It must have been a bit of a shock for you to hear that your lover is a kind of traitor.'

'Traitor?' She stroked his hair lovingly. 'I'm not sure that's the right word to describe you. What I'd like to know, though, is, are you going to get involved in other –' she searched for the right word. 'Other escapades like this? Or are you finished?'

'I don't know,' he said finally. 'I really don't know. There's this Chinese man in Shanghai – Su Bai-li – who wants me to act as his eyes and ears, so to speak.'

'An informant, you mean?'

'Yes. He wants to know what's going on among the Japanese in China. And to let him know if I think something's important.'

'A kind of spy, then?'

'Yukiko,' he pulled himself up so that he was leaning back against the bed's headrest and looking down at her naked body beside him. She modestly pulled a sheet over her waist and thighs.

'First and foremost, I'm a newspaper journalist. I investigate stories, or potential stories. Like the Takahashi Bank affair. Sometimes, these are about what's going on in China. A lot of the time, though, they involve the Japanese. In one way or another. Which means that I tend to find out things about this country and its people that I'd prefer not to know. But I can't just ignore them. It's my job to expose the truth, as I see it. And if that means some people are going to think of me as a spy, so be it. I don't see things that way.'

'How do you see them, then?' She was stroking his thigh as she listened.

'I see it as my duty to tell the truth, as I said, about my country. And my country, for better or for worse, is Japan. At least, it is for now. So when I write, I write about how I believe my country and its people should behave. I may not always be right, but I believe I have to hold Japan up in a mirror to my readers, so that they can judge for themselves what their country looks like and whether that's really how, as Japanese, they want to look to others.'

It was his turn to stroke her hair.

'That, Yuki-*chan*, is the kind of man you've chosen. Maybe he's not right for you, after all. Maybe you should be looking for someone who isn't so taken up by what's right and what's wrong. Someone who's softer, more easygoing. Certainly someone who's more settled. Someone, in other words, who isn't me. If so, I'll understand.'

He stopped talking and let the silence drift back into the room. Behind the curtains, there was the distant sound of the occasional car passing by. She lay beside him thinking. After a couple of minutes, she sat up beside him, took both his hands in hers, and started talking.

'Joao, maybe I should do what *Okāsan* asked. Maybe I shouldn't give up being a geisha after all.'

He felt a great heaviness inside him. Had his happiness all been for nothing?

'Why do I say this?' she asked herself. 'Because of my love for you, of course. But also my respect for you as a man who believes in doing what he thinks is right.'

Joao looked at her, saying nothing. Wondering where she was headed.

'If there's one thing I learned from Sister Ximena at the orphanage, it was always to do what's right. Or, like you, what I believe to be right. Because I've fallen in love with such a man, it's my duty – no, my desire – to help him in any way I can.'

She paused, looking deep into his eyes, searching for something.

'But how can I help a man who already knows what he wants in his life? A man who is as sure of himself and of the rightness of what he does as you are? The usual thing would be for me to stay in the house and make sure that my husband is properly fed and clothed. That he has a *home*. That I become the kind of woman who's behind every successful man.'

He held his breath as she paused again.

'But I don't want to be the woman behind you, Joao,' she continued.

'What do you want then?' He asked nervously.

'I want to be the woman *beside* you. The woman – remember? – who shares everything with you. I don't want to be just the recipient of your success, of everything you do at work. I want to contribute to it in any way I can. Not just as a housewife, but as a partner. That's my interpretation of what it means to be friends, Joao. It's not some kind of passive relationship I'm looking for. I want to play an active part in everything you do. I want your success to be *our* success.'

Joao had no idea how a young woman from a remote part of Japan could entertain such modern ideas. Probably Sister Ximena and her friends in Hirado. Secretly, he thanked them. What Yukiko was telling him merely reinforced what he'd known the moment he met her. She really was a remarkable woman.

'And continuing as a geisha is how you think you can best make that contribution? Is that what you're saying?'

'Why not? I'm free now. You heard what Okāsan said. I can pick and choose among the jobs I get offered. Among the clients who want me to entertain them. It may sound a bit arrogant of me to say so, but I'm good enough at my job to attract men at the very highest levels of Japanese society. They'll discuss things while drinking that only I will ever know outside the privacy of the room in which I entertain them. Right?'

'Right.'

'But what should I do with such knowledge when I think I could use it to help my country? Stay quiet? Or, like you, speak my mind, as Sister Ximena always advised me to do?'

'Not very Japanese, though, is it, Yukiko? Especially for a Japanese woman.'

'Does that matter? Do I have to spend my whole life doing what other people expect me to do as a "Japanese woman"?'

'No. Of course not.'

'Of course not, Joao. Of course, there's nothing I can do on my own with whatever information I overhear in the Sakura tea house. What I can do, though, is let you know. You're a newspaper journalist. You can act on the information in a way that I'd never be able to do. I can tell you what I hear, too, in the knowledge that you'll never betray me as your source and that, unlike your friend Doihara with Kohana, I trust you to be discrete and protect me at all times.'

'In other words –'

'In other words, if you are going to be a spy, we can be spies together. Imagine what fun that could be for us both.'

'Not fun, Yuki-*chan*. If there's anything I've learned this past week or so,

it's that spying is extremely stressful.'
　　She stretched up to kiss his cheek.
　　'Then it's better, surely, to share that stress.'
　　'And be my mistress, too, in our distress.'

PART SIX

Conflagration

'Serino-*san*, how was your trip?'

Joao hardly knew where to begin to answer Bai-li's query. It had, after all, been an eventful two weeks in Japan. To say the least. Detention and torture, followed by the scoop of his journalistic career; not to mention the Tokyo Protocol. And then there was the not insignificant matter of Yukiko.

'All right, I suppose.'

He wasn't going to give away anything immediately. Bai-li deserved to be kept on tenterhooks a little longer.

'Glad to be back in Shanghai?'

'Yes, indeed.'

'And in one piece, too, by the looks of it,' Bai-li was doing his utmost to be affable – something he had found difficult since Ch'ing-ling had left for Moscow. He felt even more empty without her support.

'Only just.'

'What do you mean?' Bai-li signalled to the waitress passing by. 'Excuse me, *hsiaochieh*, two Tsingtao, please.'

Joao told him briefly about his detention and torture at the hands of a certain Major Doihara of the Kempeitai.

'Doihara?' Bai-li was immediately alert. 'A Major Kenji Doihara?'

'Yes, that's the man, although I understand he's been demoted to Captain. Do you know him?'

'According to one of my informants, he's now in Shanghai.'

'Ah, yes. Of course. I have a suspicion I might know why he's here.'

The waitress plonked two bottles of Tsingtao beer firmly down on the tabletop, together with two glasses, and left in a huff. Maybe she didn't like being called 'Little Sister.'

Bai-li poured some beer into Joao's glass.

'Why might that be, then, Doctor Sereño?' Better to move him away from being Japanese and remind him that he was a Portuguese in a cosmopolitan city outside Japan.

'It's a long story.'

'It's still early. And I've got nothing planned for this evening.'

'If you insist.'

So Joao launched into a detailed account of what he'd learned about the Takahashi Bank, Mikawa Trading Company, Tu Yue-sheng, and the part played by Doihara and the Kempeitai in the distribution of opium-laced cigarettes sold under the brand name of Bat. Bai-li, as always, listened attentively and soon started searching his pockets for an elusive handkerchief with which to wipe the lenses of Sun Yat-sen's spectacles.

'So what you're suggesting, Joao, is that Doihara has come to Shanghai because a monthly consignment of opium is due to be shipped to Yokohama soon?'

'That's one reason, certainly.'

'Hmm.'

Joao reckoned it was time to give Bai-li what he wanted. The Director of Shanghai's Internal Affairs had been showing admirable restraint.

'By the way, Bai-li,' he said, 'I've got something for you.'

'You have?' Bai-li permitted himself a slightly nervous smile. 'And what might that be?'

'Something called the Tokyo Protocol, perhaps?'

'Really?' He took a sip of his beer to cover his excitement. 'Are you hiding it, Joao? You don't appear to have brought with you anything remotely resembling the kind of scroll I'd envisaged.'

'True, Bai-li. But you asked me to deposit the protocol scroll in a ministry archive, if I remember correctly.'

'Ah, yes. So I did. And did you?' he asked, as unconcernedly as he could. 'Deposit the protocol in a ministry archive?'

'What did you expect, Su Bai-li?'

'To be honest, Joao. Not that much. I set you an impossible task, I'm afraid – one that I was fairly convinced you'd be unable to carry out successfully. And yet you say you have something for me. Do I dare, then, to hope?'

'Only if you dare to fly with swallows' wings,' Joao replied enigmatically, before taking an inlaid enamel cigarette case from his pocket. He opened it and proffered its contents to Bai-li, who put up his hands in polite rejection.

'As you may recall, Joao, I don't smoke.'

'Don't you? What a shame! Maybe I should keep this, then.' He snapped the lid shut and made to put the cigarette case back in his pocket.

'Wait!' Bai-li put out a hand to stay him. Then, 'You didn't?' A pause. 'Did you?'

'I hope you have a little more faith in your other agents, Su Bai-li,' Joao chuckled.

Bai-li, too, smiled, as he took back the cigarette case and opened it.

'Which one?' He asked.

'The last one on the right. Make sure one of your friends doesn't try to smoke it. We wouldn't want the Tokyo Protocol to go up in flames.'

Bai-li gazed at what was in his hands for a few moments, then closed it and put it in his pocket.

'If you don't mind,' he said.

'As a matter of fact I'd like the cigarette case back once you've made a print. It was a present.'

'Of course,' Bai-li nodded his assent. 'Now, perhaps you wouldn't mind telling me about what happened in Tokyo? And I mean everything.'

So Joao did – from his first conversations with Ken which convinced him that Inukai father and son would probably help, to his meeting with Prince Saionji. He recounted again his interrogation by Major Doihara at Kempeitai headquarters and the serendipity of being driven round town by Tsuyoshi Inukai's chauffeur, whose brother just happened to be working in the archive of the Army Ministry. The only person Joao neglected to mention was Yukiko.

'Your interrogation must have been extremely frightening.'

'It was. And painful.'

'And painful, of course. As I said earlier, I never imagined you'd be able to complete the task I asked of you. In fact, I'd resigned myself to pursuing our aims without the evidence of an original copy of the Tokyo Protocol.'

Joao bowed modestly.

'I was extraordinarily lucky.'

'Yes, it seems like it.'

'I mean, you set me a virtually impossible task. You said so yourself.'

'And yet you made it possible. The sign, if I may say so, of a promising agent.'

'What do you mean?'

Bai-li began polishing his glasses yet again. Yet again, Joao wondered at how bushy his eyebrows were.

'We always need luck when it comes to spying. I can tell you from experience that, however well planned a scheme may be, something untoward almost invariably occurs. Which means that an agent lives or dies by the way he – or she – reacts to the unexpected. You, for instance, were able to turn your detention by Doihara into an advantage. Not every agent can do that.'

'As I said, I was lucky.'

'Yes, but luck isn't something that just happens, Joao. It isn't a passive attribute. Luck is something you actively create. Not consciously, of course. That never works. But by simply being there, in the right place at the right time. With the right – how shall I put it? – the right demeanour. You seem to have a certain knack.'

Once again, Joao inclined his head modestly and said nothing.

'To be honest, that knack of yours is why I asked for your help in the first place. The moment I learned from Ch'ing-ling that you'd somehow managed to get her to talk in such great detail about her past, telling you things that even I myself didn't know, I knew you'd make a good agent. A man who made his own luck.'

Bai-li put his glasses back on. He wasn't used to making such long speeches.

Joao said nothing, but thought back to the discussion he'd had with Ken back in Tokyo. *Go-en*. You made your own fate, too. Which meant that it wasn't fate as such. In the same way that luck, as Bai-li described it, wasn't luck. More an engineered advantage.

'*Kanpei!*' Bai-li said, raising his glass. 'And thank you, Joao. For confirming my estimation of your qualities. Ch'ing-ling had her doubts, you know.'

'*Kanpai!*' Joao reciprocated the other's toast. 'How is she, by the way?'

'Safely in Moscow, thank you.'

'Moscow? How long will she be staying?'

'A year. Two years? Who knows. As you're aware, there's no love lost between her and the Generalissimo.'

'I'm sure there isn't.' He had to ask. 'And Gerda? What did she have to say about me?'

'Gerda?' Bai-li gave one of his slow dimpled smiles. 'She was looking for something else in you. Something more obvious.'

'To do with my "Japanese-ness," perhaps?'

'Something like that,' Bai-li smiled again, the dimples deepening into their most attractive charm.

There was silence. Bai-li signalled to the waitress for two more beers. Outside, sleet was falling. Winter wasn't over yet.

'Bai-li,' Joao began. It was his turn to ask a favour. 'I've been following up on the Takahashi Bank affair. Remember? The local manager who committed ritual suicide the night of the Generalissimo's wedding?'

'Yes indeed.'

'I know it's not really your area of expertise, but, now that you've heard what I uncovered in Tokyo, I was wondering if you might be able to help. Something has to be done about all the drug money the Japanese are laundering.'

Bai-li nodded and paused for thought, instinctively searching for his handkerchief, which was, in fact, still on his lap. He really should learn to control his habits.

'I can see I've recruited a moral agent,' he laughed. 'Maybe the best way forward is for me to talk to Chiang Kai-shek.'

'How can the Generalissimo help?' Joao asked doubtfully. 'Unless he's going to order a detachment of his soldiers to blow up the bank.'

'His brother-in-law, remember, is Soong Tse-ven. T-V as he's known. I don't know whether you heard, but he's been appointed Finance Minister. Just a few days ago.'

'Has he? That must have been while I was on board the Hakata-maru. Is he still Governor of the Central Bank of China?'

'Very much so. It's that bit about him that I had in mind.'

'How so?'

'T-V can close the Takahashi Bank down if he so pleases. And freeze all its accounts. Including Doihara's, of course. But we need to persuade him. And, of course, everything has to be legal. I'm due to meet the Generalissimo in Nanking the day after tomorrow, so I'll consult him and let you know.'

'Thank you, Bai-li. Greatly appreciated.' Joao gathered up his cigarettes and lighter and made as if to leave.

'There's something else I'd like to talk to you about, Joao, before you go,' Bai-li stayed him with one hand on his arm.

Joao sat back in his chair waiting.

'I'd like to continue our – how should I put it? – our relationship, as and when appropriate.'

'Yes?' Joao wasn't sure if he wanted to hear more.

'Let's face it, Joao, eventually your newspaper is going to recall you back to Tokyo. Right? You are respected. And you've made good contacts with people who matter – people like Inukai father and son, and now Prince Saionji. It strikes me that your most valuable attribute is going to be your membership of this so-called Breakfast Club. Wouldn't you agree?'

Joao pursed his lips. 'At some point in the future, I suppose. Yes.'

'Of course, it will be. So, at some unseen point in the future, you're likely to get intimations in advance of what the Japanese Government intends to do with regard to China.'

'Possibly, yes.'

'Yes. Possibly. My query, then, is this. In such an eventuality, might you be prepared to keep me abreast of developments as you see fit? Not all developments, of course. Just those that strike you as being of potential interest to us here in China.' Bai-li paused, seemingly relieved at having been able to air a topic he'd found difficult to broach. 'What do you think?'

It was Joao's turn to pause in thought. In for a penny, in for a pound? Or a yen, at least.

'That strikes me as a not unreasonable request, Bai-li. So I'll do what I can. Provided I think it appropriate, of course.'

'Of course. I don't want you to feel you're betraying your country.'

'One of my countries, you mean?'

'As you say, Joao, one of them.'

'I won't. Unless I feel I have to.'

'That's settled then,' Bai-li smiled. Then changed the subject. 'So, when are you going to get married?'

'Eh?'

'The cigarette case, Joao. It has a name engraved on its lid.'

Joao had to laugh.

'You don't miss much, do you, Bai-li?'

Again the modest dimpled smile.

'I try not to. A rather beautiful name if I may say so. *Hsüeh*. I believe it's pronounced Yuki in Japanese.'

He paused again, as Joao nodded.

'I have a feeling there's a little more to the tale of your adventures in Tokyo than you described earlier. Anything I should know?'

'Possibly.'

Joao caught Bai-li's penetrating look.

'Definitely,' he conceded.

'As I said soon after we met, I've got all evening, Joao.'

The dimples were persuasive. Joao told the story of how he'd met and more or less fallen in love with Yukiko.

'Which brings me back to my question, Joao. When do you plan to get married?'

'I've no idea, Bai-li. We haven't reached that stage. Yukiko's in Tokyo and I'm here. So it's not going to happen in the immediate future.'

'No wedding reception at the Majestic Hotel, then?' Bai-li smiled.

'Definitely not. Not right now, at least,' Joao smiled, then turned serious again. 'There's something else, Bai-li.'

'There almost always is.'

'Yukiko is going to work with me. Passing on whatever information she overhears as a geisha in the Sakura teahouse.'

'Ah!' was all Bai-li said. Then, 'A useful kind of lover.'

'And well-placed informant.'

'Yes. Yes, indeed. Gerda will miss you.'

'Not yet. Hopefully, we'll still be seeing each other while I'm here in Shanghai.'

'I'm glad to hear that.'

'But what about you, Bai-li? Isn't it time you found yourself a wife?'

'You may be right, Joao,' he replied, thinking of Ch'ing-ling. 'But do you remember our dinner at the Majestic? While you cavorted with Gerda, I managed merely a shuffle on the ballroom floor.'

'What's that got to do with anything?' Joao was, once again, confused.

'Only this,' Bai-li smiled his dimpled smile. 'One should never give a sword to a man who can't dance.'

He was ushered into Chiang Kai-shek's office by a new aide-de-camp.

'Yen-ching! It's been a long time.'

As before, the Generalissimo stood up and came round from behind his large desk to greet his visitor.

'Indeed, it has, Chi-ch'ing. Might I enquire how married life is treating you? Well, I hope?'

'Very well, thank you. Mei-ling is a great support. There's so much to do here. And my new aide-de-camp is still learning his job.'

'Whatever happened to young Lieutenant Pan?'

'Disappeared. Rumour has it he committed suicide. But, if so, his body hasn't been found. His father's arrest upset him a lot, you know.'

'I'm sure it did.'

'Any news on that front?'

'Nothing, I'm afraid. The Russians seem to have clammed up completely. Not responding to any of our enquiries.'

'Hm. But tell me, to what do I owe the pleasure of your visit? I hope you have some good news for me. I need it, what with the Communists down south and factional warfare here in Nanking.'

'I have a belated wedding present for you, Chi-ch'ing,' Bai-li began, passing a silver cigarette case to the Generalissimo.

Chiang took it and noticed the initials engraved on its lid. CCC.

'Thank you, Yen-ching. But you know I don't smoke.'

'I do indeed, Chi-ch'ing. But it occurred to me that occasionally you might regard it as a courtesy to be able to offer cigarettes to your visitors. Provided they smoked outside your office, of course!'

Chiang frowned as he opened the case. What on earth was his old friend up to now?

'Lucky Strike? Thank you, Yen-ching. A portent for the future, perhaps?'

'One would hope so, my General.'

'But why American cigarettes, Yen-ching? I can buy them at any tobacco shop down the street.'

'You can indeed, my General. But not the one on the far right.'

Chiang touched the cigarette curiously.

'No? Why not?'

Bai-li drew an envelope from his pocket, opened it and spilled a large print onto the desktop.

Chiang picked it up.

'What's this?'

'A photograph of a document we talked about late last year. The Tokyo Protocol. Submitted by Gi'ichi Tanaka, Prime Minister of Japan, to Emperor Hirohito, outlining Japan's proposed plans to take over Manchuria and China,' Bai-li paused, before adding, 'Not to mention Southeast Asia and the rest of the world.'

'But that's –' The Generalissimo stopped, clearly agitated. He looked again at the cigarette case with his initials on them, and his shoulders relaxed.

'Yen-ching! You've been devious again. I remember now. You came up with the idea of this Tokyo Protocol in order to embarrass the Kwantung Army. Wasn't that it?'

'And motivate Stalin to do something about the Siberian border, yes.'

'So what are you suggesting I do?'

'First, my General, send the cigarette I pointed out to you – in a different container, of course – by courier to Moscow and have it handed to Stalin personally. Convinced that the Japanese won't attack the Amur River, he's left the Siberian border porous and undefined for too long. The microfilm should be enough to persuade him finally to pay attention to what's going on and send reinforcements to the Far East.'

Chiang sat back in his chair, his smile like that of a contented cat.

'Excellent, Yen-ching. Smart thinking. And you intend to publish this protocol, I presume?'

'Yes, my General, with your permission. I am arranging for Chinese newspapers around the country to publish the contents of the document in full, once you give the go ahead.'

'It's time we got the Japanese worrying a bit. You have my permission to proceed, Yen-Ching. Anything to get the Kwantung Army to face north, as well as south, and distribute its troops across a long stretch of terrain. That should weaken its threat so far as my own Northern Army concerned.'

'That's the objective, yes.' Bai-li took off his glasses and looked at them in his lap before proceeding. 'There is, though, something else we should keep in mind.'

'What's that?'

'It's not of direct military significance, but in my opinion important all the same. Again, we've discussed it briefly.'

'Refresh my memory, then.'

'By warning Stalin of Japan's military intentions, you'll ingratiate yourself with him. If so, he may be prepared to overlook everything that happened last summer.'

'With the communists in Hankow.'

'And Shanghai. By easing off on your pursuit of the Red Army in the south, as we discussed before, Chi-ch'ing, you assure Stalin of your unswerving loyalty to Soviet Russia should he decide to go to war against Japan. And you protect your son.'

'Ah! Ching-kuo,' Chiang sighed sadly. 'I haven't heard from him, of course. Do you think Stalin will fall for it?'

'I don't know, my General. I just don't know. But it's possible that your goodwill will persuade him to reconsider his decision to keep Ching-kuo hostage. I know, it's a long shot. But if Joseph Vissarionovich wants you to join forces with him against the Japanese, he's going to have to give you something in return.'

'Yes, of course. Thank you, Yen-ching.' Chiang seemed suddenly to be in a jolly mood, so Bai-li continued.

'I was wondering, Chi-ch'ing, whether you might be kind enough to arrange a meeting for me with Soong Tse-ven.'

'T-V? What do you want with him?'

'It's a long story. To do with the Takahashi Bank, drugs, and the

Kempeitai.'

'Drugs?' The Generalissimo looked at his friend sharply. 'In that case, let me call T-V now. If it's to do with a bank, we'd better hear what you've got to tell me together.'

Twenty minutes later, the two men were joined by China's new Finance Minister. Bai-li could see T-V's resemblance to Ch'ing-ling, and felt sudden nostalgia for the woman he loved, now so far away. T-V looked considerably less fragile than his sister, though, and perhaps less serious – to judge by the way his tie was knotted askew in his soft collar. His thick black hair was slicked back with some kind of perfumed oil that smelled of sandalwood and wealth.

Bai-li told the two men everything he'd learned from Joao, before asking them for their advice.

'This matter is for you, I think, Tse-ven. As a mere general, I'm hardly the expert when it comes to high finance,' Chiang said with a certain false modesty. 'What do you recommend?'

T-V thought for a few moments. Then,

'So far as I understand, the Takahashi Bank is no longer operating in Japan.'

'That's what I gathered from Serino-*san*.'

'In that case, the branch in Shanghai is no longer technically a Japanese bank, in the sense that it's no longer taking orders from a head office in Japan.'

'Because that head office is no longer functioning?'

'Precisely. Instead, I think it could be argued, it's technically Chinese, because it's operating on Chinese soil.'

'Even though the bank is located in the International Settlement?'

'A slight problem, I admit. But remember, it has other branches in Peking and Manchuria. And since I'm now Finance Minister for the whole of China, what I say goes.'

Bai-li appreciated T-V's ability to get straight to the point.

'Also,' he continued, 'I happen to be a member of the Takahashi Bank's board of directors in Shanghai. That may help, too.'

'How so?'

'Well, I could, for instance, call a board meeting and propose that, given the uncertain circumstances surrounding the bank's operation and ownership, its name and articles of business be changed to reflect its Chinese clientele and location. I might suggest a new name – like the Sino-Manchurian Bank, for example. Or give its Japanese name, Takahashi, a Chinese pronunciation – the Kao-ch'iao Bank. Something like that. We'll see.'

T-V stopped to sip the tea brought in earlier by Chiang's new aide-de-camp.

'I suggest we start by freezing all accounts in the Shanghai branch of the Takahashi Bank.'

'That'll create quite a furore, won't it?' Chiang laughed at the thought. 'Especially among the Japanese.'

'I'm sure it will.'

'Let them make all the fuss they like. In a couple of weeks' time, they're going to have no friends, either in China or in the West.'

'What do you mean?' T-V looked nonplussed, so his brother-in-law explained, as briefly as he could, about the Tokyo Protocol and its publication in the Chinese newspapers.

'Ah! That will definitely help,' T-V smiled, 'Especially when it comes to explaining why we've frozen all the bank's money. The Shanghai Municipal Police surely won't object, will they, Brother, if you were to order a detachment of soldiers to surround and seal off the building?'

'They'd better not. Bai-li, can you deal with that?'

'Certainly, my General.' Bai-li turned back to T-V. 'When do you suggest this be done?'

'As soon as possible. Why not next Friday afternoon, before the bank closes business for the weekend?'

A man after Bai-li's heart. Like a falcon for speed, an arrow for directness. Lao-tzu forgot to say that.

'There is, of course, another way,' he interposed.

Both men looked at him expectantly. There was always another way.

That same afternoon in Shanghai, Joao received two letters. The first, which arrived by ordinary mail, was from Yukiko. As he had come to expect, it was written in a beautiful calligraphic style and the notepaper, he noticed with a hint of nostalgia, was scented with lavender.

> Dear Joao,
>
> I'm sorry not to have written to you sooner, but I seem to have been incredibly busy since you left. Okāsan keeps asking me to entertain one client after another. 'You need the company,' she says, 'Now that Joao has gone back to Shanghai.' So I do as she asks, while thinking of you.
>
> Here, finally, there is a hint of spring. The air is warmer and we can expect the cherry trees along Kagurazaka to blossom soon. I wish we could sit together under their branches in full bloom one evening and enjoy their fragrance while drinking sake.
>
> Something happened last night that makes me take up my pen. I was, as usual, at the Sakura tea house. Inukai sensei had called for me early in the evening, but left soon after, complaining of an upset

stomach. I gave him some chamomile leaves and told him to take them as an infusion. He promised he would, but he was already so drunk he probably forgot all about them before he reached home. Hopefully, his wife will have taken care of him.

Anyway, as I was about to leave the *chaya*, Okāsan asked if I wouldn't mind entertaining two new customers who had called for a geisha. She didn't know them, but they had been recommended by another regular client, so she had agreed to allow them into the tea house on condition that they behaved themselves in the manner of gentlemen – a necessary provision given that they were both military officers of some kind.

A little reluctantly, I agreed. After all, they were paying above the normal rates and, now that I am so to speak 'freelance,' that meant I would be taking home half of what they paid Okāsan. She introduced me to two men in their mid-forties, who seemed, as I said, to be mid-ranking officers in the army or, possibly, the Kempeitai. Or both. They were polite enough, and I danced and played the usual childish drinking games to keep them amused.

Of course, they became drunker as the evening wore on and their tongues began to loosen although, thankfully, they refrained from making sexual innuendos involving me. If they had done, I would have been out of the room in a flash. Instead, they began talking in veiled terms about a kind of cigarette called Bat. It's not a brand I've ever heard of, but it seems that it is made in Japan and sold in Manchuria, if that is possible, and that each cigarette contains a drug called opium. Isn't opium something the Chinese are addicted to, Joao-*chan*? I seem to remember your mentioning it once when we were together. (If only we were together now. Then I wouldn't need to be writing this letter to you!)

It was what these men said next that prompted me to write to you. The opium the Japanese manufacturer puts in these Bat cigarettes apparently comes from Shanghai. It is shipped from a warehouse there to Yokohama on the last Thursday of every month, they said. Which warehouse exactly, I don't know, but they mentioned Mikawa Trading Company at one point, so maybe that is the connection?

I took up my pen to tell you all this because I thought you might like to hear it as a journalist. Whether it's connected with the story you're writing about the Takahashi Bank, I don't know. I just thought you might be interested.

I am, looking forward to being with you again soon. Please try to find an excuse to come back to Tokyo.

Your loving Yukiko

The second letter was handed to him in the office of the Asahi Newspaper by a Japanese consular official. It was from Tsuyoshi Inukai.

'I have been instructed to deliver this safely into your hands by the Minister of Communications in Tokyo,' he bowed stiffly and left.

The letter was written in English – presumably by Ken, and presumably to avoid careful scrutiny by any Japanese bureaucrats or censors who might have had the opportunity to open it and read its contents.

> My respectful greetings, Serino sensei,
>
> Please excuse this sudden intrusion from afar, but I hope this letter finds you well. Here in Tokyo things are much as they usually are. In case you happen to be wondering, I have asked Ken to translate my original letter into English. I hope that you will overlook my impoliteness, but it seemed the most appropriate thing to do under the circumstances.
>
> And now to the issue at hand.
>
> As you are aware, social relationships in Japan and China rely on what one might call 'give and take.' When somebody helps you out, you know that at some point in the future you may be called upon to come to the assistance of that same person, if so requested. In a way, you could say that that is what the exchange of gifts at New Year and during the mid-summer *obon* ancestors' festival here in Japan is all about. I offer you a gift to thank you for all you've done for me during the past half year, in the expectation that you will help me out in turn if I find myself in need. Gift giving, together with the relationships it underpins, is – as you are fully aware – a kind of insurance against misfortune. Social relationships, therefore, are transactional. This is something Westerners don't readily understand about Japanese and Chinese societies.
>
> In this context you may be wondering why Prince Saionji decided to help you during your recent visit to Tokyo. Was his decision to release Chiyotsuru from her debt an act of pure altruism? You may wish to think that indeed it was. After all, we like to believe that human beings are essentially good, even though we are surrounded by behaviour that categorically disproves such a Mencian attitude. But, in my opinion, there is no 'essential' this or 'essential' that. Everything we think or say or do is based on the fact that, like it or not, our lives are made up of transactional relations.
>
> Perhaps I'm jumping ahead of myself. Prince Saionji helped you, not because he thought so highly of you (which, of course, he does), but because I asked him to. Why did he agree to my request? Because, many years ago, when we were both much younger, Saionji

fell in love with my older sister, Yoshiko. He was married at the time, but wished to take Yoshiko as his mistress. Since Yoshiko herself was not averse to the proposed arrangement, my father agreed. As a result, I became the unofficial brother-in-law of an Imperial prince. And because I am his relative by 'marriage,' so to speak, Prince Saionji will do anything I ask of him; as will I of whatever he asks of me.

There is, however, a second set of relations that underpinned my own decision to help you in the first place. It is here that my son Ken's favourite topic of *go-en*, or fated chance, comes into play. Many, many years ago – long before even I was born – my grandfather was challenged to a duel by a young samurai who insisted he had been slighted by my grandfather's decision to take as his wife a young woman whom the samurai himself claimed to love. Duels were even then frowned upon, but the two men fought and, being a far better swordsman, my grandfather won. The young samurai survived, but was disgraced. In his own eyes, he had lost his honour.

He probably ought to have committed *seppuku* by cutting open his stomach in the traditional manner. But he chose not to. Instead, he married another woman who bore him a son, and that son in due course of time sired his own son who, again in due course of time, although I didn't even know of his existence, chose to join the Kempeitai. That man's name, like that of his disgraced grandfather, is Kenji Doihara.

When I first learned that you had been interrogated by a major called Doihara at Kempeitai Headquarters, I thought nothing of it. But then I remembered how, as a boy, I had heard many tales about our family's history and how one of them was about my grandfather's duel with a man named Doihara. I was intrigued. Surely, it was too much of a coincidence that the Doihara you had to deal with was descended from the one who had lost his honour to my grandfather.

But then, Serino-*kun*, you discovered that this same Kempeitai officer was using a geisha called Kohana to gather information on, among others, senior members of government and well-placed officials and businessmen. Not only this, but he actually had the temerity to be sleeping with her, in the full knowledge that I myself had taken her as my occasional mistress.

I am learning in my old age, Serino-*kun*, that the transactional part of a relationship is never necessarily immediate. It can last for generations – not always in the consciousness of those involved, but it remains there under the surface, nonetheless. It's a bit like the Cheshire Cat and its smile. Do you know the book, *Alice in Wonderland*? If not, I recommend it. Sometimes visible, sometimes receding into nothingness. The Doihara whom you had the misfortune to encounter at Kempeitai Headquarters suddenly appeared in my own life. As a result, I realised that I need to rid myself of him once and for all. Not because of Kohana, although her deception hurts my old man's pride, but because, somehow or other, Doihara has got hold of a photograph showing me in disarray in a Shanghai hotel room with Miss Gerda Weidemeyer. In consequence, he has chosen to blackmail me.

Do you see now where this letter of mine is leading you? I have no idea whether our mutual acquaintance, Su Bai-li, is responsible for Doihara's possession of the print in question. My impression from meeting him again at Chiang Kai-shek's wedding reception is that this is unlikely, but I would be grateful if you could make enquiries on my behalf.

After making discrete enquiries of my own, I have now discovered that Doihara was last month reassigned to the Kempeitai in, of all places, Shanghai! I realise that you are not a violent man, Serino-*kun* – you use brain rather than brawn when it comes to dealing with adversity – but might I humbly ask you to return me a favour by explaining the situation to Su Bai-li, and asking him to arrange for the 'disappearance' of Major Doihara? I will be forever in your debt.

I look forward to seeing you again soon. As does Ken, who says he misses his new best friend.

'You're right, Joao. Something should be done.'
He had asked to meet Bai-li more or less as soon as he stepped off the train from Nanking at Shanghai's North Station.
'The question is, what? How does one get rid of a Kempeitai officer?'
'With difficulty, I'd say. But it's not impossible.'
'How did Doihara get hold of that print, Bai-li? Surely, you're not responsible?'
'Definitely not.'
'So, who else knew about Gerda and Inukai?'
'Nobody. Except for the man who developed the film for me. He will be questioned and, in all probability, removed.'
Joao preferred not to dwell on the nature of the man's removal.
'What about the Takahashi Bank?' he asked, changing the subject. 'And the Mikawa warehouse? Can the Municipal Police confiscate the opium stored there before it's loaded onto the ship for Japan?'
'I'm sure they can. But I'm equally sure that the confiscated opium will

then make its way back to Tu Yue-sheng.'

'To be deposited once more in Mikawa's warehouse, when the time comes.'

'Precisely.'

'Is there no way, then, that we can put a stop to the Kempeitai smuggling operation?'

'I'm afraid not, Joao. We're facing the combined strength of Tu's Green Gang and the Kempeitai. Plus the Shanghai Municipal Police's unofficial cognizance. Whatever obstacles we put in their path, they're bound to find a way round them.'

'But you have something in mind, Bai-li?'

'I always have something in mind, Joao. But I'm afraid, in that respect, I'm a little like the bird that sings because it has a song, not because it has an answer to a problem.' He sighed a little theatrically. 'Still, might I suggest you find yourself a newspaper photographer? I think you'll have need of one.'

'When?'

'The twenty fourth of the month, of course. In one week's time, if I'm not mistaken. Be at the Takahashi Bank, at around midnight. Make sure you have transport to hand. I think you'll find that you need to get along Yangtzepoo Road to the Mikawa warehouse fairly promptly after that.'

Always on the move. The journalist's fate. But then standing still was always the quickest way to grow most tired.

The best place to find Tu Yue-sheng, or Big Ears Tu, was at the Donghu Hotel on rue Doumer in the French Concession. He owned and ran the place. Bai-li didn't like Big Ears, but hardly anyone else did either. He was a man to be feared – Shanghai's most renowned criminal, boss of the Green Gang, and henchman to Chiang Kai-shek, as and when it suited the Generalissimo. And, of course, Tu. It was at the Donghu that the bad and the ugly gathered to hatch their plots and run their businesses.

So far as Bai-li was concerned, the good thing about the hotel's location was that no Japanese had a hope in hell of doing anything in the neighbourhood without Big Ears knowing about it. The idea that he'd ever assist a dwarf bandit was as remote a possibility as flying a man to the moon. Unless money was involved.

Which was why he was ready to furnish the Kempeitai with a regular, monthly supply of opium. That wasn't assistance; that was business. And financial profit always came before personal likes and dislikes.

There were a couple of Tu's gang members standing guard outside the hotel steps when Bai-li arrived, but they let him pass with little more than a cursory glance. The newcomer was too soft to cause trouble.

Inside, though, was another matter. A short, stocky Russian with bulging biceps put one hand out to stop Bai-li in his tracks.

'Business?' He asked roughly.

'I've come to see Tu Yue-sheng,' Bai-li answered smoothly in Russian, 'By appointment.'

The Russian looked at him suspiciously and motioned to him to sit down in one of the armchairs in the hotel lobby. Then, having asked Bai-li his name, he made off down a corridor behind the front desk. An attractive Eurasian woman brought Bai-li tea. After setting cup and saucer down carefully on a low table beside him, she bowed wordlessly and left, her cheongsam revealing more leg than Bai-li could cope with at that time of the day.

He was finishing his third cup of tea when the Russian returned.

'Come with me,' was all he said.

Bai-li stood up and followed the man back down the same corridor, until he stopped outside a closed door and knocked. There was a grunt from within. The Russian opened the door and showed Bai-li into a comfortable room with low table and armchairs, platters of food on a sideboard, a well-stocked drinks cabinet, and two more well-proportioned Eurasian hostesses to serve them. Yet more shapely calves and glimpses of thigh.

Big Ears stood up from a leather armchair with broad armrests placed at one end of the low table.

'Su Bai-li,' he did his best to crack his twisted mouth into a welcoming smile, before flicking his opium-stained fingers for the hostesses to serve drinks and snacks.

'Long time, no see, *lo*.'

He stretched out a long, bony arm to shake Bai-li's hand. His nails were more than an inch long and, like his fingers, stained by opium. Magically they didn't dig into his visitor's flesh. One of Big Ears' well-honed arts of war.

'Take a seat.'

The feared boss of the Green Gang waved a hand in the direction of one of the armchairs, as he himself sat down. Bai-li politely accepted the offer and observed his host.

Tu Yue-sheng's addiction to opium had taken its toll. His face was pitted and mottled, a little like a honeycomb, though hardly as sweet. His eyes were empty, dull and impenetrable like a taxidermist's bird. His mouth was full and sensual, but twisted, and his ears were – as his nickname suggested – large and protuberant. He had close-cropped hair and prominent thick eyebrows, while a drooping lid over his left eye added to his rather sinister appearance. Not the kind of man you wanted to meet on a dark night.

'So what brings the Generalissimo's spymaster to rue Doumer?' Tu rasped. 'Communists again?'

'I don't think there are many of them left, are there, Yue-sheng, after last summer?'

'One or two maybe,' Big Ears gave him a sharp, almost knowing, look.

Bai-li chose to ignore any innuendo that might have been implied.

'This time, it's the Japanese who are causing the Generalissimo problems.' He paused, returning Tu's look in kind. 'And you yourself, of course, Yue-sheng.'

'Whaddya mean, me?' He growled ominously. 'I hope you're not here to insult me, Bai-li.'

'Not at all, Yue-sheng. I'm here as your guest to ask for your help.'

'Again?' Big Ears laughed loudly. 'When will Chiang Kai-shek learn to look after his own affairs? Maybe I'm the one who should call himself the Generalissimo!'

'A title that would suit you well, no doubt. You should ask him what he thinks,' Bai-li said.

Big Ears roared his appreciation.

'You're a funny man, Su Bai-li. I like that.'

'What I have to ask of you, though, isn't so funny, I'm afraid.'

'It's not? That's the trouble with things these days. Too serious.'

He took a large gulp from the cup of *shaochiu* one of the Eurasian girls had placed before him.

'So, Su Bai-li, tell me your serious story. Then I'll see how I can help. More likely if, so don't get your hopes up.'

Bai-li told his serious story. When he was done, Big Ears sat silently for a while. As Bai-li had anticipated, he didn't look entirely pleased.

'You want my boys to set fire to a Japanese bank where I've deposited a lot of my money?'

'Yes, but only after you've withdrawn it first. Two million yen, I believe.'

'Two million one hundred thousand, if you want to know.'

'Two million one hundred thousand, then.'

'And that's it?'

'That's it. Remember, nobody else knows that all the bank's other deposits are about to be frozen. If you don't agree to help, you'll lose your two million,' Bai-li paused, 'And the one hundred thousand.'

Big Ears scratched his scalp with a long-nailed finger.

'Come on, Yue-sheng!' Bai-li said encouragingly. 'When will you get another government-sanctioned opportunity to set fire to a Japanese bank? Think how annoyed the dwarf bandits will be.'

'True. But what about their go-down? I'll be setting fire to my own merchandise.'

'You will, indeed. But, as you're well aware, the Japanese will have no choice but to ask you to supply them with more opium. If you manage to get most of your merchandise out of the go-down before setting fire to the building, you'll get paid twice over. Imagine doing that every month!'

Big Ears gave Bai-li the benefit of another of his barking laughs.

'Hey, Mister Spyman, maybe you missed your vocation.'

Bai-li bowed his head in acknowledgement.

'And just to show you my, and China's, appreciation, you can have all the money in Doihara's account, too. That's another million. To cover your expenses. I'm sure he won't miss it.'

Big Ears scratched his head again, thoughtfully, his dead eyes never leaving Bai-li as he weighed everything up. Eventually,

'OK. Su Bai-li,' he stretched out a bony claw. 'It's a deal.'

Bai-li grasped Yue-sheng's proffered hand and shook it firmly. *Show me a murderer and I'll deal with him.*

Shanghailanders talked about the 'great fire' for months on end. Rather like the Great Fire of London, it took pride of place in the annals of the International Settlement's history, although there wasn't anything like that extent of destruction. After all, the scope of the fire was limited to the northern bank of the Whampoo River, from Garden Bridge where it curved sharply south down to Whashing Road, before heading off to join up with the Yangtze several miles downstream. And it only burned for a single night. Still, local inhabitants didn't stop talking about it until the Japanese attacked the Chinese part of the city five years later.

Those newspapermen with memories not befuddled by alcohol, noted that the day – or rather, night – of the great fire was ominous. It occurred exactly one year after British and American warships had bombarded Nanking to defend the foreigners living there from the rioting and looting in the city by Chinese soldiers. In what way the date was 'ominous,' though, remained as opaque as the cryptic messages derived by fortune-tellers from their *ling-ch'ien* spiritual sticks.

Accounts differed as to where the fire started. Was it the Takahashi Bank on the other side of Garden Bridge? Or was it further downriver, along Broadway, where the Japanese warehouses began? Ultimately the question was irrelevant since everything between these two points was burned to a cinder. But one thing everyone agreed on. The Fire Brigade never stood a chance. It was up against an inferno. Even if its volunteers hadn't stopped off at Cisco Joe's for a quick 'one for the road,' they'd never have been able to put out the flames roaring up into the night sky.

And when did the fires start, exactly – because they were definitely plural, not singular? Another irrelevant question in the greater scheme of things. But European men seated at the world's longest bar in the Shanghai Club were used to irrelevance. They needed something to talk about as they nursed their Stengers the following day. Local Chinese, though, knew better than to worry themselves with such questions. Instead, they simply enjoyed the sight of several dozen dwarf bandits running around in the middle of the night like headless chickens, reminding themselves – as if they needed reminding – how tasty chicken's feet were when braised in oyster sauce, garlic, ginger and sugar. A delectable snack to go with their *shaohsing* rice wine.

The answer to the second question was easy – and banal – enough. The fires started sometime on the Saturday night, of course, because that's when people heard the fire engines ringing their bells. It didn't matter whether it was midnight or 2 am. Most turned over in their beds, put a pillow over their heads, and went back to sleep. A few – young couples mainly – thought the disturbance a suitable excuse to make love, matching with their passion the fires outside. A few other sleepless souls went up onto the roofs of their buildings to get a view of what was going on.

Not that there was that much to see. The whole section of river frontage on the eastern edge of Hongkew was engulfed in flames and smoke. But smell? That was another matter. Those who watched the fires from a distance were pleasantly surprised by the rather wonderful smell – of opium, those who weren't addicts later learned – that wafted across the city and made them feel quite dreamy. If this was opium burning, there should, perhaps, be more such fires. For once, there was something to thank the Japanese for.

Not that the Japanese themselves were feeling gratitude for anything much that night. For a start, many of them lost a lot of money that they had deposited over the years in accounts in the Takahashi Bank. Whether ill-gotten gains or hard-earned life savings, everything went up in smoke. Easy come, easy go, maybe, but money didn't grow on trees was the clichéd way people described their loss. Customers consoled themselves with the fact that, while a detachment of Chiang Kai-shek's troops had sealed off the building the afternoon before, the Nationalists had been unable to get hold of the money in the bank's vaults before the fire started.

At least, that's what they thought. What they didn't know, however, was that T.V. Soong had arranged to have everything – cash, bonds, deposit box jewellery, foreign savings – taken out bit by inconspicuous bit throughout the day, through front door and back, by officials from the Finance Ministry in Nanking. By the time the fire had begun to engulf the building, the Takahashi Bank was totally empty of anything valuable – other than some office furniture and a large flag of the Rising Sun. It seemed appropriate that the latter should be consumed by flames. The insatiable beast of Japanese patriotism was for once tamed by the Chinese dragon.

At midnight, Joao was ready and waiting outside the bank building. He was accompanied by Flash Wang, a Chinese news photographer whom he had hastily recruited the day before. Of course, his name wasn't really Flash, but a Scots missionary by the name of Gordon had decided to call him that because of his penchant for using a flash bulb even when it wasn't strictly necessary. And the name had stuck, as names often do. Half a dozen years later, bored foreigners propping up that same long bar in the Shanghai Club suggested that the Chinese news photographer was the inspiration for a comic strip character that had recently hit the newsstands. A devotee of opium in his spare time, Flash – they explained with glee to any newcomer who would listen – tended to be appropriately 'spaced' out. Jolly good joke, what!

But that was by the bye. After taking photographs of the fire ravaging the Takahashi Bank, with, in the foreground, the silhouettes of panicking Japanese customers and Kempeitai military policemen, the two newspapermen got into their waiting ricksha and moved at a smart pace towards more smoke and flames down by the waterfront. This time, Joao already knew, the arsonists' target was the go-down belonging to the Mikawa Trading Company, located between Kungping and Jansen roads. As their ricksha man moved at a fair trot along Broadway East, Joao saw that the fire had spread rapidly downstream, thanks to a brisk southerly breeze, and that neighbouring go-downs were also alight.

The British taipans of both Jardine's and John Swire had already been woken in the beds of their mistresses and were by now taking the steps necessary to avoid a catastrophe. It was one thing to look on, gin in hand, as a rival Japanese company's go-down was being burned to the ground, quite another when one's own property was threatened. Because these British companies owned Shanghai, or so they believed, the taipans sent word ordering the Municipal Fire Brigade to focus its attention on the warehouses between Kungping Road and Garden Bridge. Other buildings should be attended to later, after imminent danger to British property had been averted. In fact, their orders were to no avail. The British trading houses lost as much as the Japanese.

Once they reached the corner of Yangtzepoo and Jansen roads, Joao and Flash alighted. It was too much to ask their ricksha man to risk having his livelihood burned to cinders, and perhaps his emaciated body, too, by taking them between blazing buildings to the waterfront, so they left him with strict instructions to wait at the corner and promised him twice the fare he was charging if he did so. The ricksha puller sat down on a nearby fired hydrant and lit himself a Bat cigarette, unaware that the supply of his favourite smoke was going up in fragrant fumes before his eyes.

Flash pointed down the alley to the wharf.

'Bossman, my look-see catchee good picture bund-side,' he said in his Pidgin English.

Joao nodded and followed him down to the river. The flames were fierce and almost unbearably hot, so he tied a bandanna over his mouth and nose to protect him from the fumes. A large freighter, which had been moored securely to four bollards, was now straining as the tide pulled it downstream away from the quayside. Three of its hawsers had already snapped, weakened by the intense heat from the fire in the go-down beside which the ship was moored. The last snapped as Flash focused his camera and took his photo right on cue. Living up to his name. This was a night for reputations.

As the Tobata-maru drifted slowly downstream, there were shouts behind them. Joao turned to see several men staggering out of the burning warehouse carrying large blocks of what he realised must be Tu Yue-sheng's opium. He pulled Flash's arm and, to make himself heard above the crackling roar of burning wood and falling timbers, shouted to him to take photos of the rescue operation. As he did so, however, he realised that the men were wearing armbands with the Chinese characters of 'military police' printed on them. Someone in the Kempeitai was desperately trying to save its precious cargo of opium. Flash obligingly took several shots of the sweating MPs at work.

A few yards further along the wharf were more Japanese. Not Kempeitai, but Japanese rōnin – ruffians of all sorts who had formed a line by the water's edge and were passing buckets of water across the quay to a second burning go-down. They were as useful, Joao realised, as spitting on the face of a Chinese coolie – a rōnin's more usual hobby when roaming the squalid back alleys of the city.

In the midst of all these figures shrouded in smoke was a Kempeitai officer shouting loudly, enraged at the inability of the rōnin to do anything about the flames shooting up into the night sky. The smell of opium was overpowering and probably contributed to the men's inefficiency. Flash seemed ready, too, to put away his camera and go home.

Joao was having none of it.

'Photograph that man!' He ordered, pointing at the Kempeitai officer half-hidden in the smoke of the burning embers around them.

Flash moved closer to his target. The flash from his camera bulb made the officer swivel round towards them and Joao suddenly realised who it was.

'Welcome to Shanghai, Captain Doihara!' He shouted in Japanese. 'Long time, no see *lo*,' he added for good measure in English.

'Serino!" Doihara snarled, after an initial double-take. 'What are you doing here?'

'Just doing my job, Captain.'

'Major, if you please!' A stickler for rank.

'OK, Major.'

Doihara clearly had somebody protecting him to be able to get his old rank back so quickly.

'I'm here to report on a big fire burning down Japanese warehouses. Is there anything you can tell me, Major?'

Joao took a few steps forward towards Doihara, pencil and notebook in hand. 'Any idea how it started?'

'Get away from here, Serino! It's none of your business.'

'Oh, but it is, Doihara,' Joao returned the insult. 'My readers in Japan will want to know all about this. What's Mikawa stockpiling in there that your men are doing their best to salvage?' He jerked his head towards the go-down beside them, 'Smells pretty like opium, doesn't it?'

Doihara turned and barked an order at the men behind him. Two of the rōnin detached themselves from the line of men passing buckets of water to and fro and came running forward.

'Savour it while you can, Serino. It's the last pleasant smell you're going to enjoy for a long time.' Doihara drew a pistol from the holster at his waist, as the two rōnin hovered just behind him. 'You're under arrest.'

'What? Again?' Joao asked a little incredulously as the two rōnin stepped forward and pinioned his arms roughly behind his back. Déjà vu?

'I didn't arrest you in Tokyo. Remember?' Doihara gave Joao the benefit of one of his cruel smiles, his little moustache bristling on his upper lip. 'You were merely a suspect.'

'Ah, yes. So I was. But you never told me what of.'

'Espionage,' Doihara said grimly. 'You were suspected of being a spy.'

'What? Because of something your bit of flirt, Kohana, told you? I never imagined you could be so gullible. Really, Doihara!'

'Careful, Serino. My patience is wearing thin tonight.' He still had the pistol in his hand.

'And mine, too, Doihara. So let me tell you what you'll read in the papers the day after tomorrow. A story about the Kempeitai's role in buying opium in Shanghai, having Mikawa Trading Company ship it to Japan, and then forwarding it to Teikoku Tobacco which uses the opium to manufacture Bat cigarettes. You gave me one when we first met, remember? Your second mistake.'

'Second?' Doihara suddenly was less sure of himself.

'The first was when you told me your name. You know, journalists like me tend to train our memories, Doihara.'

'So?'

'So yours I knew from an unpublished article about the Kempeitai's scheme to supply underage Russian girls to politicians in Tokyo. And your own role in devising and running that scheme.'

'Idle speculation, Serino. You've got no proof.' Doihara looked less than pleased.

'Of that particular scheme, maybe not. But of your present activities, plenty. Bank statements, photographs, witnesses. You're in deep trouble, Doihara. I can assure you of that.'

The Kempeitai officer still had his pistol in his hand, but he was waving it erratically from side to side, distracted, perhaps, by the noise and fury of the conflagration around him. The two rōnin still stood beside Joao pinioning his arms, but seemed uncertain what – if anything – their boss wanted them to do. One of them relaxed his grip noticeably.

'And then, of course,' Joao continued, regardless of the danger, 'There's all the money you've been laundering through the Takahashi Bank.'

Doihara took aim and fired, just as Joao twisted away from his captors.

Whether it was the simultaneous crashing of the go-down roof collapsing in large chunks around them, or his own uncontrollable anger that led to his pistol jerking to one side as it went off, Joao didn't know. But somehow, Doihara missed. Flash Wang, though, wasn't so fortunate. The bullet lodged in the flesh of one beefy upper arm. To his eternal credit, the news photographer didn't drop his camera. But the sheer quality and quantity of the invective that followed stopped even the Kempeitai officer in his tracks.

Joao shook himself free and moved back several steps as Doihara advanced determinedly.

'You half-caste bastard!'

He raised his arm again to shoot, but at that very moment the wall of the warehouse beside them crumbled in a fiery thunder of wood and masonry. There followed the crack of a pistol behind Joao and the gun in Doihara's hand fell to the ground. With a look of uncomprehending surprise, the Kempeitai officer stared down at blood streaming from his right hand. Then he turned on his heel and ran into the billowing smoke. Two more shots hit the two rōnin who had held Joao's arms. They fell to the ground dead.

As Joao began to turn, more than a dozen of Tu Yue-sheng's Green Gang members charged past him, heading towards the rest of the Japanese rōnin, who immediately dropped everything and fled into the thick smoke reeking of opium. There were shouts and cries as more men were killed or wounded.

'Come on, Joao, move!' A woman's voice commanded.

He turned round further to see a slight figure, looking like a ninja assassin in a black tunic, standing behind him, pistol in hand. From under her hat peeked stray wisps of auburn red hair.

Gerda.

Except, he realised as he stepped back towards her in the half-light of the conflagration's embers, it wasn't. The woman who had shot Doihara was Isa. Gerda was standing just behind her.

It seemed like there were two paths to the top of the mountain. But the view, once he got there, was the same.

'I'm glad we can still surprise you.' Gerda smiled, as she cuddled beside him in his bed.

They were in his quiet apartment backing onto the French Park. Gerda had insisted on accompanying him to his place, not hers. Isa was going off, she had said, in search of a man. Or maybe a woman. Either would do. She was in that kind of mood. But she had to make love in her own bed.

'Are we talking about what happened on the wharf earlier? Or just now in bed?'

'Both.'

'The sex was fantastic,' he said truthfully. And it had been. Like Yukiko, Gerda knew a thing or two. But in a totally different way. Where Yukiko was calm and erotic, Gerda displayed a passionate intensity, a physicality that demanded everything of her man. She seemed to accept that Joao had done his best for now, but she expected more. Like her sister.

'But your shooting Doihara, that was more than a surprise. For a moment I thought I was about to die.'

'And you would have, Joao, if Isa hadn't been there to practise her marksmanship. Doihara's a cruel bastard who stops at nothing to get what he wants. And you were in his way.'

'Yes, but how did Isa know I'd be down by the wharf? And that he'd be there?'

'How do you think, Joao?'

'Ah! Bai-li.'

'Of course. Bai-li anticipated that Doihara would try to do something to rescue his precious shipment of opium. So he sent her to deal with him.'

'It's a pity she didn't shoot him dead.'

'She could have done, of course. But imagine the fuss the Japanese consul would have made if a Kempeitai officer had been killed on his turf. Under the circumstances, it was better just to disarm him.'

'And disable him, too. He's not going to be able to use his right hand again for a long time.'

'Probably never.'

Joao held her a little closer to him. Her breasts felt soft against his chest.

'And Bai-li did some kind of deal with Big Ears Tu, it seems. You had at least a dozen members of Tu's Green Gang as back-up.'

'Mainly to carry the dead bodies into the warehouse and let them burn there. There was no point in leaving evidence lying around on the wharf, was there?'

'Definitely not. But why were you there in the first place?'

'Out of curiosity, I suppose. I didn't want my lover to be killed.'

Joao let be the illogicality of her reasoning.

'At least, you could help poor Flash Wang. I didn't realise your skills included first aid.'

'There are many of my skills you're not aware of, Joao,' she said coquettishly.

'So I'm beginning to learn. But tell me, where did Isa learn to shoot?'

'Where do you think?'

'Germany? As a child in the Great War?'

She shook her tangled red hair with a trademark infectious laugh.

'Moscow,' she said. 'We were both trained by the OGPU in Moscow. At first, they thought we'd be good only for honey traps. Typical men!' She gave Joao the benefit of another of her infectious laughs. 'But then they discovered Isa was the best shot in our intake and that, in spite of her slender and petite form, she could be pretty tough when it came to martial arts, so they started taking her seriously. When the Comintern offered her a job running a bookstore in Shanghai, the OGPU ordered me to join her. We were assigned to Bai-li.'

'Bai-li, who then ordered you to give Tsuyoshi Inukai a blow job during Chiang Kai-shek's wedding party.'

'Among other things.' She put out a hand to caress his cheek. 'I'm sorry about that, Joao. It really wasn't what I'd wanted at all. I had other plans for us that evening, but Bai-li insisted. In the end those other plans for us worked. But only until the following morning, when you opened an envelope slipped by mistake under our hotel bedroom door. I was mortified.'

'As was I.'

The two of them lay silently on her bed for a while, each in their own thoughts. Joao realised that if he was to become a spy, he would have to be far more calculating in what he did or did not do. And far colder when it came to human relations. There was no room for emotions or sentimentality. Not even with Yukiko.

'Joao,' Gerda began eventually. 'I enjoy having sex with you. It's exciting and it helps me forget some of the other things going on in my life.'

'Me, too,' he said, pulling her to him.

'But now, I gather, you've fallen for a Japanese geisha. Does she know about us?'

'Yes,' Joao said honestly. He had been true to his word about hiding nothing from Yukiko.

'So what did she say when you told her we were lovers?'

'That we should carry on seeing each other while I'm in Shanghai.'

'Seeing?'

'And making love. She doesn't object to my having sex with you.'

'A sensible woman, then,' Gerda said approvingly. 'After all, sex is just that, isn't it? Sex. It should never be confused for love.'

'That's what Yukiko said.'

'I've always thought that sex is like spying. To be enjoyed for the thrill it provides. A thrill made all the more exciting by the fact that it comes without any emotions attached to it.'

'Is that what the OGPU taught you in Moscow?'

'The OGPU?' Gerda looked puzzled. 'No, Joao. It's what my body has taught me over the years.'

'In which case, maybe your body can give mine another lesson?'

'With pleasure.'

'Which I'm looking forward to. I have a feeling this may be the beginning of an exhausting relationship.'

'But pleasurable, too,' she said, reaching between his legs.

'Definitely pleasurable.'

There was considerable furore over the Tokyo Protocol when it was first published in a Chinese newspaper ten days after the 'Great Fire' of Shanghai. Local Chinese were incensed and carried out a series of strikes in Japanese-owned textile mills, as well as an extensive boycott of Japanese goods. Some suggested that the 'Great Fire' itself, which led to the total destruction of a Japanese bank building and several go-downs on the Whampoo River, was revenge on the part of the Chinese. In a way it was, though not quite in the manner suggested. The Protocol merely confirmed local inhabitants' worst suspicions about the dwarf bandits.

Very soon, Westerners frequenting various well-heeled bars in the International Settlement debated the veracity of the Tokyo Protocol. Were its contents to be believed? Or was this merely a Chinese propaganda stunt designed to embarrass the Japanese army in Manchuria? Arguments for and against each firmly-held position raged back and forth for two or more weeks, without a decisive victory by either side – in large part because what little they knew about the Tokyo Protocol was indeed very little. None of them could read Chinese. Bar owners, however, noticed a distinct increase in the amount of alcohol consumed during these arguments and encouraged them with improvised snippets of gossip that added fuel to the smouldering embers of conviction.

But then, much to these same bar owners' delight, an English language translation of the Tokyo Protocol appeared in several American newspapers a month or so later. Now Shanghailanders had something to really get their teeth into. It became clear very quickly that those who had hitherto supported the Japanese cause now found themselves on seriously unstable ground – not surprising really, given that Shanghai itself had first been built on the shifting mudflats of the Whampoo River – and deserted in droves to the Anti-Japanese cause. Their example was followed – in certain cases, preceded – by politicians and diplomats in Great Britain and the United States who began to question their alliance with the Japanese, and shifted their sympathies markedly towards Chiang Kai-shek and the Chinese Nationalists under his command. Although the Japanese Government protested vigorously that the Protocol was a fake and that no such document existed in the archives of the Army Ministry in Tokyo, few Westerners were prepared to believe them.

In this, of course, they were justified. And yet, in the end they weren't. Two men employed as archivists in Tokyo's Army Ministry were ordered to go through every single document box filed under the headings of 'China' and 'Manchuria.' Their search was time-consuming, but meticulous. Nothing untoward – certainly nothing containing contents such as those published in the newspapers – was found.

One document box, buried in the Ministry's archive, was devoted to a 'Far Eastern Conference' held by Prime Minister Tanaka in the summer of the previous year. Its scanty contents consisted of nothing more than a conference agenda and list of participants. It didn't even contain a summary of proceedings, until one afternoon the box was signed out by a senior staff officer, kept overnight, and the following morning returned containing one additional file – a summary outlining how all those present at the conference had advocated peace with China. In a carefully-worded letter to Joao Serino-sensei, Jiro Kobayashi remarked that the whole business seemed to have been a lot of hoo-hah about nothing. Or very little, at least.

In fact, however, events transpired in such a way that the Japanese Government appeared to have been telling the truth. There was no original of the Tokyo Protocol in the archives of the Army Ministry. This came about, thanks to a second unfavourable story circulating in the foreign press about a plan by Japan's military police, the Kempeitai, to distribute opium-filled cigarettes throughout China and so make the population of that country incapable of engaging in war because of its addiction to the drug. As was wryly pointed out by the Director of Internal Affairs in Shanghai when interviewed by a newspaper reporter, the Japanese had taken a leaf out of Sun Tzu's book. The supreme art of war was to subdue the enemy without fighting a single battle.

One sidebar story in this scandal concerned a Japanese Kempeitai officer, a certain Major Kenji Doihara, who had been closely involved in the cigarette scam. His charred body, along with those of a number of other military policemen and unidentified ruffians – probably Japanese rōnin – had been discovered, it was officially reported, among the blackened timbers of a warehouse belonging to Mikawa Trading Company that had burned down during the Great Fire of Shanghai. As to what Doihara and his colleagues had been doing in or near the warehouse at such a dangerous time was a moot point, but the newspaper journalist's opinion was that they had been trying to rescue some of the opium burning inside. Photographic evidence was provided in his article to support this claim. Not that the opium could have been sent to Japan in the immediate future. The ship on which it had been destined to be loaded, the Tobata-maru, had slipped her moorings in the fire and run aground a mile or so downstream, much to the chagrin – and expense – of the freighter's owner, Mikawa Trading Company.

The apparent death of an officer of the Kempeitai meant that the file containing all records of his service activities in the military police needed to be removed from the Army Ministry archive and destroyed. The archivist assigned to extract Doihara's file felt it advisable under the circumstances to remove one record pertaining to Major Doihara — an exquisitely written document presented to the Emperor by the Prime Minister of Japan, Gi'ichi Tanaka, containing a summary of the conclusions reached by highly-placed members of government and the armed forces of Japan, following a conference on the future role of Japan in China. In this so-called Tokyo Protocol, it was agreed that Japan would invade not only China, but the rest of Southeast Asia, before turning its attention to Europe and the United States.

The archivist concerned, one Jiro Kobayashi, was of the opinion that this document unnecessarily besmirched the reputation of the said-to-be deceased Major. He therefore withdrew it before passing the rest of Major Doihara's file to a senior Kempeitai officer for inspection and subsequent destruction. Kobayashi rolled up the Tokyo Protocol and placed it in a cardboard cylinder, together with several *shunga* erotic woodblock prints that he liked to enjoy during his lunch break. One of these – a drawing by Hokusai of a woman having her vagina eaten out by an octopus – he was obliged, very reluctantly, to loan to a guard who took a liking to it after casually checking the contents of the cylinder when Kobayashi left for home that evening. The document in question then found its way, courtesy of Jiro's brother, who was chauffeur to the future Prime Minister of Japan, to an exceedingly beautiful geisha who was often to be found entertaining important men at the Sakura tea house in Kagurazaka.

The fate of the Tokyo Protocol thereafter remains a closely guarded secret, but it appears to have been passed into the aristocratic hands of Prince Saionji, *genro* and elder statesman, who from time to time liked to while away an evening in the company of the geisha known as Chiyotsuru, but whom in the privacy of his residence he called Yukiko. He particularly enjoyed her artistic skills and, if he had been pressed on the matter, would readily have admitted that he was mesmerised by the way she manipulated her fan in *nihon buyō* – a classical form of Japanese dance. He would have waxed eloquent on how the fan that Chiyotsuru wielded became an extension of her body – now a leaf blown by the wind, now waves breaking on the shore, now a mirror, now a sword. It breathed emotion, while her lissom body displayed an erotic beauty that he wished he were young enough to enjoy to the full.

One of the Prince's formal tasks was to recommend the appointment of the Prime Minister of Japan to Emperor Hirohito. In due course, when Gi'ichi Tanaka's position as Prime Minister had become untenable, owing to various scandals surrounding the Takahashi Bank, the Prince requested Tanaka's presence at the Tsukimidō moon-viewing building in the Imperial Palace. Following a heated discussion during which the Prime Minister displayed his fearless 'blood and thunder' character, he was shown evidence of his Far Eastern Conference's conclusions, and was prevailed upon by the Prince to resign. His Minister of Communications, and leader of the Minseitō Party, Tsuyoshi Inukai, was then summoned and asked if he might be able to form a government. With a deep bow that left the imprint of his forehead on a tatami mat freshly laid down for the summer months, Inukai sensei humbly accepted Prince Saionji's request. Things had worked out well for the Old Fox.

One final question surrounded the publication in English of the Tokyo Protocol. Given the general lack of interest among Westerners in what was going on in China and Japan at the time – European attention was in large part focused on Soviet Russia and its new leader, Joseph Stalin – one Japanese journalist, Joao Serino, who had broken the scandalous story surrounding the affairs of the Takahashi Bank, was surprised at how promptly an English version of the protocol had appeared in print. Who, he asked himself, as he lay naked in bed after another exhausting but exhilarating bout of sex with a petite red-head, had translated the Chinese with such efficiency? Of course, he himself could have claimed responsibility. He was, after all, fluent enough in English and Chinese, but he was too honourable a man for such dishonesty. His best guess — in fact, a correct guess – was that a cigarette that he had handed to Su Bai-li in an enamel case had somehow made its way to Soviet Russia, where its contents were revealed and a translation made. Moscow had then disseminated the English document to the United States through the Comintern, the Communist Party's international branch. The rest was child's play.

He thought of asking the naked young lady beside him for confirmation of his theory, but didn't want to spoil their post-coital contentment. Sex and espionage might go together, as she had said, but pleasure was in a realm of its own.

Author's Note

Conducting historical research for *The Tokyo Protocol* has taken me along paths that, as an anthropologist of contemporary Japanese society and culture, I had never imagined, let alone explored. I am very grateful, therefore, to all those scholars and journalists who have written about pre-war Shanghai and Japan – the people who lived there, the kinds of lives they led, and the events they lived through. In addition to a handful of historical studies of Shanghai in the 1920s, three books I found of particular help: *City of Devils* by Paul French, *Shanghai and Beyond* by Percy Finch, and *Big Sister, Little Sister, Red Sister* by Jung Chang (who was once, although I doubt she was aware of it, a colleague at the School of Oriental & African Studies, London).

Many of the peripheral characters who appear in this book are (or were) real life people: Chiang Kai-shek, Chou En-lai, Soong Ch'ing-ling, Tu Yue-sheng, Doihara Kenji, Inukai Tsuyoshi, and his son, Ken (or Takeru). Although their physical descriptions are as accurate as I have been able to manage, their words and deeds as portrayed in *The Tokyo Protocol* bear, so far as I know, no resemblance to how they behaved in real life. They are, in other words, primarily fictional.

But only primarily. Chiang Kai-shek and Soong Mei-ling did hold a wedding ceremony and reception in the ballroom of Shanghai's Majestic Hotel in December 1927. Moreover, the fact that his son was being held hostage in Moscow almost certainly did influence the Generalissimo's failure – perhaps one should say, refusal – to exterminate the Red Army in China during the early 1930s.

As intelligence officer in the Kempeitai, Doihara Kenji made systematic use of terrorism, assassinations, blackmail, bribery, trafficking and racketeering to disrupt Chinese society and weaken public resistance to Japanese aggression. One of his schemes involved manufacturing (Golden Bat) opium-laced cigarettes for sale to unsuspecting Chinese.

Finally, as mentioned in the Prologue, there was indeed a real-life equivalent of *The Tokyo Protocol* known as the *Tanaka Memorial* (Carl Crow's *Japan's Dream of World Empire* provides a translation thereof). Historians nowadays regard the Memorial as a fake, rather than as an authentic document: a masterly 'false flag' operation conceived and carried out – if Trotsky is to be believed – by the Soviet Union.

Facts, as we know, can indeed be stranger than fiction.